Malice

Malice

A NOVEL

Heather Walter

DEL REY

NEW YORK

Malice is a work of fiction. Names, characters, places, and incidents either are products of the author's imagination or are used fictitiously. Any resemblance to actual persons, living or dead, events, or locales is entirely coincidental.

Published in the United States by Del Rey, an imprint of Random House, a division of Penguin Random House LLC, New York.

DEL REY and the CIRCLE colophon are registered trademarks of Penguin Random House LLC.

Library of Congress Cataloging-in-Publication Data

Names: Walter, Heather, author.
Title: Malice / Heather Walter.
Description: First edition. | New York : Del Rey, 2021.
Identifiers: LCCN 2020015907 (print) |
LCCN 2020015908 (ebook) | ISBN 9781984818652 (hardcover) |
ISBN 9780593357255 (international edition) |
ISBN 9781984818669 (ebook)
Classification: LCC PS3623.A44683 M35 2021 (print) |
LCC PS3623.A44683 (ebook) | DDC 813/.6—dc23
LC record available at https://lccn.loc.gov/2020015907
LC ebook record available at https://lccn.loc.gov/2020015908

Printed in the United States of America on acid-free paper

randomhousebooks.com

2 4 6 8 9 7 5 3 1

First Edition

Book design by Elizabeth A. D. Eno

For Lindsey, who believed when I didn't. If any kiss can break a curse, it's yours.

And for Ashley, my very first partner in villainy.

Part I

Briar King,

You mortals may think yourselves above such counsel, but I must urge you once again to end the Vila. There was a war fought over the extermination of these beasts, though your memory is too fickle to recall it. And to welcome another—even a half-breed—into your realm will surely bring ruin. If you insist on so reckless a path as to let the creature live, know this: You were warned.

—Missive from Endlewild,
Lord Ambassador of the Fae Courts,
to Tarkin, Briar King. Age of the Rose, 976

CHAPTER ONE

Age of the Rose, 996

The golden bell above my doorframe bobs twice.

I roll my shoulders against the needling ache that settles at the base of my neck whenever that damn thing sounds. After nearly a decade of hearing it, I've come to despise the bell's shrill, tinny clang almost as much as the message it carries: A patron is coming. When it was first installed, my bell gleamed like those the Graces use in their parlors. But now, seeing as the servants conveniently forget to polish it, a mottled green tarnish clings to the thing like a scaly skin. Fitting, I think, that I should have the ugliest bell in Lavender House when I am by far the ugliest creature living inside it.

Alyce. My own name on my patron schedule glares up at me when I glance at the next appointment. Beneath it: *The Dark Grace.*

Grace, indeed. If I were truly a Grace, I'd be receiving my patrons in a sunny parlor with silk-upholstered chairs and trays of spongy, cream-frosted tea cakes. Instead, I'm banished to a converted storage annex attached to Lavender House's kitchen. It's yet another reason Cook hates me. The space was once a larder and now Cook complains every chance she gets that there isn't enough storage space in the cellar. I catch her grumbling curses at me when she thinks I'm out of earshot, as if this insufferable chamber is some kind of prize. There are no windows. A dank chill seeps through the rotting mortar, even in the summer heat. And the wretched hearth—hastily added once I opened my practice—clogs more often than not, filling my Lair with a perpetual smoky scent and smearing soot on every surface.

It's more a dragon's lair out of a story than a parlor in a Grace house. Rose dubbed it such soon after she arrived: the Lair, where the Dark Grace dwells. I hate the place so much that I didn't even fight her.

Callow ruffles as the bell jangles a second time, as annoyed as I am at the intrusion. I offer my kestrel a few meat trimmings snuck from beneath Cook's nose.

"What do you think this one wants?" Callow shakes out her white-speckled wings in a decidedly irritated fashion and nudges my hand with her head. And I suppose there's no point putting it off any longer. "Enter!"

The chamber door squeals and I can tell immediately from the footsteps that it isn't one of my regulars. They're anxious. Hesitant. A startle away from turning and bolting.

I wish they would turn and bolt.

Whispering apologies to Callow, I fix her hood over her head. She's easier to handle this way, especially around strangers. I'd found the kestrel as a chick some years ago, half-dead and starving on the sea cliffs outside Briar's main gates. Though I'm no healing Grace, I was able to nurse her back to health with what tinctures I could concoct. She's never taken to anyone else. Not that I blame her. Mistress Lavender said it would have been kinder to kill the bird, and one of the servants mistook her for a rat and nearly bludgeoned her to death. The maid was lucky I didn't return the favor.

The nervous patron hovers in my doorway, hood close around her face despite the oppressive, salt-soaked heat of late summer. The firelight flits over her features, sharpening her cheekbones. Hollowing her eye sockets. Definitely not a regular. She looks like she thinks I'm going to roast her over a spit. As if my pathetic hearth is large enough to manage that. Would that it could.

"Your Grace." The edges of her brocade cloak tremble as she scrapes a curtsy.

"What brings you here?" I stroke Callow's snowy breast with one finger, affecting the cool, detached manner people expect from the Dark Grace. I don't ask her name. Within these walls, she doesn't have one. Patrons do not come to my Lair seeking beauty or charm or wit as they would in a Grace's parlor. They come for revenge. For cruelty. Services provided at a steep price, and that price includes anonymity.

"I . . . I have a . . . cat." She stumbles. Flushes at her own threadbare deception.

I resist the urge to roll my eyes. My patrons always spare less than half a thought to crafting a decent backstory. Briar's Grace Laws prevent the use of their magic for ill will, which should directly prohibit my line of work. But I am the only Grace of my kind. And all I do is prepare the elixirs. Once the vials leave my hands, it's up to the patrons to dispose of them as they please. And as long as I don't *know* I'm party to an attack on another citizen, I cannot be held liable for my patrons' actions. Besides that, my elixirs cost three times the average rate of those of a Grace. And if I stopped working, the Crown wouldn't get its cut.

"A cat." I school my features into the neutral expression I've perfected over the years.

"Yes, a cat." She fiddles with the buttons at her sleeves. "A cat too pretty for its own good. She's getting too much attention from the other . . . cats."

Dragon's teeth, she's even worse than the others. And I once had a man tell me his own rose garden smelled too nice and was attracting bees.

"And you wish to . . ."

"I don't want to harm the cat," the woman says automatically. "I just want . . ."

"To give her a few warts?" A standard ugliness elixir.

Her gaze brightens in the gloom. How predictable. New patrons are always so grateful when I offer suggestions. I think it makes them feel less the villain. Like they didn't come here specifically to do harm to someone they've convinced themselves deserves it.

The patron nods and I motion for her to sit at a worn wooden table near the hearth as I start assembling ingredients for the elixir. Swamp water. A dash of powdered nightshade. And, for the warts, I cart over the short, boxy cage that houses my toad, Prince Markham.

The woman stammers, flinching as I plop His Highness on the table in front of her. He lets out a belchy croak.

Only the crackle of the flames and the grind of the pestle break the silence as I work. I'm grateful. Sometimes my patrons try to plump up their lies, offering needless explanations and sugarcoated stories. Hoping I'll nod along. Make it easier on their consciences. I never do. They deserve whatever guilt festers in their guts.

But this woman only chews the inside of her cheek, glancing at the door every few moments as if she's worried she'll be discovered. She needn't be. Every aspect of my craft is steeped in secrecy. Patrons book their appointments with me using a shrouded alcove around the side of the house, built specifically for the purpose. There's a little screen secured into the wall, where patrons or their servants can murmur their needs to our house manager, Delphine. She even takes the payments through a slot and allows aliases on the bookings, a practice forbidden to the other Graces. If Delphine guesses who the patrons are, she's paid well enough to keep her mouth shut.

My current patron, who calls herself Mistress Briar—how original—seems to have forgotten about the great care Lavender House has taken to protect her identity. Despite the Lair's cold, sweat beads on her upper lip and she dabs it away with a lace handkerchief. She jumps every time Callow moves on her perch. Ignoring her restlessness, I hold a long needle over a candle flame, and then with a quiet apology, I pierce one of Prince Markham's warts. He gurgles in protest as a few drops of his blood, so dark they're almost black, fall into the waiting vial. I add it to the rest of the mixture.

Now for the most important piece. With a small scalpel, I press down on my finger. A line of green blood—the source of my power—wells. I count to three, inhaling the faint scent of woodsmoke and loam that is my magic, as it dribbles onto the other enhancements. Immediately, the mixture hisses. I stir it with a long spoon until a cloud of black smoke erupts from the mortar. My patron covers her slender, highborn nose and coughs.

"For your cat." I raise an eyebrow, pouring the elixir into a vial and sliding it across the table. "The more you use, the more warts she'll get."

She nods and pockets it, not daring to say another word, not even deigning to thank me.

As the door snicks closed behind her, I curse the familiar sickening feeling that settles like hot coals inside me. I should be used to these requests by now. I can't even count the number of ugliness elixirs I've produced over the years. And I'm bound by the Grace Laws to satisfy my patrons' needs.

But the woman's abrupt dismissal still stings, as does every other slight I've endured since I began working in Lavender House. My patrons pay good coin for my services, but not one of them would willingly meet my eye if they passed me on the street. I am reviled and despised for the very reasons I'm sought out. A figure of dark, evil magic. A member of a race all but stamped out. A Vila.

A monster.

CHAPTER TWO

"Honestly, if I have to shade Lady Dulcet's eyes lavender *one* more time." Rose selects an apricot tart from a tiered stand at tea that afternoon. Her fluffy rat of a dog, Calliope, whines at her side. "Today was the third appointment this month."

"It's in honor of the princess, surely," Marigold chimes in, slathering a healthy layer of jam onto a scone. "It is her birthday."

"I don't care what it is." Rose sucks sticky orange filling from her fingers and slips a scrap of ham to Calliope, who slurps it up and begs for another. "Lady Dulcet should understand that it will take more than one of my elixirs to maintain the beauty of someone of her . . . circumstances."

"You mean age." Laurel doesn't even glance up from the book that's balanced on her knees. "And be careful. You've had to make Lady Dulcet three elixirs in a month. People will think your gift is Fading."

Like me, the Graces draw power from their blood. But

while my blood is the green of the Vila, the Graces share the golden-colored blood of the light Fae of Etheria, the Fae courts beyond Briar's northern mountain border. Centuries ago, the High King of the Fae, Oryn, and the Briarian ruler entered into an alliance agreement. In exchange for the humans' aid during the War of the Fae, the Etherians granted Briar the Graces. Born of human women, the Graces possess only a fraction of the power a full-blooded Fae can wield. The Etherians have mighty staffs said to be able to command the sea currents or turn straw into gold. Their long lives skirt the boundaries of immortality. But the Graces' gilded blood can only produce charms and blessings when added to an elixir. And eventually, that golden blood Fades to a dull silver color. The Fade is slow at first, usually starting at around age thirty. A Grace will begin to need more drops of her blood in each elixir. Strands of her vibrant hair will turn silver, as will the signature golden hue of her eyes. And then, the most feared sign of all, flecks of silver will appear in her blood. After that, it's only a matter of time before the Grace's gift is spent and she endures the rest of her life as powerless as any other mortal woman.

I imagine my own green blood will Fade one day, as I'm not full-blooded Vila. But I don't care half as much about losing my power as the Graces do. I've seen Rose picking through her hair when she thinks she's alone, looking for the dreaded telltale silver in her roots. And if she's overzealous—crafting too many elixirs or increasing the dosage of her blood to heighten their potency—her gift could Fade well before her time.

"Don't even dare." Rose's golden eyes narrow to slits.

She's been marked as one of the most skilled beauty Graces since she Bloomed five years ago, consistently ranked in the top quarter of the house standings each year. "Mistress Lavender will dock your coin for spreading such lies."

"And what will she do to you?" Laurel lazily flips a page. "For speaking ill of a patron?"

Rose's pink curls begin to vibrate. I smile into my tea.

"And what are you so pleased about, *Malyce*?"

After so many years, I would have thought myself immune to the ugly nickname. But humiliation flames in my cheeks anyway. Rose watches me with her perpetual haughty smirk as she drops another sugar cube into her teacup.

"Well. Are you going to sit there and gawp at me?" She drums her nails against the linen tablecloth. "Pass the cream."

Scowling, I reach for the pitcher. But not before I use the tines of my fork to open the small wound on my fingertip, earned from crafting elixirs that morning. I let a pearl of green blood fall into the cream before Rose can see. She accepts the pitcher carefully, making sure not to accidently brush hands with me, and chatters to Marigold about inane court gossip.

One heartbeat. Two. I suck the tip of my finger, tasting the leather and damp earth of my magic. The next time Rose sips her tea, her lips come away black. She chokes, spewing a stream of filth across the table.

"You stupid Vila!" Rose slams her fists on the table. The dishes rattle. Her pearly teeth are now coated in pitch. Laurel covers her shocked laughter with her book.

"I'm not a Vila." Not entirely, anyway. Though my exact

heritage is unclear, it's obvious from my outward appearance that I am at least half human. The other half, though . . .

"You're right." Calliope yaps and growls, her wispy-haired ears lying flat. "You're worse. You're a *mongrel*."

The room goes silent. Even the buttery afternoon sunlight dulls as a cloud passes by the arched windows. Laurel and Marigold dart nervous glances between us. They're wondering what I'll do next. Make boils erupt on Rose's skin? Tie her tongue into a knot? Anger surges inside me. I want nothing more than to do exactly what they expect of me. To live up to my reputation. The Dark Grace. Dealer of black wishes and evil deeds. But I don't get the chance.

"Graces!" Mistress Lavender sails into the room, clapping twice. "That's quite enough."

"It's her fault. Look at what she did to me!" Rose bares her inky teeth. Her tongue looks like a garden slug.

Mistress Lavender sighs, beleaguered. "Alyce, really."

"This is intolerable," Rose continues. "I cannot be expected to work in a house that—"

"Rose, go and clean up."

"But—"

"I trust you have your schedule from Delphine. You don't want your patrons to see you looking like that." Mistress Lavender straightens her bodice. "I'll deal with your sister."

"She's *not* our sister." Rose flings her napkin onto the crumbly pastry remains on her plate, pinches Marigold's elbow, and stalks away, her dog trotting at her heels. Laurel follows mutely behind them, shooting me a sympathetic look.

"I don't understand you, Alyce." Mistress Lavender perches in the always-empty seat beside me. Her gaze—silver now that she's Faded—is tempered with accusation. "Why do you insist on making a target of yourself?"

"Me?" My blood begins to heat. "Rose hates me. All of them do. I'm too . . . different."

The word presses against my eardrums and my temples begin to throb. My "sisters" are Graces, able to grant hundreds of prized attributes with mere drops of their blood. I study the reptilian green veins marring the backs of my hands. Next to the Graces, I'm like the sludge staining Rose's teacup: a nuisance someone else has to clean up.

"That may be." Mistress Lavender risks a tentative touch on my arm. The amethyst ring on her first finger, denoting her status as housemistress of Lavender House, glints. "But you earn your keep in this house. You have value, Alyce."

I snort. "Curses?"

"All magic has a purpose." A refrain I've heard a hundred thousand times. As if it's possible to somehow gloss over the fact that the purpose of my magic seems to be to do harm. "And it isn't as if you lack for patrons. Lavender House rose three rankings once you Bloomed. Surely that's worth something. Even to you."

I clench my fingernails into my palms. It isn't.

There are about twenty Grace houses in Briar, each with anywhere from three to thirty Graces. Every year, the Grace Council—a handful of noblemen selected by the king and tasked with regulating the Grace system—determines the rank of those houses based on a number of factors: the tabulation of each house's yearly earnings, accuracy and precision of its Graces' elixirs, growth from the previous year, patron loyalty, and a hundred other things, it seems. Official rankings are announced at the Grace Celebration thrown at the palace each spring. High-ranking houses accrue royal favor and increased patronage. Exceptional Graces and housemistresses are recognized with gifts and more desirable house placements. Mistress Lavender, obsessed with earning a position at a more prestigious house, drills our weaknesses into us at every opportunity.

"I don't give a dragon's ass—"

"Mind your attitude, my dear." Mistress Lavender squeezes a warning into my shoulder. "That's no way to speak of your house. You earn triple the coin of your sisters. Why don't you spend some of your wages on . . . well . . ." She looks around the room, like the answer might be written on the floral-papered walls. "Perhaps you'd like to wear something a trifle more . . . becoming?"

Yes, because a change of dress would instantaneously reverse the ostracism I've endured for twenty years. But at least Mistress Lavender didn't suggest letting Rose try to alter my appearance or Marigold school my manners with one of their elixirs. My childhood was riddled with excruciating failed attempts to conceal my macabre blood, resculpt my bones, and cool my temper. They all slid off me like oil from water, leaving me exactly as I am now: stringy, jet-black hair that refuses to stay in any sort of passable arrangement; dry, tissue-thin skin; a figure as flat and bland as dry toast; and a temperament that's only festered over the years.

"I don't need new clothes." I've no patience for such fripperies. And, in truth, I think my patrons enjoy seeing me this way. A hideous half-Vila in stained, musty clothes.

"Well." Mistress Lavender pats a stray silver ringlet back into place. Before she Faded, our housemistress was gifted in wit. And I know she's trying her best to access the dregs of that power and sway me to her side. But the attempt is useless. I'll never be like the others.

"I just wish you wouldn't be so contrary. I'm sure there's some sweetness in your core. We just have to tempt it out." She examines the ratty tips of my hair, lines bracketing the corners of her mouth. I angle away from her. "In the meantime, will you please stop baiting the others? You only draw more attention to yourself."

I start to argue that I don't bait everyone. Just Rose. Sometimes Marigold. And only when they deserve it. But at that moment, the glass-paned double doors of the dining room burst open. Rose barrels through, waving a gilt-edged parchment. Marigold tumbles in behind her, warm brown face flushed beneath her glittery powder.

"It's from the palace!" Calliope nearly trips over Rose's feet as her mistress twirls with delight. The dog's tiny nails skitter over the parquet floor. "They've added a ball to Princess Aurora's birthday celebrations!"

Mistress Lavender snatches the invitation out of Rose's hand.

"Oh, it will be wonderful!" Marigold begins dancing with an imaginary partner. "It's been ages since we've had a grand party. Her other birthdays have been positively grim."

She isn't wrong. Parties and balls are commonplace at the

palace, especially for the Graces, who seem to be invited to such gatherings every week. But since the deaths of the crown princess's two elder sisters, the birthday celebrations the royal family has held in honor of their remaining daughter have been lacking. Last year, there was only a dinner to which a select few were invited. Rose wasn't one of them, and we heard about it for weeks.

"Dragon's teeth, why did they wait so long to announce? We've no time to prepare."

As if Rose doesn't have a wardrobe full of ridiculous outfits she buys with all the coin she makes. Just the other day, she came downstairs wearing a hat with an actual bird's nest secured into the netting, with three jewel-speckled eggs glistening inside it. Eggs that, thanks to some innovative Grace magic, hatched a trio of twittering diamond canary chicks every so often. I was half tempted to untether Callow and let her use the thing as a roost.

Rose begins ticking things off on her fingers. "I'll need a new gown, of course. And slippers. Do you think Madame LaRoche could have them ready in time?"

Mistress Lavender peers at her over her half-moon spectacles. "This says the ball is in a week. A new gown so quickly would be quite the request, Rose, dear."

"But I'm a favorite of madame's. And I give her enough coin to deserve the effort." She frowns. "Perhaps an elixir will encourage her to get me what I need."

"That isn't allowed and you know it," Laurel chides from across the room. Tall and willowy, Laurel's beauty isn't gaudy and overdone like the other Graces'. Though always well-dressed, the wisdom Grace makes no effort to procure expensive clothing or jewelry. Her emerald-green hair is tied in a neat, uncomplicated braid, deep black complexion free of the golden powder the other Graces apply liberally to their faces and necks. Sometimes I even catch her with ink or enhancements smudged across her forehead. "Graces aren't permitted to bestow personal favors."

"Don't quote the Grace Laws at me." Rose glowers. "You'd grant a favor to Madame LaRoche in a trice if she could give you something you craved badly enough. You just don't care about fashion."

"Laurel is right," Mistress Lavender intercedes. "Payment is always required for our services and not"—she holds up one finger as Rose begins to argue—"in the form of gifts or favors. The Grace Laws are very clear, Rose. You can't go about flouting them. It's for your protection, as well as for fairness's sake."

Just after the War of the Fae, when the Graces were new to Briar, wealthy nobles would buy Grace children, lock them away, and force them to work only for their own families. Some even tried to extract the Etherian magic from the captive Graces' blood and replicate its power. These horrible practices led to the establishment of the Grace Council and the passing of the Grace Laws, which are still in effect today. Last I checked, there are over four hundred Grace Laws, and the council adds new ones whenever it sees fit.

Some of the laws are fair enough: Graces are required to be paid for their services, which is where Rose gets her coin to buy slippers made of sea glass and rare cloudlike ostrich plumes imported from other realms. Briar is also obligated to care for its Graces once they Fade—like providing a housemistress placement, a good marriage, or a stipend. But some laws are unpopular even among the Graces, when they dare to complain about them. Rose hates the law forbidding her from showing bias toward any one patron or family, thus thwarting her scheme to bribe Madame LaRoche into completing her gown in time for the ball.

It's an extraordinary occurrence when Rose doesn't get her way, and I have to cover my mouth to hide my grin.

"What are you smirking at, Malyce?" Rose sneers in my direction. "You don't even get to go to the ball. They'd never let something like you ruin a royal celebration."

Some*thing*. Rage claws up my chest. I shouldn't let Rose provoke me like this, but I can't help it. She knows every weakness. My fingers twitch. I want to wipe that look off her face and use it to scrub the floors.

"I don't see why she can't go to the ball." Laurel reads over Mistress Lavender's shoulder. "The invitation is addressed to the Graces."

"She's not a Grace." This time it's Marigold.

"I'm known as the Dark Grace. Even at the palace." I don't give a dragon's tooth about the ball. But I don't want them to be right.

The honeyed tint of Rose's skin flames bright copper. Marigold splutters something unintelligible. And Laurel curves a slow smile. We're not exactly allies, Laurel and I, but she's never hated me the way the other two do. I nod my thanks.

Mistress Lavender clears her throat and removes her spectacles, silver gaze studying me carefully. "I'm delighted to see you taking such an unprecedented interest in Grace activities, Alyce. Though I'm not entirely sure the invitation *is* meant for you."

"It isn't." Rose grips the back of a chair so hard it looks like it might buckle. I wonder if I could come up with an elixir to make her glossy pink curls fall out, one by one. "She's never even gone to a Grace Celebration. Why should she be invited to the princess's birthday?"

"That may be true. But simply because she's never accompanied us to a Grace Celebration doesn't mean she would not have been permitted to attend one. I have always excused her on account of, well . . ." Mistress Lavender clears her throat. "Now, however . . ." She taps the edge of the parchment against the tabletop. "I suppose, as long as you're caught up on your appointments and other duties, I see no reason why you should not go with us."

I think I see steam billow from Rose's nostrils. Marigold lets out a cry. They both try to speak at once, but Mistress Lavender raises a pale white hand to stay them. "We must be inclusive, Graces. Alyce is under my protection, and it's my decision if she goes."

"Some party this will be," Rose grumbles. "No one will be able to enjoy themselves. Everyone will be too afraid she'll curse them. A Vila skulking in the palace, indeed."

"That's quite enough. I'm sure you all have patrons coming. Or has Delphine been slacking in her duties?" Mistress Lavender pockets the invitation and begins steering the others out of the room, but not before Rose's words twist into me with painful precision.

Even in an evening gown, the guests will know who I am. What I do. Already, when I move through the Grace District, the crowds part around me like I have some kind of plague. What will it be like for me in a ballroom?

A nudge on my elbow brings me out of my thoughts.

"It's a masque." Laurel speaks close to my ear. "If you don't wish it, no one need know you were ever there."

A masque. A night where I can shed the identity of Dark Grace and become anyone I wish. The idea creeps over me like the sun rising over the sea. And I decide that the Dark Grace—no, Alyce—is going to make her first appearance at a royal ball.

CHAPTER THREE

The next week is the busiest for Lavender House that I can remember. Patrons flock to our Graces, eager to dole out exuberant amounts of coin for Rose to smooth the bumps on their noses and plump their lips. For Marigold to enhance their dancing skills or lilt their shrill laughter. Even Laurel is beset with nobles wanting to know the perfect gift to get the princess or the style of clothing they should wear to the celebration.

And the Dark Grace is not forgotten. For every name Delphine pens on the Graces' schedules, there seems to be two on mine. It's all the usual demands—elixirs for hair-thinning and unriddable stenches and unsightly rashes. Anything a patron might think of to give themselves an edge against the perceived competition they'll face at the ball.

"It's utterly demeaning." Laurel massages her temples in the main parlor between patron visits. It's Friday and we've seen more patrons this week than in the last month. Delphine can barely manage to fit everyone in our schedules. Her huge appointment book sits open on her desk in the alcove, quill still dripping with ink where she left it to snatch a bite from the kitchen. And it's not only Lavender House: All of the Grace houses are reeling. "Is this the worth of my gift? To help a vapid patron decide whether to wear pink or blue?"

As per the Grace Laws, Laurel cannot refuse a paying patron. It's another way the Grace Council contrives to keep the Graces from showing bias among their patrons. Any Grace who refuses to use her gift—unless she has express permission—is punished. Usually, a larger portion of her profits are forfeited to the Crown and Grace Council, who already take their healthy cut of coin. But some Graces are brought to trial and face much steeper consequences. The last trial was a year ago, and the Grace in question was placed in a strict punitive house where she is monitored at all times to ensure she's following the laws.

"You won't be griping once you can order more of your precious books." Rose bustles through the doors, stuffing a pastry bulging with strawberries and cream into her mouth. She flops onto a jade chaise and Calliope seems to materialize out of thin air, leaning her front paws on Rose's knees and wagging her plumy tail.

"At least I'm not wasting my income on clothes." Laurel lifts an eyebrow.

Even without an "encouraging" elixir, Madame LaRoche was able to accommodate Rose's request for a new gown—and Rose has done nothing but blabber about the fine details since she returned from the clothier's. The monstrosity of silk and lace is blushing peony, the exact same shade as Rose's hair, accented with seed pearls and rosebuds and trimmed with a fine layer of real, whisper-thin gold. I don't even want to imagine the cost.

"I'm not wasting my income at all. You might not care about this house's standings, but I do. No patron will visit a beauty Grace if she doesn't look her part. Do you think anyone would bother to book appointments with me if I dressed like Alyce?" She scoffs, but I ignore the jab. "I want everyone in the realm to see that I'm simply swimming in coin. In fact . . ." Rose whips her schedule from her bodice and brandishes it at us. I can hardly see the parchment for all the times and names. "I've told Delphine to shorten my appointments so I can accommodate more patrons."

Laurel pulls back from the schedule as if it has fangs. "Why are you trying so hard?"

"I don't know why you don't try harder." Rose scoops Calliope into her lap and nuzzles her nose into the storm of white fur. "Don't you want a larger house? A wider following? Invitations to the palace?"

I suppress the urge to groan, caring less than the pus from one of Prince Markham's warts about any of those "rewards." Part of the annual Grace Celebration includes a Blooming Ceremony, which is when the new Graces demonstrate their skills and are assigned both a house and a preliminary fee by the Grace Council. In order to keep competition between the houses fair, Graces are placed evenly throughout the district, regardless of the type or strength of their gift. In fact, lesser houses like ours often receive the more talented newly Bloomed Graces so that we might have a chance of keeping up with the larger houses. But a Grace's placement is by no means permanent. Like the house-mistresses, a Grace can be reassigned or even request a transfer from the Grace Council. Rose has been trying to wheedle her way into Willow House for years, even though they already have an exceptionally gifted beauty Grace—Pearl.

With several dozen Graces sharing the same type of gift, it's no surprise that the rivalry between them can be fierce. Pearl has an enormous following. She earned the most coin out of all Graces last year. There are even hints that she might replace one of the Royal Graces, those so talented they're given apartments at the palace and fees that can only be afforded by the richest nobles and the royal family.

"I'm happy to work less and let my gift linger." Laurel pours more tea.

"Then Mistress Lavender can just leave you to wallow here when she earns her promotion." Rose leans back so her head rests against the plush curve of the chaise. "I plan to be her prime Grace at her new house."

"If you haven't Faded by then."

I thought I'd said the words too quietly to hear, but Rose jerks upright like she's been stabbed, eyes smoldering amber. Calliope yips as Rose shoves her to the floor. My pulse speeds up. For a moment I think Rose might use her perfectly polished nails to tear into my face instead of the silk upholstery she's currently strangling. But then her shoulders soften.

"Alyce." Her voice is sweet enough to make my teeth ache. "Would you be a dear? You clearly have nothing to do and I need some enhancements." She withdraws another sheaf of paper from a pocket at her waist and holds it out to me. Even from here, I can see that the writing takes up both sides. A trip to the apothecary to fetch the ingredients is bad enough so close to the ball, but then I'll have to lug the heavy sack back through the Grace District. And I'm already tired from my own day.

"I have a patron coming."

"Really?" Rose raises her eyebrows. "Shall we check with Delphine?"

I bite my tongue, gaze darting to the appointment book. I've finished for today. My morning was full to the gills, but it's midafternoon and the nobles are busy getting ready for dinners and parties. I could have a walk-in, which sometimes happens. But Delphine would just tell them I'm otherwise engaged and schedule a later appointment. Still, that doesn't mean I have to be Rose's errand girl.

"We have servants to do such chores."

"Oh. Is that not what you are? Forgive me." She smiles, snakelike, and I fight the impulse to stuff that list down her throat. "But since you are free and all the servants are busy helping the *Graces*." She bobs the paper in my direction, as if offering a treat to her insipid dog.

Laurel looks at me, a question in her eyes. I consider just walking away. But then Rose would only whine to Mistress Lavender, who would then probably have me fetch what Rose needs anyway, along with everything on everyone else's lists. And then Rose would have the satisfaction of both winning and seeing me scolded. I grit my teeth and yank the paper out of her hand hard enough to rip the corner.

At least this way I'll get a break from her company.

Rose's list is filled with the usual enhancements. Flowers like juniper and mountain laurel and others that we don't grow in our own garden. There are also robin's eggs and crow feathers and birch wood. Unlike the Etherians themselves, who wield their magic with their staffs, a Grace must employ enhancements to shape her elixirs. So when a patron wants their eyes shaded a certain color—as with Lady Dulcet's frequent requests for Rose to turn hers lavender—a Grace might take the desired hue from a plant and mix it with her own gilded blood. Laurel uses sage and yew and mint in her elixirs to stimulate different parts of her patrons' minds.

I also need enhancements, though I have nowhere near the store of knowledge about my own abilities that the Graces enjoy. Grace magic has been studied since the first Fae-blessed infant appeared in Briar. The number of Graces born per year varies—sometimes as many as twelve and sometimes none at all. But always female and always marked by a shock of vibrant hair, golden eyes, and golden-colored blood to match. Once identified, the infants are given over to the care of the Crown and raised in nurseries, where they spend their first fifteen years learning their craft and determining the nature of their gift. Eventually each is presented at the Blooming Ceremony to begin her work.

But that was not my story. There was no bittersweet parting as my parents handed me off to the Grace Council and accepted their stipend. No coddled childhood in a nursery with Grace mothers coaxing and sheltering my burgeoning gift.

I was discarded. A squalling infant brought to the Grace Council by a fishmonger in the Common District. All Mistress Lavender told me about the man was that he vehemently swore he wasn't my father and that he claimed to have found me bundled into a basket in a deserted alley near the harbor. No one knows how I got there, or why I was left, or who my true parents might be. And though my blood carried a spark of magic, I wasn't permitted to taint the other Grace children in the nursery with my presence. Mistress Lavender volunteered to take me in—persuaded by a bump in salary, no doubt—and sequestered me in the attic room of Lavender House.

Twenty years later, I'm still there.

The Grace pennants in the pink, yellow, and green of our house snap above me as I push the front door open. Almost without my bidding, my gaze travels to the coral-tinged tips of the Etherian mountain range in the north, the border between the mortal lands of Briar and the Fae courts.

In Briar itself, the only magic that exists is that which the Graces and I provide with our blood. But every soul in the realm knows the stories surrounding the Etherian lands. It's said that the soil in the Fae courts can sprout anything from treasure-bearing trees to treacle-petaled flowers, each one grown from the seed of a whispered wish. That birds sing the future in their melodies. That fish can grant a heart's greatest desire if swallowed whole when caught. Nearly a thousand years ago, Briar was only a barren wasteland. But that didn't stop countless mortals from sailing across the Carthegean Sea, marching through our future realm, and trying to breach the mountains and claim the magic of the Fae.

The Etherians soon grew tired of pushing back army after army. And once Briar was established—the only mortal realm on this side of the Carthegean Sea—the first queen swore to protect the mountain border from encroaching humans. As part of this alliance, the Fae granted Briar permission to mine Etherium—a magic-rich mineral found in the heart of the Etherian Mountains. The ground-up powder can be used to cure ailments, enhance beauty, and I've even heard that a strong enough dose can bring feelings of euphoria. With the healing Graces in Briar, we have little need of Etherium's medicinal properties. But the nobles in the Grace District like to keep vials on hand in order to nurse wine-soaked heads, and small dishes are always provided for patrons to enjoy in the Grace parlors. But the true bliss the mineral brings is in its lucrative overseas trade. The realms across the Carthegean Sea can't get enough Etherium. And our seemingly endless, exclusive supply is the reason Briar boasts the title of wealthiest realm in the world.

But not even Briar's ocean-deep coffers grant us the right to set foot beyond the mountains. Etheria belongs to the Fae alone. It's a restriction that many of the nobles complain is unjust. Some, usually drunk, even claim that they would explore Malterre, the land where the Vila once dwelled. If I look closely enough, I think I can see the shadows dance in the distance. Hear the cry of a lonely raven and detect the pungent bite of sulfur.

The home of my ancestors.

Malterre is abandoned now, salted with a poison that wiped out nearly all of the cursed race of Vila when humans and Etherians banded together to end the War of the Fae. But the fact of their near extinction does not curb the gruesome tales still circulating about the creatures. That the Vila plucked mortal infants straight from their cradles and replaced them with changelings. That they lured humans to their lairs and used them as slaves. That a mere look from one could turn your blood to ice or stop your heart.

These stories prey on my mind every waking moment. They dig their mutinous claws into my very dreams. I see them etched into the expressions of everyone who has the misfortune of crossing my path.

And with every slurred oath uttered behind my back, I am reminded:

I am half Vila. And everyone in Briar wishes I were dead.

CHAPTER FOUR

Even in this summer's humid breeze, I will not leave the house uncloaked. Laurel argues that the practice makes me even more conspicuous when all the ladies are in silks and light lace shawls and working their fans to keep cool. But she has never had to navigate the streets as the Dark Grace.

Before venturing off into the Grace District, I steal around the back of the house and fetch Callow, knowing she will be grateful for the fresh air. Mistress Lavender doesn't approve of my taking my bird with me when I travel the district, but I don't care. Callow's talons are a familiar, comforting pressure against my shoulder, and she helps keep people at bay.

As we weave through the district, the homes of the upper nobility and the other Grace houses soar overhead, all columns and ironwork and huge windows that dazzle in the bright, sea-salted sunlight. The streets are lined with poplars and hydrangeas and azalea bushes that give off a rich, sticky-sweet scent. With such lush surroundings, it's hard to believe the level of poverty that exists beyond the thick stone walls to the east in the Common District, a labyrinth of drab buildings that houses those who can't afford the ornate residences of the Grace District. Merchants, servants, and even disgraced nobility are all relegated to the Common District, unable to cross into the glittering world of the wealthy unless on official errands. In fact, the only shops permitted in the Grace District are those belonging to upscale clothiers like Madame LaRoche, merchants of fine goods, and apothecaries like Hilde.

I don't bother to try to hail a carriage. They wouldn't take me with Callow on my shoulder, and this close to the princess's birthday celebration, they're all overburdened anyway, teeming with passengers worrying over errand lists twice as long as mine. Besides, I find the drivers unfathomably annoying. Either they refuse to stop for me, or they spend the entire drive quaking in fear that I'll use my Vila blood against them. The last trip I took almost landed me in a ditch after I popped my head through the front window to amend my destination and nearly frightened the driver to death.

Liveried servants scuttle around the horses' clopping hooves, earning colorful oaths from the coachmen. In all the tumult, everyone is too busy even to notice me, only wincing when they draw too near and Callow snaps at them. I encourage her to bite their noses off.

The crowd carries me closer to the royal residence than I'd like. The palace, a behemoth of turrets and spires and battlements, looms over the Grace District. It's carved out of the very rose-stained stone of the Etherian mountain range, which rises at its back. I've heard the entrance to the Etherium mines is below the palace itself. Crates of the powdered mineral trundle away toward the Common District and the harbor to be sold overseas, or to be bottled and stocked at the apothecaries here in the Grace District.

Near the palace's elaborate gates of solid white gold stands the towering bronze statue of Leythana, Briar's first queen. The sun gleams against her broad shoulders. The Briar crown—a wreath of brambles and roses and thorns—sparkles on her head. Droplets of gold track down her forehead like melting wax, a symbol of the Etherian blood that blessed her rule.

Leythana's is a story I know well. During the time before Briar, when the mortals would send their futile campaigns across the Carthegean Sea, a Vila snuck into the court of the High King of the Fae and stole his staff.

High King Oryn was furious. The staff was the instrument of his power, and all of the Fae courts trembled to think what a Vila would do with that prize. But not even the fiercest Fae warriors dared to go into Malterre and retrieve the staff for their king. The Vila's land—saturated as it was with dark magic—would poison any Etherian who set foot in their domain. And so Oryn set a challenge.

The mortal who managed to retrieve his staff would win the right to rule the empty borderland. It was an arrangement that suited the High King well, as the victorious mortal would serve as warden to the Fae border, thus putting an end to the constant onslaught of foreign armies trying to breach the mountains.

It seemed a simple challenge to the knights and princes and even kings who were valiant enough to make the quest. But those men focused on threats and brute force to recover the staff, killing the Vila and laying siege to Malterre. Every one met his death in battle.

Until Leythana.

Using her own mind as a blade, Leythana negotiated her way into Malterre under the flag of diplomacy. This was a woman who was rumored to mount the heads of her enemies on the masts of her ships, but not a single drop of blood—mortal or Vila—was spilled in her endeavor. She convinced the Vila to return the staff to the High King. Established her own truce with the dark creatures, promising that Malterre would remain unmolested while she ruled Briar. Once Leythana returned to Etheria with the Fae staff, Oryn was so grateful that he fashioned a wreath of bramble and thorn, gilded it, then blessed it with his very blood. It was a blessing that symbolized the Fae alliance, promised Fae protection, and ensured that only the new queen's heirs could rule Briar from that day on. The crown itself would kill any usurper.

As a child, when I was subjected to every manner of experiment to determine how a half-Vila infant had appeared in Briar, I dreamed of what it took for Leythana to earn that crown. Our first queen was a warrior. Legend says she sailed into the realm she was destined to rule on ships constructed of dragon carcasses, their great wings fashioned into sails and their enormous jaws roaring at the bows.

I'd read and reread Leythana's story until it was written

on my heart. Repeated it to myself when the healing Graces came, their brutal, cold hands holding me down while they drew vial after vial of my blood. Pictured myself wearing that Fae-blessed crown as they dunked my head under vats of Etherium-seasoned water until it filled my lungs. Pretended that as they poured countless sticky-sour tinctures and serums down my throat I needed only to endure. One day it would be worth it. One day I would be like that first queen—untouchable.

Someone hurtles past me so fast he drops his bundles, jarring me out of the cesspool of my memory. Callow screams and he fires off complaints and curses at me, then I see myself mirrored in his gaze and he begins spluttering terrified apologies instead.

And once again I'm reminded that my imaginings were nothing but childhood fancy.

I'll never be a heroine like Leythana. In Briar, I'll only ever be a villain.

Hilde is the one woman in Briar who doesn't treat me like I'm a pile of horse droppings on the street. Perhaps that's because she sees her fair share of oddities in her line of work. Or because she's like me, in a way. Both of us pinned by circumstance in a place we don't belong. I visit her personally for my own enhancements instead of enlisting a servant to fetch them like the other Graces do.

She waves from behind her counter as I enter, the little bell on the door jangling merrily. A few of her other customers glance up. I let my hood fall around my shoulders and scowl at them. The shop is empty in seconds.

"Always one to make an entrance." Hilde shakes her head. Sweat glistens on her tawny brow, and she wipes it away with a long, lean-muscled forearm. In a realm where nearly everyone sports Grace-gifted features, Hilde is refreshingly plain. Her black hair, sprinkled with gray, is swept into a messy bun beneath her cap, and fine scars—the marks of her trade—etch themselves across the backs of her hands and along her fingers.

"Sorry." I settle Callow on the counter and unfasten my cloak. The scent of enhancements is so thick I can taste the earthy sage and the tang of citrus, laced with the undercurrent of coppery blood. "I didn't mean—"

"They'll be back." Hilde shoos away my apology. She fishes a few dead beetles from a jar for Callow, who gobbles them up as if she hadn't already eaten her weight in venison trimmings this morning. "I'll not be lacking for the coin, I can tell you that much. Not with everyone losing their minds over that ball. Now what can I get for you today, Alyce?"

I hand over the list. Hilde doesn't flinch as her fingers brush mine.

"This isn't your usual sort."

"It's not for me." I don't even try to keep the salt out of my tone. "Rose sent me."

Hilde snorts. "I see. High and mighty Grace too busy to come here herself?"

"But never too busy for Madame LaRoche."

"What a surprise." Setting the parchment on her counter,

Hilde begins filling the order. I let my attention drift. Dried plants hang in bundles from the eaves—sachets of periwinkle and yellowed bouquets of calla lilies and leathered strips of birch bark. Vials of every shape, size, and color crowd the shelves. Stuffed wildlife with glass eyes snarl down at me from high corners. Hilde's pets, she calls them.

"I don't see why you let them order you about." The apothecary's voice is muffled as she roots around in the back stores. "They aren't any different than you are."

"You know that's not true."

"Why?" She reappears, half of Rose's order stacked precariously in her arms. "Because your blood is green and theirs is gold?" She wrinkles her nose. "I've never liked gold much myself. Too gaudy."

"I don't think the rest of Briar agrees with you." I begin helping her pile the items into a sack. "They started a war over it once."

"The rest of Briar can take a dive off the Crimson Cliffs as far as I'm concerned."

A strangled laugh escapes me.

"What? So they can. Obsessed with charm and beauty and whatever other fripperies those Graces can dish out. Mark my words, Alyce. When the Etherians created the Graces, they weren't doing us a favor."

I stifle a groan. Hilde and her conspiracies. She's been breathing in too many of her potions. Graced children are the most coveted in the realm. Expecting mothers, especially those in the Common District, pray that the Etherians will visit and Grace their unborn babies.

"More of your stories, Hilde?" Callow pecks at a glass case filled with withered snake carcasses and I nudge her away.

"Don't sass me, little miss." Her honey-brown eyes narrow. "If you used your brain, you'd know I'm right. The entire realm has gone mad for Grace elixirs. Nobles rip one another to bits to get a particular shade of hair or a clever tongue. It's a Fae trick, girl. They're laughing at us from their courts. Same as when they set that challenge."

Confusion rumples my brow. "You mean the challenge to win the Briar crown?"

"And do you know of any other challenge set by the Fae?"

"No." I grab a handful of small vials and stuff them into my sack. "But I don't see why you think it was some kind of trick."

"When have the Fae done anything that didn't suit their own interests? Mortals mean little enough to their kind. Why should we? We're gone in a blink and they live nearly forever." Hilde tosses another beetle at Callow, who snaps it out of the air and chitters with delight. "And now that poor princess reduced to a breeding mare—having to pop out heirs in order to keep the throne secure. Last heir, indeed. You see how much the Etherians care about her plight."

There's nothing poor about Briar's royal family, but I keep that back. Even around Hilde. "Maybe. But I still think Leythana deserved to rule Briar. I read about her campaigns before she came here. Did you know that she overthrew the Cardon King because of the way he treated his people? That's why the island isn't a monarchy anymore. And her crew was mostly women—they all had a say in what missions they undertook. Things would be better in Briar these days if the queens had followed Leythana's lead."

Hilde places a hand on her chest. "I had no idea I had such a devout follower in my shop."

Something burns in my chest, and I try to smooth it away with a shrug. "I know my history is all."

"Indeed." Hilde taps her sorrel-stained fingertip on the lid of a jar. "I imagine you know far more than I do. But I ask you this, Alyce: Was it a victory Leythana won, when they put the Briar crown on her head? Or a curse?"

Curse. The word slithers between my ribs. And a scar just to the right of my navel twinges. I clench my fist to keep from touching it.

"I'm the only one cursed around here."

"Are you? I hadn't noticed." She opens the jar and frowns. "Damn. I'm out of robin's eggs. Your precious Grace will have to do without."

I chew my lip. If I go back without every item on Rose's list, she'll throw a fit.

"I'll get them myself, then." There are some thickets outside Briar's main gates where I've gone before to gather robin's eggs. It shouldn't take long.

Hilde grunts and folds the list in half, passing it back. "Sounds like a fool's errand."

"I'd be a fool if I give Mistress Lavender any more reasons to scold me." I reach for the sack, but Hilde snags my wrist. There's an unfamiliar seriousness to her expression.

"There's a reason you're drawn to the first queen," she

says. "I know a bit of history, too. Enough to guess that there's power in you, girl. More than you realize. I look forward to the day when you wake up and start using it."

The apothecary's words follow me as I make my way to the stone walls that divide Briar into the Grace and Common districts. There's a line of merchants and servants queued at the gate, wagons being inspected by Grace District guards to ensure against smugglers and thieves. For once, my appearance works in my favor. It's not uncommon for me to visit this district on my way to the main gates, and I'm allowed to bypass the checkpoint without the proper papers, slipping through a side door with hardly a nod from the guard.

In the Common District, grimy houses and storefronts are packed together like pickled fish. My reputation known even in this filthy place, I keep to the alleys, dodging grubby sheets drying on clotheslines and clusters of chickens that scatter at Callow's elongated shadow. Too often, I've been chased by a pack of local children who think it amusing to use my back as target practice for rotted fruit or pails of dirty wash water. I keep my hood tugged down.

But even my heightened awareness is not enough to bury Hilde's ridiculous prediction. She spoke as if my power was some kind of blessing. But my heritage has been drilled into my head since I was old enough to comprehend it: I am part Vila. My kind was ruthless and unfeeling and driven out for good reason. I deserve to be punished for their crimes.

Even so, an inexplicable boldness flashed through me at

the apothecary's touch. What if Hilde is right? What if I can do more than the Graces? When I was first learning how to use my gift, we found that my power is unpredictable at times. Without enhancements, Grace blood does little more than sparkle. But a drop of mine can act all on its own. Healing Graces used to dread treating me because my blood was known to cause burns or sores if it dripped on their skin. The bowls they used for my bloodletting would often rust or corrode. And then there's what I did to Rose at tea a few days ago. A terrifying part of my soul whispers that I can do far more than spoil a jug of cream. That I want to.

After the guards at the main gates wave me on, I try my best to drown this feeling in the sea breeze. The coastal landscape of green earth and craggy rock has always been a refuge for me. Out here, there are no Graces or patrons or house standings. Only the Carthegean Sea swallowing the horizon, a depthless azure that stretches all the way to realms I've only read about.

Sometimes Laurel jokes that I would be a wisdom Grace if my blood was gold, for I devour every atlas and geography text I can get my hands on. According to those books, Briar is the smallest realm in the world. We've only the Grace and Common districts and a smattering of homesteads outside the main walls. Other realms boast a seemingly endless expanse of villages and cities and landmarks. I remember tracing my fingertips along the ribbons of blue marking the rivers. Measuring the lakes with the pad of my thumb. Connecting the dots denoting the towns like constellations, testing their names on my tongue and imagining what the citizens living within those places might look like or sound like or believe. In Tyrna, a landlocked queendom ten times our size, they worship dozens of goddesses. One for every season and emotion and aspiration. In Cardon, the small island now governed by several influential families, decisions are made by debating and casting votes. And then there are the tantalizing, undiscovered places just waiting to be explored.

A bell rings in the distant harbor, where Briar's great ships are moored and swaying on the waves. High on their masts, golden flags emblazoned with the Briar rose snap and ripple in the wind. From their bows jut dragon heads, an homage to Leythana, their jaws wide and grinning. As if the creatures cannot wait to be untethered and set loose on the sea.

Not for the first time, I wonder what it would be like to be aboard one of those ships. To feel the scrape of the salt wind on my cheeks, nothing but ocean in front of me. To see the glimmer of the palace fade behind me forever. To never hear the words *Dark Grace* uttered again.

But the Grace Laws forbid any Grace from leaving Briar, even after she's Faded. The Crown does not want other realms accessing a Grace's blood, golden or silvered, on the chance that the Etherian magic could be used against us. The Grace Council went so far as to train packs of hunting dogs to sniff out Grace blood. Each ship is searched before it leaves port. Any Grace found belowdecks is severely punished.

But I am not a Grace. The thought flames hot. I smother it.

Beyond the harbor, heat undulates against the Crimson Cliffs. With sea-slicked rocks the color of wet mortal blood, the cliffs are named for the time before Briar existed, when the light Fae used the power in their staffs to summon squalls and tidal waves to shove back the human ships that dared trespass, sending them to shatter against the garish rocks as if they were no more than wooden playthings. It's said that the seabed around the cliffs is nothing but bones and rusted swords and ghostly hulls.

A shiver races between my shoulder blades.

Once Leythana was crowned, the realms across the Carthegean Sea didn't dare antagonize the ruler who'd won the Etherians' challenge and earned the Fae alliance. And, centuries later, none want to jeopardize their stake in the Etherium trade by souring their relationship with Briar.

But wealth is the only legacy Leythana left behind.

As her reputation was enough of a deterrent, Leythana waged no wars against invaders. Even so, she and her early descendants built up a formidable army and navy—the envy of the world, if the stories are true. But as time passed, the warrior queens softened. They saw little use for a strong defense when the Etherium was security enough against any foreign threat, so the military funds were diverted to tasks such as beautifying the Grace District and constructing a new palace. And worse, the queens began carving up the hard-won power Leythana bequeathed to her descendants. Slice after slice of royal authority was served to their greedy husbands, who turned a blind eye to the growing hunger of the Common District and the unchecked depravity of the nobles. Our current queen is nearly powerless next to her husband, King Tarkin. Though she's the heir of the most powerful woman in the world, Mariel is hardly more than a figurehead. A mere dragon on a bowsprit—hollow on the inside.

What would Leythana think now, if she could glimpse the future her efforts had wrought?

I think she would burn it all down.

CHAPTER FIVE

The robin's eggs are easy enough to find, though the hunt takes me farther away from Briar's outer walls than I've been in a while. I don't mind the extra time away from the Grace District. Callow agrees, ruffling her feathers and letting out a satisfied shriek. She hates the Lair as much as I do. When I'd first found my kestrel on these cliffs, my heart broke at the thought of someday setting her free. Lavender House is not equipped with a mews, and I am untrained in falconry. But as she healed, it became clear that Callow would not be returning to the sky. One of her wings was too badly injured. And so she remains with me, denied the freedom that is hers by right. A gull calls overhead as if mocking her. Talons needle into the flesh beneath my gown.

"Don't listen," I tell her. "We have each other."

As much as I enjoy visiting Hilde, I've always preferred fetching my own enhancements to buying them. When I first began practicing my gift, I devised physical challenges for myself as a distraction from the loneliness I experienced within the walls of Lavender House. They started small, with scaling trees and balancing on boulders. Then I started pushing myself to reach even the highest nest within the spindliest branches, where the elusive, dark-mottled eggs of a carrion crow waited, or wriggling into the narrowest burrow to scavenge weasel whiskers and discarded badger claws. I almost never lost this game, no matter how impossible the errand.

But the robins' laying season is nearly done. Rose would have to make do with just two of the bright-blue eggshells. Once I pack the fragile things away, I stretch my arms over my head and breathe deeply, letting the briny, humid air warm me inside and out. I wish I could listen to the sea from my attic room in Lavender House. There all I can hear is shouting and wheels against stone. The bustle of the servants and Rose's grating laughter.

A familiar shape in the distance catches my eye. Perched high on the sea cliffs, it might look at first like nothing more than a mountain of rubble stacked in the vague shape of a castle's tower. But I know the story. It's a relic of early Briar. Not of the original palace—those ancient bones still stand beside the new monstrosity. This structure was built before there were Grace and Common districts. Possibly before even the main walls were constructed—during the years in which Leythana and her first heirs allowed their subjects to settle wherever they chose. It must have been a wealthy home, if the surviving tower is only a piece of it. But it was built too close to the cliff's edge and, over the centuries, the strong sea squalls from Briar's coast began to chip it apart, stone by stone. It's been abandoned for generations. Uninhabitable, except by the ghosts said to haunt its hollow halls.

Ghosts. Ridiculous.

Still, I've always felt a strange pull to the place. How fitting would it be, the Dark Grace living in the wretched castle tower? Not that I'd ever be allowed to leave Lavender House before my gift ran out. But once it does, the Grace Council has to grant me lodging somewhere. Out here, I'd never have to worry about visitors again. It's a sweet enough thought to have me checking the angle of the sun. Calculating how long it would take for me to get to the tower and back. And then I'm on my way toward the ruins.

Clumps of trees patch the landscape, their roots clinging to the cliffside like giant spider's legs. Their branches provide only the barest shade to combat the heat of the sun. Gulls call back and forth overhead, riding a sticky, slow-moving breeze that does little to circulate the cottony air. Before I'm halfway to the tower, my dress is plastered to my skin. Sweat beads down my neck and across my back. The sack filled with Rose's order is heavier with each step.

But the trip to the ruins is worth it. Just before the earth drops away, the black tower staggers into the sky on its wobbly legs. Pieces of the roof have fallen off or caved in. Black vines snake in and out of broken windows like the arteries of some gargantuan creature. I love it.

The door is the only part of the tower still relatively intact. It's made of oak, with various crests and patterns I don't recognize carved into the silty surface. I set my sack down and transfer Callow—who has much to say about being left behind—to a fallen log nearby and secure her jesses to a limb. And then it takes three hard shoves of my unhappy shoulder to get the door to give. The rusted hinges scream an iron-laced peal. Even then, I achieve only a hands-breadth sliver of space between the door and the frame. I suck in my breath and angle myself through.

The chamber within might as well be a tomb. A crumbling stone staircase hobbles up the side of one curved wall. Judging from the mezzanines, the structure has three floors, their railings furry with moss and draped with cobwebs. Tattered banners still hang from the beams, the shredded hems billowing in the sea breeze. And there's a perpetual echo of the roar of the ocean, which is plainly visible through a wide, gaping hole in the far wall, where a hall must once have connected the tower to the rest of the manor.

Movement to my far right snags my attention, coupled with a sound too heavy to be a rat or a snake. It seems I'm not the only one who thought the black tower looked inviting.

"Who's there?" I fight to keep the tremor out of my voice. I have no elixir ready to use in my defense. Even if I did, the Grace Laws forbid it. And the people of Briar would string me up if I harmed one of their own. I'd be at the bottom of the sea before sunset.

I squint in the gloom and take one step forward. Two. I think I can make out the shape of hunched shoulders. The sheen of dark eyes.

"Please." The voice is raspy, as if it hasn't been used in some time. It's a man's, I think. And the accent is strange. Clipped and clean despite the scrape of gravel in it. Perhaps even foreign. "I mean you no harm."

Adrenaline hums through me. "Come into the light, then."

"I . . . cannot." He wheezes, choking on his own tongue.

"Why not?" I pick up a rusted iron bar and test its weight.

The darkness shifts, churning like the waves of the sea outside. A man's shape begins to emerge. Tall and lean. Peeled from the darkness, as if the very shadows had cobbled him together and given him life. Tendrils of black unspool from his arms, from his hair, like a child's unruly curls. Even his eyes are a bottomless jet black, haunting and desperate.

My heart thunders against my ribs as I scramble backward. But the floor is slick with brine and my feet slip. With a yelp, I tumble onto my backside, pain lancing up my spine as the iron bar clatters against stone.

"Forgive me," the stranger says. "I did not mean to frighten you."

He moves closer, still refusing to step into the sunlight, and his features begin to solidify. Broad shoulders, strong jaw, chin-length hair falling in inky waves around pronounced cheekbones.

One unnaturally pale alabaster hand reaches out as if to touch me and I scuttle away on all fours.

"Are you . . . real?" His throat bobs.

It's not the first time someone has asked me that question—typically drunken imbeciles I encounter at night. Anger quickly replaces the panic sawing through my lungs.

I shove myself up to stand, rubbing at the sore spots on my elbows and palms. "Of course I'm real. What kind of question is that? You can see me, can't you?"

"Yes, but—" He swallows and it looks like it hurts him. "It has been a long time since I had a visitor. Nearly twenty years."

Twenty years. Something scratches at my brain. "That's not possible. I've never heard of anyone living in the tower."

A ghost of a smile tugs at his lips. "I was put here to be forgotten."

Liar. "If I can open that door, you can. There's nothing keeping you here."

"No. I—" He looks at the halo of light at the entrance like a drowning man spotting a piece of driftwood. A muscle flickers in his jaw. "I am bound to the darkness of this tower."

A wave pounds against the cliff. That's impossible. But I study the charcoal shadows twining around his ankles, clutching him as tightly as chains. His dark cloak, rippling slightly in a current of wind incongruous to the breeze I feel. The way he is so careful not to step into the shafts of dappled sunlight sneaking through the cracks in the roof. My mouth goes dry.

An enchantment. But who and, most important—"Why?"

"A punishment." He winces.

"For what?" I press. "It would take strong magic to bind you here. Surely you did something worth remembering."

"It is strong magic," he confirms. And I note the rigid set of his shoulders. His shadows sharpen to spears. "I—it was during the war." He sinks to his knees, one hand clutching his chest. "Please, I cannot say. It is forbidden." A horrible gurgling sound escapes him.

"All right." I rush forward before I can stop my feet, understanding flooding through me in a rush. "The enchantment keeps you from speaking of it?"

He nods, gulping down air.

"Dragon's teeth," I whisper, kneeling beside him. A tingling suspicion raises the hair on my nape. The only creatures I know to be capable of such magic are the Fae. But they can only summon light magic—surely not this sort. Even so, I have no desire to trifle with them, one in particular. And yet—if the stranger's crime was so terrible, he would be known. There would be chains and guards and locks. I wouldn't be able to just stroll inside his prison on a Friday afternoon. "You mentioned a war. Do you mean the War of the Fae?"

He grunts something like assent. And he must, for there isn't any other war in Briar's history. But that was centuries past. And this man has been rotting in here ever since? It's impossible. And yet . . . here he is.

"Does the enchantment keep you from telling me your name?"

"K—" He heaves a ragged breath. "Call me Kal."

"Kal." I test the name on my tongue. "I'm Alyce."

After a few more hacking coughs, Kal calms. He looks at me, a fine line wrinkling his forehead. "You look. No. It cannot be." He scrunches his eyes closed and opens them again. Without warning, he seizes my forearm and yanks me toward him.

"Let me go!" But he's stronger than I imagine. And so

painfully cold. Like frosted steel through the sleeve of my dress.

He examines the tracks of green on my wrist. "You are Vila."

An all-too-familiar shame trickles down the back of my throat. "Half."

"Your mother. Who was she?" His grip tightens.

"I don't know," I admit, heat burning in my cheeks. Perhaps this man is telling the truth about his captivity. Even the youngest child in Briar knows the story of the Dark Grace, and I don't appreciate being made to retell it. "She left me. When I was an infant."

"Twenty years ago."

A cold that has nothing to do with Kal prickles across my shoulder blades. The sea crashes outside. "How do you know that?"

He smiles, a real smile this time. He glows with it. "Because I knew her. Lynnore."

The breath leaves my body. *Lynnore.* For twenty years I've wondered, haunted by the specter of parents who abandoned me near the harbor like I was no better than a basket of rotting fish. I pictured my mother a hundred thousand ways. Weak and destitute, hoping someone would take pity on her cursed child. Indifferent and shrewd, willing to cast me off for her own gain. Terrified and lost, having birthed a defective Grace and too afraid to claim it.

And now those ghosts have a name: Lynnore.

"Why should I believe you? My mother left me to die in an alley. If you were her friend, then—"

"She did not leave you." The prisoner's black eyes flash.

"Lynnore entrusted you to a woman in the Common District, where you would be safe while she came here to help me. Free me from this tower. And then we were going to leave together—all of us."

A wind whistles through the cracks in the stone. The fishmonger. He could have had a wife. I imagine the woman waiting with me as the hours ticked by, apprehension building. And then, when my mother never came back for me, she panicked. Her husband would have wanted nothing to do with a hideous infant and her unknown powers, and so he delivered me to the Grace Council. Which means my mother might have walked these very stones. Smelled the salt and the mold and the reek of fish. It takes me a moment to find my voice and I struggle to disguise how much Kal's words have affected me.

"She was—she was Vila?"

"Only partly. Like you. Oh, Alyce. I can see her in you. The same mouth and nose." He lifts my hand. "The same fingers."

I remove myself from his grasp and retreat farther into the sunlight. "Why would she have wanted to help you?"

Hurt flits across Kal's features—an expression I know well from the number of times I've been brushed off or shoved aside—but he continues. "They did not know about her Vila blood. She disguised it well. And she found me here, much as you just did. We were kin, in a way, as both of us hailed from Malterre. And she understood the cruelty of this prison. No one deserves this fate."

"But how did she hide from the Fae ambassador? I couldn't."

Endlewild.

A full-blooded Etherian appointed to the royal household and tasked with holding together the alliance between the Fae courts and Briar. It was he who recognized my Vila blood when I was dumped in the lap of the Grace Council. He who led the experiments to see if I was Vila enough to kill, or just a darker version of a Grace. My insides wither at the thought of his golden Fae eyes and bark-like skin, brown and grooved like that of an oak, and that same pain from Hilde's shop resurfaces. This time, I can't help but press the heel of my palm into the place on my middle.

"She appeared human. More so than you do," Kal adds quietly, as if worried it will offend me.

"Is that why she never came back for me? Because it was easier for her to hide?"

"They killed her." He grinds his teeth. "The beasts. It was just after she attempted to sever my bindings. But the power of the enchantment was too great. She went back for you. We would try again another day. I was watching her return to Briar as I always did, and they intercepted her. I do not know how they knew she was here. Or how they determined what she was. There was some kind of argument, and then they threw her into the sea. These abominable shadows rendered me powerless to stop them. And you—I thought you were dead, too."

"Beasts? Who do you mean?"

It couldn't have been Endlewild—then there would have been no questions about my origins when I turned up in the Common District. And I doubt it was the king's men. But Kal's mouth just opens and closes, the bones of his neck straining as he struggles to speak. Callow screeches outside, and it seems to knock a dose of sense into me.

I have no reason to trust this man. No proof that what he says is true. "This is too much. I have to go."

"Wait! I can help you. I know the power that runs in your veins. The gift of the Vila."

I pause mid-step. "The curse, you mean."

His dark brows knit together. "Is that what you think? What they told you?"

Against my own instinct, I find myself rushing on. "What else can it be? All I can summon is ugliness and pain."

"Alyce." I've never heard my name spoken that way before, with compassion, and it almost hurts. "You are so much more than that."

"What am I?" The question is barely more than a whisper, an aching need that's plagued me since I was old enough to understand the extent of my otherness. "You said my mother looked more human than I do. Why? I'm part Vila, but what about the rest? Do you know?"

"I do." A tide of Kal's shadows rolls toward me, sizzling when it reaches the sunlight. "Are you certain you wish me to tell you?"

No. But I can't seem to turn away, either. And so I nod.

"You are a Shifter. Just like me."

CHAPTER SIX

I'm not sure how I got back to Lavender House.

As soon as I'd regained my senses, I fled the tower. Away from Kal. Away from the brand he seared into my back.

Shifter.

The word rings in my head, echoing off the curves of my skull until it swallows every other thought. Before the war, Shifters were one of the many creatures drawn to Malterre by the darkness of the Vila's power. And like all the rest—Demons and Imps and Goblins and more—Shifters are bloodthirsty monsters. But Shifters are more than just vicious. They're manipulative and cunning. They can turn themselves into whatever form they wish: beasts with the head of a wolf and body of a griffin. Beautiful maidens who lure their victims in and slit their throats.

I read one story in which a Shifter bargained with a mortal—a year of the human's service in exchange for a pair of wings. The human was unaware that a Shifter can only change its own body. And so after the year was up, the Shifter fashioned a pair of wings out of wax and fixed them to the human's shoulders. Overjoyed, the mortal leapt off the nearest cliff. He soared over the waves of the Carthegean Sea, but the wings soon melted in the heat of the sun, sending the unwitting mortal to crash into the water and drown.

I cannot be a Shifter.

If the prisoner spoke true, why wasn't I killed, like all the other Shifters I'd read about? Destroyed before they could wreak havoc on the realm. Why did the Briar King let me exhale a single breath once he knew of my existence?

The questions rend me to ribbons. Corrupt my dreams when I stumble into spurts of sleep. In the swirling images, fur sprouts from my skin and my teeth lengthen into fangs. I try to run, but my legs are fins or spindly spider's legs and I cannot move, only *scream* and—

Something slams into my shoulder hard enough to throw me halfway off the bed.

"Get up, you useless creature."

I catch myself before I fall to the floor and then wince against the white blur of the morning. A shadow looms over me.

"How am I supposed to treat my patrons without ground peacock feathers?"

A petal-pink curl dangles in front of my face. Rose. She tosses a broken vial at my fingertips, and I'm barely able to jerk away before the shards lodge in my skin. I groan, hefting myself upright. That damn sack. In my flight from the black tower, my clumsy hands had dropped it more than once. I'm surprised only the one vial was smashed.

"I'll get another." I rub the sleep from my eyes.

"Oh no, you won't." Rose taps her slipper and the bells sewn onto the toes jingle. "I've already sent a servant. But it will come out of your wages. Mistress Lavender said."

I doubt that, but I'm too groggy to argue. "That's fine. Get out."

"Someone woke up on the wrong side of the bed." Glass crunches under her heel.

"*Someone* was dragged off the wrong side of the bed."

"It's your own fault if you're lazy. I've been up for ages. Already had three patrons."

"How's your blood looking?" It's a low jab, but an effective one. Twin splotches, like gilded dandelions, erupt on Rose's cheeks. "Finding any silver specks?"

"My blood looks far better than yours." She sneers. "I'd jump off the Crimson Cliffs if I had green in my veins. Do everyone a favor."

"Careful, Rose." I rest my chin on my knees and grin. "You never know what the Dark Grace might do. Poor thing. Your teeth are still a bit gray around the edges."

She snaps her lips closed and whirls, the bells on her shoes tinkling.

"Speaking of patrons," she calls over her shoulder. "Yours have been waiting for the past half hour."

The door slams behind her and I bark out a litany of curses, rushing to pick out a fresh dress. The black wax seal of Delphine's schedule, still waiting to be broken, glares at me from the floor. A servant must have slipped it under the door on their rounds to wake the Graces. But I'd been sleeping too deeply to hear their knock. Dragon's teeth! Mistress Lavender hates for patrons to wait; it makes them more likely to bring their business to another house and lower our standings. And even if I am the Dark Grace, the only one in the realm, she insists I adhere to the same standard of service as the others.

I rake a comb through my lank, oily hair and splash some water on my face. The reflection in my spotted mirror isn't inspiring. But I drag myself downstairs anyway, stuffing a breakfast roll in my mouth and ripping open my schedule before heading to the Lair.

"Alyce, really," Mistress Lavender chides, herding me through the kitchen. "The ball is *tonight*. The house cannot afford any mistakes."

I mutter a few apologies while she continues to rant about duty and service and Lavender House's rank, then I scuttle out the door.

For the rest of the day I entertain patrons: I whip up elixirs to leaden nimble feet. To tarnish lustrous skin and snub graceful noses. To replace a pleasant singing voice or musical laugh with the squawk of a crow. It doesn't matter if the victims have already employed the service of a Grace. My magic is stronger, a fact we learned when it was decided that I was to open my own practice and the Grace Council was testing the limits of my power against the Graces'. A Grace can attempt to cover the effects of my elixirs, but the darkness always bleeds through. The ill effects of my magic Fade eventually, but they cannot be completely undone, not even by the healing Graces. Much as I abhor being the Dark Grace, my blood's power to thwart the Graces' always gives me a rush of victory.

It's not until evening that I'm finally stoppering my last vial. The patron is already dressed in his finery for the ball and is quick to depart. My bones ache, fingertips sore from where I've slashed myself over a dozen times already. It's all I can do to feed Callow and haul myself back to the house, desperate for a bowl of whatever Cook has waiting in the kitchen. The smell has been making my mouth water for hours.

"Dragon's teeth, but you look a fright!"

My mood only further sours as Rose sweeps into view. She looks like an elaborately decorated dessert in her cascade of silk skirts and pearl-studded ringlets. She whips a matching fan out of her reticule and waves it under her nose with distaste. "And what have you been cooking up?"

"Toad piss." I shake my skirts in the hopes that the dirt and soot will spoil her gown. "I'll be sure to add some to your bottles of scent."

Rose glares and steps away from me. Marigold flounces in behind her, dressed in frills of daffodil silk. Heavy gold limns her eyes. Grace powder sparkles on her brown shoulders.

"You aren't ready!" She feigns shock, an ivory-gloved hand at her breast, then deals a conspiratorial smirk to Rose.

"I had patrons." I divide a look between them, confused. "Why didn't you?" This close to the ball, they should have been swamped.

"Oh, we've been finished for simply hours." Rose twirls

her fan. "Delphine arranged it. A courtesy so that we could prepare for the ball."

"I was granted no such courtesy. My last patron just left."

"Really?" A tiny crease digs between Rose's brows. One of the peach-colored ostrich plumes on her fan brushes against her cheekbone. "An oversight, I'm sure."

Marigold titters. "It's a shame you won't be ready."

A bell chimes from the drawing room, announcing the arrival of their carriage. Marigold links arms with Rose, who bestows an infuriating wink upon me. "Good night, Alyce. We'll tell Mistress Lavender you've decided to stay home."

My blood grows so hot I think my skin might be glowing green as their bustles round the corner toward the front door. This is Rose's doing. She probably bribed Delphine to shift my appointments until the last possible moment. It wouldn't have taken much coin. Every servant in this wretched house hates me. It would be useless to involve Mistress Lavender. I can't prove anything. And I'll never be ready in time. I haven't even thought of what to wear.

Part of me wants to go as I am now, just to spite them all. Show up on the palace doorstep in my sweat-stained, reeking gown with remnants of enhancements still caked under my fingernails and smudged on my face. A picture of the deranged creature they think I am. See if they have the gall to turn me away.

But they would turn me away. And Rose would revel in it. I'd never live it down.

And so I turn my attention to the trays of leftover tarts

from today's Grace sessions. I fill a plate—blueberry, raspberry, cardamom—piling them as high as I can, and head up to my attic room. I didn't want to go to the ball anyway, I remind myself. Wouldn't have even thought to go if Rose hadn't rankled me. But now—

There's a heap of fabric on my bed that doesn't belong there.

My mouth freezes around a bite of creamy filling. I swallow quickly, setting the plate down on the top of a side table.

Folded neatly on the twisted coverlet of my bed is the most beautiful dress I've ever seen. It's onyx silk, overlaid with a sheer, gossamer fabric that shines like spun moonlight. Beads of jet dance in intricate patterns down the bodice. The sleeves are the same silvery fabric as the skirt and cut to fall next to the hem, like long, delicate wings. Next to the gown is a mask, one large enough to cover the wearer's entire face. Black, silver-dusted ostrich plumes protrude from the forehead and there's a stiff veil of black and gold netting gathered around the eyeholes, thick enough that it will obscure the midnight color of my gaze.

Beneath the mask, a note:

No one need know.

L

It takes several attempts to convince a servant to both help me into this gown and flag down a carriage to take me to the palace. Her name is Lorne, I think. And I can tell by her puckered lips and pinched brow that she doesn't think I should be going. But after some convincing, her own fear of the Dark Grace wins out and she finally begins unlacing my work dress.

The new gown fits like a glove. Laurel must have spent her own coin to have it made for me. It's the nicest gift I've ever received. The only gift, actually. An unfamiliar surge of emotion swells beneath my breastbone as Lorne does up the fastenings at the back of the bodice. Perhaps Laurel is fonder of me than I thought.

Lorne pins up my hair in a fashion she slyly comments will flatter me, which I take to mean it will hide the oil and dirt I didn't have time to wash out. Because the style isn't particularly flattering—just tightly braided and coiled at the crown of my head. She adds a healthy dusting of Grace powder as well. It itches where it sticks to my chest and neck.

By the time she's finished, the carriage is already waiting. Lorne fastens the mask to my face, then helps me navigate the stairs in my tissue-thin skirts, pausing at the front door. She hesitates, then opens up a closet and pulls out a Grace cloak. One of Rose's that she hardly ever wears. It's gold taffeta trimmed with mink. Gems bright as petrified sunlight are studded down the back, patterned in the Grace sigil of a blooming Briar rose wreathed in laurel leaves. I argue with her at first. The powder is one thing, but to wear the sigil feels too close to flouting the Grace Laws.

But Lorne refuses to budge.

"If it's the Graces invited to the ball," she insists firmly, "you should go as a Grace."

She steps away, revealing my reflection in the foyer's full-length mirror. I don't recognize the figure standing before me. My green-veined skin is completely hidden by the black, elbow-length gloves and the lace at the neckline of my bodice. Lorne even tied a thick ribbon strung with a pearl pendant to disguise the nest of veins at my throat. And the mask covers everything else, even the black of my eyes. If I tilt my head in just the right way, I could swear they burn gold. Dressed like this, I could be anyone. A real Grace. As much as I despise the Graces' spoiled, vapid ways, this new identity locks on to my skin like armor.

I stand straighter, shoulders back and chin high, as I've seen Rose do countless times. Lorne adjusts the cloak, fluffs my skirts one last time. And then I glide out into the night.

CHAPTER SEVEN

The driver is uncommonly kind to me as he navigates the maze of cobbled streets. The palace waits in the distance. Even from here, I can see the gilt-capped turrets spiking into the stars and the dragon gargoyles roaring from the eaves. When Leythana was established as Briar's first queen, the early citizens of her new realm decided that the mountain face would provide the best material with which to build her new palace. Over the following decades, they carved out a few modest wings to serve as the royal residence. But as the queens began relegating their duties to their husbands, the Briar Kings soon decided that those old wings were too sparse and drafty for their liking. The palace of the wealthiest realm in the world should be the envy of every foreign ruler. And so they began expanding and refurbishing and constructing, until the only bit of Leythana's original palace is now a narrow wing that juts off to the side of the newer structure like a stony, sleeping beast. It looks lonely, the dark windows like hollow eyes in the moonlight. Like the eyes of someone else I recently encountered.

"Have you ever met the princess?" the driver asks, snapping the reins.

"No." A firework bursts above our heads, glittery fuchsia and cerulean ash drifting over gabled rooftops.

"Shame about the curse on her. She's a pretty thing, as her sisters were. Would've thought they'd find her true love by this point."

My skin tingles, as it always does when there's talk of the curse. It was a Vila who cast it, taking her revenge on the realm that destroyed her lands in the War of the Fae. All heirs of Briar would die at the age of twenty-one, a curse designed to wipe out anyone living under the protection of the Fae-blessed Briar crown. The Etherians intervened, of course. Unable to destroy the Vila magic, they softened the curse so that it could be undone by a true love's kiss. Even so, dozens of princesses have met untimely deaths, including the current crown princess's two elder sisters. I remember their funerals. The first was when I was only a child, hardly able to understand why the heavy bells tolled day and night, or why Briar was draped in black for months. But the second daughter died just five years ago. I watched the royal family send her out to sea on a floating pyre. Waited on the cliffs with the rest of the Grace District, until the flames were only a distant blaze on the horizon.

I tighten my mask.

"How old is she now?"

He maneuvers around a corner. "You don't know? I thought everyone did."

I'm grateful he can't detect the burn on my cheeks. "Yes, I—well, it's hard to keep track." *When you don't care.*

He laughs at that, flicking the reins again. "Right you are there, Your Grace."

I flinch at the honorific. For the first time in my life, it's not spoken to me with contempt or loathing, but with respect. I'd imagined the change would feel triumphant. Instead, slime slides down my spine and I fight to keep my shoulders from bowing inward.

"Her Highness is turning twenty."

One more year, then. It makes me sad, though I can't fathom why. The royals have never shown kindness to me, unless you count not executing me when I was an infant—an event Mistress Lavender assures me was discussed. But my name is never listed among the honors announced at the yearly Grace Celebration. I was not recognized at a Blooming Ceremony when I began accepting patrons. And if I wasn't disguised, I have no doubt they'd find some reason to turn me away tonight. Mistress Lavender said herself that she didn't know if the invitation included me. And I know the truth in my heart: The Dark Grace is meant to lurk in shadows, keeping the nasty secrets of the nobility. They do not wish to see me in the light.

For the rest of the trip, the driver prattles on about his family. He boasts a brood of six children, apparently, who hope to find work in the Common District, the boys on ships if they're lucky. I'm only half listening. We're passing the manor houses of the minor nobility, those who aren't favored with a suite of rooms in the palace itself. Servants' shadows flit in the glow behind drawn curtains. They'll be heading back to the Common District once their chores are done. No one from that district receives an invitation to royal functions. And I wonder how those servants feel about being excluded from the glittering world they help maintain. If the aches in their shoulders and feet and backs throb with resentment as mine do.

But those servants are soon forgotten when we reach the palace gates. Torchlight laps at the white gold filigree and Briar roses. Sweat spots on the palms of my new gloves. The waist of the gown digs into my ribs, the lace at my neckline prickling against my skin. The driver helps me down, and I'm thankful for the support of his calloused hand. These satin slippers pinch places usually unbothered in my worn leather boots. I'm certain the guards are watching me with suspicion. Without Mistress Lavender here to prove that she allowed me to attend, I half expect that someone will spring from the bushes, rip off my mask, tear the cloak from my shoulders, and send me home in disgrace.

But as I approach the entrance, the men stationed there give only a stiff bow at the waist, the kind every Grace receives in greeting. And then I'm being waved through. Into the palace. As a Grace.

If I thought the parlors in Lavender House were atrociously overdone, it is nothing compared to the palace's ballroom. A massive stained-glass window devours one wall, a vibrant mosaic arranged in a life-size rendering of the royal emblem:

a dragon in flight. A scarlet Briar rose blazes on its chest. Its giant ruby eyes seem to pin me inside the entrance, as if it knows I don't belong. Candlewax drips from golden sconces and dazzling chandeliers, servants flying from one to the next to replace them before the lights gutter out. Tendrils of smoke drift lazily from tiny pots of burning incense, which produces a honeyed, floral scent meant to combat the tang of sweat and perfume, but only serves to nauseate. The marble floor is shot through with amber and encrusted with amethysts and opals, the royal colors. Trays overburdened with goblets of bubbling wine and bowls of plump fruit and shallow dishes of shimmery pink Etherium powder float by on the arms of liveried footmen.

And there are people. Everywhere.

Aside from my excursions in the Grace District, I've never seen so many in one place. Their costumes are ridiculous. One woman is dressed as some kind of sea nymph. Painted shells dangle at her ears and throat, and her gown is an opaque turquoise with candy-scaled fish embroidered into the folds of her skirts that seem to leap and dive as she moves—fabric clearly designed by the innovation Graces, who can use their elixirs to give extraordinary abilities to inanimate objects. Several others wear translucent wings strapped to their shoulders that flap back and forth in lazy tempos. Masks are adorned with Grace-grown chrysanthemums that wither and rebloom into varying hues every few seconds. Some of the men have bottlebrush tails swishing behind their waists and tiny, twitching fox's ears secured to pomade-crusted heads.

There's scarcely room to move as I push slowly through the ballroom doors, which are a staggering two stories high and accented with gems of every color, and into the party. A servant materializes from thin air and unfastens my cloak before I can stop her, mumbling something about where to retrieve it later.

Without my cloak, I feel totally exposed. I glance around, standing stock-still. A rat caught in a trap.

But no one is staring at me.

Adrenaline surges through me. There are no crushing judgmental gazes. No derisive whispers slithering into my ears. The guests pay me no more attention than they would a sitting room chair. As if I were as ordinary as possible. As if I *belong* here.

Footsteps still unsteady, I begin to maneuver my way along the outskirts of the ballroom. Conversation and laughter and music clash in an overwhelming cacophony of sound. The hard edges of the jewels in the floor bite into the soles of my slippers. I wave away the endless trays flung toward my face, knowing I wouldn't be able to keep a single mouthful of it down.

Something knocks against my elbow.

"Pardon me." A man takes a fluid step back from me and bows. His mask covers only the area around his eyes, which are the bright blue of the Carthegean Sea in summer, and are filled with something I don't see often: pleasant curiosity. *About me.* "Are you here alone?" He scans our tight perimeter, searching for my companions.

"I—yes," I admit, unable to snatch a quick enough lie.

"Well, we can't have that. Allow me to introduce myself." He bends again. "Lord Arnley."

Arnley. I've heard that name. I think his family has patronized Lavender House before, mainly for Rose. Those eyes certainly indicate the work of a beauty Grace.

"You are a vision this evening." His gaze sweeps from the hem of my skirt to the tips of the feathers on my mask. "Your costume so obviously complemented my own attire that I felt compelled to seek you out."

He motions to his waistcoat, a deep black that matches his jacket. Diamond cuff links stud each sleeve. A silver cravat, the same shade as the gauzy overlay on my gown, puffs out from his chest. Suspicion begins to build behind my sternum. He sought me out? Has he been watching me? Had Laurel devised our meeting as some cruel joke?

"Such an exquisite mask," he continues, oblivious to my wildfire pulse. "But it denies me the privilege of viewing your face. May I?" He reaches a hand toward the ribbon behind my head. I jerk away, needing much more space between us.

"I prefer not."

"A woman of mystery, I see." He leans close enough that my nose tickles at the fizzy, peach-cream scent of wine on his breath. "My favorite kind."

My toes curl inside my slippers, my tongue glued to the roof of my mouth. Is this flirting? No one has ever spoken to me this way before.

"May I at least have your name?"

A name, damn it all. I had not thought of another name.

Alyce is common enough, isn't it? Or do they all know me? Alyce, the Dark Grace. *Malyce.* A blast of trumpets saves me from having to answer. The crowd quiets, turning to the dais at the front of the ballroom.

"The Briar Queen!" shouts a wiry man in purple-and-white livery, stamped with the royal dragon emblem. "Mariel. Queen of the realm, Warden of the Fae Border and Defender of the Graced." He bangs the gilded end of a cane onto the floor. A tiny dragon rears atop its head, a garnet Briar rose flashing like a beating heart on its chest.

Like a wave in the sea, the mass of nobles and Graces dips and bends as the royal family sails through a private ballroom entrance. And though the Briar Queens have forfeited nearly every one of their duties to their husbands, entering a royal function before the king is one of the few privileges that remain for Mariel.

It seems even this small slight irritates the Briar King. He storms through the doors a step behind his wife, resembling an overinflated balloon. Even his crown is almost comically large, likely made so in order to eclipse the wreath of bramble and thorn his wife wears. Fat square-cut rubies glimmer on the speared tips. His purple cape, trimmed in ermine, only adds to his girth as it billows behind him. A matching doublet is almost invisible beneath the mounds of gold and jeweled chains draped around his neck. As soon as possible, he maneuvers Mariel behind him, dwarfing her in every way. And I can't help but notice the tightness to her features tonight. The restlessness in her step and the way her fingertips tap against the king's sleeve as she clutches his arm.

It's clear soon enough what has her so agitated.

Behind the royal couple, the crowd begins to murmur—a tall, graceful young woman glides into view. The Princess Aurora.

In the books I've read over the years, I learned that there are kingdoms that insist on a male inheritance. Elder or more capable daughters are passed over in favor of a son to manage a kingdom. I've always thought the practice idiotic, the same as inheriting by birth. Look how well it worked for Leythana's line—warrior queens diminished to pretty ornaments.

But though it's widely known that Tarkin yearns for a son, he married a Briar Queen. And Briar Queens—due to the Fae blessing on their crown—only have daughters. It's the same magic that causes Graces to be born female.

The princess's feet hardly seem to touch the ground as she follows her parents onto the royal dais. A gown of embroidered violet silk hugs her body, its color deepening impossibly to midnight blue as she moves. And every movement is visible. The long length of her waist. The curve of her hips. The soft line of her lower spine as it plunges into a back cut far lower than any I've seen here tonight. Or ever.

Whispers begin circulating immediately.

"Scandalous."

"Improper."

"The dressmakers will be in a tizzy tomorrow."

A smile tugs its way from the corners of my mouth. I don't know what I'd expected from the princess, but a rule-breaker wasn't on the list. It's strange to hear such things uttered about someone who isn't me. But undeniably satisfying.

"As we all know"—the king's deep voice quiets the undercurrent of chatter—"the curse on our beloved Aurora has yet to be lifted."

More shifting from the crowd. Aurora stands straighter. Her spun-gold hair, accented with the oranges and coppers and reds of the rising dawn, cascades beneath the slender diadem marking her status.

"But we will not lose hope," the king continues. "In fact, tonight we welcome a suitor."

"Not another one." Arnley snags a wineglass off a servant's tray, then scoops a heaping spoonful of Etherium from another and mixes it into his drink. "The poor girl should at least have a rest at her birthday party."

I'm about to ask what he means when the cane bangs again.

"His Grace, Duke Prichard. Earl of Theonlay and the Western Provinces of Yesalt."

Yesalt. A northeastern kingdom on the other side of the Carthegean Sea, my brain supplies. It's no surprise. Briar Kings are almost always foreign princes, hungry to wrap their fingers around the Etherium mines.

A sickly-looking man sidles in, clearly doing his best to look regal and not like a caught fish. He's failing.

"Oooo another duke." Arnley scoffs and downs his glass.

Suitors for the crown princess are always male, even though couples of the same gender are common in Briar. There are several nearby, like the pair of women just behind me with their arms draped around each other's waists. They wear twin gowns of cornflower organza, accented with sashes made of Grace-gifted butterflies fluttering down the backs of their skirts. But while Briar's citizens may engage in whatever romantic entanglement suits them, the immediate royal heirs are forbidden from such affairs until succession is established. Daughters are required to carry on Leythana's line, and *husbands* are required to get them.

Duke Prichard gives a stiff bow to the onlookers, then another as he nears the royal family. Aurora just stares at him. The queen jabs her daughter discreetly in the ribs with an elbow until she deigns to scrape the barest of curtsies.

"Your Grace. Welcome to Briar." It is the most unwelcoming welcome I've ever heard. I rather like it.

"Thank you, Your Highness." His red, bulbous nose practically touches the floor as he bows. "A very happy birthday to you. You look simply resplendent tonight."

"Resplendent?" I hear someone nearby echo. "How long do you think he practiced that line?"

Aurora inclines her head the smallest possible degree. Candlelight washes over her skin, a bronze-kissed cream. Luminous. Grace-gifted, without doubt.

"Please, Your Grace." King Tarkin snatches Aurora's free hand in the awkward silence that follows and offers it to the duke. "Secure the future of our realm."

The princess doesn't withdraw her hand when the duke's envelops it. But every inch of her remains locked in stone. Duke Prichard takes a hesitant step toward her. Another. Until he's standing closer than he should be.

And then the whole court holds its breath as he leans down and plants a kiss on her lips.

My jaw drops to the floor. The princess was just kissed. In public. By a complete stranger. And no one seems to be batting an eyelash. I'd known the royal curse had to be broken by true love—even that she had to be kissed—but I had no idea it was such a spectacle. An entire court gawking as a man she's never met puts his lips to hers. A strange, uncomfortable sympathy for the crown princess writhes in my belly.

A few taut moments pass, the duke still clutching Aurora's hand as if he might break the curse with the force of his will alone. And then she gently frees herself, unbuttons the sleeve of her gown, and displays her forearm to the audience. The room lets out a disappointed sigh.

There it is, stamped into the princess's otherwise flawless skin: a Briar rose surrounded by bloody thorns. The curse mark borne by each of Leythana's heirs until they either find their true love or . . .

The king claps the dejected suitor on his shoulder, dismissing him, and the musicians begin playing again. But not even the music can mask the frantic whispers of the court or smooth the queen's pinched brow. In fact, the only person who seems the least bit undisturbed is Aurora herself. Far from anxious, the princess appears . . . relieved.

And I might be imagining it, but I think I see a smile ghost across her face.

CHAPTER EIGHT

"Well, I say she made a lucky escape." Arnley tosses back another glass, this time with an even larger dose of Etherium mixed into the wine. A few other nobles join us, eyeing me sideways but saying nothing. "I'm not sure being stuck with that one would have been much better than succumbing to the curse."

Titters of laughter.

"Oh, Arnley, you are horrid." This voice I know. It slices straight through my chest.

Rose.

She saunters into our circle, silk gloves concealing her predator's claws, and loops her arm through Arnley's. Her mask is barely a mask at all, just a thin strip of golden tulle resting across her eyes and secured to an elaborate headdress in the shape of a swan. Crystals glisten like drops of water on its feathers. Of course she wouldn't want her identity concealed—it might mean she's not the center of attention.

"I feel sorry for the poor thing. Such a beauty. All that Grace magic simply wasted if she doesn't find someone within the year. Just like her sisters. And she is the last heir."

In other realms, there can be any number of claimants to a throne. A cousin or nephew or even a favorite can be named successor in place of a direct heir. In Cryseria, whenever the monarch dies, a trial by battle is the method of crowning the new ruler. It's something I'd love to witness if I ever manage to leave Briar. Here, the Etherian treaty is clear—only Leythana's blood can wear the crown of bramble and thorn. Before the curse, perhaps it was possible for some distant relation of Leythana's to take the place of a reigning queen's daughter. Not anymore.

The first years after the curse were turmoil. Because the Vila's magic was so powerful, so steeped in hate, all of Briar's potential heirs bore the curse mark, no matter how far down they were in the line of succession. Women who had already reached their twenty-first year suddenly dropped dead when it turned out they hadn't found their true loves, a nasty revelation for husbands and wives whose royal-blooded spouse abruptly perished. There was so much death that it was decreed that only immediate heirs were permitted to produce daughters—and only once crowned. For many of the royal daughters, the restriction meant little—it was soon discovered that the magic in the Vila's curse kept them barren until the curse was broken. Younger surviving princesses could adopt children, and many did. But the blood that carried the curse had to be contained.

And now there is only Aurora.

"Please." Arnley swats her words away, diamond cuff links twinkling. "One way or another, the crown *will* find a head."

Rose hisses at him to be quiet.

Questions riffle through my mind. What does Arnley mean by that? I don't remember reading about an heir crisis in any of the books on Briar's history. There was certainly nothing about what would happen if Leythana's descendants died out. Are there measures in place? Not that I particularly care.

"She's a beauty, perhaps," a woman chimes in, bringing me back into the circle. She's a Grace, I can tell by her massive arrangement of sapphire hair, roughly in the shape of a beehive. Tiny gilded bees, another gift from the innovation Graces, hover and buzz around her towering braids. "But so brazen. That dress."

"I love it," Rose proclaims, adjusting one of the feathers on her headdress. "I'm going to have Madame LaRoche make an exact copy for me. In red."

"I'd certainly like to see that." Arnley's voice is closer to a purr, thick and a little slurred with the wine.

"Arnley." Rose smacks him with her fan. "You shameless flirt. Come, the music is changing. You owe me a dance."

Yes. I push the thought out with all my might. *Go and dance. Far away from here.* But Arnley's attention swivels back to me, sending my stomach to my toes.

"You know I'd never skip a dance with you, Rose." He grins and gently extracts himself from her talons. "But I'm afraid I've been utterly enchanted by this mysterious guest."

Six pairs of eyes pinion me to the jewel-crusted marble.

This feeling I know well. My mouth goes dry as my pulse kicks up. Dragon's teeth, I was a fool to come here tonight. What was I thinking?

"I never—" I begin, ready to push him off.

But Rose tilts her head at me, drawing her fan through her fingers like a blade. "I don't recognize you."

Damn it all. Stupid, foolish me.

"Isn't that the point?" The beehive Grace laughs. "It's a masque."

Rose's face twists. Even a grimace looks lovely on her. Her tiny nose twitches, as if she can scent the deception, and the vise of my bodice seems to cinch. "But I would still like to know the lady who has captivated our dear Arnley." She combs a jagged-edged gaze up and down my body. "You appear to be a Grace, but I don't know you. Are you newly Bloomed? How many came out at the last Blooming Ceremony?"

The other Grace counts off on her fingers. "Ten, perhaps? I've lost track."

"Yes, and the Grace Celebration was months ago. Why haven't we seen you before?"

"I—" The edges of the eyeholes in my mask begin to darken. I feel a strong arm wind itself around my waist.

"Don't be jealous, Rose." Arnley waggles a finger at her. "It's unbecoming. You know how much I adore surprises. Let this one linger awhile longer." And with a dashing grin at me, the courtier steers me away.

• • •

Dancing with Arnley is equal parts terror and euphoria. As he navigates our place among the couples on the dance floor, I try to argue that I'm a horrible dancer. I'm unpracticed. Dancing with me will only make him look the worse for choosing me. Almost as idiotic as I am for coming to the palace in the first place. But he's deaf to my protests. And it turns out it wouldn't have mattered if I'd swallowed one of my own lead-feet elixirs.

Though clearly touched by the wine, Arnley glides me over the marble as easily as a ship skating across a calm sea. I find myself completing spins and twirls, dips and hops. Heat bursts where his broad hands land on the cobweb lacing at the back of my gown. Other couples watch us through the slits in their masks. But he pays them no mind. His Grace-gifted eyes never leave mine, their sapphire color depthless in the light of the hundreds of candles.

"Is this your first time at the palace?" he asks as he pulls me close. Under the floral headiness of the wine on his breath, I catch the scents of leather and spiced tobacco, not entirely unpleasant. "Aside from your Blooming Ceremony, of course."

"No." I immediately wish I could reel it back. I'm sometimes called to assist the dying, using my elixirs to ease their pain and make their passing swift. My least favorite kind of errand. But I've never been to this part of the royal residence. Never been welcomed inside as a guest. Only as a necessary evil.

"Really?" His grip tightens at my waist, lightning darting between my ribs as he hoists me into the air. No one has touched me like this before. Not willingly. "And yet we've never met. How curious. But you are a Grace." His gaze flits to the Grace powder Lorne caked in my hair. "Which is your house—or are you staying here, at the palace? But I suppose you can't be one of the Royal Graces. I'd *definitely* know you."

"No." I curse myself for not having thought of a lie. "House—"

We whirl past the royal dais, where a new figure watches the festivities with ill-concealed disdain. His skin appears peeled from the trunk of an oak tree, riddled with currents of bronze. His hair is neatly tied at his nape, the coarse strands—presently boasting the summer colors of dewed green leaves and jewel-bright berries—change with the seasons. But his eyes are steady. Always the stark, molten gold of a Grace. Yet he is not a Grace.

Endlewild. The Etherian ambassador to the Briar Court.

The light Fae live long, practically immortal lives. Endlewild is only the second ambassador to reside in the realm since Leythana's reign began. But though his placement here might be considered by many to be a luxury, it's clear that the Fae lord views his tenure a prison sentence. He's dressed in Briar court fashion, but the sigil of the High Court of the Etheria—laurel leaves twined together around an iridescent orb—is embroidered on his doublet. And he stares down at the party guests as if they're clusters of rodents. His spindly fingers curl around his staff, a rough-cut, unpolished birch branch. An orb like the one stitched in the High Court's emblem pulses at the top, swirling with his magic. With hardly a word from Endlewild, that staff could erupt with power. Smash me to bits.

The area just to the right of my navel throbs, where a garish half-moon scar, the perfect imprint of the side of Endlewild's staff, rests. It's a remnant of one of his more aggressive attempts to use his light magic to clear my blood of evil. I remember the way that orb felt as he'd pressed it to my skin. The smell of scorched flesh and the white-hot agony. Those unforgiving, knobby-boned fingers clamped around my wrists as I begged and begged . . .

The next step is a surprise. I stumble into a woman whose bustle and train are made out of actual peacock feathers. Arnley catches me, apologizes on our behalf, and adjusts our course with a damnably charming wink. "Don't let that spoilsport bother you. Awful creature. Honestly, I don't know why he shows up to these things if he hates the rest of us so much."

I've heard Rose express similar sentiments. Though they share the same golden blood, the Etherians want little to do with the Graces they create with their blessings. To the Fae, the Graces are part of an alliance agreement. An end to the war that almost destroyed Etheria. But they're bitter about having to share any part of their magic with the humans. Though technically kin to the Fae, the Graces have no claim on the magical power that threads through Etheria. Their human heritage taints their gilded blood, the same way that the Vila taints mine.

"We were talking about your house." He sends me spinning and reels me back in, and I try to steady my breathing and let Endlewild blur into nothing. "Let me guess. Lark

House? They had an influx of newly Bloomed Graces at the last ceremony."

Gold dances like a flame among the Graces on the dance floor. It flashes in the swish of satin and the jangle of bracelets. The dozens of honeyed eyes skirting around us.

"And what is your gift?" Arnley bends me into a graceful dip, one of his eyebrows quirking up as his hand on my back drifts slightly lower than it ought to be. And I can't help but notice the cleft in his chin. The shadow of stubble on his jaw. "You're certainly filled to bursting with charm. And wit."

He *is* shameless. The musicians reach the end of this dance and begin another, but Arnley doesn't change partners. He repositions his arms and twirls me in time to the faster tempo.

"Or perhaps." He steps behind me and lifts me up, the words tickling the crook of my neck. "A pleasure Grace?"

I blaze hot and cold at the same time. Pleasure Graces are gifted in the more . . . intimate arts. I can see a few of them now. Crimson-lipped and full-bodied. Several of them are wearing more Grace powder than gowns, like living, gilded statues sipping fizzy wine and fawning over ruddy-cheeked nobles. It's of little surprise that a few of those men sport the Grace sigil pinned to their lapels, denoting their status as members of the Grace Council.

"Certainly not."

Arnley laughs. "Not a pleasure Grace, then. That's all right. I've never needed one." He trails a black-gloved finger down my jawline, just under the ridge of the mask. "Not charm or wit or pleasure. You must be—"

"A *mongrel.*"

My head yanks back hard enough to crack my neck. My arms pinwheel, hands batting at thin air.

"What are you doing?" Arnley flings the question at someone else, rescuing me before I topple over.

But it's too late. Ribbons snapped, my mask slips from my face and meets the craggy facets of a sapphire embedded in the floor. I stand staring at the ruined pieces. The false diamonds glisten, like petrified tears. A peony-pink heel grinds mercilessly into the feathers.

"I knew I recognized that cloak when you walked in." The dancers nearest us, two fox-tailed men, slow to a halt. "You've no right to wear it."

Arnley's grip is still tight on my arms. Protective. "Rose, what are you . . . ?"

"*Look* at her, Arnley."

He leans away. I feel rather than hear his sharp intake of breath. And then his hands loosen. He backs away instantly, as if he's been burned.

"The Dark Grace."

An all-too-familiar muttering ricochets through the crowd. My arms lock around my middle, as if I can shield myself. As if I could do anything to prevent what I know is coming.

"That's right, Arnley." The venom in Rose's voice is sticky-sweet. "You've been dancing with *Malyce* this whole night. I hope she didn't curse you."

I drag my gaze up. And I would have thought that twenty years of enduring a realm's hatred would have prepared me for the expression on Arnley's face. Fear mixed with revulsion. Blanching, he scrubs his hands against his trousers. My eyes begin to sting.

Vaguely, I realize the music has stopped. It seems the entire ballroom circles our trio now, gasps rippling from the inside out as the news of my identity spreads. I catch a glimpse of the ladies I'd seen before. They lean into each other, even the butterflies on their gowns stilling.

"You thought you could come here and be one of us?" Rose laughs, brittle and cruel. She stomps on the mask again. Ebony shards spin wildly in every direction. "You'll never be. You don't belong here."

On the royal dais, Tarkin rises, clearly debating whether he should have me forcibly removed by the guards. Mariel shrinks into his side. But it isn't the Briar King who turns my guts to pudding. It's the Etherian ambassador, the orb of his staff glowing hot as his magic builds. He stares me down, thin lips pressed into a line. I can smell his loathing from here.

Anger and humiliation ball up inside my chest, stabbing their thorns into the underside of my flesh. Into my bones. Until my vision tinges red. I want nothing more than to give these people exactly what they so clearly desire. Spit my cursed blood in their faces and watch them shrivel. Poison their wine. Murder their children.

But I am not fool enough to think I would live beyond my first strike.

And so, coward that I am, I pick up my skirts and sprint toward the first door I can find, a parting tide of party guests in my wake.

CHAPTER NINE

I run until one of my infernal slippers tears and sends me sprawling. Rage boils in my veins. I snatch up the shoe and hurl it as far from me as possible. My dress is in shambles. The skirt is torn where my throbbing knees met the ground, the fabric billowing like shredded cobwebs.

I force down breaths soaked in earth and dew and pace back and forth between the manicured hedges on either side of me. No matter how hard I dig the heels of my palms into my eyes, I can still see the courtiers. Rose's triumphant smirk as Arnley staggered away from me. The horrified expressions of the women with the butterfly sashes. I knew better than this. That I could never be one of them. And yet I let myself hope that just for one night—

I'm a fool.

A fountain gurgles just ahead. I splash chilly water on my face, letting it dribble down my cheeks and drip off my chin. It leaves a gritty residue, which has me blinking in surprise. The water from the fountain is no longer clear, but a black, sticky mud. My palms sting and then I'm hit with the smell of woodsmoke. Damn everything. I must have cut my hands when I fell, and my blood in the water caused—I suck my teeth—*this*.

Dragon's teeth. Of course it did. The sludge spewing from the fountain is just like the soured cream at tea. Like the time I'd fallen down the stairs as a child, broken my lip, and the spots of my blood on the rug in the hallway chewed the fabric to ash. This is what Vila blood does. It destroys everything it touches.

Riding the fresh wave of my anger, I shove both hands into the murky filth. Steam rises instantly. The blackened water roils and coughs and spits over the varnished white sculptures of leaping fish and bathing maidens, leaving them ugly and distorted. Exactly like me.

"It's true," a soft voice says behind me. The fountain calms. "You're the Dark Grace."

So someone followed me. Eager to get a glimpse of the mongrel. I count to ten as I release a slow breath, willing myself not to react. To bite back whatever snide remark dances on my tongue. When I turn, I need not worry about words at all.

Princess Aurora, the amethysts in her diadem reflecting the moonlight, stares back at me. "Well? Aren't you?"

It takes me a moment to remember how to speak. This close, the princess is breathtaking. And she should be. At their births, the royal daughters are besieged by the Graces, each vying for the chance to offer their gift and curry favor. Even if the princess had been born with straw for hair and bloodred eyes, her faults would have been remedied by nightfall.

"I—yes. Your Highness." I cobble together a curtsy, gaze flicking behind her, where there must be guards stationed.

"We're quite alone, I assure you." She nears me, trailing one graceful hand along a hedge. A faint scent of apple-blossoms and the peach-drenched wine from the celebration fills the garden. "I often come out here when I want a break from the court."

I have no idea how to respond. What does one say to a princess? If her parents knew I was alone with her right now they would—I don't even want to know. "It's . . . nice."

She steps back as a mud bubble erupts and splatters my gown. "That fountain has seen better days, though."

I cringe at the dark brown liquid frothing at the base. "I'm sorry," I begin quickly. "I didn't mean—"

"I actually like it better this way." She taps a fingertip to her chin. "Yes. It's much more entertaining than anything the innovation Graces could have crafted."

An awful sound between a laugh and a choke bursts from my mouth. I clamp my hands over my lips to smother it. Aurora pretends not to notice.

"Is that all you can do? Muck up fountains and horrify courtiers? It doesn't seem like the sort of power that nearly vanquished the light Fae." She watches me closely for a few beats. And then, softer, "I'm sorry they were so rude to you."

She sounds sincere. I've never heard an apology uttered for anyone's treatment of me, not one that wasn't wrenched from Rose's lips at Mistress Lavender's insistence. I'm not sure what to make of it.

"I'm ashamed of them," the princess says. "Would you

like them banished? It's the least I can do. The insult was given at my party, after all."

It takes me a moment to realize she's teasing me. Another of those clumsy, mortifying laughs punches through my lungs.

She grins. "Very well. Once I'm queen, it's done."

Quiet settles between us. I pick at the ruined parts of my dress. It feels far too tight now under her scrutiny, the seams like bars of a cage.

"I've heard stories about you," she says finally. "You're not as green as people claim." She leans in. "A little pale, perhaps. Not a typical Grace, certainly."

I stiffen as the familiar feeling of being found wanting expands in my chest. So she came to marvel at the half-Vila Dark Grace. Like I'm one of the creatures in the royal menagerie. "We can't all be Grace-gifted."

She doesn't miss the vinegar in my tone. "Oh, no. I mean that as a compliment. The Graces are so vain."

Another surprise. "You really think so?"

She tosses her hair over one shoulder and bats her long eyelashes, an exact copy of one of Rose's gestures. "You can hardly expect otherwise, I suppose. The Fae magic goes right to their heads. The Royal Graces are the worst. They seem to think that because they live here, they can cluck over me and pour their newest elixirs down my throat. The witty ones are fun sometimes. And wisdoms aren't so bad, when they're not trying to prove you wrong. But the rest are absolutely tiresome."

I let my shoulders drop, drinking up her words like honey. I've never met anyone besides Hilde who dislikes the Graces.

"And the sycophants who dote on them are worse," she goes on, striding around the fountain and examining it like it's a piece of art. "Don't feel too bad about losing Arnley's interest. You would have lost him anyway, even if you weren't the Dark Grace. Once he'd gotten your mask off, if you catch my meaning."

I do, and it makes the ridges of my ears burn. Graces are forbidden from romantic or intimate relationships until after they've Faded, but the way Rose was hanging on Arnley. The jealous twinge in her jaw when he danced with me. Had she—I'd rather not know.

"I wasn't interested in him."

"Good." She wends her way back to me. Moonlight slides over the bits of red in her hair, turning them a burnished copper. Her gown shimmers over every inch of her body, as if she wears the sea itself. "My parents threw him at my head years ago. I was relieved when he wasn't the one. The royal children would have had dozens of half-siblings."

I nearly choke. The Grace from earlier was right. The princess is nothing if not brazen. I find myself thawing toward her.

"How often do they—" I fumble a bit, wondering if it's a delicate subject. "Throw someone at your head?"

She laughs, a musical sound that illicits an answering call from a nearby nightingale. "Since I was barely more than a child. A few a year then, as I was the youngest. But now it's nearly one a day."

"Once a day? You have to—to *kiss* total strangers?"

"More than that after tonight." She shrugs. Fiddles with

the chain on her collarbone. "Now that this is the last year. And my sisters . . ."

She trails away and sympathy bats at my heart. Aurora was as young as I was when the first princess died—only a child. Even so, she likely witnessed her elder sisters welcome and kiss every suitor. How many, I wonder? She probably knows. Probably counted and hoped and held her breath in anticipation. And it all meant nothing in the end.

"I'm sorry." It doesn't feel like enough.

"Everyone is." A firefly rides the next current of breeze. The light from the spark of its body snags on the jewel at her throat. Glides over the exposed skin of her shoulder, so different from mine. Pure and unbroken and lovely. "I wish I could be like you."

"What?" I suck in air too fast and cough. That's something I never thought I'd hear coming out of anyone's mouth, much less a royal's.

"I do." There's not a trace of doubt or mockery. "Destroy things and . . ." She drops her voice, studying the fountain. "People, even. Let out what simmers inside me. But I can't. I'm too well trained. Ever grateful and graceful and—" She glances my way and a blush paints her cheeks. "Forgive me. I'm rambling."

"No." I dare a step closer. "I know exactly what you mean. I wanted to bring the ballroom crashing down after Rose— Well, you saw what she did. So many times I want to . . ." I look down, worried I've said too much already.

A gentle touch lands on my arm. Heat shoots through the silk of my glove. "We're not so different, are we?"

I meet the princess's gaze, a lump in my throat. "No. I suppose we're not."

"A princess and a Dark Grace. Quite the pair." She scoops up a glob of mud with a fingertip and inspects it. "You've ruined my favorite fountain, you know. Those are sculptures of me." She gestures to a marble maiden. Sludge oozes down its waist and drips from the crook of its elbow.

Damn everything. "Are they really? It's your favorite?"

"No." She laughs again, flicking the mud away. "But it is now. It's absolutely my favorite thing in this entire palace."

Princess Aurora herself helps me to steal away into a carriage without having to walk back through the viper's pit of a ballroom. I'm home well before the others, drifting in on the cloud of joy Aurora cultivated in the gardens. I never thought I'd meet anyone who understood even a sliver of what it means to be me. Especially not a princess.

But the sight of myself in the mirror, the reflection in the servants' eyes as I return, sends me crashing back to reality. I barricade myself in my room, peeling off the dress, the gloves, the one remaining shoe. Part of me feels guilty for spoiling the surprise Laurel clearly worked hard to achieve. But it isn't me who should apologize. It's Rose.

Rose who deals out my humiliations as easily as hands of playing cards. Rose who takes great pains to ensure I feel every bit of the hatred the realm harbors for me. And as I burrow into the safety of my coverlet, I begin to devise how, exactly, I will return the favor.

CHAPTER TEN

The rest of the household returns well after midnight. I hear their carriage clatter up the drive. The orders shouted to servants and the trudge of dance-weary footsteps. No one comes to check on me, not even Laurel, which makes me strangely sad. She probably feels it's best to leave me be. And she's right.

Exhaustion pulls my eyelids down, but I don't let myself sleep. Not yet. Instead, I remove the tiny key hidden in the false bottom of my dressing table drawer and open a trunk of relics from my childhood. Old dresses I've outgrown and books Laurel lent me and didn't want returned. The embossed title of one volume stares up at me in the weak light of my candle. This one did not come from Laurel. And it was not a well-meaning gift. Endlewild brought it. I remember the way those Fae eyes glinted as he tossed it at my feet.

Dark Creatures of Malterre.

I trace the letters, wings flapping in my belly.

"Forget not what you are" was all he said.

Not who—*what*. He'd wanted me to read the sections about Vila. Horrible stories about human sacrifices and kidnapped children and blood rituals. Tales that would frighten me. Make me understand what would happen to me if I ever used my power against Briar. But Vila are not the only creatures described in this book.

The spine creaks and the smell of dust and old paper greets me. My trembling fingers find chapters on Nyxes and Imps and Goblins, all creatures who once lived in Malterre but were driven to extinction at the end of the war.

Here, toward the end of the book. The Shifters. My eyes move so quickly I can barely take in the words.

> Like the Fae, it is believed that Shifters live long—perhaps even immortal—lives. It is difficult to discern the exact lifespan due to the changeable natures of the creatures. Though there have been no reported sightings of Shifters in their native form, it is believed that they have no exterior body hair. They may also possess multiple sets of breathing apparatuses, including gills as well as humanesque noses, so that they may Shift easily from land animals to water. Skin may also be covered in scales. And blood, when extracted, is a thick, sticky black. Similar in viscosity and color to the ink of a Carthegean Squid.

That isn't me, I tell myself firmly. I don't look like that. I have green, Vila blood. Not black. But my gaze darts involuntarily to the backs of my hands. I may not have scales, but my skin is always dry and flaking. And while I have hair, it's pitifully thin and lank. A good yank away from falling out completely.

But if I *am* a Shifter as Kal says—I could change into anyone I wanted to be. I could leave Briar behind forever.

The thought is so sweet it dissolves like spun sugar on my tongue.

The Grace Laws, my mind screams. *The dogs.* The ones trained to sniff out Grace blood and keep them from being smuggled out of the realm.

But I am not a Grace.

Once dawn breaks, I'm up. The others won't bother to rise until at least midday and Delphine can burn my schedule for all I care. Not even the kitchen staff is awake. I stuff a sack full of pastries, nick a loaf of bread and some cheese, settle Callow on my shoulder, and leave the house before anyone's the wiser.

Brine and sea salt scrape the inside of my nose once I pass through the main gates and turn toward the black tower. Fat clouds are rolling in from the horizon, promising a downpour. It's a gray, miserable morning, the mist so thick I could cut it with a knife. The perfect post-ball day for the nobles to laze about in their beds, nursing their wine-soaked heads with vials of Etherium and forgetting about the Dark Grace.

I will not forget.

I will not be humiliated like I was last night. Never again.

A sour taste lands on my tongue as I try, and fail, to tamp

down the images from the ballroom. Arnley's disgusted stupor. Rose's twisted delight. I cling to another instead, as if it's a piece of driftwood floating in a raging sea: Aurora's moonlit face as she studied the fountain I'd muddied. Even now, the sound of her laughter skips across the waves.

Will she have a line of suitors waiting for her this morning? Another longer one tomorrow if her true love isn't found? My blood chills at the thought of such a curse. She must have kissed most of the men in the realm by now, entirely against her will. I shake my head to clear it. The princess was an unexpected relief when I'd needed it most. But she is a royal and not my concern. If I see her again it will be at her wedding. Or her funeral.

The encroaching storm front makes the black tower even colder and gloomier than my last visit, the sea pounding against the cliff as if it has something to prove. I enter cautiously, slipping in a few places where the worn stone is covered in moldy slime. Callow squawks her complaints.

"Kal?" His name is buried under the sound of the sea and the distant rumble of thunder. The hair on my arms begins to rise.

"You came back."

There's a ripple to my left. Kal appears, his hair mussed and eyes bleary, as if my arrival woke him. As the darkness unspools from his frame, Callow screeches and flaps unevenly to the ground. I soothe her with a few scraps of meat.

"I did not think you would." The shadows waft in smoky tendrils up and down his arms. Wind around his neck and burrow into his clothes.

"You said you could teach me about my power." I keep a healthy distance between us.

"I can." He watches Callow, who has grown bored of us and is hunting between the cracks in the stone for more snacks. "You have a kestrel?"

I'm in no mood for distractions. "What do you want for your information?" I thrust the sack in his direction. "I brought food."

He shakes his head. "I cannot eat. The enchantment keeps me—the way that I am. And I require no payment to train you."

Distrust flares like a match striking. Nothing is free, I've learned that well enough. I lower the sack, narrowing my eyes. "Why not?"

Kal stares at me. Shadows dart between the crooks of his elbows. "We are kin. And I knew your mother well. She would want you to understand your worth."

"Would she?" I search every crevice of his face, bracing myself for the next question—one that surfaced in the dead of night and hounded me for hours. "You said she came here twenty years ago—before I was even born. That you were going to leave here with her. Are you . . . did you and she—"

"No, Alyce." One corner of his mouth rises. And I can't decide whether the feeling in my gut is relief or disappointment. "You and I are related only through our breed of magic. This enchantment prevents me from . . ."

My neck burns. "You don't need to go on."

Kal clears his throat. "Very well. Your mother discovered

me just as you did. And she trained with me for the same purpose you are here now."

"You said she tried to free you and died for it. Would you ask the same of me?"

A wave crashes against the tower and Kal looks longingly to the horizon. "I will not ask anything you are not willing to give. I am alone here." The shadows encircle his wrists like shackles. "It is enough to have some company for a time. To honor Lynnore. And then, when the time is right, if you feel that you could sever my bindings—" He lets out a shaky breath, as if the thought itself is too fragile to entertain for long. "I would be in your debt."

I turn his words over and sideways, looking for evidence of deceit. "How are you so sure I'm a Shifter? I have a book that says Shifters have gills and hairless bodies and—"

He raises an eyebrow. "And I take it the author saw a Shifter in its true form?"

Silence is all the answer Kal needs.

"I thought not. Shifters almost never inhabit their original shapes. Only those so young they have not yet learned how to Shift. They embody a form similar to that of one of their parents." His expression softens with regret. "You resemble Lynnore so much it hurts."

The cry of a gull slices through the air.

I chew my lips, unwilling to accept what he says as truth. That Endlewild was right—I'm no better than the monsters in the book.

"If you train me, will you help me leave Briar?" The desire that's wrecked my heart since I first watched the ships leaving the harbor and knew I could never board one.

"If you let me teach you . . ." Kal inches as close as he dares. Callow skitters sideways, flaring her wings. "Your power will be unstoppable. You could bring the Etherian Mountains tumbling into the sea."

A tremor at the base of my skull tells me this is too good to be true. But I want to believe. So very badly. A bell sounds from the faraway harbor, warning of the coming storm. One day, I could be aboard one of those ships. Not the Dark Grace. Just Alyce. Sailing toward a new life.

"All right," I say at last, smothering logic and instinct with both hands. "Prove that you can do what you say."

Kal's smile is a slash of white in the gloom of his shadows. "We will begin with your Vila magic. It will be hard for you to Shift at first—you have been in your human form for many years. Some Shifters, when they are too long in one shape, forget how to change back."

"You mean—will I never be able to Shift?"

"Do not trouble yourself about it now. Typically, such a thing only occurs when a Shifter spends too long as an animal. The primal instinct takes over. But tell me of your Vila magic. How are you accessing your power now?"

"Like the Graces do. I craft elixirs with my blood."

"Like the Graces . . ." Kal blinks at me a few times, his mouth opening and closing. My shoulders hunch up to my ears as he studies me. "Give me an example."

Licking my lips, I tell him about my last run of patrons. The elixirs for blemished skin and limp curls and frumpy figures, each sounding pettier than the last. He listens without speaking until I finally run out of steam. Callow's wings brush my hem, and I know she senses my anxiety. The heavy clouds have finally begun to fissure. Rain drizzles through the gaps in the ceiling. One fat drop lands on my nose. I swipe it away.

Kal clasps his hands behind his back, bristling as he paces. "This is exactly what I mean. The Graces have wrangled you into their mold. Repressed your true power."

An unwanted memory resurfaces. A tight circle of Graces, flinging whispers back and forth as I lay strapped to a bed. A basin rests under each of my arms, catching streams of my blood. Already, my mind is fuzzy. The room blurs. But I can still hear them.

"Do you think that's too much?"

"No. The Lord Ambassador said we must bleed it out of her. Her blood is that terrible color because of the toxins. The touch of evil. It must be obliterated."

A wind rips through the tower. The stones groan.

"But the Vila are . . . were—"

"Lies." Kal wheels to face me, his shadows sharpening to knifepoints. "All of it lies. I will not have you repeating such filth about your own. Vila blood is worth ten times that of the Etherians. They require those despicable staffs to command their magic. But you—if you have half the power of Lynnore, you will be formidable."

Thunder rumbles again, closer now, echoing in the emptiness of the tower. My mother carried the same loamy blood that beats at my wrists. A power that could be my key to escaping Briar. The sea churns, pitching waves against the base of the cliff as the storm lumbers inland.

"What do you mean?"

"You are not like those vainglorious Fae bastards, the

Graces. They are forced to drain themselves to access their magic. But you are better than that."

"You don't know what you're talking about." I turn away. "They . . ."

Another memory rears its ugly head. I'm soaked and shivering after they'd dunked me in an ice bath laced with cleansing elixirs and Etherium. Pinned my shoulders as I'd fought and flailed against the vise of panic squeezing my lungs. The fevered, impossible count to one hundred before they finally allowed me to surface. Their hushed conversation as I retched the frigid water back up.

"Something's wrong."

"How long was she under?"

"Too long."

"Not natural."

And one that I don't want to think about, but that punches through anyway.

"Is it kinder to just put her down?"

"They tried everything to bring out my power."

Kal is close enough to touch me. "Everything they knew." He lifts my chin gently. "Which cannot be much."

That coaxes a weak smile from my lips.

"Your power is in your blood, Alyce. As with any Vila. You have lost some of your connection to it because you live in the borderlands and not in Malterre where you belong. The realm of your ancestors was thick with dark magic. You could have tapped into it as easily as breathing."

"That's why the humans wanted Etheria before Leythana's reign."

"Yes. In their ignorance, the mortals believed the power

in the Fae courts was tangible. Able to be scooped up and contained. Like an elixir in a bottle. It is not so simple. The magic in Etheria is a living thing, as it was in Malterre." He takes my hand and traces the stark veins at the inside of my wrist with his alabaster fingers. I don't pull away. "You are trueborn. You have more than one way of accessing and guiding your magic. Magic that, in your long life, will not Fade. It cannot be bled out and expended the way the Graces' can."

"More than one way? All I know are my elixirs. Without enhancements, my power won't act as I wish."

"Would it not? Have you never noticed your power working outside of an elixir?" Kal reads my expression. One eyebrow quirks. "Perhaps there has been some sign?"

I tell him about the jug of cream I spoiled. The fountain. The frequent complaints of the healing Graces when I was a child that the effects of my blood were unpredictable and disastrous. It took years before my elixirs started working, and even then the results were often unexpected. Noses grew bumps when hair was supposed to brittle. Toes turned stubby when warts were meant to sprout.

Kal is grinning at me before I've finished. "That is because your blood was not meant for elixirs, Alyce. You have never required enhancements to shape your magic."

I think of all the years I spent testing boiled nettles against carrion crow feathers for a proper ugliness elixir. Mixing swamp water with crushed nightshade. "That can't be true."

"It is," Kal says simply, stoking my frustration. "Your power centers on intent. From what you have told me, it sounds as though you *wanted* your elixirs to work. And it was that desire, once it was given proper direction, that steered your elixirs. Not the enhancements."

"No." My tone is sharp enough that Callow bridles. "I never wanted to be the Dark Grace. No one would—"

"But you did want the experiments to stop. The torture."

The scar on my middle throbs.

"Yes."

One of Kal's shadows creeps forward, curling as though it would caress me. "Do you not see? In your own way, you wanted your magic to behave like a Grace's. And you wanted it so badly that your power obeyed. You used your true gift without even realizing."

The crash of the ocean presses against my eardrums. I despise the Graces. But how often did I look in my own spotted mirror and wish I was one of them? How many years did I yearn for my magic to be like theirs?

"If I don't have to employ enhancements, then how else do I wield my power?"

"Magic is everywhere," Kal explains, his shadows lively and eager. "Even humans carry a spark of it in their fragile, fickle souls. All you need to do is reach out and find it. Twine it with your own, and you can control it."

Lightning flashes through the gap in the wall and suspicion sends a tingle down my spine. My skepticism must show in my face.

"Try for yourself." The storm heaves overhead, the bellies of the clouds deep and rolling. "Your mother likened her power to a tether that lived inside her. An invisible limb, if you will. And she said the magic in other things had their own shape as well. Often, she described them as beating hearts. Some stronger than others. All you need do is find that heart." He points overhead. "There happens to be a perfectly good source of magic at your fingertips."

"The storm?" He can't possibly be serious. "No one can control the weather."

"Maybe not. But you can control magic. You can already sense the energy pulsing in the air. It will be a small thing to send your power out and find the heart of the storm."

It doesn't seem like a small thing to me. A raindrop splatters on my forehead, as if to taunt me.

"Close your eyes," Kal says. "Trust me."

Doubt gnaws at me, but a whisper-thin hope sings through it. The Graces shackled me with their gilded chains since the moment I was delivered to the Grace Council. If I can do what Kal says, nothing could stand in my way.

"Feel the charge in the air," he continues, pacing in the shadows. "Find the magic."

I squirm, catching only drizzle and the briny wind. "I don't know what that feels like."

"You mentioned turning the water in a fountain to mud. What were you feeling then?"

"Anger," I answer immediately. "Pain."

"Yes. Your magic has much to do with emotion. *Feel* something, Alyce. Deep inside. Here." His hand presses against my abdomen. I gasp. "It will answer you."

Letting Kal brace me, I try to follow his direction. Every slight and insult and humiliation I've ever suffered comes hurtling back to me. The mask crushed beneath Rose's shoe. The pointy-toothed smiles. The jeers. Rage builds, hot and strong behind my breastbone. There's something else there, too. Something I've never noticed before. A thrumming of darkness, thick and taut like a tightly braided rope. It seems to coil and uncoil at my attention, like Callow pacing on her perch. I concentrate harder and it stretches and lengthens—exactly as my mother described. Another thought and the cord of my magic snakes out of my body and through the air, wriggling past the cracks in the ceiling and out into the clouds. The scents of woodsmoke and loam and leather flood my nose, stronger than I've ever smelled them. I can even taste something like charred wood on the back of my throat.

This can't be real. I would have known if I could do something as miraculous as this. And yet that rope of dark magic obeys as I tell it to veer this way and that. To find what I seek. In fact, my power seems to know what I want better than I do. It navigates the leaden clouds, darting and diving like a fish in the sea until—

There.

My power brushes against another, the impact cold enough to shock. Where mine is a long tether connected to my soul, this one is a knotted ball of energy. An angry thing that hums and vibrates in time with the thunder rolling through the tower.

It's the storm.

The realization hits me like a slap in the face and my power retreats at my own surprise. But I summon my courage and push it back out. Bid my new dark limb to fist around the storm's heart. I feel the faint pulse of the storm. The crackle of lightning and the patter of rain. Hazy, bumbling things that could be the storm's thoughts drift in and out of my consciousness.

Come. I push the command through my own tether and into the storm as hard as I possibly can. My entire body is warm and buzzing. I feel well and truly alive for the first time since I can remember.

The heart of the storm resists.

Come!

A deafening clap of thunder rattles my bones. Callow screams. White flashes across my eyelids. And then the clouds above the tower empty their contents on top of our heads.

CHAPTER ELEVEN

Though I wouldn't have dreamed it possible to crack a storm cloud like an egg, flooding the black tower with rainwater up to my knees, Kal says it was a simple feat. Natural forces like storms are brimming with magic. Their hearts are louder, he'd said, and therefore easier to find. And it *had* been easy. There were no special incantations. No delicate mix of ingredients, as I use for my elixirs. Everything I thought I knew about my power was false—just as Kal claimed.

Once the rainwater drains through the gap in the wall and back into the sea, I spend the rest of the day experimenting with my newfound abilities. Finding the storm's heart was simple compared to seeking out other sources of magic—like those in the fallen stones of the tower. It takes a full hour for me to rouse the magic in even one small rock and send it skipping across the waves. The power of the sea breeze is slightly easier. I can tame its evasive heart after a few tries, making small cyclones dance between our ankles.

But like a muscle that's never been used, my power soon tires. And the deeper a heart of magic is buried within an object—as with the stones—the more control it takes to command. By the time I'm done practicing, there's a hammering behind my eyes and a strange weakness in my mind that softens my brain until it feels like putty. My whole body aches, as if I've run up the Etherian mountain range and down again. Even so, I am exhilarated. And when I at last begin to wander home through the humid haze of the storm's wake, Callow still bristling over nearly having drowned when the storm emptied on her back, I vow to show Briar exactly what the Dark Grace can do.

I return to Lavender House through back alleys dark enough to hide my face and enter through the kitchen. Cook and the servants have already cleaned up from dinner, but I find an apple and don't even bother wiping the juice from my chin as I inhale its tart sweetness. I'd eaten all the bread and cheese I'd taken to the tower and am still ravenous. That was another thing Kal warned me about: As my magic wakes, I'll need more food to fuel it.

I'm more than happy to oblige my hunger and begin rooting around the kitchen, hunting leftover tarts and treats to appease Callow. But a few moments later, Mistress Lavender's screeching can be heard from the main parlor several doors down. It kills the rest of my appetite. I bid Callow keep quiet and tiptoe closer to the kitchen door, then out into the hallway, melting into the shadows.

"But where *is* she?" The question bounces off the papered walls. "I can't send the servant back empty-handed. There will be consequences. The house will be—"

"Here she is. Lurking, as always."

Dragon's teeth. I'm usually excellent at hiding. The servants typically glide right past while I'm eavesdropping, as if I'm no more than a window treatment.

Because you're a Shifter, a nasty part of my mind whispers.

Marigold glares, hands planted on the waist of her honeysuckle dressing gown. "And she has that filthy bird."

Mistress Lavender explodes into view, silver ringlets springing in every direction. One cheek is still rouged. Her painted lips are smeared, coral pink smudged onto her chin. Someone interrupted her evening toilette. My stomach sours. This cannot bode well for me.

"Alyce, where have you been?" She doesn't even wait for a response as she grabs my arm and tows me into the parlor. Callow clicks her beak and ruffles her wings, and I struggle to calm her. "Delphine had to reschedule three patrons for tomorrow, so now you're double booked. If you disappear like that again, you'll owe the house for the lost time. Do you understand me?"

I mumble my assent, seething at Marigold's haughty smirk. A servant I don't recognize waits in a corner, wringing a wine-colored cap in his hands. I'm not sure if his nervousness is because of Mistress Lavender's fuming or my own presence.

"And you're needed at the palace. At once."

"Why?" The servant, a jittery slip of a boy, isn't wearing royal livery.

"It's Duke Weltross." Mistress Lavender drops her voice, shoving a rumpled paper into my free hand while keeping a wary eye on Callow. I register the burgundy seal of the duke's house and my heart clenches. His wife, the duchess, is often a patron of Lavender House, one of Marigold's. And I'd heard her husband was ill. I did not think he was ill enough for my sort of treatment. "The duchess sent word. He's in a bad way, Alyce."

I don't have to open the summons to know what Duchess Weltross wants. A swift, gentle passing for her husband. Freedom from her duties as nursemaid. The queasiness that always accompanies my terminal patrons already begins to churn and the ache in my temples increases by tenfold. Dark Grace. Bringer of death.

"My kit is downstairs" is all I can say.

"Marigold, go and fetch it," Mistress Lavender instructs. "And take the bird with you."

"But I—" Marigold gapes at Callow like she's a dragon instead of a tame kestrel. But Mistress Lavender doesn't let her finish.

"Go! And don't dawdle. She's late enough as it is. I'll fetch her cloak."

My limbs feel made of lead. I want to refuse this errand. I'm better than this. More than the villain they've created. I close my eyes, consider tapping into the magic of the wood and stones and mortar of this house and bringing it all down around their ears.

But I do not. Because I'm a coward.

And so I transfer Callow to Marigold's trembling arm. My poor kestrel looks as happy about the situation as I am. Marigold winces as Callow's angry talons pierce the thin silk of her dressing gown, and then she sulks off, muttering to herself and watching Callow like the sullen bird might peck out her eyes. I hope Callow does.

"Where have you been all day?"

The voice makes me jump. I hadn't noticed Laurel when I came in. She's tucked herself into a reading chair, the embroidered Briar roses on her wide sleeves gleam in the soft light of a swan-shaped lamp at her side. Her book is still open on her lap.

"You look terrible."

I almost laugh. Laurel. Graced in wisdom, but not tact.

"I've been out."

"Obviously." Her stoic gaze lingers on the mud stains splotched up to my knees and the windblown mess of my hair. "If I'd known you insist on making such a state out of *all* your clothes, I never would have given you that dress."

Guilt snakes up my throat. I never thanked Laurel for what she did. "I'm sorry about that. And I—" I pause, unused to giving apologies that I mean. "I should have told you how much I appreciated it. The gown was beautiful."

Laurel shuts her book. "You seemed like you were having a good time in it."

"Yes." Happiness ghosts through me, remembering the way Arnley had whirled me around the dance floor. How he looked at me like I was some radiant courtier. And how that look had withered. Laurel guesses the direction of my thoughts.

"Rose is confined to her rooms when she doesn't have patrons." One corner of her mouth quirks. "Mistress Lavender didn't want to punish her in front of the court to protect the reputation of the house, but she received quite the tongue-lashing all the way home."

"Well, that's something." Not enough. But better than nothing.

"And her wages are forfeit until the dress *and* mask are paid for. And they were very expensive."

A sliver of satisfaction cuts through my resentment. The punishment won't harm her Grace standings, but it will keep her from adding to her precious wardrobe. "Now I'm sorry I missed the look on her face."

Laurel's grin widens. "It was quite entertaining."

A warm moment passes between us, one I'm not used to sharing with a Grace. "If Mistress Lavender gives me the money, I'll pass it along."

"Keep it." Laurel waves away the offer. "You're owed more than that for the night you endured."

I'm not sure what to say, and so I'm silent, balling up the summons in my fist.

"Rose was wrong." The silk of Laurel's dressing gown rustles. "You're not hated, Alyce. Not by all of us."

The crisp points of the crumpled parchment dig into my palm. "Not by all," I answer. "But by enough."

• • •

This time, I am not welcomed at the swirling gates of the palace. The Weltrosses' servant leads me through an achingly familiar back entrance. I remember my first visit through these cloistered halls. My knees could hardly hold me and my hands slipped on my kit, knowing I was here to end a life. Torn about whether or not I could do it.

The Grace Laws regarding these services are gray at best, and the Grace Council has conveniently neglected to clarify them. While Grace magic can't be used to intentionally cause harm, the definition of *harm* is loose. After all, Graces can only produce blessings and charms with their Fae-blessed blood. Rose couldn't use her beauty gift to hurt a fly. But Laurel, for instance, could potentially employ her enhanced wisdom to discern the best way to cause someone pain or the best strategy in battle. Treasonous practices when used against Briar.

Since I am half Vila, mine is the only power able to inflict direct, premeditated harm. And while I can't sell a poison knowing that it would be used to murder someone in good health, giving that elixir to the terminally ill or injured is a different matter. I don't know how Mistress Lavender first thought of the practice, or if it was even her idea at all. But once my skill in the darker arts began to manifest, the task fell like an iron weight on my shoulders. For an exorbitant amount of coin, one can hire the Dark Grace to ease a passing. The patron must be known to be near death—too far gone for either a healing Grace or Etherium to have any effect—and there must be witnesses. But I can do it.

No, I am *required* to do it under Grace Law.

Even though I don't want to.

Even though it only solidifies my reputation as a murderess.

It is a reputation that crests behind me in whispers and black looks as I'm led through the labyrinth of stairs in the back of the palace. Servants, arms laden with silver tea trays, bottles of wine, cheeses, and fruits, scuttle like mice. They give us a wide berth, some of them almost tripping over their toes as my identity registers on their faces. I keep my hood raised, as if the material could shield me from their razor-sharp judgment.

The Weltrosses' chambers are in the wings closest to the older, abandoned part of the palace. But nothing of Leythana's first home is evident here. The apartments are huge and lavish, filled with gilt-framed portraits and frescoed ceilings and crystal chandeliers, their iridescent prisms cut in the shape of delicate roses. But the reek of stale sick and creeping death tarnishes the finery. I don't know how the duchess stands it, especially as the acrid scents mingle with the candle smoke and earthy, burning herbs some healing Grace probably recommended. Herbs that are by no means helping.

The duchess has the decency to greet me herself when her servant announces my presence, leaving the duke's bedside and approaching me with wary footsteps. He's been like this for days, I can tell immediately just from the circles ringing the underside of both of her eyes. Her scarlet dressing gown is wrapped tightly around her frame, which is all sharp angles and jutting bones. The light from the fireplace shines against her warm black skin, highlighting the gaunt hollows of her cheeks.

"I did not know what else to do." Her voice is strained. Exhausted.

Part of me wants to take one of her too-thin hands in mine. Soothe her and tell her she did the best she could. That her husband will be out of pain soon. But then her nose wrinkles slightly as she takes in the rainwater stains on my dress and the other evidence of my afternoon at the black tower. I didn't have time to change before leaving Lavender House, much less even wash my face. I grip my kit harder.

"There must be another witness," I tell her. "And his doctor."

The duchess murmurs something to the servant, who flits away and returns with two others in tow. Dr. Renault is one. I recognize her sallow white face and badgerlike features from some of my other visits. The other person is a round woman who keeps sniffling and dabbing at her eyes with a handkerchief.

"This is the duke's sister," Duchess Weltross says, indicating the weeping woman. "Surely her presence as witness is sufficient?"

I nod and direct my next question to Renault. "Has everything been done to assist this man?"

She watches me stiffly from behind a veil of disdain so thick it ripples. The weasly woman has never liked me. Doctors rarely do. In truth, any physician could accomplish what I do in these cases. My blood makes a poison more potent, more efficient, but anyone can kill a dying person. They choose to relegate this task to me in order to save themselves from it.

"Yes," Renault snaps, turning up her nose at me.

"And you're certain he is beyond your skill?" I love asking that question. Forcing them to admit they've failed at something. That they had to come to me.

"He is beyond anyone's skill. Except *yours*."

Ignoring the insult, I turn my attention to the duke's sister. "And do you know of any reason he should not be allowed to die? Any person wishing him dead?"

It took years of schooling my features into neutrality for this part of the process. More than once, I've had my suspicions about disgruntled wives or husbands and friends with grudges. And I've seen my share of patrons who exhibited signs of long-term poisoning. Blackened tongues. Sallow skin laced with brittle veins the color of nightshade berries. But I am not paid to investigate possible murders. So when the bereft witness just shakes her head and prattles off a string of blubbery nonsense through her handkerchief, I make my way to the duke.

He's in worse shape than I imagined. Each breath he takes is a shuddering, wet rasp. His lips are cracked and white, the insides lined with garish streaks of red. Blood trickles down the side of his mouth. The duchess wipes it away with a gentleness that tugs at my heart.

"Duke Weltross." This is the most important part. "Do you wish to die?"

Sometimes the patrons can't reply, they're so far gone. And the answer doesn't truly matter. All that counts is that I asked the question. The duke moans. His body twitches. And then, to my immense relief, he nods.

The next part should be quick. I have an elixir ready: belladonna and valerian and foxglove, mixed with a few drops of my blood. A swallow from the patron, and it's all over. But my hands hesitate on the lid of my kit, remembering what happened earlier with Kal. How I'd found the heart of the storm and commanded it to my will. What was it Kal had said—that even humans have a spark of magic in their souls? I watch the labored rise and fall of the duke's chest.

What if I could help him? Heal instead of harm?

It isn't possible, my mind hisses. *You're Vila. Your power is bred from pain and despair.* Evil—exactly like Endlewild always claimed.

But Kal said a Vila's power is ten times that of an Etherian's. He didn't seem to think they were the wicked creatures I've been raised to believe. My power hinges on intent. What if I could use that intent differently? I could banish my reputation as the Dark Grace tonight.

I set my kit down.

Placing my hands on the duke's husk of a body, I try to look like I know what I'm doing. No one says anything, but there's a shift in the room as the duchess and the doctor share a glance. I shove away the prickly feeling of their unsettled energy, then relax the tension in my shoulders and breathe.

"This isn't your usual method." Dr. Renault disrupts my concentration.

I open one eye. "Have you been taking notes?"

She scowls, but doesn't answer.

I refocus on the fading heartbeat beneath my palms. On the magic that must be flickering somewhere between the duke's failing organs and bird-frail bones. I send my own magic out carefully, curious tendrils poking and prodding as it seeks what I want.

The gentle crackle of the fire seems to dull. My magic darts between the duke's ribs and burrows into his throat. He moans and stirs, enough so that the duchess steps forward, distraught, but the doctor holds her back.

I've almost given up when I find it. Where the storm's magic was violent and throbbing, the duke's is thin and shivering, so faint I'm surprised I feel it at all. Do all mortals possess such small scraps of magic? It's soft as a ball of spider's silk. The scents of juniper buds and sun-warmed stones—scents that must be linked to the duke's magic—tiptoe alongside those of the wet earth and charred steel of my own power.

I take in a breath and exhale. Test and nudge with my newfound limb, trying to bend the human magic to my desires. *Life, health, healing.* The windowpanes creak in the night wind. The duke's body grows warmer under my fingertips. Hope flares behind my sternum. I press harder on his magic.

And then the duke coughs.

Something hot and sticky spatters across my face, stinking of copper. My eyes fly open, magic reeling back into my body like a snapped string. The duke's face is purple. His eyes bulge. Deep, glistening crimson soaks the coverlet. He lets out a horrible croaking sound, his whole body seizing. And then he falls back against the pillows, his gaze glassy and vacant.

A terrified scream rips the room in half.

CHAPTER TWELVE

The doctor wastes no time. The duchess is wailing, her frenzied cries punctuated by hollow, painful-sounding gulps of air. Two maids ricochet from corner to corner, rushing between their mistress and the round woman, who has collapsed on the rug in a boneless heap. Renault grabs me by my upper arm hard enough to bruise it, shoves my kit into my hands, and bullies me out the servants' entrance.

"Your housemistress will hear about this," she promises.

And then the heavy door slams in my face.

Alone in the dim corridor, I can only stare at the blank oaken panels, the thud of wood against wood still resonating as the events of the last few minutes replay.

What had happened?

I'd found the duke's magic, grasped it with my own and manipulated it the way I had with the storm and the stones in the tower. Had I pushed too hard? Did I use my magic too quickly after exhausting it?

It is because you are Vila, that hideous voice inside me growls. *And an utter fool.*

Guilt burns my throat like strong drink. There'd been so much blood. The duke's eyes had almost burst out of their sockets. What had I done?

I keep my head down as I retrace my steps through the passages. I just want to leave as quickly as possible. Never come back.

Something solid crashes into me, toppling me off balance. My kit clatters to the dusty floor. Glass breaks. Perfect. Another reason for Mistress Lavender to be angry.

"Idiot." Useless, bumbling servant. I hope he's scared out of his wits when he sees who I am. "You'd best be prepared to pay for that."

"Oh, I am sorry."

But that is not the squeak of a frightened boy. I straighten dizzyingly fast, nearly dropping the kit again.

Princess Aurora blinks at me from under her hooded cloak.

"I—you—what are you doing here?" I back away. "This is the servants' passage."

"I'm aware. I live here."

"I know that," I begin again, sharper than I intend. Then, remembering myself, "Your Highness." I drop into a threadbare curtsy. "I'm just surprised."

"Clearly." She motions for me to rise, a smile in her voice. "What are you doing here? You're not a servant. I thought—" Her breath hitches and she leans in. "What happened to you?"

At first, I think she's talking about my dress. But she's staring at my face. My fingertips go to my cheek and come away crimson. The duke's blood. Dragon's teeth. Shame scalds the ridges of my ears and I scrub the flecks of blood away, biting my tongue until I taste woodsmoke and loam.

"I'm summoned to the palace sometimes—"

I don't want to go on. Don't want to see the look in her eyes when she realizes what I am. But I also don't see the point in lying. She'll find out one way or another that I'm exactly what Briar deems me to be.

"To kill people."

Aurora inhales sharply, surprise or horror or both rippling over her features like torchlight. But she doesn't break my gaze. "I've heard that rumor."

"It's true." My jaw sets, bracing for rejection. For her to summon her guards and have me escorted to the dungeons.

"I'm sorry. I don't imagine it's an errand you enjoy."

I'm sure that I misheard her. She can't possibly be taking my side. Again. But she doesn't waver. Doesn't even flinch. In fact, I think I detect genuine sympathy in the down-turned corners of her mouth.

"No." Exhaustion and humiliation overtake me. The kit rattles in my hands. "It isn't."

She looks like she's about to say something else, but a flurry of hurried footsteps echoes down the corridor. Aurora links arms with me and starts herding me forward before I can utter a word of protest.

"Let's get out of here."

"Why? Who are we running from?"

"No one probably." She grins a wicked grin. "But possibly my guards."

"Your—*what*?" I try to break free, but she won't budge. This is exactly what I need. To be discovered with the crown princess in a deserted servants' alley. Add kidnapper to murderess on my list of offenses against the Crown. "Your Highness, I cannot."

"Oh, hush up and keep moving. I do this all the time."

Aurora steers us seamlessly through the passages. My heart is racing at the thought of being found, the scar on my middle blazing. But we pass no one. And what seems like miles later—I've given up trying to count the forks and turns—the princess finally pulls to a halt at an ancient door in the oldest part of the palace. With a wink, she extracts a tiny golden key from the inside of her bodice and unlocks it. The moldy wood swings wide without a sound. She must oil the hinges herself. It doesn't look like anyone's used this place for decades.

We push aside the moth-eaten remains of a tapestry to reveal a vast, shadow-steeped chamber. My eyes squint, adjusting to the gloom. The only source of light trickles in through high, circular windows that are more grime than glass. Chalky moonbeams paint the rotting railing of an upper-story gallery. A spiral staircase, ironwork rusted. Furniture with springs poking out and dusted with cobwebs. And rows and rows of shelves.

"Books?" I forget myself so much that I set my kit down and start drifting toward them.

"It's the old library. One of the last relics of the first palace." Aurora lights a fat, waxy candle and trails me. "I do my best for the volumes in decent shape, but some are beyond my help." She selects one that may once have had a red leather cover, but is now faded to dingy brown. The pages are yellowed and crumbling. She clicks her tongue and replaces it.

"They didn't move the books when they built the new wings?"

She shakes her head, the bits of auburn in her hair catching in the candlelight. "Only the ones the *illustrious masters* thought necessary." Her nose scrunches. "Masters who didn't even bother to keep this place up. It's horrid in the winter. Frost gets in through the windows. Damp in the rain." She frowns. "It should be a crime."

Laurel would certainly agree. I think her emerald head might explode if she saw books neglected in such a deplorable manner.

"How did you find this place?" I wasn't aware that midnight excursions to abandoned libraries were high on a princess's itinerary.

"It's always been difficult to keep me locked in my rooms." Aurora laughs and inspects a low shelf. "I figured out how the servants were coming and going as a young girl. After that, it was easy."

"And no one minds?" I raise a skeptical eyebrow.

"Oh, don't worry. As the third daughter, I was largely ignored. I didn't even think I would have children before—" She breaks off, her fingers stiffening around the warped spine of a book as the ghosts of her sisters drift past. "After

Cordelia and Seraphina . . . when it was just me, I made sure to be caught for plenty of other offenses. Sneaking out of my window or the front doors of my chambers. Putting on ridiculous disguises." The fluidity returns to her shoulders. "Anything to distract my guards and masters from what I'm really doing."

"Which is coming here."

"You don't sound impressed."

"It's just"—I struggle to keep my face serious—"when I think of a princess sneaking out of her rooms, trips to an ancient wing of the palace don't exactly come to mind. Unless . . ."

"Unless I'm meeting a lover."

My cheeks heat and I become fascinated with the nearest book, unsure why the idea of the princess trysting makes me so bashful. "That."

"Well, as you can probably guess, it's *not* that." She taps at the place where her curse mark rests under her sleeve. "My curse is quite intact, as you must have noticed."

"A lover wouldn't have to be your *true* love," I say, surprising myself.

"You sly thing." She shoves my shoulder gently. "Don't you think I've endured enough kisses from strangers?"

"Of course you have," I say quickly. "Forgive me, Your Highness."

She bats the air. "Enough of that. I'm Aurora to you."

"Aurora." The syllables are full and bright on my tongue, tasting of summer berries and fizzy wine. My heart stutters. "Have you found anything interesting, at least?"

"Oh, yes." She flops onto a divan. Dust erupts from the

faded blue silk and glitters in the shafts of moonlight. "All kinds of texts on the realm's old history. I don't know why the masters didn't care more about this place. There should be a historian in here, keeping track of things."

"Old history? Like Leythana?"

She sits up straight. "You're interested in Leythana as well?"

"Who wouldn't be? A queen who earned her crown by right, not just inheriting it like some lazy—" I realize my mistake too late and skid to a stop. "I'm sorry. I didn't mean . . ."

"No." She rises and moves to a column, tracing tiny diamond-shaped patterns in the gritty surface with a fingertip. "I know exactly what you mean. And I agree."

"You do?"

"In fact, that's why I'm here. In a way. I want to be like Leythana. Not just an ornament, as my mother is. I want to be fierce and worthy." She pauses, looking as though she's debating whether to continue. And then the next words come out in a breathless whoosh. "And so I come here at night to try to find something to break the curse."

I'm certain from the way she worries with the edge of her sleeve that this is the first time she's spoken her dreams aloud to anyone.

"You want to break the curse," I repeat slowly. "Without your true love?"

"Yes." Those violet eyes shine. "I want to earn my crown myself. Not hand it over to the first man who kisses me correctly." But then her shoulders hunch. "You must think me a fool."

"Not at all. I admire you. You're nothing like . . ." I grapple for the right words, but they swish through my mind, slippery as eels. "What I thought."

Her smile rivals the starlight. "I take that as an extreme compliment."

"It is." An inexplicable shyness nips at me and I fumble for a distraction. "Have you made any progress?"

"Not much," she admits. "I've been poking around in volumes about the War of the Fae. Especially those about Vila. If any creature knew how to break the curse, it was them."

A chill rumbles through me. My ancestors. Aurora doesn't notice my sudden interest in a cracked magnifying glass I find on a side table. She glides away into the shadows. The light from the candle bobs and I can hear her mumbling to herself as she hunts.

"What are you doing?"

Instead of answering me, she reemerges with a huge black book tucked under one arm. Streaks of dust and dirt darken the hem of her nightdress and there's a smudge of something gray on her face. An insane part of me wants to wipe it away. "This one's in passable condition."

She nudges it into my arms and I smear away the caked dust on the cover with my cloak. *Vila in the War of the Fae,* it reads. A barbed lump forms in my throat.

"Are you sure you should be reading this?" I doubt the royal couple would be pleased to find their daughter dabbling in this corner of the realm's history.

Aurora ignores the question. She tracks one hesitant fingertip down a line of green on the back of my hand. "Are you the last one, do you think?"

My skin ignites beneath her touch. I step away from it, unsure how to answer. It was a Vila who cursed the royal family. Robbed her of her sisters. I grip the book so hard it might cave into itself. "I have no idea."

She looks at me for a long moment. "I don't care that you're Vila."

I half expect the floor to open up and swallow me whole. And I half wish that it would.

"You don't mean that."

No one could mean that. Not in Briar.

"You didn't cast the curse," she reasons.

"But it could have been—" Not my mother. Not even her mother. But somewhere down the line, I could be related to the Vila who did. The princess doesn't let me finish.

"It happened so long ago, Alyce. All we can do is live with the consequences. I'm much more interested in breaking the curse than seeking vengeance."

There's no bitterness there. No vehemence. It puts the realm to shame, myself included.

"Besides," she continues lightly, "you're far too interesting to hate. Your power is fascinating. What you did with the fountain was incredible. What else can you do?"

Do I tell her? I know better than to tell Mistress Lavender or even Laurel about Kal. But what about Aurora? She trusted me with her secret. The words are on the tip of my tongue.

"Can you turn my guards into toads?" The question throws me off balance. "That would be very helpful."

I consider this, wondering if I can use my magic to alter a human's shape. I am part Shifter after all. Then again, things had gone so horribly wrong with the duke. "I don't know. I don't think so. But I can give them warts."

"Perfect." She beams. "Do so—they'll be horrified, the vain creatures. And keep the book. See if you can spot something I missed. I'd love a second opinion, especially from someone with Vila heritage."

"I can't." I thrust it back at her. A book like this, stolen from the royal library and detailing how my ancestors nearly defeated the Etherians in the War of the Fae, could not be discovered in my rooms. I don't have the protection of a crown. "And you know more about my heritage than I do."

"I insist." She crosses her arms, stubbornly refusing to accept it. "If I know more about the Vila than you do, it sounds like you have some reading to do. And I insist that you return the book as well. It gives us an excuse to meet again."

I should leave the book, no matter what she says. It's too dangerous to keep. But fool that I am, I hug it to my chest, thinking only of the fact that she wants me to read it. That she cares about what I think.

And that she wants to see me again.

CHAPTER THIRTEEN

I don't leave Aurora until the silver moonlight blushes to the pale peach of dawn. The sleeplessness of these past nights is beginning to wear on my bones, but I wouldn't trade it for anything. We talked for hours. Aurora told me about her days in the palace, the suitors and the parties and how badly she wishes her life could mean more than flaunting new gowns, favoring the right courtiers, or obsessing over the best Grace elixirs. She wants Briar to be as it was during the reigns of the early queens—no districts dividing the poor and the wealthy. Women serving on the small council and in other key government positions. Like Laurel, she believes the Graces are little better than servants, wasting their gifts for Briar's greed. She vows the Grace Laws and even the Grace Council will drastically change when it's her turn to rule.

I didn't divulge much about my own life, wanting to leave it behind me for a few precious hours. Instead, I entertained Aurora with little demonstrations of my magic. Now that I understand better how my power works, it's easier to control. With it, I can make the candle flame burn green. Grow a fleeting pair of horns on a mouse we catch. For Aurora's benefit, and to keep my true gifts hidden, I make a show of using the elixirs in my kit. But I'm not sure she would have noticed if I hadn't, she's so enchanted with every trick. It is both a relief and a terror to be around someone who doesn't consider me an abomination. Applauds my power instead of shrinking from it. And I find myself daydreaming about the possibility that the princess will become Queen Aurora. A Leythana for the new age. Perhaps the world could be different. For everyone.

But these hopes smolder to ash when I return to Lavender House.

I sneak through the early-morning bustle of the kitchen, glaring at any curious looks the servants throw my way. Starving, I toss two fresh pastries into a cloth, licking the cinnamon glaze from my fingertips as I tiptoe up the stairs.

But I don't manage a single creaking footstep before I come face-to-face with Mistress Lavender. She doesn't look much better than she did last night. Her hair is coiled at her nape, but wisps of it escape the pins and writhe in the currents of air. Her clothes are slightly askew, the bodice crooked and improperly buttoned.

"Alyce." Her eyes burn molten steel. "You're just coming back from the palace?"

"I'm not taking any patrons today." The words are out of my mouth before I can stop them, and the boldness sends adrenaline rushing through me.

Mistress Lavender drums her fingernails against the balustrade, the sound like shots firing. A cloud of her cloying namesake scent floods the stairwell, suffocating to the point that my eyes water.

"I should say not." She brushes a silver strand out of her face. "It's barely past breakfast and yet Delphine informs me that they've all sent word canceling their appointments. Would that have something to do with Duke Weltross?"

The shame from last night creeps up my spine. "You know."

"Of course I know. Dr. Renault came herself, in the dead of night, to tell me what you did." She pauses. Tension snaps between us. Damn that weasel-faced doctor. "And then I'm sure she spent the rest of the small hours spreading her gossip. What were you thinking, Alyce? The Weltross family has been loyal to this house for decades, though they could easily afford one of the Royal Graces. I won't be surprised in the least if your sisters suffer because of your inexcusable lapse of judgment, not to mention the coin you will lose us. The next Grace Celebration will be upon us before we know it. We cannot afford such a stumble."

"They're not my sisters." I begin to crush the pastries in my grip.

"How can you say that?" Mistress Lavender descends a step, looming over me. "You share the same magical blood. You work together for the good of this house—"

"The same blood? I'm part Vila. And you saw what Rose did to me at the ball."

"She's been punished for that." A manicured nail jabs at my chest. "And *you* are forbidden to do"—she splutters, flustered—"whatever it was you did last night."

For a heart-stopping moment, I want to tell her that I won't be Briar's puppet anymore. That I will not be controlled. But I only bite my lip. The truth is that I don't want to do what I did last night. Don't want to cause that kind of torture to anyone, ever again. And so I nod.

"Good." Mistress Lavender smooths her skirts, relief softening her shoulders. "I assured the doctor that this was nothing but an accident. And it will *never* happen again." She tips my chin up with two fingers. "With any luck, your patrons will return."

"And what of the damage to our house's reputation?" A draft of summer rose and calla lily floats down the stairs and I cringe.

Mistress Lavender turns. "This does not concern you, Rose."

"It most certainly does." Slippers crusted with what looks to be a thousand minuscule seashells tap impatiently on the top landing. "I won't sacrifice my standings because of her stupidity. She should have to compensate us for the lost income."

"I don't blame you for worrying about income," I feign sympathy, "when you're paying for the dress you ruined."

Rose blanches beneath her gold rouge, her lips drawing into a tight line. I can see the wheels behind her eyes spinning, contemplating her next move.

"That's enough." Mistress Lavender angles her body between us. A Grace bell chimes in a parlor. She checks the watch she wears on a chain at her waist. "Rose, that's yours I believe. We don't need to add tardiness to the litany of this house's recent faults."

Rose says nothing, just stomps down the stairs, checking my shoulder as she passes. Her blush-colored skirts swish and I step on a pair of embroidered sea horses on her hem. She yanks herself free with a curse.

"This feud between the two of you must stop." Mistress Lavender rubs her temples. Creases web out from the corners of her eyelids. "It's bringing nothing but shame and ill will. Do you want to be the lowest-ranking house? Because we're on our way to that, I assure you. We have nine short months until the final house standings are determined."

"Tell her that." I jerk my chin at the door of Rose's parlor.

"I have. And now I'm telling you. It ends. Today. Aren't you tired of it? The constant battles and sniping? None of the other housemistresses have to deal with such nonsense."

I highly doubt that, but say nothing. And I am tired. But making peace with Rose won't ease my pains. Only leaving Briar can do that. Even so, arguing with Mistress Lavender will get me nowhere. "I'll try."

"Thank you." She pats my shoulder awkwardly, then starts down the stairs. "Rose said the same. I'm sure between the two of you, we'll have a much better arrangement."

I roll my eyes behind her retreating back, stuffing an entire cinnamon roll into my mouth. It's gone cold, the glaze slimy. Yet another disappointment for the day.

But as I trudge up the stairs, laughter trills from a parlor. Rose's. I press myself against the balustrade, leaving sticky fingermarks on the polished wood. I can just hear her chatting with her patron, effervescent and charming as always. I eat the other pastry, chewing slowly, considering.

I learned my lesson with the duke; I'm no healer. I am Vila. And perhaps it's time to use my power the way I was born to do.

Holding my breath, I slink down the steps, avoiding the noisy planks of wood I've catalogued over the years. I hug the wall, pressing myself so close to the green-striped paper that I can see Rose fully through the slit in the door. She's beaming her brilliant Grace smile, complimenting her patron on inane things like the shape of the woman's eyebrows and the shade of her face powder. The patron coos and china clinks as she sips her tea.

Rose fusses with her mixture. Reaches for the long rose-headed pin she will use to draw her blood. Three sparkling drops fall like liquid sunlight amid the other ingredients. A puff of ocher smoke erupts from the bowl, and then Rose pours everything into a goblet and passes it to her patron.

The woman's plump, greedy hands grab for the glass, jeweled rings glinting in the morning light that streams through the tall windows of Rose's parlor. She takes no pains to appear ladylike. Two gulps and I know it's gone. I think I even hear a muffled burp.

I release a shaky, silent breath. Close my eyes and concentrate the way I did when I sent my power out to find the heart of the storm. It will be harder this time. I have no idea what I'm looking for. Do I focus on Rose or the patron? What will the magic in the elixir feel like? I wish Kal were here to guide me.

But it doesn't take long. Perhaps because my magic recognizes that of the light Fae. Or because Rose's gift is actually as potent as she believes. But my own darkness bumps against the silken gold almost instantly. Unlike the duke and the storm, Rose's magic isn't like a heart. It's a thrumming cord, like mine. A riot of glittering sparks. If I breathe deeply, I can just catch the honeyed floral scent that must be the light Fae power. In a moment, it will find the heart of the patron's magic and shape it as the elixir bids.

But not yet.

I wind the dark limb of my magic around the shimmering strip of Rose's power. Hers is warm and solid. But it's malleable. I bid the bands of my magic to burrow like snakes into Rose's gift. Exhilaration swells as my power obeys. I inhale woodsmoke and charred iron. *Weaken,* I push the command with all my might. *Become ugly. Monstrous.*

Rose's gasp is all the confirmation I need that it worked.

"What's wrong?" The patron sets the glass down.

Even through the gap in the door, Rose's shock is evident.

"I—" She fumbles with the instruments on her table, upsetting a jar of crushed mint. "We did not quite achieve the right balance." A smile plasters itself on her face, her voice too high. Too desperate.

"Let me see."

"Not yet. Allow me—" There's a plea beneath her words the patron doesn't miss.

She snatches up a hand mirror before Rose can stop her. There's a moment of jagged-edged silence, shattered by a shriek. And then a dull *thunk* as something drops to the ground.

"What have you done?" The question feels like a slap, even to me.

"I—I don't understand . . ." Rose is close to tears. "It's never—"

"The rumors about this house are true." There's a rustle of silk as the patron rises. A smack of wood as her chair topples. "You are cursed. Either that, or your power is Fading."

"No, please—"

But it's too late. Angry footsteps storm across Rose's parlor and I melt into the nearest corner. In her haste to leave Lavender House, the patron looks right past me. But I certainly see her. Her skin has thickened and puckered, mirroring the exact shade and texture of an orange. Craters the size of pinpricks are visible from her hairline, over her face, and down her neck. I clap a hand over my mouth, hardly able to contain my glee.

I did that. With *my* power. Stole Rose's Grace magic. Made a patron speak to her the way they all speak to me, contentious and spiteful. A delicious mix of elation and wonder surges as Aurora's question from the library comes soaring back.

What else can I do?

CHAPTER FOURTEEN

No one can figure out what went wrong when Rose gave her patron the skin of an orange. Or when the next patron leaves with hooves for feet. Or when the next sprouts hay instead of hair.

Rose is beside herself. She blames me. I can hear her tantrums even in my attic room. But she has no proof. Healing Graces have been to the house twice to examine her for signs of poisoning, the only thing they believe could be the culprit. But her blood is as golden as ever. They give her healthy doses of Etherium just in case, and I have shown her nothing but sugarcoated concern, clicking my tongue and murmuring condolences whenever our paths cross. Mistress Lavender is quite pleased at my change of heart.

But two days and a handful of sabotaged patrons later, I catch Rose alone in her parlor after half her day's list canceled. Her hands are shaking as she tries to practice her craft and her eyes are limned scarlet from weeping. I decide she's had enough.

For now.

Done with wreaking havoc on Rose's appointments, I turn my attention instead to the book Aurora let me borrow. I keep it in the locked chest hidden in my wardrobe so the snooping maids won't find it. Its pages are in terrible condition. Whisper-thin and cracking at the edges. My head aches with the effort of squinting at the faded, cramped ink.

Some of the pre-Briarian history I already know. Since before Briar's founding, the light Fae have occupied all the lands beyond the Etherian Mountains border. Most of the Fae world is a mystery to Briar. Endlewild, the Graces, and the Briar crown itself are our only connections. But we do know that there are seven Fae courts of Etheria—the Lesser Courts and the High Court, where the High King Oryn rules. He is the most powerful Fae in existence. It's said his light magic pours from the High Court into the others, pulsing like a second heartbeat and giving life to nymphs and sprites and winged Fae steeds. Wood harvested from Fae birch groves can be crafted into bows that never miss a shot. Sand from the shores of their lakes can be blown into enchanted glass that lets the viewer see into other worlds.

And just as the humans thirsted for that power and sailed across the Carthegean Sea to claim it, darkness was attracted to the magic of the Fae. Long before Leythana arrived on her dragon ships, Demons and Shifters and other such creatures stalked the borders of Etheria, believing that if they could consume the blood of an Etherian, they could harness the light Fae power. Oryn and his courts were diligent in crafting defenses to keep such creatures out of their realm. But eventually a Demon succeeded in tricking an Etherian, luring her away from her court with the distressed calls of her kin.

When the Fae female drew close enough, the Demon pounced, sinking his teeth into her tender flesh and feasting on her golden blood. But the Demon did not absorb her power as it thought it would. And the Fae was strong. Using her staff, she slew the creature and tossed its carcass out of Etheria as a warning to others. But not before the damage was done. Evil had bitten into her soul. Soured her magic.

She had become the first Vila.

As her wounds festered, the Fae's power began to change. Her gilded blood turned the color of hemlock. Her hands and feet grew claws. Her skin, once polished and smooth like a silver birch, began to peel and rust. Tiny bones, like thorns, sprouted from the tips of her shoulders, along the ledge of her collarbone, and across her forehead like a crown. In her new form, the Vila's footsteps scorched holes in Etherian lands. Ambrosia groves wilted and died beneath her fingertips, the fruit crawling with maggots. Rivers were poisoned when she tried to scrub herself clean, fish and sprites and water nymphs floating as shriveled husks when she emerged. Horrified at what she had become, the despairing Vila hid at the edge of the Fae realm, allowing no one to touch her for fear her darkness would spread.

It did anyway.

Soon her dark power consumed the Vila. It seeped into the land she inhabited, a place dubbed Malterre for its barren trees and silty earth that hummed with evil and stank of carrion. The Vila's heart hardened. She grew resentful of the light Fae she once loved, believing that they had forgotten her. And she discovered that her Vila magic was far more powerful than that of her kin. Powerful enough to make them regret what they had done.

Bent on revenge, the Vila snuck into the Etherian courts in the dead of night, luring males into her lands and using her magic to compel them to mate with her. Before long, she produced a brood of cursed Fae just like her. With each new Vila offspring, their power grew, bleeding out and decimating the Etherian lands.

It was no surprise when, centuries later, the tension between the two races erupted in a war. Formidable as they are, the Etherians were no match for the dark magic of their fallen kin. They couldn't even set foot in Malterre, where the toxicity thrummed beneath the ground and leached into their bones and stopped their bright hearts.

The light Fae turned to their only ally: Briar. It was well known that humans could venture into Malterre without the consequences endured by the Fae. They'd done so since before Briar existed. With the help of the Etherians, the mortals could poison the Vila lands, driving out the malevolent creatures and all other abominations for good.

But the time of the warrior queens had long ended. And the reigning Briar King was greedy. He knew that Leythana's alliance agreement stipulated only that the ruler of Briar must protect the Fae border against *mortal* attacks. It said nothing about Vila. And so in exchange for his army, the

Briar King bid his wife demand the most precious gold of all: the power of the light Fae.

The bargain the High King Oryn struck created the Graces. And I understand now why Hilde believes it to be a Fae trick. When negotiating the bargain, the Briar King was clumsy with his words. He probably thought he would get to choose the form of the Etherians' gift, such as his own immortality or access to Etherian lands or some other prize. Instead, Briar received the Graces. Random children who, though they carry the gilded Etherian blood, can only access its power by draining it.

I trace my fingertips along some of the illustrations in the book. Vila. Tall, lanky things with tips of bone jutting at all angles. This one is described as female. Bone spikes protrude from her knuckles and cheekbones. Like the light Fae, her skin appears as tree bark. She could be cut from the trunk of a yew, with wide, almond-shaped eyes that gleam emerald, just like her blood.

But the only mention of the curse cast by the Vila during the war is the ruin it wreaked on Leythana's line. The rampant, swift deaths of the potential heirs and the struggle to contain its spread. I may not know much about my heritage, but I'm relatively certain that the key to breaking that curse forever lies with the Vila who cast it. But she isn't even named in this text. And try as I might, I can't silence the needling apprehension that I'm somehow linked to her. Somehow responsible for the magic that might kill Aurora.

There's only one person I can think of who might have answers.

And so on the third day that a patron schedule does not arrive in the morning, I put together a sack of food and return to the black tower before Mistress Lavender can decide I'm more useful assisting the servants.

Kal is already waiting for me when I arrive.

"You did not bring your companion."

"No." After what happened the last time I'd trained with Kal, I decided to leave Callow behind. She was more than slightly annoyed, and I have the beak-shaped lances on my hands to prove it. "But I'll tell her you asked after her."

A shadow brushes my arm, almost playful.

I slough off my pack and roll my shoulders back with a groan.

"That looks heavy," Kal says. "When you learn to Shift, I can teach you to strengthen your muscles. You will be able to carry far more than that with ease."

"When can we start?" I rub at the sore spot at the crook of my neck.

"Now, if you like." His shadows coil around him, betraying his eagerness. And once more I'm struck by what a lonely life it must be for Kal. I complain about my attic room and the resentment of a realm, but Kal has been chained to darkness since the war. Alone for twenty years before I showed up. And who knows how long before my mother arrived. "Have you been practicing at all? Any of your Vila magic?"

"Yes." He'd love to know how I terrorized Rose's patrons. But before I can tell him, I recall another patron. Duke

Weltross, his eyes glassy and bloodshot, his fragile human magic obliterated beneath my steel-dipped power.

I want to forget the duke. But the words press against the back of my teeth until I have no choice but to spit them out. "I was with a patron. He was sick—dying. I wanted to use my magic the way you taught me. To heal him." The smell of coppery blood and rancid bile stings my nostrils. The sounds of the duchess's screams twine with the wind. "But . . ."

"It went horribly wrong."

"How did you know?"

Kal moves as close as the darkness will let him. "Because that is not your gift, Alyce. Vila cannot wield light magic, regardless of intent."

I let out a breath and slump onto a fallen beam. "I thought that's what you would say. But I wanted to be wrong."

Stone crunches under Kal's boots. "Why?"

"Because"—my cheeks burn with the admission—"I wanted . . . I wanted to be different. I don't want to be a monster."

Kal reaches for me, but I'm too far in the sunlight. "You are nothing of the kind. You should be proud of your power. Who else can boast that they punctured a storm cloud with their will alone?"

Unwelcome tears pool, hot and bitter. "And what good did that do anyone? I can only summon pain. Destruction."

"Who told you that?"

"No one has to tell me," I rush on. "It's in every look flung my way. Vila are the worst sort of creature. Everyone knows it."

He crosses his arms. "Everyone?"

I swipe my forearm across the infuriating dribble at my nose, jerk Aurora's book out of my sack, and practically throw it at him. "Enough that there are whole books on the subject. How awful and vicious the Vila race was."

"Not was," Kal corrects, flipping through the pages. "You still live."

"Dragon's teeth, I'm in no mood for wordplay." A wave pounds against the cliff.

"Are you not?" He snaps the book closed. "Because that is all I see in this book. Lies and trickery. And yet you write it on your heart. Demean yourself because of the opinions of"—he opens the front cover and sneers—"the illustrious Master Walburn. What gives him the right to tell you who you are?"

I don't know how to answer that. It's never occurred to me to question the source of the information in my books. But Kal is right. Master Walburn was employed by the royals. Trained, as I was, to despise the Vila. I think of the book Endlewild gave me when I was a child. Who wrote it? Another Etherian who wants me dead?

Without warning, Kal throws Aurora's book through the gap and into the sea.

"Kal!" I leap after it, catching myself just before I tumble over the edge. "Why did you do that? It doesn't belong to me."

"If you want a history lesson, I will provide one." Shadow laps around him like flame. "But I will not have your mind poisoned any longer. Your mother would be ashamed."

Dragon's fucking teeth, Aurora is going to murder me. I dig the heels of my palms into my eyes. "Fine. If you're such the expert, tell me what really happened."

There's a smile in his voice, the bastard. "I am so glad you asked. Tell me, as you are so well-informed, how the first Vila came to be."

Gritting my teeth, I ramble off the version that now rests at the bottom of the sea.

"Wrong," Kal interrupts before I've finished. "The light Fae was attacked by a Demon, that much is true. But she did not exile herself because of some selfless desire to save her kin." He laughs. "Her court abandoned her."

"What?"

The Etherians are known to be crafty, but they are unfailingly loyal to their own. For a light Fae to be cast out of their court is unthinkable.

"Oh, yes. Not the story you know, is it? After the Demon attacked her, the Fae was tainted in their eyes. Her own kind banished her to the edges of Etheria. But she had mated with a high-ranking member of her own court. A powerful Fae lord who would not forsake her. He went with the fallen Fae. Loved her. And chose to turn his own blood Vila."

A wind gusts through the tower.

"You're saying that a Fae *lord* willingly gave up his power? To be Vila?"

A slow grin spreads across Kal's face. "He was not the only one. Over the centuries, many Fae elected to leave their courts and go to Malterre. Why would they not? Vila blood was more powerful than that of the Etherians. In Malterre, they were not bound to the strict order and etiquette of the Fae courts. They were free."

Free. In the distance, a ship's bell rings.

"And so, the Vila offspring. They weren't—" My chest burns just thinking of what I'd read in Briar's books.

"Incestuous bastards?" Kal's shadows sharpen. "No. The suggestion that the first Vila's offspring mated with one another to produce more of their kind is yet another slander. The Etherians were furious when their own took up with the Vila. And so they spun stories like the one you told me to try to keep others from going to Malterre."

"But Etherians can't lie," I argue.

"No, but they misdirect. Spreading rumors is one of their favorite pastimes. Stay here."

"Where are you going?"

But he's already dissolved into the darkness, leaving me spinning in a tide pool of my own questions. Should I believe Kal? I have no reason to doubt him. He's only ever helped and guided me, which is more than I can say for almost every soul in Briar. I've seen for myself how much Endlewild hates me because of my blood.

"Another book for you." Kal materializes so swiftly that I startle. He holds out a leather-bound volume that looks in remarkably good condition for having been kept in this tower.

I take it with caution, running my hands over the cover. There's no title, only an emblem stamped onto the leather. It looks somewhat like the sigil Endlewild wears, entwined laurel leaves curving together around an orb. But where the Fae lord's is elegant—soft curling edges and shimmering color—this one is all sharp angles. The laurel leaves look closer akin to teeth, jagged-edged and brittle. And the orb is cracked, with something that might be blood oozing through the craggy break. "Why should I trust it?"

"A very good question." One of Kal's shadows grazes my cheek. "You do not have to trust it. But I can tell you that it came from Malterre. It is the history of the Vila, written by one of their own. Grimelde, a scribe from the court of Targen. I knew him. He managed to escape Malterre after the war and left it with me."

"He didn't free you?"

"He could not. Though he promised to return with reinforcements. That we would rebuild Malterre." There's a touch of bitterness in Kal's voice. "I have not seen him again."

"I'm sorry."

"It matters little now." Kal's shadows unspool and waft toward me. "I think you will find many answers in his words. Vila were not the monsters the Etherians would have you believe."

A wind sighs around us, laced with the hint of an early autumn. I tug my cloak closer. "But then why did the war start?"

"Why does any war start?" A gull laughs as it soars past the tower. "The Etherians abhorred the Vila for their difference. For the fact that their magic was the stronger breed. Vila power takes light magic and distorts it. And they loathe you for it."

The scar on my middle aches, and I imagine that I can feel Endlewild's grip bruising my arms as he pinned me down and held his staff to my skin. More than ever I'm certain that the book the Fae lord gave me was another instrument of his torture. That he wanted me to believe I was an abomination. Unworthy of even the air I breathed.

The angle of the sun has changed, casting me in shadow. Kal closes the distance between us in two sweeping strides.

"History is written by victors." He cups my face in his ice-cold hands. Frost tickles my nose. "Embrace your gift. Your heritage. Such wild, untapped power. You are perfect."

No one has ever, *ever* called me that word before. And I can't help the sob that thunders up my throat. Kal pulls me close, tucks my head under his chin. I let my arms wrap around his waist, not even caring that it feels like I'm embracing a solid block of ice. That his heartbeat is slow and irregular and so faint I might be imagining it.

"It is the Graces who are monsters," he says softly, his wintry breath on the shell of my ear. "For letting you believe such things about yourself."

Long-held pain and resentment bleeds out of me, scraping me clean. Until I am an empty, hollow husk. I do not know what to say. What to do.

"I will never treat you so poorly." Kal pulls back and tips my chin up. I see nothing of deception in his onyx gaze. Only appreciation. And caring, something I hardly recognize.

I wipe my freezing, wet cheeks with my sleeve. "Teach me, then."

• • •

I return to Lavender House in the early evening, after a grueling training session.

I'm still not ready to Shift, and so we focused on my Vila power. Kal explained that it was easy for me to sabotage Rose's patrons because I wanted fiercely to punish her. My intent was strong. But I must learn to steer my magic the way a rider controls her horse. And like any fledgling rider, I'm thrown on my ass more often than not—especially when the magic of another object is difficult to find. Which is why the small rock Kal bid me sculpt into a beastly gargoyle turned out as a lumpy, larger rock. And then the sword he wanted me to forge from a thorn was just a dull, rusty dagger. By the end of it, my head was pounding and my muscles spent.

Even as my body screams for a hot meal and my own bed, I'm anxious to delve into the book Kal gave me. The pages seem to whisper to me from my sack, begging to be read. And so I don't even notice when Mistress Lavender and the others are waiting for me in the main parlor.

"What have you done now?" It's Marigold who pipes up first, her lemon-drop hair done up in a honeycomb cluster. Golden powder crusts her bronze cheeks.

I look from one to the next. Marigold and Rose are watching me like cats with cornered mice. Laurel with an expression that might be sympathy. And Mistress Lavender taps a cream-colored roll of parchment against the arm of her chair, her face pinched with worry.

The sack slips off my shoulder. Do they know where I've been? About Kal? About my magic? I hand my cloak off to a servant, trying to hide the tremor in my limbs.

Delphine slides me a sly glance as she pretends to be arranging tomorrow's schedules at her desk, crisp envelopes clacking on polished wood.

"I don't know what you mean," I attempt, as evenly as I can. "I had no patrons and I spent the day gathering enhancements."

Rose scoffs, exchanging an eye-roll with Marigold. I breathe a hope that no one asks to look in my sack and discovers Kal's book.

"It appears you're wanted at the palace." Mistress Lavender says slowly, as if she can't quite believe it herself.

"To be punished." Rose smirks.

"You don't know that." Laurel rearranges the hunter-green taffeta skirts of her gown—a gown too fine for an evening at home. Why is she dressed like that? And Mistress Lavender is wearing her official Head of Household golden sash. Embroidered lavender flowers dance along the hem. The Grace seal, picked out in amber stones, shines in the lamplight.

"The royal family is hosting an intimate dinner, to which we are invited." For all her obsession over rank, I would think Mistress Lavender would be elated. Ours is one of the minor Grace houses, and we're rarely afforded such exclusive invitations. But she's looking at the missive like she hopes its contents might have changed. "And your presence is specifically requested."

She passes the letter to me. I gape at the words as if they're written in a foreign tongue. But no. There it is. An extra line just after the others' names:

A new shot of adrenaline hits my bloodstream. Summoned—to a dinner? That has never happened. I wasn't even included in the Blooming Ceremony when I began using my gift. I've never attended a Grace Celebration. I find Laurel's curious gaze, but she just lifts her eyebrows.

"It's because of the duke." Marigold is quick to fill the silence. The tiny hummingbird baubles dangling from her ears sparkle. "You killed a member of the nobility. They'll probably execute you."

Rose nods in agreement, and Mistress Lavender throws them both a scathing warning. "Graces, that's enough. To my knowledge, His Majesty is not in the habit of lopping off heads after dessert."

Marigold pouts. "What about before?"

"It is however"—Mistress Lavender's attention swivels back to me—"quite an unusual situation. You've never been named before. I don't know what to make of it. Do you, Alyce?"

All I can do is shake my head. Why would the king want me at a dinner? Does *he* know about Kal? About my true abilities? Has he finally decided to do away with the Dark Grace? My thoughts strike against one another like pieces of flint, goading a flame that will burn me up.

But I have no time to sort them out. Mistress Lavender rings her bell and I'm carted off before I can argue any further.

CHAPTER FIFTEEN

It takes three highly disgruntled servants working on me, but I'm dressed and ready faster than I believe possible. One of my stiffer black gowns is deemed passable, but Mistress Lavender had it made for me years ago. I despised the thing and never wore it, and now the sleeves don't quite reach my wrists and the hem is too high to be fashionable. Next to Rose and the other Graces I look like I'm going to a funeral—for someone I hated. My hair refuses to stay pinned in place, the greasy strands slipping out and sliding at odd angles down my neck. The dress couldn't be aired out before I put it on, so I smell faintly of cedar wood and musty satin. Rose makes sure I know it, wrinkling her nose and coughing into a frothy lace handkerchief the entire carriage ride. Marigold, for her part, acts like I'm not even here, jabbing me with her elbow each time she "rearranges her skirts."

I'm too lost in my own worries to care, the clopping of

the horses' hooves matching the iron-clad rhythm of my heartbeat. Laurel keeps offering me encouraging looks, but they do little to inspire me. I still feel like I'm on my way to the scaffold.

At the palace, we're quickly ushered inside. Mistress Lavender tugs out the royal invitation and holds it in front of her like a shield, clearly expecting to need to explain my presence. But the guards make no move to stop me. Don't even acknowledge me, save for stiffened shoulders and the barest of winces when I draw near. They must have been warned, which makes me even more nervous.

Rose performs an elaborate show of calling out to every courtier we meet on the way to the royal wing, tossing out empty compliments and reminding them to book appointments with her well in advance. To anyone else, she would seem the picture of confidence. But I catch the anxious, too-high pitch of her laugh. The way the Briar roses on her bracelet jangle with each overly enthusiastic wave.

And I see the way the others respond to her as well. Whispers hidden behind gloves and fans. Condescending smiles from other Graces. Dark, suspicious glances flung behind her back like blades. I haven't meddled with her patrons since I caught her crying in her parlor, but the recent incidents have left a scar on her reputation. I almost feel sorry for her, especially since it's my fault she's suffering.

And then Rose veers in just the right way to make me stagger into a statuette of a bronzed dragon. Pain lances up my side as the corner of the marble pedestal finds my hip bone. Maybe I'll slip an ugliness elixir into her tea.

The décor in this part of the palace is just as nauseating as in the ballroom. Like the rest of the newer wings, the royal private residence was commissioned when the Briar Kings decided that Leythana's original home had grown too drab for the richest realm in the world. They spared no expense in the renovations.

Instead of sconces, tiny gilded dragons—likely designed by the innovation Graces—line the halls, spewing fire from their miniature snouts. Elaborate arrangements of Grace-cultivated Briar roses burst into bloom in opal-veined vases, petals shifting from lavender to indigo to scarlet. Ornate tapestries woven with scenes of Briar's history adorn the walls. I'm drawn to one in particular: Leythana being blessed by the Etherians, her crown dripping with glittery gold. There's another beside it showing the mortal army poisoning Malterre during the War of the Fae. Vila cower and shrivel at the soldiers' feet, mouths open in wrenching screams. The magic from the innovation Graces makes it appear as though their green blood is still flowing. That the humans are still laughing, victorious. I look away.

Mistress Lavender halts in front of a pair of glass doors featuring a mosaic pattern that's an exact, smaller copy of the dragon in the ballroom. She announces herself and her Graces, but her voice falters a bit when she gets to me.

The herald's flat brown eyes widen as he takes me in, and my palms begin to sweat. But he says nothing, only turns in a forced, mechanical motion and slams his dragon-headed cane onto the marble floor. The doors swing open.

"Mistress Lavender, Housemistress of Lavender House, and her charges, their Graces Rose of Beauty, Marigold of

Charm, and Laurel of Wisdom. And"—I think I hear him swallow—"the Dark Grace."

I sense the movement in the room before he steps aside to grant us access. The private dining hall is only about the size of a few of our parlors put together, but a thousand times more intimidating. A dais looms at the other side. King Tarkin and Queen Mariel are already seated at a table with carved dragons for legs, the polished top balancing on the tips of their taloned wings. Servants with plates of hors d'oeuvres hurry back and forth, pretending not to notice my entrance. There are about five or six other tables in front of the dais. One holds the handful of Royal Graces. The wreaths of gilded laurel crowning their vibrant heads gleam as they regard me with curiosity mixed with repugnance. At the other tables, dozens of jewel-laden necks crane in my direction, wine flutes and spoons freezing on the way to gaping lips.

My breathing comes fast and sharp, sawing in and out of my lungs like one of Cook's serrated knives. I lick my lips, finding them chapped and cracked because I'd picked at them so much on the way here. There is nowhere to look. Nowhere to go. My brain screams at me to turn around. Flee whatever is waiting for me here. I take a half step back, preparing. And then a voice cuts through the tension.

"You came!"

A blur of crimson brocade comes barreling from a hidden corner of the room, too quickly for me to move out of the way. She is upon me in an instant, grasping my shoulders and giving each cheek a quick kiss.

"I hoped you would."

"P-princess Aurora." A sharp jab in the ribs from Laurel reminds me to drop into a curtsy, as the rest of them have already done. Murmurs of "Your Highness" ripple like waves.

"What did I tell you about that?" she whispers, drawing me back to stand. "Thank you for attending our dinner," she says to the others. "And for bringing our dear Alyce."

I wish there were a way to capture the look on Rose's face as she gawks between us, her painted mouth hanging open so far I can see the back of her throat.

"*You* invited *her*?" Her face goes white, then splotched with amber. Matching blossoms explode on the exposed skin of her chest. "Here?"

Mistress Lavender pinches her elbow.

"You seem surprised." Aurora links arms with me. "Now come, Alyce. Take a turn with me before dinner."

Laurel deals me a grin as the princess guides me away. But the rest of them are horror-struck. And I can't say I feel much steadier. My limbs are like rubber. Muttering and stares follow us with every step.

"You invited me?" I repeat, willing my focus to stay on the Briar roses embroidered on the heavy damask drapes. The busts of former queens, their crowns of bramble and thorn glazed with candlelight. The gentle cadence of lutes being played in a corner. Anything but the needling attention of the other guests. A servant hiccups as he passes us, almost dropping his tray of thinly sliced meat folded to look like dragons. I've never missed my hooded cloak more.

Aurora gives my arm a shake. "How many times must I say it? *Yes.*"

"But—" Doubts and questions buzz like a stirred hornet's nest in my mind. "Why?"

She blinks at me. "I want my book back. You promised to return it."

Dragon's teeth, the book. I bite down on my tongue so hard I taste the loam of my blood. How exactly do I tell her it's at the bottom of the Carthegean Sea?

"Don't look so worried." She laughs, attracting even more stares. "I'm only teasing. I wanted to see you again. Is that so strange?"

Yes. Extremely strange. "But—"

"If I'd known you were going to interrogate me the entire night, I'd never have invited you." She sighs, steering us around a stuffed peacock perched on a pyramid of fruit. Its cascade of tail feathers brushes the floor. "But I did, because you're the one person at court I can stand for longer than half an hour."

"That can't be true," I argue, relieved that the subject of the book is momentarily forgotten. "And I'm not at court."

"You should have seen the men I had to kiss this morning. One of them insisted on prattling on about the cattle breeding trade in his kingdom, even *after* his kiss didn't take." She shudders. "I think he still believed there was a chance we'd get married."

We're nearing the royal table. Another guest has slithered in. Endlewild sits to the right of the king, pushing an assortment of quail's eggs around his plate with a gilded fork. Snippets of their conversation float above the din.

"I'm commissioning a new trade ship, Lord Ambassador." Tarkin motions for more wine. "I've heard that the Fae can weave fabric of such quality that it never tears. That it could be used to craft a sail that does not even need wind to steer it. Is that true?"

Endlewild spears the yolk of one egg and watches it ooze over his plate. "My kin are capable of many feats unknown to mortals."

Tarkin's mustache twitches. "Perhaps. But answering my questions directly has never been one you've accomplished during your lengthy tenure." He drinks deeply. "How much would such fabric cost? Surely Briar can afford the expense."

But the Fae ambassador doesn't reply. He watches me instead. Aurora and I round the front of the dais. She curtsies quickly to Queen Mariel, but I am frozen in place, as if pinned by Endlewild's gaze. Like I'm an insect that has wandered onto his dinner plate, and he has me between the tines of his fork.

Somehow I manage to bend my knees into the appropriate obeisance, the scar on my torso aching.

"I insist you come more often to save me from such company." Aurora leads me away, but I can still feel the Fae lord's attention sizzling like a brand into my back. "And I'm dying to know what you thought of that book. Did you find anything? Do you think—" But the sound of a gong cuts her off. Aurora grimaces. "Damn. I'm sure they sat you with the Graces, though I do wish you could be with me. Perhaps we could arrange . . ."

"No, I—" *I'd rather die than share a table with Endlewild,* I don't say. It's bad enough sharing a room. My dress suddenly feels even tighter. "I'd better do what's expected."

"All right," she relents. "But find me after dinner. There'll be a reception in the drawing room. Or come to my chambers. A servant will tell you the way. Promise."

She's gone before I can answer.

I am seated with the Graces, the royal table mercifully at my back. I also notice a healthy amount of space between myself and the two Graces seated next to me. One is Pearl, Rose's rival beauty Grace at Willow House. Her hair, done up with rhinestone-studded combs fashioned to look like starlings, is a unique shade of opal. Varying hues of turquoise and coral and citrine dive and then resurface in the candlelight, the colors made even more breathtaking against the dark umber of her skin. She's been Rose's chief competition for years. Rose pretends to be friendly with her, but I know she'd rip out the other Grace's golden eyes and mash them into an elixir if given half the chance.

The other, I learn, is Narcisse. From the lacquered bell charms at her ears and on her bracelet, and the lilt of her laugh, I assume her gift is music. Graces like her are almost always put to work entertaining wealthy households and bestowing pleasant singing voices on patrons. I'll probably have to sit through Narcisse's recital later this evening. At least there will be plenty of wine.

Pearl and Narcisse's easy chatter dies a sudden, gruesome death at my arrival.

"So." Pearl adjusts the monstrous sapphire ring on her finger, a gift I heard she received from the Grace Council in honor of earning the most coin last year. Rose squawked about the thing for weeks, and I don't think it's an accident that Pearl is wearing it now. "A royal invitation for the Dark

Grace. Has that ever happened before? Narcisse and I receive simply stacks of them, for one party or another. But you—I never would have thought it possible."

"Nor I." Rose sips her wine, sharing a loaded look with her rival. I'm so happy I can unite them in their distaste for me.

"And how exactly did you achieve such an honor? The royal family is very exclusive when it comes to these dinners. I was surprised to see even our dear Rose here tonight."

"Yes," Narcisse chimes in. She pats at her chignon, which boasts the reds and golds and coppers of living flame. Grace powder sparkles on her white shoulders. "It seems as if you're quite the favorite with the crown princess."

I take a gulp from my own goblet, if only to buy myself time. The wine is too sweet, more like honeyed nectar. I'm tempted to dump a spoonful of Etherium into it from the crystal dish at the center of the table. Anything to help me get through this night.

"What's wrong?" Laurel drums her fingertips against the table. "Jealous?"

I could kiss her. The Graces frown, glancing over at the cluster of Royal Graces, who are talking comfortably at their table. The Royal Graces represent the pinnacle of Grace talent. Almost every Grace harbors a healthy dose of envy about their status. There are around five Royal Graces usually, each with a different gift. They serve at the palace until they show signs of Fading, and then they're moved to a lesser house once a stronger Grace is selected to replace them. Though the Grace Laws technically forbid the monopolizing of a Grace for one family or person, the Royal Graces are so powerful and charge so much for their elixirs that only the wealthiest nobles can afford them. But, in order to preserve fairness among the houses, Royal Graces are exempt from house standings until they are excused from royal service.

When they're not working, these Graces enjoy throwing extravagant parties and dinners in their palace chambers. I've heard Rose griping about how seldom she is invited to the gatherings. Though lately her complaints have turned to energetic gossip about how one of the Royal Graces might be Fading. If it's the beauty Grace, the vacancy she leaves is one Rose might actually kill for.

"The Dark Grace is hardly our competition," Pearl drawls. She selects an hors d'oeuvre from a passing tray that looks like a crystalized Briar rose and nibbles on a petal. "Besides, I'm sure it's a fleeting fancy. The princess is young and sheltered. A fascination with such a . . . creature is understandable. She's never seen anything so grotesque."

My ears begin to burn, the cord of my magic quivering. I fight the urge to send it out and make that beautiful Grace hair fall out of her head.

"Or perhaps she murdered someone the princess hated." Marigold laughs, shoveling another spoonful of a custard-like mold into her mouth. "Like with Duke Weltross."

The table freezes.

"Oh, that was a gruesome business, wasn't it?" Narcisse leans in, one of her belled earrings tinkling. "Do tell us, Alyce. What happened?"

"It was an accident." I keep my eyes down, but my white napkin becomes the bloodstained sheets from that night. I dig my nails into it, probably poking holes through the linen.

"Was it?" Rose swirls her goblet. "You never did explain."

"Because it's none of our business." Laurel again. "And it's not as if you haven't had your share of accidents lately."

Rose flinches like she's been slapped. Pearl's catlike attention cuts across the table. "That's true. I'd nearly forgotten. How are you coping, dear?" She reaches to pat Rose's wrist in a manner that could only be described as predatory.

"They were—" Rose takes a visible breath, the lace at her neckline fluttering. "Flukes. My enhancements were probably soured."

Marigold nods. "Exactly. Rose's gift is as strong as ever, as our standings will prove."

"Well, I hope you've punished the servant responsible. Such *accidents* could mean everything at the next Grace Ceremony."

Rose speaks through gritted teeth. "I plan to."

My heart skips, and I take another sip of wine against my better judgment. It's smoother than the last time. My head buzzes.

"Even so." Pearl runs her thumb over her ring. "We can't ignore the fact that such . . . flukes could be a sign that your gift is weakening."

Rose goes perfectly still, the knuckles holding her goblet stretching white. I worry that the glass might shatter. "I'm fine. I worked on Lady Eleanora earlier today. She turned out beautifully."

"She did," Marigold chirps. "Absolutely stunning."

"That's so good to hear." Pearl grants them a cloying, condescending smile as she spoons Etherium into her wine. "Briar would certainly hate to lose such a gifted Grace."

A line of servants marches through a side door. A footman sets a dish in front of each guest, then they sweep away the cloche coverings in one unnervingly synchronized motion. Venison, drizzled in herbed butter, all served on golden plates.

Except mine.

A throbbing starts behind my eyes as I stare down at the silver plate. No one even bothered to polish it. Tarnish dims the edges, mottling my reflection. Like the bell in my Lair.

"Forgive me, Dark Grace." The man's voice is close to my ear, shaking slightly. "We had no more golden plates for tonight's dinner."

I swallow. This room is pure opulence. The vaulted ceiling is painted as the night sky, studded with what are probably real diamonds. The fireplace is large enough to walk into, carved with intricate designs of ambrosia fruit and Briar roses intertwined with the king's and queen's initials. Gilt cutlery and jeweled goblets drink the candlelight. There are less than a dozen Graces here tonight. Three times as many are usually present at a more formal dinner. And so I know that they did not run out of gold plates. That someone told them to deliberately not give me one.

To exclude me.

"And what about you, Alyce?" Pearl's voice is hardly audible over the rushing against my eardrums. I force my stiff neck to turn to her. "Do you think the incident with the poor duke is any indication that *your* power is Fading?"

The rapt attention of the table falls on me like a wet woolen blanket.

Without once breaking my gaze from Pearl's, I pick up my fork and knife and saw into the venison. It's tender, cooked rare. I can smell the red juices that burst from beneath the skin and pool on the plate, iron and salt and spices. It spills out of my lips and dribbles down my chin as I stuff a hunk into my mouth. My own reflection glares back at me in the gold saucers of Pearl's eyes, the only Grace plate I'll receive tonight. My lips are bloody. Crimson tracks down my neck. Smears across my teeth.

I bolt down the half-chewed meat with a sloppy gulp.

"What do you think?"

CHAPTER SIXTEEN

The rest of dinner progresses at the pace of a garden snail. No one says much as the other courses are whisked in and out of the room, although Laurel did raise her glass to me after my stunt with the venison. By the time the herald announces that we should progress to the drawing room, the other Graces can't remove themselves fast enough.

Endlewild disappeared after a dish of some sort of gelatinous meat, thank the dragon, and so I don't have to bear his silent, piercing scrutiny any longer. Before trailing after her parents, Aurora locks gazes with me and completes an elaborate series of hand gestures that I take to mean *find me later*.

A swarm of servants is ready for us in the drawing room, bearing trays of swollen cream puffs piled into pyramids, succulent glazed pastries topped with sugared violets, delicate tarts dusted with slivered almonds, and—if it's possible—

more wine. The Graces are quick to partake, seating themselves in clusters on claw-footed sofas and satin divans and launching into frenzied, whispered conversations. All of which are probably about me. I stick to the darker corners, searching for Aurora. Desperate for some friendly company after the agony of dinner.

"Walk with me."

But that voice is not the princess's.

To my horror, Queen Mariel seems to peel herself from the frescoed walls. I'm immediately grateful that I took the time to wipe my face clean of the venison juice. My dress, however, is another matter. I can still smell the gamey spices and there are oily blotches down my bodice.

I sink into a deep curtsy, head spinning with the remnants of wine and the sheer impossibility of this situation. But the queen gives me little time to recover. With a gesture Rose sometimes uses with Calliope, Queen Mariel indicates that I should follow her through a set of glass doors and out into the night.

"My daughter seems to have taken quite a liking to you." The sounds of clinking crystal and falsetto laughter fade behind us as Her Majesty leads me along a white-and-purple-tiled porch. The palace gardens roll out from the steps in a riot of lilies and topiaries and manicured paths. There's a clean, sweet scent to the night. Fireflies ride the wind, which is brisk now that autumn is creeping in.

"I—" I fumble. "I am honored to have her favor."

It seems the right answer. Queen Mariel inclines her head a fraction. "I would like to know your intentions."

Intentions? No one has ever asked me that before. "I'm afraid I don't understand."

The queen wheels to a stop. "What do you want with my daughter? You are the Dark Grace. There must be some motive."

"I— I just want—" The air is suddenly too close. The fabric of my gown sticks to my back. "Your Majesty, I only— I want to be her friend." The words sound so foreign. So utterly unbelievable. I have no friends. No one would choose to be mine.

The queen watches me for a long moment, twisting one of the garnet rings on her slender fingers. I can see Aurora in the curve of her bronze-kissed cheek. The height of her forehead. The way she bites her bottom lip when she's thinking. Then she turns and keeps walking, leaving me to hurry behind her burgundy skirts.

"My daughter is young. Impressionable. She has not seen much of the world." She lifts her chin higher, quickens her pace. "And this may be the last year of her life, if—" Her voice cracks.

"I understand, Your Majesty."

"Do you?" She stops again, so abruptly I almost trip over my own feet. "I'm not sure that you do. Aurora is the last heir. Every moment, every second of her life must be funneled toward securing her throne and breaking her curse."

A cold, slick feeling sloshes in my stomach and I'm worried the venison will resurface.

"She does not have time for cr—" Mariel catches herself, but I know what she was about to say. *Creatures. Animals.*

"For anything else. For *friends*. I have lost two daughters to the curse." She rubs at the inside of her forearm, where her own mark once rested. "I will not lose another. And I will not be the last Briar Queen."

My jaw aches from clenching my teeth together. There's a burning behind my eyes, but I will not show weakness. "I want her to rule as well." And I mean it. Briar needs a queen like Aurora would be. Like Leythana.

"Good." Moonlight glints silver against the tips of the thorns on her crown. I have no doubt she'd impale me with them if she could. "I do not know what happened with Duke Weltross." When I open my mouth to respond she raises her voice. "And I do not care to know. Such matters are for the king to deal with."

So there *was* a conversation about me. A nightbird sings sweetly from its perch, the sound so incongruous to the tension humming between us.

"But I will not have my daughter, the crown princess of Briar, mixed up in such matters." She pauses, letting her words sink their teeth deep. "I trust that from this day forward, you will remember your place."

There is nothing to say. Nothing I can do but drop into another curtsy, the marble tiles blurring. "Yes, Your Majesty."

"We will not have this conversation again, Dark Grace."

I bite my lips to keep my words locked inside them and wait until the clacking of her slippers has faded before I rise from my position. Because that was not a warning. Not a threat. It was a promise.

After the queen is gone, all I can do is seethe. I press my forehead into the cold veneer of a column, but it does nothing to ease my temper. Nothing to extinguish the rage licking my insides like tongues of flame. I want to tear this palace down, stone by cursed stone. Find every heart of human magic and grind them all up like I do enhancements beneath my pestle. I want—

Feeding off my desire, my power explodes out of its cage and dives for the first target it can find. It careens into a rosebush, plump Grace-grown blooms lolling their heads in the breeze. The plant's magic is nothing more than a wriggling worm against mine, filling my nose with the scent of summer rain and velvet petals.

Dragon take these roses. This entire realm, saturated with its own self-importance and willing to smother the rest of us under its greed. A tingling starts in my toes and surges upward. My blood sings through my veins. The scent of charred stone and flint floods my lungs.

At my slight push, the rosebush triples in size, stems growing as thick around as my arms. The leaves sharpen, edges barbed. Soft lavender petals darken to a red like wet mortal blood. Jagged-toothed thorns cut through the meaty flesh of the stems. The branches sway and groan in the breeze—a sound like a growl. Like the whole bush is a beast waiting to strike. And it *would* strike, I realize, if I wished it to. I could command one of those branches to tighten around someone's neck until it snapped. Bid the thorns to shred their skin and arteries to ribbons.

The grisly image startles me back into the present. My

magic loosens its grip and ebbs away. What a fool I am, using my power this close to the palace. To Endlewild. The fountain was an accident. But this—this is dangerous. No one can know the true extent of my power.

I turn back to the porch, smoothing my skirts and schooling my face into neutrality. Panic slams into me like an icy wave. A shadow lurks in the doors of the drawing room, huge and hulking and most certainly King Tarkin. His face is in darkness.

But even from here, I see the white gleam of his smile.

I cannot breathe. Not as my feet fly across gravel paths to the waiting carriages, where I demand to be taken back to Lavender House. Not as I hurl myself upstairs and claw off my gown, snapping at the servants to leave me be.

Seams pop. Fabric rips. It isn't enough. I can still see Tarkin leering at me in the night. Endlewild watching my every move like a wolf about to pounce. The same way he looked at me every day during his "treatments." I rip the coverlets off my bed and flip over the mattress. Grab one of the pillows, tear the cover apart with my teeth, and yank the feathers out in fistfuls. The washbasin shatters when I heave over its table, the sound of breaking porcelain undeniably satisfying. The wardrobe is too sturdy to take much damage from my bare hands, but I kick and pound at it anyway. Throw open the doors, toss my pathetic dresses to the floor, and attempt to stomp them into the floorboards.

When I have run out of things to destroy, I crumple amid

the mess. Sweat drenches my back and neck. Feathers float around the room and stick to my skin. It is only then that I let myself weep. Sobs wrack me for what feels like hours, days. Until my eyes are swollen and my throat raw and my chest aching. It's been a long time since I cried like this. The last I can remember was when I was a child, after sessions when I was locked in Endlewild's frigid, dank chambers for long stretches of time. Burned and pricked and reminded with every horrified glance how different I am. How freakish.

I cry until I can't anymore, nothing but soft whimpers escaping my salt-stained lips. And then there is only darkness.

Before dawn, I push myself up from the wreckage and clean up what I can. Mistress Lavender will dock my wages if she sees the state of my room. For the first time since my appointment with Duke Weltross, a schedule arrives when the servants make their rounds. I suppose word of my invitation to the palace wormed its way through the Grace District. If the king and queen see fit to dine with me, the nobles must feel far more comfortable soliciting my wares. I squeeze the black-sealed parchment in my fist, wanting nothing more than to feed it to a candleflame. But that would only bring more trouble.

Downstairs, the Graces are taking breakfast. Sunlight streams in from the side gardens, searing against my tear-crusted eyes. The tempo of the hammer in my head increases.

"We couldn't find you after dinner." Marigold wastes no time, dunking a strawberry the size of her palm into a bowl of whipped cream. "We thought you'd been called for another 'appointment.'"

Laurel's gaze darts up from the open book balancing on the edge of the table.

"No." I serve myself a boiled egg and a thick slice of toast. Food is the last thing I want, but I'm weak and dehydrated and know that I'll need my strength to get through the day. The others watch me closely, clearly expecting me to explain. I don't.

"Well then." Rose fusses with the tie of her fuchsia dressing gown, then slips a scrap of bacon to Calliope, who accepts it and trots off in glee. "Where were you? I think I saw the *queen* spirit you away. And I can't imagine what she would want with someone like you, if not commanding a service."

The toast tastes like ash, but I chew slowly, deliberately, breathing so that I don't visibly bristle. Marigold titters into her napkin.

"Actually, the queen did speak with me." I dab at my mouth. "It seems one of the Royal Graces is Fading."

Rose and Marigold suck in a breath in unison. Marigold leans forward, elbows on the tablecloth, oblivious to the way her long dandelion sleeves are trailing into the butter dish.

"Really? Which one?"

"She didn't say." I give a noncommittal shrug. "But Her Majesty is searching for a replacement."

Rose's teacup is frozen midway to her lips. "Surely she hinted at someone?"

"Oh, yes. She has her mind quite made up."

"And?" The word sounds more like a creak of rusty iron.

I drizzle honey into my tea.

"She asked if *I* might be willing to fill the role."

Rose's china cup drops back to its saucer. Tea splashes onto the tablecloth. She snatches up her fork so fiercely I think she might stab me with it. "Liar."

"I suppose you'll never know." I pop a few blueberries into my mouth. "Unless you wish to ask the queen herself. At one of your own private audiences."

Rose's chair falls over as she launches from her seat. Calliope comes skittering back into the room, yipping at whatever perceived threat upset her mistress.

"One day, you'll get what you deserve." Rose's pink curls vibrate. And then she's gone in a storm of swirling silk and ribbons. Marigold glares at me and follows, but not before swiping a last pastry from the basket.

"My gift compels me to tell you you're treading on thin ice." Laurel doesn't even look up as she speaks. "You're a sheep among wolves, Alyce."

"Am I?" I start in on my egg, hand trembling slightly from the rush of so thoroughly enraging Rose. For a heartbeat, my nails appear as claws as I pick off a bit of shell. "Or am I the wolf, and they're the sheep?"

Laurel's golden eyes meet mine, sharp against the dark black of her face. "I imagine we'll find out soon enough."

CHAPTER SEVENTEEN

Over a month passes without incident. Without any additional invitations to the palace. Not that I care. Aurora sends me several notes, but I feed them to the hearth in my Lair. I've no wish to trifle with the queen. Aurora is a princess, and I'm a . . . someone princesses definitely do not associate with. She'll forget me in time—just as Pearl predicted. Better sooner than later.

When free from my duties as the Dark Grace, I spend my time at the black tower, practicing with Kal. Things are progressing far slower than I'd like, which makes the day I'll be able to leave Briar seem nothing but a blur on the horizon. But my abilities, Kal continues to remind me, are improving. And that blur will eventually solidify. And then I'll never have to bother with self-serving nobles or enhancements again.

I console myself about my extended sentence in Briar by reading the book Kal gave me. The roots of my hair prickled when I first dared to open it. I was certain that Endlewild somehow knew what I had and that he was going to swoop in at any moment and cart me off to the palace dungeons. Or worse. But as the pages and hours of the night flew by, I forgot those fears and became lost in my own history.

The author, Grimelde, dedicates the book to his mistress and lady of the court, Targen. It seems that, like the Etherian courts, those of Malterre were governed by a single, powerful leader and a small inner council. In his book, Grimelde describes pieces of the early history of the Vila and how they contributed to the founding of his own court and the rise of its current leader. But the stories I read here are nothing like the nightmares I encountered in Briar's books. No stolen children or human slaves.

According to Grimelde, the Vila were iron-willed creatures who could rival any of the light Fae in intellect or skill. Targen's court even attempted diplomacy with the Etherians. She sent envoys to treat with the High King of the Fae in an effort to establish relations between the courts of Malterre and Etheria. Of course, the High King Oryn rejected their advances, disgusted by the Vila race. But Grimelde states that many of the light Fae did not share Oryn's sentiment. They craved the stronger power of the Vila and chose to change their blood from gold to green. Humans even visited Targen's court, both before and after Briar was established, in the hopes of gaining access to the dark magic of the Vila. The groups of mortals formalized, calling themselves the Nightseekers, and they were welcomed among my ancestors. Though they could not be transformed into full

Vila, they were taught simple rituals and spells even a human's small spark of magic could manage.

And there were other creatures who called Targen's court home. The Goblins, who were driven out of the caves of the Etherian Mountains by the light Fae and forced to flee. The Imps, who were captured and used as slaves in the Fae courts. And then there are the Shifters. I can't drink in those words fast enough. Shifters were essential to the courts of Malterre. With their changeable bodies, they were perfect for serving as the Vila's spies in Etheria and even in the realms across the Carthegean Sea—which is what Kal must have done. It was a high honor to employ a Shifter in a court. In most places in the world, Shifters were tortured and executed if caught. But in Malterre, they were celebrated, valued, something I know little about. In fact, in Targen's court, every race was allowed to select a representative to sit on the small council. Every voice was heard.

I trace the words of Grimelde's dedication: *To Mistress Targen, whose dark power fuels the hearts of so many.*

Kal claims I shouldn't trust the information I read in Briar's books. But should I trust this one? I wonder if he'd given it to my mother as well. If she'd touched these pages and tried to answer the same questions that tumble through my mind. I'd give anything to be able to ask her.

But I can't. And if Kal is to be believed, it's because someone in Briar killed her. They would likely kill me, too. Endlewild would if he knew I possessed this book.

As the weeks pass, I read and reread the volume until the ice of my fear and doubt begins to thaw, replaced with a growing curiosity about the other half of my magic. The Shifter in me. The key to escaping Briar.

There's only one person who can tell me how to use it.

"Teach me to Shift," I tell Kal as soon as he surfaces from the shadows. It's early evening, and I'd muttered an excuse to Delphine about fetching enhancements as soon as my last patron left. I settle Callow on the remains of a rotting table.

"Happily. Though, if I may ask . . ." Kal studies me, his shadows curving into question marks. "What brought this sudden desire? The last I remember, you were unsure of your Shifter heritage."

"You were right. I've lived the lies Briar fed me from the day I drew breath. But I'm tired of being treated like a caged pet, let out only to entertain those who despise me."

That's how they treated me at the dinner. Pearl and the others—looking at me like I was an animal allowed indoors. Aurora is the only one who ever—

But no. The queen made it clear that I won't be seeing her again. There's no point remaining in Briar now.

"Did something happen?" Kal asks carefully.

"Nothing that hasn't happened a thousand times before." But it's so much more than that. Aurora was—*no*. It's no use dwelling on what might have been. "I thought I had a friend," I admit. "I don't."

Kal crouches, extending a tentative hand to Callow. She nips it in her *I will tolerate you* fashion. "One of the Graces?"

I shake my head. Those amethyst eyes surface, filled with

laughter and mischief. The dawn-colored silk of her hair set against that flawless skin. "The Princess Aurora."

"The—" A stray piece of glass cracks as Kal abruptly straightens. I never told him about my summons to the palace. Or about the abandoned library. Callow flaps her wings in disapproval. My fists clench at my sides, expecting him to begin berating me. Reminding me of the royals and their history with our kind. He doesn't. "The crown princess."

Gulls cry in the distance, as if even they think it's a ridiculous idea.

"That's what I said."

"Forgive me, Alyce. That is—given your heritage—a strange choice of friend."

"I know that." The back of my neck heats. "And I said we're not friends."

Kal's shadows draw closer. They nibble at my ankles. Wend around my waist. Ice dances down my torso as his hand lands on my shoulder. "She was cruel to you."

"Not her," I answer automatically, cutting him off. "She would never . . ." But I can't finish. "It was Queen Mariel." And so many others.

"Ah. That does not surprise me." Kal tucks a lock of hair behind my ear and I'm tempted to lean into him, starving for the connection of another person. The need is so much greater now that I've experienced what it's like. "But it is for the best."

I jerk away from him. Callow returns to my side and clacks her beak, sensing the downturn in my mood.

"Hear me, Alyce." Kal's chest appears in front of my nose. I inhale the scent of winter nights and frostbitten trees.

"Perhaps the princess is kind. Perhaps she even cares for you. But she will never understand you. Not as I do. And when the time comes, she will turn on you."

"She would not."

"Alyce." He says my name gently. Almost like a caress. "Which of them has not?"

The truth slices through me, quick as a hot blade. I think of Mistress Lavender, who acted as though I was the cause of the animosity between myself and the other Graces. Even Laurel, though she speaks up for me from time to time, did nothing when Rose revealed my identity at Aurora's birthday masque. Hilde is kind enough when I visit her shop, but could I run to her if I needed help? Would she stand by me if the king decided Briar had no more use for a Dark Grace? I don't know.

"Au—" Her name snags and I clear my throat. "The princess isn't like them." I parcel the words out carefully, watching him for signs of disagreement. Of anger. "She wants to abolish the Grace Laws and the Grace Council when she's queen. She wants a new Briar."

"Does she?" Kal's stance remains fluid and easy. His tone light. But I detect the undercurrent of disdain in the way his shadows jerk. "I hope she succeeds. But I think you will find that much is lost in the ascension of a princess to a queen. Especially a Briar Queen." He picks up a diamond-shaped pane of charred glass and sends it sailing out of the tower, a spark of bottle-green against the backdrop of the sea. "She may not even survive to her coronation."

That ugly thought rears its head. Queen Mariel was adamant that Aurora would find her true love and secure

Leythana's line. But what if she doesn't? No. I don't want to think about that. And it shouldn't matter. I'll be gone by then. But I can't stop thinking about it—about *her*. The way she called me Vila without revulsion. Took my arm in front of everyone.

"Do you know who cursed her?" The question wriggles its way free of my heart. "The name of the Vila wasn't in the book you gave me."

One eyebrow quirks. "I was wondering when you were going to ask me about that book. You have been so silent that I worried you might have sent it to join the other." He gestures at the gap in the wall. "Could this be the reason you are embracing your Shifter magic."

I shrug and move past him, looking out at the sea. "I'm still not sure what to believe. I only know that denying my power has brought me nothing but misery. And I won't be a prisoner here any longer."

"Good. But the book from Malterre was written before the war. The Vila in question was not notable then. And you will not find her in any of the books in Briar, either. She was stricken from the annals of the realm." His shadows sharpen to spikes. Callow scuttles out of his way. "After the curse was enacted, it was treason to even utter her name."

"But you know."

"Even I cannot speak it." A grim smile stretches tight across his lips.

"It's part of the binding enchantment." Disappointment rushes through me. "And you're sure there's no way to break the curse?"

"Quite sure." Kal nods, tossing a flat stone from hand to hand. "She was a powerful one, that Vila. Bent on vengeance. Only she could undo the curse. However, even if she wanted to, it would be risky."

"Why?"

"You know that Vila magic hinges on ill intent. Breaking a curse, even one cast with their own power, is an act of mercy. She could have tried to retract her work. But it might not have ended well."

The briny tang of the wind smells suddenly like copper. Like the duke's blood on my face. His death was caused by the best intentions. "And now she's dead."

"Not even Vila are immortal. Most of the time, their magic outlives them—as with the curse on the princess." He holds out his arms, indicating the shadows around his wrists. "And my own enchantment."

I blink in surprise. Had he just told me it was Vila who bound him here? But why would they have done that when their courts treated Shifters with honor?

"Do you mean . . ."

"That is quite enough for one evening. I would much rather spend our time teaching you how to Shift."

I don't want to let the subject go, but the enchantment won't let him tell me anything else. And the curse won't be my concern for much longer.

Kal begins pacing the perimeter of the tower. "Shifting is easy once you know how to do it. It will be more difficult for you, as a half-Shifter. But I am certain you will thrive."

"That makes one of us," I grumble.

"Doubt will only weaken you." He motions for me to join him, rolling his shoulders back. "Like everything else I taught you, Shifting is about intent. Think of what you want and command your magic to do it."

"Impossible. I would have Shifted a hundred times by now if it were that simple."

"Why?"

"Because . . . because I've wished so often to appear . . . different." Gooseflesh rises under my sleeves, recalling the hours spent in front of my mirror, detesting the reflection inside. The thousand wishes I'd whispered as a child, desperate for my looks to alter. To wake up one day and resemble the Graces. Even a regular human. Anything but what I was.

"Those are wishes. Flimsy, hollow things." He flicks his long fingers, as if shooing an annoying gnat. "Think. Young Shifters manifest their gifts in strange ways before they fully grasp the magic, as your own blood did when you described what happened with the fountain at the palace. Has there ever been a time when you changed? Even in the slightest?"

"No." But the answer is too immediate and my mind starts wading back through memory without my bidding. My ability to hold my breath underwater when Endlewild and the healing Graces were testing my power. The way the servants glance right over me when I eavesdrop, as if I have blended into the very walls. Even gathering the damn carrion crows' eggs, when I can climb higher than any human ought to.

My breathing shortens. Kal reads the lines of my face.

"I thought so. You change now when you need to, at

your power's unwitting command. But *you* are in charge of your power. Not the other way around."

Kal must scent my uncertainty. He circles me.

"Do you trust me?"

"Yes." Kal has cultivated my gifts. Not tried to drown or bleed them out of me. The puckered half-moon scar on my stomach sears as though freshly made, the phantom pain hitting every nerve. I grit my teeth against it.

"Then try."

Mustering the dregs of my confidence, I find the cord of my magic, the scent of loam and woodsmoke swelling. At first, my grip slackens, unsure of what I want and how to wield this new ability. Then I look down at my hands. The reptilian blood and nearly translucent skin that has plagued me since the day I was born. Marked me as a monster. As an *other* no one wanted.

"Tell it what to do," Kal coaxes from beside me. "Do not wish. Command."

Keeping a hold on my power, I picture Laurel. She is seamless and polished. Effortlessly elegant. I dare to imagine myself in the same fashion, and tell my magic to obey. At first, there's nothing. No invisible limb curling out of me or a thrumming of power. But then the tips of my fingers begin to tingle. My ragged, bitten fingernails lengthen into identical pearly half-moons. The dry, scaly surface of my skin smooths and glows. It happens so quickly I jerk back in surprise, losing my control. The illusion vanishes.

"I— I *Shifted*." I don't know whether to be awed or horrified.

"Almost." Kal puts both hands on my shoulders, directing my focus to him. "Try again. This time, change everything at once. You will know when it is done."

My magic is waiting for me, warm and buzzing behind my sternum. Eager to be used.

I want to be beautiful, I tell it.

It only wiggles. That was too close to a wish. A mere suggestion. Setting my jaw and steeling my spine, I try again.

Beauty. I don't picture anyone in particular. Just the idea, pushing it out with everything that I have. To my utter amazement, my magic responds like a horse spurred into a canter. Heat races from my toes to the crown of my head. My bones stretch, a gentle tugging sensation that feels almost comforting. My scalp prickles, hair rising and rearranging as if caught in a sea breeze. Muscles go warm and rubbery, the way they do in a hot bath. The scent of woodsmoke and wet earth wraps around me like a blanket, mixed with something else. Appleblossoms, I think. And spring rain.

And then everything stills. I can feel the cold, salt-soaked wind stinging my cheeks. I blink my eyes open, sleepy and disoriented. I'm taller, I think. Almost eye level with Kal. He is staring at me, his mouth hanging open.

"What is it?" My pulse speeds up. I flex my hands, finding that long, slender fingers have replaced my own. There's no trace of my Vila blood. My shoes are too big. The bodice of my gown looser. The floor tilts and I think I will faint, but Kal catches me around the waist and guides me closer to the gap in the wall, where the russet-streaked sunset is lighting up a shallow puddle on the stones.

"Look," he says, herding me forward when he gets too close to the light.

I am numb and shaking, but force one foot in front of the other. Lean over the molten amber mirror. The woman looking back at me widens her eyes. Opens her mouth in a soundless scream. And then the floor hurtles up, meeting my shoulder with a sharp crack before the world winks out like a snuffed candle.

Because it was not my face in the water.

It was Aurora's.

CHAPTER EIGHTEEN

The next day, all I can think about is Aurora's reflection where mine should have been. The gentle slope of her nose. The hollow of her unmarred throat. I find myself looking for her in every mirror, startled when it's my own sallow face in the glass.

I'm so distracted that I'm a half-hour late for one patron, and another has to ring the bell until it practically snaps off its cord before I answer. Three broken jars of enhancements later, I'm slogging through teatime, unable to eat a bite as Rose's vapid court gossip washes over me.

"Alyce?"

When I look up, I find that the entire table is staring at me. My ears burn.

"Sorry," I mumble, stirring another sugar cube into my tea and grabbing an apricot tart in the hopes that the jolt of sweetness will keep my mind from drifting. Marigold snickers.

"As I was saying," Mistress Lavender continues, "Delphine will be rescheduling your afternoon patrons." She slides an envelope across the table, her eyebrows arching up over her half-moon spectacles. "You have a summons from the palace."

The flaky pastry crust balls in my mouth and glues itself to the back of my throat.

Day summons are rare, the court preferring me to ease their loved ones into death beneath the shroud of nightfall. Accidents happen, I tell myself. Sudden illnesses.

But then I see that the parchment bears a violet wax seal imprinted with a dragon in flight. The royal crest. The apricot jam sours on my tongue.

"Don't keep them waiting," Marigold croons.

I don't bother to fire back a retort. And I don't trust my voice even if I had one ready. I leave the rest of my plate and drag myself to my Lair to get my kit, then trudge through the streets of the Grace District. This autumn is colder than most. Everyone else is already wrapped in their early winter furs, but I feel nothing of the chill. Only the sharp-footed dread picking its way along my scalp. Is it Queen Mariel? Has she decided to do more than simply warn me away from her daughter? Or Endlewild—I shudder at the thought of what the Fae ambassador might want.

At the servants' entrance, I present the summons. But I am not escorted through the usual halls. This time, we break right, directly into the royal wing. The dragon crest glowers at me from every column and windowpane. Other servants and courtiers abruptly change direction when they spot me.

My escort unlocks a door to a set of back stairs, and we climb higher and higher, until sweat beads along the back of my neck and between my shoulder blades.

Unnervingly stoic, at last he slows, then ushers me through another narrow entrance. I stop short, face-to-face with a monstrous set of doors carved to look like the rough hide of a dragon. Stone wings flare out from either side of the frame, covered in golden armored scales. A neck as thick as my torso rears up from the tip where the doors meet, the ruby eyes on its head glinting in the torchlight. The handles are taloned feet, with Briar roses branded into the soles. Its jaws are opened in a scream, its mouth huge enough that it could snap me in half.

I shiver, imagining my own emerald blood dripping from between those polished teeth.

Quite against my will, I am pushed inside. And I immediately realize it was no ornamental choice that the doors resembled a dragon. That it seemed as if I was walking into the belly of a beast to enter this room.

Maps line the walls, Briar and several realms beyond the sea. Trade routes and ocean currents. Diagrams of beastly warships and lighter ones built for stealth and speed are pinned beside them. A huge ebony table, the wood shot through with silver, dominates most of the room. It's littered with papers and waxy candle nubs and discarded quills, their inkpots left carelessly open to dry out. Maps are spread here, too, with bronze markers arranged in intricate formations.

This is the king's room. The war room.

As per her alliance agreement with the Etherians, Leythana and her heirs cultivated a military renowned throughout the world. But the later queens grew lazy, preferring to spend Briar's significant coin on gowns and parties and placating their husbands.

Tarkin, though, is different. Before breaking Mariel's curse, he came from Paladay, a landlocked northern kingdom on the other side of the Carthegean Sea. It is a country famed for its horse trade, as well as its insatiable desire to expand its borders. And the Briar King clearly inherited Paladay's lust for glory. The War of the Fae was over long before Tarkin came to power, and we've had no hint of conflict since. But Tarkin shovels coin at his army as if war could be declared any day. Briar's forces have tripled in size since he married Mariel, though they have little enough to do but train in the yard, patrol the mountain border, and stage mock battles from the Fae war.

But that knowledge does nothing to calm my rabbit-quick heartbeat as I discover the floor-to-ceiling windows along the right wall. All of Briar sprawls out beneath my unsteady feet: The pastel domed and gabled rooftops of the Grace District, its elegance bleeding dry at the barrier marking the gray, gritty Common District. The thick outer walls of the realm. The sea, vast and unyielding, blurring in smudges of turquoise and indigo on the horizon. Ships the size of my fingernail cutting through the choppy water or bobbing in the harbor. There are no panes on these windows, only clear, unbroken glass, giving the illusion that this room teeters on the top of a cliff. That those inside it are far above, ruling from an unimaginably high vantage point.

And that those rulers could easily toss their enemies over its edge.

"Do you like it?" I wheel around, my kit slipping in my hands, then sink automatically into a low curtsy. The Briar King watches me from a corner. I hadn't even heard him come in. "The glass is said to be sound against even dragon's fire. I had it forged specially."

The thought of the expense makes my stomach roll. There have been no records of dragons in Briar since Leythana sailed in on her ships. And for all we know, those dragon carcasses were just a story.

"Are you hungry? Would you care for some wine?"

He motions to a back table laden with fresh fruits and buttery cheeses and a decanter of claret so dark it's almost black. All of it probably poisoned.

"No, thank you, Your Majesty."

"Suit yourself." He pours himself a healthy glassful, though beneath the shadow of his beard, his sandy white skin is ruddy with a flush of wine. "You must wonder why I've summoned you."

Wind gusts against the wall of glass until it groans. I inch as far away as I can, trying to ignore the nauseating image of myself plummeting into the eaves of the Grace District.

Tarkin strolls idly along his table, adjusting the markers on the maps. "It occurred to me, after the incident with Duke Weltross, that your *singular* abilities may be underappreciated."

I knew I had not heard the end of the duke.

"I consider myself quite foolish, actually. I knew when

you were discovered that you were special. That your . . . unusual . . . blood would serve Briar well. It's why I didn't kill you, though I was certainly advised to do so." A slow smile spreads across his face that raises the hair on the back of my neck. "I applaud that decision even more so today."

Somehow, I don't take that as a compliment. "I don't understand your meaning." I set my kit down and begin rooting through the vials. "Perhaps Your Majesty would like an elixir—"

"No, Dark Grace." He closes the lid of my kit. The amethyst on his signet ring glitters. "You are too modest. I heard that you ended the duke's life with a mere touch."

He is too close and I wish for something to steady myself. But I refuse to let the Briar King see me weaken. "The duchess was grieving. Confused. As was everyone else in that room."

Tarkin resumes as if I hadn't spoken. "I also heard of a fountain that started spewing mud some time ago. The royal gardeners were quite perplexed."

Dragon's teeth, I'm an idiot.

"And then"—the smell of the wine and the spice of roasted game wafts from his breath—"at our dinner. When you turned a royal rosebush into some kind of vicious plant. I saw you with my own eyes. Am I also confused?"

He lifts one eyebrow, looking at me like I'm a particularly elusive stag he's just taken down. I resist the urge to grab his magic and bend it until he crumples like a used rag.

"Please." Tarkin pulls out one of the chairs at the table. "Sit."

The last thing I want to do is sit. But I doubt how much longer I can stand, and so I allow myself to perch lightly on a chair.

"I believe we're starting off on the wrong foot." Tarkin refills his glass. "I am not repulsed by your Vila blood. In fact, I quite admire it."

Something between a snort and a laugh escapes me before I can stop it. "If that's true then why am I treated as if I have some kind of disease in this realm?"

Tarkin examines one of the thick medallions on his doublet. "Not everyone at court is as enlightened as myself." I suppress another snort. "Lord Ambassador Endlewild, for example."

Ice water floods my limbs. The look the Fae lord gave me the night of the dinner—that I was something to be scraped off his shoe—still haunts me. I've no doubt he was the one who counseled the Briar King to end my life.

"You do not like him," Tarkin guesses.

I hate him more than words can express. But I must tread carefully. "I have no issue with—"

The Briar King waves me off. "You do not need to lie. I share your sentiment."

Another surprise. One I'm not sure I like.

"The Lord Ambassador is always so dour. Acting as if his position is a prison sentence instead of one of the most coveted in the realm. I've tried to have him replaced multiple times since I married the queen." He sighs, drinking deeply. "To no avail."

For the first time in my life, I feel a shred of sympathy for

Endlewild. One dinner in the midst of the Briar court was torture enough for me. And he has to endure it every day of his unnaturally long life. But that twinge dissolves in the throbbing of my scar. "We have different reasons for our distaste, sire."

He chokes out a laugh. "Quite. And you should thank the dragon that you are not full-blooded Vila. And that your power did not manifest under the Lord Ambassador's scrutiny. He would have insisted on your death. Or killed you himself. But I embrace your abilities. And I want to use them—for the good of Briar."

It takes every ounce of self-control to keep my expression neutral. "In what way?"

Tarkin's jeweled chains clank as he moves. "I will send you commissions. I take it from what I've seen that you are capable of producing far more than simple elixirs."

There's no point in denying it. I continue to use enhancements with my patrons to avoid suspicion. But I won't tell the Briar King everything. Dragon knows what he would have me do if he knew I could Shift. I merely incline my head.

"Good. You will craft such things as I need. And in return I will reward you handsomely. Coin at first, titles and prestige later."

Titles? He must be mad. The small council would never approve it, and the Grace Council would have a fit. Mariel would rather see me thrown into the sea. He must think me an idiot if he imagines I will believe such a promise.

"What things might you need?" I venture.

"Does it matter?" His mustache twitches, the only sign

that I'm grating against his infamous temper. "I'm offering you wealth and power and influence. Other courtiers would kill for such an opportunity."

"I am not a courtier," I counter. "And the Grace Laws prevent me from causing intentional harm."

Tarkin's small mouth screws into a snarl. I brace myself, expecting that ringed hand to leave welts on my cheek. Expecting the guards to be called to haul me to the prison cells beneath the mountain. Instead, his expression softens. It is far more terrifying than a slap.

"Do we really need to concern ourselves with such petty trifles?"

I grip the arms of my chair until I feel the blood drumming in my fingertips. Those "trifles" have kept me bound to Briar for the last two decades.

"*You* will harm no one," he reasons. "And no one else will know of our arrangement. That's rather the point. I'm prepared to pay you triple your normal rate, off the ledgers. It won't help you much in the Grace standings, but perhaps we will see about awarding you your own house. Chambers in the palace, perhaps. You would be an asset here."

I'd rather live at the bottom of the sea. But something else about Tarkin's offer is ridiculously appealing. Three times my rate, and I don't have to give any of it to Lavender House. My gaze travels out the windows, over the grid of buildings and homes, to the sea and into the endless blue of the horizon line. Ships crowd the harbor. With enough gold, any one of them might take me away to a new life. Still, it would mean submitting to a monster.

"I've no wish to be an assassin."

The Briar King picks up one of the markers on the table, a bronze horse with an armored rider. And it's then that I manage a closer look at the maps. The coastline arching like a bow on the far eastern edge. The mountain range to the north. And a hazy, pale pink area far beyond. Etheria. What would the Briar King be doing with maps of Etheria? There are also smaller pewter markers in patterns tracking haphazard paths through the mountains. Pinpointing areas that make no sense to me.

Tarkin slams the marker down. I flinch.

"Do you wish to be rich?" he asks. "Do you wish to tread on the bent backs of all those who have wronged you? Lord Endlewild, perhaps. The Graces, who treat you like a feral dog even though your power far surpasses theirs."

I can hardly breathe around the desire that courses through me. Yes, I want those things.

"You shall have it," Tarkin promises. "That, and more. Work with me, Dark Grace. Together we can bring about a new age in Briar."

The call of a seagull penetrates the glass, sounding like hope and freedom and everything I've ever wished for.

But this is a bad business. I don't know what the Briar King is plotting, but it's dangerous. The very idea should be enough to turn me away from him. But for once, I could use my title for my own advantage. If Briar loses a few nobles along the way, it will not be my hand that poisons them. Not really.

Tarkin reads my acceptance in the lines of my face. He rubs his thumb over his signet ring. "As I thought. You can expect your first commission shortly."

CHAPTER NINETEEN

When I return to Lavender House, the Graces are busy with their evening patrons. I tiptoe past their parlors, hoping to slip out to my Lair unnoticed. Callow will be peevish at my long absence. And I'm exhausted, my mind still reeling from Tarkin's offer and the new, impossible predicament I find myself in. The last door is slightly ajar—Rose's. The night lamps have been lit, but there doesn't seem to be a patron waiting for her inside. I press closer, catching the clink of metal on glass. The fizz of enhancements reacting.

Keeping to the shadows, I position myself so that I can see into the bright slit of light. Rose is sitting at the table. Alone. She's heaping scoopfuls of a bright silver powder into a bowl. I recognize it immediately.

"What are you doing?" I shove into the room. She yelps. The metallic shavings go flying onto the floor.

"Get out of here! You're always lurking, you filthy beast."

She sweeps some of the spilled powder into her palm and adds it to her brew. "This is my parlor."

"I know what that is." Before she can react, I swoop over to the table and pluck her bowl out of reach.

"Give that back." She bares her teeth.

"Bloodrot"—I keep the bowl behind my back as she swipes at me—"is dangerous for a Grace. For anyone."

The leaden shavings in Rose's bowl are believed by some to extend the longevity of a Grace's abilities. Bloodrot is a blood thinner, and so a Grace will dose herself with the stuff in the hopes that less of her blood will be required to create an elixir, thus keeping her from Fading before her time. But that logic is ludicrous. First of all, manipulation of a Grace's gift—by anyone—is illegal and carries a steep sentence with the Grace Council. More than that, the quicksilver powder is called bloodrot for a reason. Too much causes sickness. The metal poisons the organs, settles in the heart and ossifies. And it's far more likely that a Grace will misjudge her dosage and bleed out if she so much as suffers a nick in the right place.

"You could die from using this."

"And you'd know all about how to kill someone, wouldn't you, Malyce?" Her eyes are so wild and livid they seem to tinge crimson. But I don't take her bait. I duck under her outstretched arms and bolt across the room.

"I won't let you kill yourself." I'm panting now, the bowl wedged between my stomach and the back of a winged armchair.

"I'd rather be dead than lose my gift." She lunges around

the side of the chair. "Do you know what happens to a Faded Grace?"

"There's nothing wrong with—"

"Nothing!" The word rises into a screech. "No one gives a dragon's tooth about a Faded Grace. No patrons, no invitations. Faded might as well mean dead."

"The Crown is obligated to care for you. What about having your own house like Mistress Lavender? Or all the Graces who've married and—"

Rose laughs, a brittle sound that makes the hair on my arms rise. "Oh, yes. That's what I want. To be tethered to a spouse who only wants me for what I used to be. Or put in charge of a bunch of Grace brats when I won't even be able to—" The rest of the sentence crumbles. Rose wheels around before her tears start to fall, but I can see her shoulders shake.

My mouth opens and closes, but nothing comes out. This is a foreign place. Me, in the position to comfort my greatest tormentor. Guilt gnaws at my conscience. It's been more than a month since I interfered with one of Rose's elixirs, and I thought she'd let the incidents go once her patrons returned. I had no idea she was resorting to such desperate measures. How long has she been dosing herself?

I edge out from behind the chair. "Rose, I—"

"What in Briar is going on?" Mistress Lavender barrels into Rose's parlor, bright silver splotches on her white cheeks. "Delphine could hear your shouting from the front of the house."

Rose wipes at her face. In half a heartbeat, her breathing

has calmed and her expression is neutral, making my head spin with how quickly she can throw on the mask of nonchalance. "Nothing. I was just showing Alyce a new enhancement."

Mistress Lavender's lips pucker, gaze flicking between us, scenting the lie. Rose gestures for me to return her bowl, daring me to tell Mistress Lavender what she was doing. But I won't. It's her secret. I have enough of my own. And so I pass the bowl back. She's careful to keep the contents out of view.

"Well," Mistress Lavender says after a few charged seconds, her battle stance relaxing. "It's nice to see you two working together for a change." She pats at her tight chignon and tugs down her bodice. "But do be quieter about it in future."

"Of course," I mumble.

"And, Alyce, dear. There's a patron waiting for you downstairs."

Walk-ins are the worst sort of patron. Usually, they arrive in the heat of an argument. The elixirs they request are particularly vicious, skirting the line of what's permitted within the Grace Laws. I grit my teeth as I trudge out to my Lair.

The patron huddles near the hearth. A woman, I think. Her shape is hidden beneath the folds of a garnet cloak. Callow ruffles her wings at the sound of my footsteps, and the patron turns and lowers her hood.

I trip over my own feet. "Your Highness!"

"Do you keep all your patrons waiting this long?"

"How did you—why did you—" Clumsily, I slam the door shut behind me and draw the bar, certain Mistress Lavender or someone else is about to find me here with the crown princess of Briar and how much trouble that will bring.

But why would they? No one ever ventures into my Lair. Especially not when I have a patron. Anonymity is the largest chunk of my fee. The rush of adrenaline ebbs.

"I could think of no other way." Aurora—*Aurora,* I have to repeat it in my mind—ambles the perimeter of the dank chamber, picking up odd-shaped vials of deep plum valerian syrup and jars of pickled nettles. She peers at me through a bright vermilion liquid, her eyes ten times the size they should be. "You ignored my notes."

Callow paces back and forth on her stand. I go to her, fishing a scrap of meat out of a bucket and watching her gobble it down. "I'm sorry."

"Are you?" The question stings. Aurora folds her arms across her middle. She's hurt, I realize. She thinks I didn't want to see her.

"Yes." I focus on the brittle-edged silk of Callow's feathers beneath my fingertips. "I wanted to come, but—" The rest floats away. I don't want to lie to her, but I also don't want to implicate the queen. "I wasn't sure another meeting was what you wanted."

"Why would I have sent the notes if it wasn't?"

"Because you're a princess. And I'm . . ." I start fidgeting with various instruments strewn over my worktable, rearranging them in no particular order. "Me."

A hint of appleblossom and gardenia tickles my nose. Clean, heady scents that don't belong here. The princess plants herself across from me.

"I enjoy spending time with you. I don't know why you find that so difficult to believe."

Because no one else has ever wanted to. Except Kal. I drag my gaze to Aurora's, finding the bared soul of someone who has never had to question her place in the world. A long-frozen chamber in my heart begins to thaw.

But then the queen's threats float back to me, laced with the crackle of the fire.

"Even if I wanted to"—I return my attention to the worktable—"I can't."

"Why not? I have plenty of coin to pay you."

The hot wax of my insides solidifies in an instant. I almost forgot—she had to pay Delphine in order to be admitted. And part of that payment will trickle down to me. Pearl's comment from dinner strikes home, that the princess is only fascinated with me because I am grotesque. "Because I'm a pet you can toy with and then throw away when you're bored?"

I storm to the hearth and snatch up the poker, taking out my anger on the half-crumbled logs. The fire coughs and spits black soot. The smell of ash burns against my throat.

"I didn't mean that. I just— I thought this was how it worked with the Graces."

"You can't just pretend to be a patron." I'm being harsher than necessary, but I don't care. "And I don't know how I feel about you paying to spend time with me. As if I'm some kind of— of pleasure Grace."

A few beats of strained silence thrum.

"I didn't think of it like that." Her voice is small. "I'm sorry. I wanted to see you again and you wouldn't come to me. You left in such a rush after dinner. I can guess why."

Swiping my sleeve over the soot on my brow, I set the poker down. But I don't look at her. Don't admit what happened.

"I'm not an idiot." Aurora puts herself in my way when I try to slide past. "I know how my mother can be. Do you think you're the first friend she's chased off?"

"I have absolutely no idea."

"Why do you think I told you to meet me in the servants' halls? Slipped my guards and came here? I don't pay to see all my friends, you know."

Some of the tension between my shoulder blades unspools. Aurora wanted to see me badly enough to plan out the particulars.

"Though, I admit, something to turn my guards into toads would have been most useful." She notices Prince Markham on a nearby table and sticks her finger through the slats of his cage, rubbing his warty head. He lets out a sound that might be a toad purr.

"I can't do that with an elixir." She frowns. "And I can't go back to the palace. Not to see you. Not even in secret. Your mother was very clear."

"I'm sure she was," Aurora grumbles. "When I was little, it was the servants' children. The second one of us started spending too much time with a kitchen girl or maid's daughter, my mother would pack that family away to another post. Especially the boys. Once, I pointed out that any one of them might be our true love and I was locked in my rooms for a full day." She picks up a handful of black toadstools and lets them fall back into their bowl. "Of course, that wasn't as bad as the time I suggested one of the *girls* might break our curse. For that I got a week."

I bristle, but can't explain why. "But they might have. There would be no shame in it. I've never understood why your suitors have to be men. The early queens used to take consorts of both genders."

"Yes," she agrees. "The early queens also never married. They would have children with multiple men sometimes, as it suited them. Until Catalina."

That's a name I haven't heard in a long time, though I know it well. A Briarian marquess broke Catalina's curse, and she was besotted with him. But he had ambitions beyond that of a consort. If Catalina wanted him, she would have to marry and remain faithful to him. Catalina was so in love that she penned a marriage contract immediately, and even appointed her new husband to be lord commander of the military. It seemed an innocuous title at the time, when the realm knew only peace. But her decision soon proved a dangerous precedent to set. Every other queen followed Catalina's lead, marrying their curse breakers and carving up the various pieces of sovereignty, until only crumbs remained.

"But Catalina's actions don't explain why you're restricted to kissing men," I argue, surprised at the force in my own words. "You should be able to marry whomever you choose. Heirs can be conceived in other ways."

"I need someone like you on my council one day," she

muses, smiling. My cheeks heat. "And you're right—which is why the early queens never bothered with marriage. Truthfully, I think there have been instances in which a princess's curse was broken by a woman. But they were quickly covered up. I imagine the poor girls were probably lesser nobles or servants, even. Easily paid off and sent away."

"But *why*?"

"Do you know of a Briar King who would willingly give away his title to a woman?" Callow stirs and flaps her wings, as if the idea is preposterous even to her. "And there is . . ." Aurora pauses, "another story."

The fire chews away the logs.

"Do you know the island of Cardon? It's in the Southern Sea."

"Just below Ryna, yes. That's the one Leythana liberated. It's ruled by several families now instead of a monarch."

"Exactly. A Cardon son came to Briar to try to break the crown princess's curse. Among his retinue was his sister, Corinne. Well." A chair creaks as she sits and motions for me to join her. "The son's kiss did not break the curse. But Corinne and one of the younger Briar princesses—Eva—got along quite well. So well, in fact, that Corinne broke Eva's curse."

I shake my head. "That can't be right. I've never read anything about that."

"You wouldn't have." Aurora smiles wryly. "I only know because my mother told me during the week that I was confined to my chambers. It's rather a family secret."

A big one, it seems. And I wonder how many others are

buried inside the palace walls. Old skeletons packed bone to bone. "What happened to them—Eva and Corinne?"

"The Cardon family was furious. They demanded that the son they sent marry the younger princess immediately—after all, there was a chance that Eva would one day be queen. And they commanded Corinne to return home. Couples of the same gender were not as accepted in that realm."

"Oh." I think of the women with the butterfly sashes at Aurora's birthday. "But Eva didn't marry him?"

"No." Aurora picks at the laces of her bodice. "She refused the match. She said she would marry her true love, no matter the consequences. She threatened to stow away in the ships taking Corinne back to Cardon if they tried to keep them apart."

"Did she?"

It's a long moment before Aurora speaks again. "They threw themselves off the Crimson Cliffs instead."

A high, tinny note rings in my ears. "They did *what*?"

"I suppose Eva knew that even if she did go to Cardon, she would be in danger. As Leythana's heir, someone would want to get a child on her or hold her ransom—especially if her elder sister died." The wind groans down the chimney. "In any case, it was a disaster. Cardon threatened war and Briar's small council scrambled to cover up the scandal. In the end, it was decided that princesses would be formally restricted to male suitors. What happened with Eva made it clear enough the *inconvenient situations* that could arise with another woman involved. Cardon still receives a yearly shipment of Etherium as payment for their loss."

"And so your parents would rather you die than have a woman break your curse?"

Aurora laughs, but it's bitter. "Well, when you say it that way, it really does sound horrible." She rubs the curse mark on her forearm and watches the hearth. "I know they only want to protect me. To protect the crown, but . . ."

The fire pops.

"What does happen"—I dig my toe into a smoking ember on the floor, not wanting to entertain the thought, but unable to escape it—"if you die?"

"I'm not exactly sure," she admits quietly. "I've overheard my parents arguing about the subject. In truth, there won't really be a problem until after Mother's death, when there are no more Briar Queens. The Etherians will have to be involved at that point. It's their blood that blessed our crown. They won't ally with anyone else. But the small council and the other advisors keep me out of any discussions or negotiations they're having with Etheria. I suppose they think it shouldn't matter to me. After all, either I break the curse or I'll be dead."

She laughs a little again, but I don't join her.

"It does matter to you, though. I know how much you want to rule."

"Yes," she says. "And I think I should be allowed to practice. Try my hand at diplomacy and dealing with the High King Oryn. In case I don't die." She deals me a grin. "But if I do . . ." She tugs at the pendant hanging from her necklace—a tiny gold dragon. "I imagine there will be another challenge."

Another challenge. It seems unthinkable. Briar will be in chaos.

"Of course, Father thinks the whole crisis is the fault of the former queens. He says there shouldn't have been restrictions placed on royal births—even if it meant more women would die if they didn't break their curse." She screws her lips into a snarl that very much resembles one I saw in the war room. "Such a mistake would never happen in Paladay."

He can sail right back there.

"They might keep me out of their council meetings"—her amethyst gaze snaps back to mine—"but I'm determined to begin making some of my own decisions. And one of them is to come here. And see you. If you don't object, of course."

It takes me a moment to find my voice. "No."

"Good. We can figure out something with the money I leave at the front. Donate it to the Common District, they need it well enough."

The last of my anger melts. She *would* think of something like that.

Aurora crosses the room and raises a tentative hand to Callow. "Who is this?"

"My kestrel. Callow." I dig out another treat and show her how to feed the bird. "I found her on the cliffs when she was just a chick. Her mother abandoned her after her wings were broken. No one wanted her. Mistress Lavender said I should just leave her."

"Leave her to die?" Aurora pets the speckled fluff on Callow's head.

"They wanted to do the same to me." I shrug. "An ugly Grace infant with green blood."

"I'm glad they didn't." She lowers her hand and it brushes against mine. Sparks shoot up my wrist. "Callow is lucky to have found you."

"We found each other."

I smile at my kestrel, once again struck by how similar we are. Both of us broken castoffs. Kept in the shadows, unable to fly. Callow tilts her head, as if she understands my thoughts.

"I'm sorry for her, though," Aurora says. "It must be a miserable existence. To be caged your whole life."

The lines of her body pull taut beneath her cloak. She knows something about that fate, I think. Beneath the crown and the lavish ballroom and expensive clothes, Aurora is little better than the Graces. A servant to the Crown instead of wearing it.

But I might be able to do something to help her.

"I have an idea. Since you *are* a paying customer." I scurry along my shelves, plucking up bottles and jars and setting them on the worktable.

Aurora resumes her pacing around the room. "I wish I had chambers like this."

"You want a lair?" I drop a dollop of magnolia-bark paste into a mortar, then sprinkle lavender heads on top, grunting as I mash it all together. "A cold, wet room that constantly stinks of smoke and blood?"

She laughs. "Remember, I like the abandoned library."

"True." A long tip of the valerian syrup completes the

mixture. I stir everything together and funnel it into a small vial. "For your guards. A sleeping draught. It's not an elixir, but a little bit in some tea will do the trick. Or coat a needle with it and prick them, if you're feeling bold."

"Oh, I'm always feeling bold." Aurora winks and my heart skips.

She reaches for the vial. Our hands touch again. My scaly skin juxtaposed with her bronze-kissed glow. Light and darkness. Monster and maiden.

"Aurora." I want to keep the words back, but I can't help them. "Are you sure you don't mind—me being part Vila? After—"

"I've already answered that." She twirls the base of the vial on the table. "Whoever that Vila was who cursed my family, she was not you."

"But I share her blood. Her curse killed your sisters. It might—"

"Enough." She sits across from me. "I'm sure I can come up with a long list of humans evil enough to rival a Vila with a grudge. It's over, Alyce. There's nothing to do about it now."

I let her words sink in, a warmth that has nothing to do with the hearth reaching its fingers through my veins. Callow mutters on her perch in what might be approval.

"Did you find anything in the book I lent you?"

I shake my head, hoping she doesn't ask to have it back. Damn that Kal. "Nothing of consequence. Nothing about—her."

Aurora rubs at her temples, resting her head against the

back of the chair. Firelight laps at her neck, dancing in the hollow of her throat, and an insane part of me wonders if that fragile place feels as soft as it looks. "I thought as much. In a decade I've come up with nothing."

"But you've been working alone," I argue, willing my attention away from her skin. "You've been doing the best that you can." I try to imagine if I'd never found Kal. I'd have been reduced to whipping up elixirs for the rest of my life.

"It's not enough." A wind rattles down the chimney and stirs the fire. Aurora sits up straight. "Alyce."

I'm not sure I'm going to like what comes next.

"Do you think you could help me?"

I don't.

"Help you—break the curse?"

"Yes." She leans forward. The golden dragon on her necklace glitters. "You have the same blood as the Vila who cast it. Perhaps you can do something to break it."

An image of the duke rears in my mind. Of the wicked, beastly rosebush. The stench of sulfur burns in my nose. "I don't—that's not how my magic works."

"How do you know if you haven't tried?"

A nagging instinct tells me to keep silent about Kal. About my true powers. "I just do."

"Please." She reaches across the table and tangles her fingers in mine. "I have less than a year left. I have to try everything."

"If there was something that could be done with my blood, they would have used it already. Trust me—there were plenty of tests completed when I was a child." I wrench free, the scar on my middle tingling. "It could go very badly. You could get hurt."

Kal promised as much. That even if the Vila wanted to remove Aurora's curse, it would be risky. And I'm not willing to gamble with her life.

"And I will die if I do nothing."

I rake my hands through my hair, frustration and guilt warring within me. This is madness. I'm just as likely to kill the princess as to break her curse. But—if I am in any way responsible for the curse on her family, I owe her this. Before I take the gold her father will pay me and leave Briar forever. But how could I possibly—

Kal's book.

Aurora reads my expression. "You have an idea. I knew you would. What is it?"

Dragon's teeth. But there's no going back now—not when she's scented the secret. "You have to promise not to tell. Swear it. This could put both of us in real trouble. Worse than getting locked in your rooms for a week."

She huffs. "Don't you trust me?"

No. Yes. My fickle heart can't make up its mind. Once again, I'm dizzy with the feeling Aurora gives me. Like plunging toward the sea and hoping you'll grow wings before you hit the surface. Against every scrap of reason, I retrieve Kal's book and hand it to her.

"What's this?" She begins flipping through the pages.

"It's a book." I clear my throat. The fire crackles. "Written by a Vila."

Aurora gapes at me, then back at the book with heightened interest. "A Vila wrote this? Is there anything about my curse?"

"No. It was written before the war, by the scribe at one of the courts of Malterre. But it's the only link I have to my past."

"It must be very important to you, then." She pauses. "Thank you for sharing it with me."

I shy away from her, both elated and terrified at once. "It's just a book. And it probably won't even help. But . . ." I guide her to the sections where Grimelde discusses the arrival of the Nightseekers. "Humans used to go to Malterre and learn dark magic. Maybe you've seen something related in the old library?"

Aurora traces one fingertip over the Nightseeker emblem. It's the same as the one for the Vila, except there's a raven perched on top of the broken orb. "This symbol looks familiar." Her brow scrunches as she thinks. "Yes. I've seen it stamped on a chest in one of the alcoves. But I've never bothered trying to open the lock. I thought there were probably just candles or something inside."

"It might be locked for good reason," I warn her. "The Nightseekers were tolerated before the war, but they must have been wiped out with the Vila."

She grins. "I suppose we're about to find out."

CHAPTER TWENTY

The Briar King had not been exaggerating when he promised my first commission would arrive quickly. I find it as soon as I open my Lair the next morning. A nondescript box waits on my worktable, along with a black envelope. My heart pounds at the sight of the dragon seal on the parchment, at the thought of one of the king's minions skulking about this place. How did they get inside? Besides myself, only Delphine and Mistress Lavender hold keys to this room. But I suppose there's little that can stop the Briar King from having his way.

I hold my breath, bracing for the Briar King's first request as I break the seal and unfold the parchment. The missive is short:

The drinker forgets all matters as instructed
by the king. Deliver in a fortnight.

A drinker? Two weeks? I unlock the box. My breath catches. There's a chalice inside, silver with scrollwork around the rim. It's not as fine as the crystal flutes served at the royal dinner. This one is simple, meant to blend in with the other dishes. One even a servant might use.

Tarkin wants me to curse this? My mind sifts through a hundred possibilities as to how to accomplish it, each of them more unlikely than the last. Kal said there's magic in everything—even a chalice? And how do I make it erase someone else's memory?

But these are questions for later. A fat velvet sack rests at the bottom of the chest. I untie the strings. Three times my normal rate of gold glistens in the light of my hearth. Gold that will carry me across the Carthegean Sea. Away from this life forever.

It's just under a week before I see Aurora again. She secures my last appointment of the evening, under the name "Mistress Nightingale," and arrives right on time.

"I was right!" She hefts a burlap bag onto my worktable and begins digging through it. "The chest in the library did contain books about the Nightseekers. I suppose we're lucky the masters left that place alone. These would have been burned if they found them."

She thrusts one under my nose. It has the raven emblem stamped on the cover.

The apple pastry I'd been eating suddenly tastes of ash. "I take it you've read them?"

"As much as I could. They're filled with little spells and rituals. Some of them look like nonsense. But here, this one is for summoning." She shows me a diagram of a large wheel labeled *Summonus*. Beside it, a list of ingredients and instruments and instructions that might as well be written in a foreign language. "Do you think you could manage this? It might summon the Vila who cast the curse. She must be able to break it."

"From what I know about my magic, that's a dangerous game," I hedge, wiping my butter-stained fingers on my skirt. "Vila power can only be used for ill intent. Curse breaking is too pure."

"What harm could it do to try? These books were written by Nightseekers. They learned from the *Vila*." She taps the wheel on the page, impatient. "Surely using your own breed of magic isn't too much of a risk."

Dragon's teeth, she's stubborn. But I can see I'll get nowhere trying to dissuade her. I change tactics. "Your curse was cast centuries ago. We can't summon a dead Vila."

"No." Aurora riffles through her stack of books, undeterred. A tiny crease forms between her brows and the peach-pink glimmer of her tongue appears as she concentrates. "But Vila and Fae don't die the way humans do. Look." She gestures enthusiastically at an illustration of a dense forest. The trees are silver and obsidian. "This was a battleground during the War of the Fae. Both Etherians and Vila died there. Trees sprouted from the remnants of their magic." She points to the fruit in the branches, like hanging gems. "Trees that grew apples stuffed with rubies or plums laced with nightshade."

A tremor ripples through me. Is that what will happen to me when I die?

"And here." She flips a few pages. "A lake in Etheria where a light Fae drowned. If you drink from it, you gain immortality."

"These sound like legends. Has anyone actually seen these places? Know anyone who drank from that lake?"

She closes the book with an irritated thump. "You said you would help. And if we use the ritual to summon the Vila's magic, maybe we can find a way to reverse it. You're the best shot I have."

She nudges the summoning ritual under my nose again with a pleading expression and I heave a sigh. She might be right. The Vila may not be able to overturn the curse herself. But if her magic could be located, perhaps it could be destroyed. And then Aurora's curse would be ended for good.

At Aurora's unrelenting insistence, I find myself at Hilde's the next day with the copied-out list of ingredients we need for the summoning ritual in hand. I still think it's a terrible idea to attempt the thing. But Aurora was so certain. At least if we try and fail, we can forget the whole business and she won't blame me.

"What chewed you up and spit you out half-eaten?" The apothecary drums her beet-stained fingers on the countertop and cocks her head at me.

My shoulders hunch. Aurora said she'd be back as soon as she could, and so I'd spent the rest of the night poring over the ritual's instructions. Dark circles smudge beneath my sleep-deprived eyes. My hair sticks to my scalp in greasy clumps.

Another customer, pimple-faced and gangly, slides me a sideways glance before deciding he can finish his business later. The shop bell clangs behind him.

"Have those Graces sent you again?"

"No." I pass her the rumpled list of what I need, written so hastily the ink is smeared. "I'm here for my own enhancements."

Hilde peers at the list, fishing out dingy spectacles from an apron pocket. "Trying to make me go blind, I see." She points. "Is this bogswort or beetle brains?"

"Bogswort," I answer, reddening. "Obviously." I've never heard of beetle brains being used as an enhancement.

"Don't sass me, little miss." She slaps the list down and sets to work filling my order. "Keeping busy, I take it."

"Extremely."

"That nasty turn at the castle didn't keep 'em away for long, eh?"

At the mention of the Weltross incident, I squirm, becoming suddenly fascinated with a selection of peacock feathers Hilde has displayed on the counter. "No."

"Oh, don't mind me." Hilde chuckles. "I don't hold it against you. Anyone who comes knocking on *your* door deserves what they ask for. And not in a pretty-wrapped silk package."

I forgot how much I appreciate Hilde's wisdom.

"But tell me." She returns from the back of the shop,

passing over three jars filled with various shades of powder. "Is that all the Dark Grace has brewing?" The wrinkles on her brow deepen. "You look like a sailor blown in by a hurricane, but there's still a spark in those eyes."

I look away, at anything but her knowing honey-brown gaze.

"Has my Alyce found a special someone?"

"Absolutely not." I busy myself with stuffing the jars into my sack, fire bursting from the tips of my toes and lifting the roots of my hair. "Don't be daft. It isn't allowed."

"Daft am I?" Hilde's voice curves. My pulse rockets up my throat. The last thing I need is a rumor like that to get started. Rose would give me no peace. "I must be mistaken," she says at last, sly as a cat. "You don't have to share your secrets with old Hilde."

She stops me from shoving the last jar into my sack with one tawny, scarred hand over mine. "But you do know, Alyce." Her tone is soft. Almost motherly. "If there is someone, I hope they deserve you."

From anyone else, I would expect that comment to be cruel. That the apothecary means she hopes the object of my affection is as wicked and hated as I am. But there's an openness in Hilde's features. The pressure on my hand is reassuring. Safe.

"Don't let them make you into their monster. Not the Graces. Not anyone."

"There's no one." The lie is salty.

"Very well." Hilde sighs, pulling on her familiar mask of indifference. She reexamines the list. The corners of her mouth turn down. "Deathknot? Why do you want a thing like that?"

I rearrange the jars in the sack. "Do you really want to know?"

She watches me for a moment. "It's not your usual sort of thing. Deathknot gets people into trouble, to my knowledge."

"*Trouble* doesn't sound like the Dark Grace's area of expertise?"

The moment hums between us. Hilde rubs her thumb along the edge of the list. And I'm worried she might refuse me. But then she turns on her heel and stalks back into her stores. Muffled grunts and curses fill the room, and she re-emerges with a fat glass container in both hands. The lid is covered with dust. Inside is the most hideous thing I've ever seen. Like a black root of some huge, deadly plant. Knotted, as the name suggests, and riddled with green, furry scabs. Tiny white hairy things poke through the leathery skin and writhe in the fluid.

Glass scrapes against the worn wood of the counter as the apothecary slides the deathknot over to me. But she doesn't let go immediately.

"Remember what I said, Alyce. About monsters." The words are low, spoken in a tone that wakes something deep in my core. "Take care you don't become what they think you are."

CHAPTER TWENTY-ONE

My deadline for the king's commission looms like a storm, and I still have no idea how to manage it. I've thought of coating the chalice in an elixir—like how the innovation Graces use their elixirs to create enchanted fabrics and ornaments and flowers. But even if it worked, the effects of such an elixir would eventually wear off.

Kal would know what to do.

Unfortunately, my patron schedule prevents me from visiting him during the day. And I expect Aurora to return to my Lair immediately. But apparently not even she is capable of absconding from the palace every night. When there's no Mistress Nightingale booked on my schedule late the next evening, I whisper a hope that she doesn't call on me unexpectedly, finish with my last patron, and sneak away.

"What troubles you?" Kal asks as soon as I arrive.

The sea is as agitated as I am. It churns and then launches

itself into the cliff face, spraying up the outer tower walls and through the gaping hole in its side.

"I don't know how to curse a chalice—or anything for that matter," I say after I've finished telling Kal about the king's commission. I sit on a stairstep and Callow flaps unsteadily from my shoulder. "The only thing I can think to use is an elixir, but—"

"Elixirs?" Shadows curl around Kal's ankles. "You have known for some time that you do not need those to command your power. The Vila who cursed the royal line certainly did not simply wrap up a vial of 'curse water' and bid the princess to drink it."

I bristle, even though I know he's teasing. "How else am I supposed to get my power to manipulate a human's without my being near them?"

"Your magic hinges on intent—that's the only thing that matters. Your elixirs worked because you wanted them to work. Because your blood carried your command. It is not the most direct way to use your power, but it can be very effective—as with the curse on the royal line."

Icy flecks of spray land on my cheeks and I swipe at them. "You're saying that if I can't reach a heart of magic, all I have to do is smear my blood on something and it's cursed?"

"Your blood holds your intent, Alyce. It lends a spark of your power to whatever you curse." He laughs at the scowl on my face. "Is that so difficult to believe? When you have spent over half a decade crafting—what are they called? Ugliness elixirs?"

The tower groans against the sea wind.

"Those wore off," I argue. "The king wants something far more powerful."

"And why do you think your power weakened so quickly when you were serving your *patrons*?" He sneers at the very idea of the nobles.

I begin to pace. Callow complains when I tread too close and interrupt her feasting among the grainy mortar. She snatches an insect out of the air and crunches it in half. "Because I wasn't using it properly?"

"Maybe." The buttons on Kal's doublet shine in the night. "It could not have been because you desired your elixirs to weaken?"

The next wave roars. "Because I . . ."

Dragon's teeth. My elixirs worked because I commanded my power to behave like the Graces'. And the effects of the Graces' elixirs Fade. I never intended to permanently harm anyone. My power understood that.

"Yes, Alyce." Kal grins. "The stronger the intent, the stronger the curse."

A shudder runs through me. The Vila who cursed Aurora's line must have been crazed with bloodlust. I shake myself a little.

"Try it yourself." Kal gestures around the chamber, at the graveyard of broken furniture and debris. "Choose something and curse it."

I consider my options. A rusted chair. A rotting beam. Not particularly inspiring.

"Curse me if you will."

"No," I answer automatically. When I was first learning to use my power, that's exactly what I'd had to do. Mistress

Lavender was certain I could command light magic if I only tried hard enough, and so she ordered me to charm the maids and the cooks, the way the Graces do when they're practicing in the nurseries. But I produced only scaled faces and garbled voices and hunched backs. The attempts wore off, as they always do, but the effect on my reputation was long-lasting. And why it used to be that we couldn't get many servants to stay at Lavender House for more than a month. "You've had enough cursing for one lifetime, I think."

Something glimmers near Callow. I kick a few stones away, revealing a small hand mirror covered in cobwebs and brine. I wipe it clean with the hem of my cloak, frowning at my own spotted reflection within. And then I remember something I read about Etheria. That mirrors crafted from the sand of their lakes can be visual portals to other worlds. My Vila power couldn't create something like that. But perhaps I could do something else.

Before I can talk myself out of it, I dig out the small knife I keep in my sack, draw my blood, and squeeze a single drop of it over the glass.

"Give it some direction," Kal coaches. "Intent."

"Whoever looks in this mirror," I begin, even as doubt chews away at my resolve, "will see their deepest fear."

Blood the color of hemlock splatters on the glass. And then it vanishes. A plume of emerald smoke unfurls from the surface. The tarnished silver is warmer to my touch than it should be, the glass undulating like water in the frame. As if my blood brought it to life.

Holding my breath, I tilt the mirror toward my face. For

a moment, all I see is myself. But then my reflection ripples. The angles of my face sharpen, my cheekbones lengthening and stretching until twin points of bone protrude above each ear. Spikes of bone erupt along my collarbone and above my eyebrows like the peaks of the Etherian Mountains. My eyes blare green fire and a charge blazes up from my toes, filling my lungs with the smell of woodsmoke and leather and another scent that isn't mine.

I am *her.*

The realization tears through me like an arrow striking home. The Vila who cast the curse on the royal line. On Aurora. My mouth opens and tips of jagged yellow teeth gleam. Lips curve into a smile without my bidding. Screaming a curse, I hurl the mirror across the tower. Glass explodes when it meets the stone of the opposite wall. Callow shrieks and hops away.

"What did you see?" Kal nears me slowly.

Numbness tingles across my scalp and I wrap my arms around my middle, needing something to hold me together. "Am I as bad as she was?" I whisper. "For working with the king? For cursing innocents?"

"Is that who appeared to you?" His shadows brush my skirts. "The ancient Vila? You have no reason to be frightened of her. She cannot harm you."

"It wasn't just that I saw her." I shut my eyes at the image of my bones morphing into hers. Of the feeling of otherness inside my skin. "I *was* her. She became me somehow—or I her."

Kal grips my elbows in his strong, cold hands. Bracing

me. Darkness cocoons us both, veiling the rest of the room. "The people you will curse—are they innocent?"

"I don't know. Maybe."

"And how many of them have come to you for their own desires, uncaring how it affected you? That it enslaved you?"

My chest tightens. "Too many to count."

"This arrangement with the Briar King is a means to an end, Alyce. It may not be pleasant, but it is your way out. And I vow to you—whatever happens, I am your ally. Your own kind. You are not alone."

Heat replaces the frozen current of my blood. I lean in, clasping my arms around his neck and pulling him close.

"Thank you."

I stay at the black tower until dawn blushes against the whitecaps. Autumn has fully spread its roots, an undoubtedly harsh winter soon to follow. I make it back to Lavender House in time to change my dress and prepare for the day.

And the first thing I do is curse the king's chalice and send it to the palace.

CHAPTER TWENTY-TWO

When I break the seal on my schedule a few days later and find an appointment with Mistress Nightingale booked for late in the evening, anticipation buzzes through me. Given how determined she was to attempt the summoning ritual, I thought Aurora would have returned by now. But her duties at the palace must have kept her away. And it doesn't matter now. She's coming.

Slogging my way through the other appointments is torture. I busy myself with small things in between each patron—feeding Callow and updating my notes. But no matter how much I will the time to pass, the hours ooze slowly along like honey in winter.

And so it's particularly frustrating when the princess is late.

First a half hour. Then an hour. Delphine is growing angrier by the minute, I'm sure. She'll want to be getting home before the weather changes. Briar's infamous autumnal storms have begun lumbering in from the sea, making the Lair even more unpleasant than usual. The wind barrels down the chimney and sends embers skittering across the floor. The stale air is saturated with the stink of mold, and a thin layer of silty grime coats every surface.

With every rumble of thunder, my mind devises a new reason behind Aurora's tardiness: Someone found out about our meetings. She's ill or got lost in the storm. Or, my vicious thoughts keep circling back to what must be the truth—she's grown bored of me. I was an amusing distraction, but my novelty has worn off. Exactly as I knew it would.

My bell rings.

I'm at the door in two heartbeats, and Aurora hurries in, pulling her scarf from around her face and slamming the door behind her against the gales. I'm so relieved I'm nearly dizzy, scolding myself for thinking the worst of her. And then, more than that, for even caring what Aurora thought. I'm letting her get too close. But I have no idea how to push her away.

"I'm sorry," she says, dumping her sack of books on the worktable. "My mother insisted I dine with her tonight. And then she refused to let me go, wanting to discuss the *new developments*."

"New developments?"

She's soaked to the bone and I fetch a blanket for her. She slumps into a chair in front of the hearth. "A suitor." She rolls her eyes, wringing out her hair. "Elias, a younger son of Ryna."

"Ryna." The kingdom directly above the island of Cardon—where Corinne had come from and broken Eva's curse before they . . . I wrench my thoughts away from the Crimson Cliffs and the broken bodies beneath the sea. "Ryna specializes in . . . silk production?"

"I'm surprised you know that." Aurora feeds a few dried beetles to Callow, stroking the kestrel's snowy breast. "Silk and astronomy, apparently. Some of their scholars compared the star charts from the night I was born to the prince's. And it's a match."

I dislike him immediately. "What does that mean?"

"Dragon knows." Aurora groans. "But most of all it means that he will be coming here. Mother is sure he's the one."

Dislike sharpens to hatred.

"But you're not."

"I don't particularly care." But the angle of her shoulders tells a different story. "Elias was extended a royal invitation years ago, but he refused. Now that the stars have spoken, his parents are forcing him to come. But I wager he wants to make the journey about as much as I want his slimy lips on mine."

I throw a handful of peppermint leaves and cinnamon cloves into a mug to make her a tincture. "You don't know that they're slimy."

"They're all slimy." She scoots closer to the fire. "All the more reason to break the curse myself. Send the star-chosen prince right back to his scholars and his silk trade. Have you collected what we need for the summoning ritual?"

I chew my lips as I fuss with the kettle, my gaze flitting to where the deathknot stews in its brackish fluid.

Aurora doesn't miss it. "What is that horrible thing?"

"Deathknot." A patch of moldy fur on the deathknot's bulbous end glares at me. It's better that we just leave it in its jar. Better yet, drop it into the sea. "I picked it up from Hilde, my apothecary. It's for the ritual."

She needs no further explanation. The chair teeters as she flies across the room and snatches up the jar. "This looks like it could have come from Malterre itself." She inspects every angle, fascinated and terrified at once.

Kind of like how she feels about you, that voice whispers. I smother it.

"It probably did. I don't think Hilde has ever had someone ask for it."

"Well, what are we waiting for?"

"It's not quite that simple." I push the mug into her hands and open the Nightseeker book, examining the looping script and faded diagram of the ritual for the hundredth time. "Are you certain about this? Because I'm not. This magic is clearly forbidden—I don't know how your father would feel if he knew we were using it. But I imagine he wouldn't approve."

She sips the brew. Nods. "That's fair."

"It's not just me I'm worried about," I go on. "You, too."

Aurora watches the jar as she thinks. "I know. And you're right."

Relief blooms in my gut, then just as quickly wilts at the look in her eyes. They're determined and sure. Reckless.

"I'm worried about what will happen if we don't use the book." She sets down her mug. Her scent of appleblossoms twines with those of my enhancements. And I'm surprised at how much I've come to expect it here. "If I'm gone, what will happen to the realm?"

"I thought your mother was working with the Etherians. There must be some plan." How can I make her understand?

I don't want to hurt her. Don't want to see her face as the duke's was—lips limned in blood and eyes glassy. "This is dangerous. It could—"

"Kill me?" She laughs. "So can the curse. I know you're trying to protect me, Alyce, but I'm tired of feeling that my fate rests in someone else's hands. Someone I don't even know. That's what killed my sisters—waiting and hoping. I won't follow in their footsteps. And if I die because I'm trying to take some control over my own life, so be it."

Dragon's fucking teeth. I know exactly how she feels. It's the same as my secret lessons with Kal. My arrangement with the king and my plan to take the gold he pays me and run.

"Fine." I pour more water into her mug. "But the ritual only works if you have a connection to the person, or spirit, summoned."

She sits back down, frowning. "We don't have anything like that."

"Actually . . ." This is the part I dreaded. "Because the Vila cursed you, I think we do." Aurora gives me a puzzled look. "I think we could use your blood."

"You want my blood," she repeats. "For the summoning ritual?"

From her lips, I can hear the idiocy of the suggestion. A flush creeps up my neck.

But Aurora only picks up the nearest paring knife. "How much?"

We spend the next half an hour preparing. The diagram from the book must be drawn on the floor, a difficult feat since the stones are perpetually damp. I scatter sage and yew and other herbs inside the faint chalk lines. While I work on that, Aurora tends the fire, bringing my large iron kettle to a boil. The rain pounds against the walls of my Lair, rivulets of icy water sneaking in through loose stones and dripping down the chimney. The fire hisses and smokes.

"I doubt this will work," I repeat, inspecting the curve of one of the lines. The design is not quite as well drawn as it is in the book. It's clumsier and smeared in places where the chalk refused to stick to the wet stone. But passable. I hope.

"It's worth a try."

"That's what the mortal armies used to say about invading Etheria."

She ignores me. The steam from the boiling pot glistens on Aurora's cheeks and tangles in her hair, curling the tiny wisps at her forehead. Even doing the work of a scullery maid, she's beautiful.

I roundly scold myself for staring at her and add in the other ingredients. All that's left is the deathknot. My chalk-covered fingers slip on the lid of the jar, and it almost crashes to the ground. But Aurora catches it.

"Last chance to turn back," I say.

Instead of an answer, she grins. And then she slides the deathknot into the pot.

A sound like nails screeching against glass pummels into my skull and reverberates in the sockets of my teeth and the joints of my jaw. We both scream, clapping the heels of our palms over our ears. Terror spikes through me, and I'm sure that a servant will hear the commotion and come to investigate. But after what feels an eternity, the damn thing quiets.

Ears ringing, I settle Callow, who is flapping her wings and shrieking, and fetch the knife from the worktable.

Aurora offers her arm, pulling up her sleeve. "You do it."

"It shouldn't require much. Just a nick." I take her hand, marveling at the softness of her skin. For a moment, I let myself trace the lines of her palm, following a long arc to the hummingbird pulse at her wrist.

"Is something wrong?" she asks, breaking me out of my trance.

My thumb freezes. Cursing myself to the bottom of the sea and back, I shake my head and position the blade so that it's poised at the place I think will hurt the least. Then hold my breath and push down.

Red blooms instantly. A color so different from the green of my own and the gold of the Graces. It looks like liquid rubies. Aurora winces. Quickly, I tilt the tiny wound over the pot and let a weak stream of crimson fall into the brew.

The room is still.

There's the sound of the rain above. The distant echo of thunder rolling down the chimney. The creaking of the house in the wind. The flames beneath the kettle and the boiling of the water. But other than that—silence.

I check the diagram. Consult the book.

"Are you supposed to say something?" Aurora presses close, reading over my shoulder.

"I don't know. I think the ritual is supposed to be enough."

She pokes the contents of the pot. "Wait. We added my blood because it carries the curse. But what about yours?"

I look up from the page. "Mine?"

"It carries the Vila magic." She lifts a shoulder. "Maybe the ritual needs an extra push."

My blood is the last thing I want to add to this concoction. For all I know, it will burn Lavender House to the ground. Curse Aurora double, if such a thing is possible. But she is already fetching another knife. Herding me closer to the kettle.

"This isn't wise."

"I don't know why you're so afraid of your own power." She holds my hand over the kettle and for some foolish reason, I don't fight her.

"You don't want to know."

"You said yourself, it probably won't even work. What's the harm?" But she waits until I nod before slicing open my skin. Gently, like she's cutting a pat of warm butter.

Emerald blood wells and drips into the brew.

And then the entire room burns to life.

White, blinding light erupts from the chalk lines of the diagram on the floor. I stagger backward, throwing my arms over my face. A gust of wind whips around us, throwing glass bottles from the shelves. Book pages fly back and forth like storm-tossed birds. Aurora is pressed against the far wall. The fire goes green, flames leaping all the way up into the chimney.

Callow screams from her perch, jerking hard enough to break her tether. She half flaps, half careens to the ground as glass smashes around her. I grapple for the nearest thing I can find, an empty bucket, and upend it over the kestrel before she's injured.

A low moan begins to swell, raw and guttural and entirely inhuman. Using the edge of the table to steady myself, I haul myself through the currents of wind and lock my arms around Aurora. Hers clamp around my shoulders hard enough to bruise.

"What's happening?" she shouts into my ear.

I wish I knew.

The fire pushes higher, creating a wall of green flame. Within it, I think I can see the outline of a face. My breath halts. It's the same face I saw in the mirror I cursed. Wild eyes and a wicked, smirking mouth. Dagger-tipped teeth flash as the flames dance, and a strange, ethereal voice wends around us.

"Find me, my pet."

I dig my fingers into Aurora's back as a scream wrenches free from my lungs. And then, just as suddenly as it all began, everything stills. The flames vanish in a cloud of smoke. The chalk on the floor chars to ash. And there is no voice but mine and Aurora's, both of us still braced together, panting and breathless.

Aurora lets go first, gaping at the destruction of the room. Yellowed, ripped-out pages flutter to the floor. Shards of glass glitter in pools of sticky syrup. Fingers of thick, black smoke slink from the rim of the pot, filling the Lair with a putrid stench. My stomach sinks, mentally tallying up the coin it will take to replace what's been ruined.

"What was that?"

I stiffen at the question, my knees still trembling.

"I don't know."

The lie is easier than the truth. I was sure the ritual was superstitious nonsense. Even if it did work, I thought we might get a glimpse of where the Vila's magic still dwells. A cave or barren field in Malterre where she must have died during the war. But this—this is the second time the Vila appeared to me. The first, in the mirror, was easy to dismiss as an illusion. But tonight—I'd called and she'd answered.

"There's power in you. More than you know." Hilde's words come back to me, the syllables warping until they sound like the shrilling of the deathknot.

Needing a distraction, I free Callow from the bucket and return her to her perch. I attempt to feed her a scrap of meat, but she snaps at my fingers and sets to fussing with her tousled feathers. She'll not be forgiving me anytime soon.

Aurora stares at the hearth, its embers still an unearthly shade of green. "Have you ever seen a fire do that? Do you think it was the Vila? The one who cast my curse?"

"If it was, we're no closer to discovering her magic." That much is true. The Vila's cryptic message was utterly useless. My head begins to ache. This was my own fault. What had Hilde said—that the deathknot brought nothing but trouble? I should have listened.

"I'm sorry about the mess." Aurora rubs at her forearm. The thorned-rose curse mark beneath her sleeve. "But I . . . I wanted to hope."

I busy myself with picking up broken bottles, unable to meet her gaze any longer.

Because as much as I feared the ritual, I'd wanted to hope, too.

CHAPTER TWENTY-THREE

The sinister face from the fire reemerges in my dreams. Laughing at me. Opening its mouth to swallow me whole. Shred me to ribbons with its gnashing teeth. I sit bolt upright, heart pounding. The sweat-soaked bedsheets cling to my legs. My fingers ache from clenching the pillows. I force down heaving, uneven breaths, an overripe taste like rotten fruit in my mouth.

Dragging a hand through my damp hair, the previous night comes back to me. It had taken hours to clean the mess, especially since I insisted Aurora return to the palace right away. She wanted to stay, but I couldn't have her discovered missing. Not after what we'd done. Not with her hand cut by my knife and her blood mixed with mine in a Nightseeker ritual. And so it wasn't until the first call of a morning lark, the autumn dawn bright after the storm's fury, that I'd made it back upstairs to my own bed, every muscle throbbing.

And now it looks like it might be close to noon. The sun through my window is warm for this time of year, and the sounds of the Grace District babble below. Errand boys call back and forth. Carriages rattle along the cobblestones. But if it's so late, why hasn't my schedule appeared? I throw myself out of bed as quickly as my body will let me, tug on a fresh dress, and splash some water on my face. It's nowhere near the level of grooming I need to cover what happened last night.

"Here she is." A grating voice intercepts me at the top of the stairs. Marigold scowls at me from the lower landing. "What were you doing last night?"

My hand flies to the railing before I topple over it. Did I sweep up the ash from the diagram? Had I left the Nightseeker book out? My head is still too fuzzy to remember.

"Why did no one wake me?"

"Mistress had to cancel your patron appointments because of the intolerable reek from your chambers." As if to illustrate, Marigold lifts a silk sachet dangling from the butterscotch sash of her gown and presses it into her nose.

"The . . ." I breathe in deeply. There it is. The awful stench from whatever the ritual did with the deathknot. I must have inhaled so much last night that I'm immune to it.

"We've barely been able to keep it out of the parlors. And you're lucky the food in the kitchen wasn't tainted." She leans forward and sniffs. "Ugh! And you smell even worse."

I'm so relieved I sink onto the stairsteps, leaning against the vined carvings on the railing slats. The tip of a wooden leaf pokes into my forehead.

"Tell her how terrible she smells, Rose." Marigold flaps her handkerchief in my direction as the sound of slippered footsteps nears. "Simply awful. The stench will never leave us."

Not a muscle of Rose's face moves. She picks at a starfish-shaped brooch pinned to her bodice. The citrine gems gleam in the shafts of sunlight flooding the entry hall. And I notice something else, too. The sallowness of Rose's skin. Her cheeks are gold, but only because of an artificial rouge. Her eyes are sunken and dulled, a result of the bloodrot. Apprehension twinges in my chest, wondering how much she's taking and how often.

As if reading the assessment in my gaze, she narrows hers. "Malyce smells no different than usual." And then she melts away.

"Alyce, what in Briar!" Mistress Lavender pushes through the vacancy Rose left. "I've had servants scrubbing your parlor all morning, but still we cannot rid ourselves of this blight."

I stand up again, trying to keep my guilt from showing. I'd put everything away. Positioned things so that it looks like my stores are full. Though I'll probably have to use my own coin to replace most of what's lost.

"I— I was experimenting with a new elixir." I keep my tone even. "One of the enhancements reacted badly." That part isn't even a lie.

"I should think so." Mistress Lavender waves her own sachet beneath her nose, eliciting a smirk from Marigold. "Needless to say, you won't have any patrons today. We'll keep some cleansing herbs burning in your hearth. Delphine will reschedule everyone for tomorrow. And I'm sorry to do it, but if any of them cancel, the coin for their appointment will come out of your earnings. I'll not have the house suffer for your foolishness."

Marigold looks like she might burst into flame with glee.

"I understand." I incline my head even as the punishment stings. Given that my patrons will traipse all the way to Lavender House to learn that I'm unavailable, it's highly likely they'll decide the errand isn't worth repeating. But I remind myself that I could be facing far worse than lost coin.

Mistress Lavender mutters a few more things to herself, then steers Marigold away, ranting off a list of tasks that need to be done.

"You do reek." Laurel glides out of her parlor and I jump. How long had she been listening?

"I think we've covered that." I roll my eyes and start back up the stairs.

"Not of whatever nonsense you just lied about."

My heart kicks. "What are you talking about? I used—"

Laurel waves away my words. "Keep your secrets. You have little else of your own."

Her answer surprises me, as did the dress and the mask she left for me what seems a lifetime ago. But I still do not trust her fully. She is a Grace.

"You smell of old books. You have for a while now."

I almost laugh. Leave it to Laurel to detect such a scent.

"I think they're wrong about your gift," I say, raising my sleeve to my nose and breathing deep. All I smell is charred deathknot. "You have the nose of a bloodhound."

She tilts her head at me. "What have you been reading? And where did you get it?"

"I thought I was allowed to have my own secrets."

"Perhaps." Her yew-stained fingertips beat out an impatient rhythm against the lacquered wood balustrade. "Could you bring me some?"

"Books?"

"Yes. I get so little opportunity to explore older texts. If you don't want to say where you got them, bring me a few."

I turn her request over in my mind. So simple, and yet it sends alarm bells clanging through my brain. It makes sense that a Grace gifted in wisdom would want rare books. Laurel's parlor walls are lined with shelves, stuffed to bursting with texts she's devoured. But I can't give her the Nightseeker volumes. Or any about Vila. And to refuse would only whet her appetite further. Lure her to snoop in my Lair. I try to read the look in her golden eyes. Laurel is different from the others. Maybe not my friend. But not my enemy, either.

"Very well," I say at last. I'll have Aurora bring a few harmless volumes. "Give me time. But I will."

The lingering stench of the deathknot does not recede enough for me to receive patrons the next day. A headache masses like a storm inside my skull as I think of the tripled appointments I'll have to squeeze in to make up the time when the chamber is finally clear. And of the coin I'll lose. But I'm grateful for another day to rest.

Callow perched on my shoulder, I spend the early hours of the morning gathering any enhancements I can find outside Briar's main gates to replace common ingredients that were lost in the wake of the summoning ritual. A cheaper solution than going to Hilde's. And then I go to the tower and visit Kal.

After turning a few pebbles into winged stone birds and coaxing them to fly around the tower, we focus on my Shifting.

It's getting easier, but my abilities are budding at best. Kal was right, my early Shifts happened out of need and desperation, and so they came and went without my even noticing. I missed the telltale tingle of bone drifting and muscle reshaping. But I suppose I should have realized. When I was a child, and I would squeeze myself into the impossibly small corners of the cellar in order to hide from the ministrations of the healing Graces. When, stomach growling after they'd forgotten about me, I could sneak unseen into the kitchen and make off with an entire pie, I always thought I was simply being ignored.

Actual Shifts are much more difficult to maintain. The command must be given and upheld, and my grip is weak and my control unpredictable. I can employ a new face for a half an hour perhaps, before my hold on the magic tires and the illusion slips. Now that I know what to look for, I can always sense it. Cheekbones itching under my skin as they settle back into place. Scalp burning as my hair flattens and brittles.

And it's not just other humans I can impersonate.

Kal is teaching me to summon the ears of a rabbit, which let me hear almost all the way to the gates of Briar from the black tower. Then the fins and gills of a siren, so I can breathe underwater. Even wings. These animalistic features are the most difficult to conjure, and I can maintain them for only a few heartbeats before they vanish. Kal says it's because I've been in my human form my entire life. It's the same as when the Shifters remain as animals for too long and forget how to use their magic. My own instinct doubts the Shift, making the magic wilt.

"What is it?" I ask after a round of turning my fingers into claws. Callow dislikes these Shifts, always scurrying out of my way and ruffling her feathers at my new shapes.

"Nothing," Kal says, as though he has not been watching me like I'm a glass teetering on the edge of a table. "Only—you seem distracted. Is something wrong?"

I pinch my thumb and forefinger against the bridge of my nose. Dark clouds gather on the horizon, changing the pressure in the air. All I've thought about since the ritual is the Vila and the curse and the hundred thousand lies salting my life. I'm not surprised Kal can sense my unease. And I want to tell him about how the Vila appeared . . . again. He would know what it meant. But then I would have to admit to helping Aurora. And I'm too afraid he would see that as betrayal.

"Nothing more than usual."

"Are the commissions from the king weighing on your conscience?" The shadows wither and swell around him, wrapping around his waist and crawling over his shoulders.

"No." Although I did receive another just this morning. A ring the king wishes to cause temporary blindness to the wearer. The request is unsettling in and of itself, but it infuriates me that I have no idea how his servants are getting into my Lair. The thought sears like grains of salt pressed into a wound. "I'm just tired."

"We can stop for today."

Heaving a sigh, I let myself sink onto the stump of a stone column, exhaustion dripping from every pore. Callow returns to my side, her tawny body brushing my shins.

"You are strong, Alyce." Kal slips through the shadows and sits beside me. "It will not be much longer until you can escape this place. Your Vila magic is progressing nicely. And soon you will be able to hold a decent Shift."

I hope he's right. Although leaving Briar doesn't quite feel as cathartic as it used to. I don't wish to remain as the Dark Grace and the Briar King's secret puppet. But Aurora. My skin tingles, recalling the smoothness of her palm. The apple-blossom scent of her hair. The soft curve of her neck as it meets her shoulder.

Dragon's teeth. I realize I've been staring at Kal, picturing the crown princess. Mortification burns up my chest and I try to focus on something—anything—else.

But then a line of red on Kal's neck snares my attention, and my brow furrows. The Shifter is shades of black and white. A creature carved from smoke and alabaster. I've never seen him wear color. Without thinking, I put my finger to the slash beneath the collar of his high-necked doublet.

There's a chain hidden there.

"What is this?" I try to tug it free.

Kal angles away from me. "Nothing to concern you."

But that will not do. I reach forward again, but his frigid grip catches me. "No, Alyce."

"Show me then."

He opens his mouth to refuse, but I stare him down.

"As stubborn as your mother." He grumbles something else, but I can't make it out. He yanks open the onyx buttons of his doublet, exposing the too-pale skin of his chest.

The chain I felt rests against his collarbone, ending in a medallion the size of my palm. The jewel, if it is a jewel, is unlike anything I've ever seen. Like a rough-cut, smoky emerald. Light and darkness writhe inside it like tangling snakes. I press closer. Raise my fingers to touch it, but Kal's close around them.

"No."

"What is it?"

A muscle in Kal's jaw works. "It is"—he takes a breath, every word a struggle—"what binds me here."

The sea breaks against the base of the tower with a roar, sending spray through the gap in the wall. Callow complains when a shower of seafoam lands on her back.

"What binds—" I focus on the pendant, watching the sifting movement of the liquid jade and indigo inside it. The colors bend and dive and whorl. Exactly as the shadows do around Kal. And suddenly I realize, it is the same magic. A collar, holding him inside the tower.

Foreboding spiders its way along my scalp.

"Much more effective than iron chains, as it turns out." Kal's smile is grim.

"You can't remove it?" The question sounds painfully weak coming out of my mouth. Of course he's tried. He shows me his hands, palms up. Scars I never noticed before stretch in a horrible lattice across his skin, silvered and about the width of the chain. Burn marks, faded with time. Centuries. My stomach twists.

"There are measures in place."

"But why did it . . . ?" I motion toward the blistered skin beneath the medallion.

"That is what happens when I try to step into the sun. Or when I attempt to leave the confines of this tower." Kal's hand drifts toward the chain, then drops. His shadows spike and coil. "A few days ago, part of the roof caved in and my leg was pinned under a beam. I managed to free myself, but not quickly enough to evade the sunlight."

I swallow. This tower is nothing but a skeleton. How long before the rest of it tumbles into the sea? As if in answer, a stone rattles loose from the upper floors, the resulting echo like a death knell.

"You'll burn," I whisper. "The enchantment—it's meant to kill you."

He studies me closely, a thousand emotions flickering over his features. "I am not your responsibility."

But it feels like he is. Both he and Aurora, on opposite sides of an ancient war, depending on me to survive. I want to save them both, but I can't help but feel that by allying with one, I'm damning the other. Beyond the gap, whitecaps churn as the dark, heavy underbellies of the storm clouds heave toward shore.

"I wish you would tell me what troubles you." Kal's voice

is gentle, the way one might speak to a spooked horse. "Remember, we are kin."

If he only knew. I close my eyes against my own warring desires. The sea breeze tastes of brine and coming rain and my own bitter cowardice.

"The only thing that's troubling me is the thought of you trapped in this place." It's true enough. I take his hand in mine. "You will not die here. I vow it."

Kal smiles, but it's sad. And I can see in the obsidian of his eyes that he knows there's more and that I'm deliberately excluding him. Guilt lashes my heart.

But it's his next words that hurt the most.

"Please do not make promises you cannot keep."

Part II

Daughters,

It is not only Fae blood which blesses your crown. It is mine. It is every other queen's—spilled in one way or another—to grant you your throne. There are those, spurred by greed, who would rob you of this inheritance. Be wary and vigilant. Wise and fair. Do not lose yourselves in the sea of wealth and power to come. Surround yourselves with loyalty and love. And if nothing else, remember this:

That which is given oft cannot be regained.

—Lost letter from Leythana, first Briar Queen,
to her heirs. Age of the Rose, 45

CHAPTER TWENTY-FOUR

"Give me that." Rose snatches an envelope out of a servant's fingers before he can deposit it on Mistress Lavender's place setting at breakfast.

"It's addressed to the housemistress." The poor thing is more mouse than boy. Clusters of freckles collide with one another as his brow furrows. I sip my tea.

"Do you see her here?" Rose glares at him with a look that could singe hair.

The servant wisely bows and leaves.

Rose breaks the violet-colored seal and unfolds the missive. She hasn't applied her rouge yet, and so her cheeks are a sickly shade of pale yellow. Next to Laurel and Marigold, each sporting a healthy, golden Grace flush, Rose looks like one of my terminally ill patrons. It's winter now, some three months since I caught her with the bloodrot. Even longer since the last time I interfered with one of her patrons. But it doesn't seem like she's let up on her dosage.

"It's official," Rose breathes, passing the scalloped-edged

announcement to an impatient Marigold. "The Royal Grace is Fading. And quickly, by the wording of that message."

"Which one?" Laurel cracks her boiled egg with the back of her spoon, her attention glued to her book.

"Beauty," Marigold squeaks. Then she squeals, clapping her hands together and throwing her arms around Rose's shoulders.

"How sad." Laurel picks bits of shell from the egg. "How ever will the royals survive?"

"Don't think I can't read your tone." Rose untangles herself from Marigold's strangling embrace with a grimace. "You're jealous."

"Quite." Laurel snorts. "I'd like to serve in the palace as much as Alyce would."

I cough around my pastry at the mention of my name.

"The Dark Grace *does* serve in the palace," Marigold sniffs. "But few survive her 'appointments.' "

I swallow hard, the unchewed crust scratching down my throat. "I'd like to be left out of this."

"Oh, don't worry. You will be." Rose daintily dabs at her mouth. "The queen has decided there will be a contest to determine the most skilled of the beauty Graces. The winner will succeed the Fading Grace."

"I suppose you're going to compete?" I raise a sly eyebrow, raking my gaze over the circles under her eyes. The bones of her neck showing through her lemon-tinged skin.

"Of course I am. And you can all thank me for it when you receive the bump in standings after I win." She grits her teeth, making a visible effort to keep her anger in check. Compared to our early years together, Rose has been downright pleasant toward me of late. I suppose she's worried I'll tell Mistress Lavender what she's doing with the bloodrot. She needn't be concerned. I have much bigger secrets.

"I'll thank you now," Marigold pipes up. "You will invite me to the palace, won't you? Often? You won't forget?"

"You'll have to beat Pearl." The name is soft on Laurel's lips, but it might as well have been a dagger flung into Rose's chest. She slams her napkin down.

"I can charm circles around that haughty—"

"Good morning, Graces." Mistress Lavender bustles into the room, bringing a thick swell of the cloying scent of her namesake that burns in my nostrils. Calliope sneezes from her post at Rose's feet. But before the housemistress can even settle into her chair, Marigold is babbling, regurgitating the details of the morning's events as she thrusts the palace's letter under Mistress Lavender's pointed nose.

Laurel and I exchange a smirk. But then I notice Rose and my stomach sinks a little. She does not look the part of a confident Grace, poised to take her place among the royals. She looks weak and ill and so very frightened.

I excuse myself without another word.

"I don't envy the subject of those thoughts." Aurora's voice brings me back to the present late that evening. She appears regularly as clockwork now. Twice a week, on the nights her guards play cards and descend into drunken half-wits. I find myself wishing they would do so more often.

After breakfast, I'd returned to the Lair to find yet another commission waiting. A solid gold bracelet the king bid me curse to paralyze the wearer. Its mahogany box glares at me from where I'd stashed it on a shelf.

"Is something the matter?"

"No." Another lie piled atop countless others. I have enough to build the black tower twice over. "Just a hectic week."

"I think I witnessed your handiwork at court." Aurora selects a miniature jam tart and pops it into her mouth. "One of my mother's ladies, a skilled dancer, could do nothing but stumble over her own feet once a single note of music was struck."

I cringe, remembering that particular elixir from a few days ago. Another lady-in-waiting commissioned it. But I can't divulge that.

"It was quite the entertainment," Aurora says around her next bite. "I ordered the most complicated dances played the rest of the night and kept throwing partners at her."

I can't help but laugh, shaking my head at her strange sense of humor. Pearl's words from so long ago come back to me, though. That Aurora is only interested in me because I'm vile and hideous. I bite down on my tongue until the thought fades.

"Oh, and have I told you about the prince's letter?"

"Prince?" I scramble to keep up. She hasn't mentioned a prince lately. Except—"You mean the Ryna prince? The one whose star chart matches yours. He's writing to you?"

"Apparently we're supposed to be getting to know each other." I might be imagining it, but it seems she won't meet my gaze. "Even if he isn't the one who breaks my curse, I suppose it can't hurt to establish diplomatic relations."

Maybe not. But a pang lands between my ribs, even as I scold myself for being unreasonable. It's no business of mine to whom Aurora writes. Or why. And yet she's never spoken of the other suitors this way. The thought of her writing this prince—sharing her secrets and reading his flattery—festers.

"What sort of things do you discuss?"

"He's as dull as can be expected." She's looking through Kal's book again, studying an illustration of an Imp using its magic to turn a pile of stones into a steaming feast. An Imp's power is small in comparison to the other creatures that once lived in Malterre. Typically, Imps can only manage little feats like mending things or conjuring food or drink—which is why they were once used as slaves in Etheria. Their magic wasn't dark or strong enough to harm the light Fae. But while summoning a feast may seem more a blessing than a curse, the Imps are full of their own special kind of tricks. I wouldn't be at all surprised to learn that the decadent food in the illustration turned back into stones once eaten. "But he did tell me of a practice in his kingdom that quite interests me. All of the silk workers in Ryna are given a small claim to the trade's profits. The prince writes that, as a result, the workers care more about producing the best silk possible. That they're happier and work faster."

I have to admit that it's a good idea—grudgingly. I've seen some of the wretches who mine Etherium for the nobles, half-starved and miserable. Many don't even look old enough to have left their mothers. And the Common District is so poor. They certainly don't see any of their masters' coin.

"I want to implement that system here," Aurora rushes on. I love seeing her this way—the same breathless passion as when she told me her plan to break the curse. "I want to bring it up at the next council meeting, but my secretary keeps forgetting to add me to their agenda. I've told her a hundred times that I need to start participating in political affairs. But, dragon's teeth, she's so absentminded. I'll never get anything done."

Absentminded. A thought taps at the edges of my mind. The chalice the Briar King bid me curse causes memory loss. It could be a coincidence, I tell myself. Aurora's secretary could be forgetful for other reasons. And why would Tarkin bother cursing such a woman? Surely he would view her as insignificant. Aurora told me that not even the small council takes her role as future queen seriously. Not until she breaks the curse, at least.

But perhaps that's the point. What if Tarkin used the cursed chalice on Aurora's secretary specifically to keep his daughter out of political matters? If he's trying to cripple her rule before she even takes the throne—or to prevent that rule entirely?

My instinct screams at me to warn her. But that would mean admitting I have an agreement with her father. And confessing my true powers and perhaps even revealing my meetings with Kal. I can't betray him that way. And more than that, I doubt Aurora would still come to see me if she knew the truth. I've become accustomed to having a friend, and it's like breathing clean air after years of sucking down the brackish odor of the Common District. I don't want to give her up just yet.

"Any luck with that book?" I ask, steering the subject

abruptly away from pesky, star-chosen princes and people I might have unwittingly cursed.

The summoning ritual was ages ago, but we've found nothing else that might aid in breaking the curse. Against my better judgment, I attempted several other rituals from the Nightseeker book. One for cleansing, in the hopes that we could clear the curse from her blood, but it only suffocated us in a haze of sage smoke so dense I could chew it. And another to reverse a binding, which promptly unraveled the hem of Aurora's gown and popped the seams of her sleeves. Aside from those, the princess has swallowed dozens of antidotes for poisons and hexes. But the deadly Briar rose on her forearm has stubbornly refused to budge.

The only experiments I've outright refused to conduct again are any rituals that use my blood. After what happened with the summoning—after seeing the ancient Vila—it's far too risky. I have no idea what else can be called by my power. And no amount of her clever reasoning will convince me otherwise.

"No." She frowns down at the sketch of the Imp. "I still don't understand why the Etherians hated these creatures so much. I'd love to employ someone who could magic me a cream puff anytime I wished."

I laugh. "The Etherians hate a lot of creatures without reason."

"Like you." The fire crackles. I don't answer. "Did you know that the light Fae are born with their hearts in their mouths?"

"Their mouths? Which book told you that?"

"One I found in the new library, actually. Father is fascinated with the light Fae and collects everything he can about them—which isn't much. Apparently, the source of Etherian power is called a heart. When a Fae child is born, the heart is blown out of their mouth and into an orb of enchanted glass. That orb is kept safe until—"

"It's placed on a staff," I finish for her, picturing Endlewild's unpolished birchwood. The scar on my middle aches.

"Yes, exactly. The staff houses their power. Their magical heart, if you will."

Like the sources of magic I find with my Vila abilities.

"Does that mean if the heart is broken, they will die?" I ask darkly, imagining what it would feel like to smash the glass of Endlewild's staff and watch the life drain out of his eyes.

Her brow furrows. "I'm not sure."

For a while, there's only the sound of the wind in the chimney and Callow's gentle rustling. And then—

"What do you think it feels like to die?"

"What?"

Aurora lifts one shoulder. "I have two hundred and forty-five days before I find out."

She might as well have punched me in the stomach. I had no idea she was counting the days. No idea how little time we have left.

"You don't know that." But it's a flimsy hope and it cracks around the edges.

"It's not that I particularly mind dying," she continues. "But I think I will very much miss living. I was never meant to wear the crown, but I can think of nothing else now. I want to do something more than simply throw balls and order gowns." She thumbs the corner of a page. "I think I might be good at ruling."

"You *will* be good at it." Tentatively, I press my hand to her forearm, bracing for the cringe beneath her sleeve. It doesn't come. "You will be queen. And you will give the Etherium miners a share in the profits and clean up the Common District and put women on the small council and do everything else you promise. You'll be as great as Leythana was, and they will love you for it."

She smiles, soft and melancholy. Placating me, but not believing me. "If I am, I will not let my husband reign in my stead, as the other queens have done. I don't care if the Ryna prince breaks my curse. He'll never have my throne."

My heart soars at hearing her talk like that. "I pity the man who tries to manage you."

I expect her to laugh, but she pulls away. "In truth, I don't know whether I wish for the curse to be broken—" She pauses. "Or not broken."

"You don't want the curse to break?" I repeat slowly. "That means you'll die."

"I know. But you don't understand. All those suitors. Some of them are nice enough. Charming, even." She twines a long lock of her burnished gold hair around one finger. "But they're strangers, Alyce. And the line grows longer every day."

Her gaze is closer to lavender today, glistening with shades of bright, terrified blue. There's a sharpness in her features that reminds me of a cornered animal. I know it well. I've seen it often enough in my own reflection.

"The curse is supposed to be broken by true love. But look what that 'love' has caused. Queens sign over Leythana's legacy to their husbands. Eva and Corinne killed themselves." Her throat works. "And then look at my parents. My father broke my mother's curse, but do they seem like they're in love?"

I can say nothing. It's hard to imagine anything like love beating beneath Tarkin's duplicitous skin.

"Maybe it was true love once. But somewhere it soured. And when I think of having to spend the rest of my life trapped with someone I no longer care about"—she hesitates, but only for an instant—"I might rather die."

"Don't say that. Briar can't lose you."

I can't lose you, my heart whispers.

Without thinking, I move beside her and scoop her limp hand into mine. Her fingers are cold, but heat rushes through me, skipping across every nerve. It is the same dizzying feeling my magic gives me, and I lean into it.

"If I do reign"—Aurora's voice takes on a hard determination—"things will be different for you. They will not call you Dark Grace anymore. You will be Alyce. Just Alyce."

"Just Alyce," I echo, the words like sugared pastry crust on my tongue. Light and sweet and utterly impossible. But I gobble down every bit anyway. Even though I know I'll be sick.

"Advisor to the queen."

I yank myself free of her grasp, staring at Aurora like she's grown horns. "You don't mean that. You can't—"

"You are speaking to your future queen." She lifts her chin and looks down her nose at me in the exact manner her mother achieves. "And I can do whatever I like. I desire to have only the brightest minds at my table. There's no one more deserving."

Heat stings behind my eyes.

Much can change between the ascension of a princess to a queen, Kal had said. And I am leaving Briar. Aurora might soon be dead.

But there's no help for it. I feel as though I've drunk too much fizzy wine: tipsy and effervescent. And for the first time, I let myself envision it: Staying here. Aurora on the throne. Not needing to Shift to hide my face because I am elevated to a new rank. Respected. With Aurora, I could bury the Dark Grace without having to step foot on a ship.

"Will you accept, Alyce?"

Doubts and questions and a hundred thousand other thoughts send me reeling. But Aurora is my anchor. She takes my hand, interlacing our fingers, and I can't tell which wildfire pulse is hers and which is mine. I let my gaze linger on an errant curl that brushes the ledge of her jawline. I want to touch it. The soft spun-gold and the warm silk of her skin. Her lips part and I find myself leaning in, unable to feel anything but a rampant, reckless desire.

A draft of frigid wind slams into my back as the door to the Lair opens.

CHAPTER TWENTY-FIVE

Aurora springs away from me, drawing her hood close to her face and fleeing to the other side of the chamber. A cold panic explodes through every limb. We've been discovered. Aurora's guards have followed her here and will take me to the dungeons. The queen will have my head for defying her instructions.

But it's Laurel.

She hovers like one of Kal's shadows just inside the Lair, golden eyes like fireflies in the darkness. My mouth opens, emitting a sound between a whimper and a croak.

"Delphine retired for the night," Laurel says, dividing a look between me and Aurora's trembling back. "Your door was unlocked. I assumed you were free."

Damn it all to the sea and back. No one's come looking for me before.

"I— I am. The appointment ran longer than expected, but the patron is leaving."

Aurora has her scarf around her face and looks like she's about to bolt for the door.

"If that's a 'patron.'" Laurel crosses her arms. The walls of the Lair creak.

"Who else could it be?" The last syllable curves to a squeak. I clear my throat.

"Your book dealer, obviously." She points at the table, where a stack of the princess's latest haul is haphazardly arranged. "Is one of those for me?"

The books. Relief washes over me in a giddy wave, spilling out in a nervous screech of a laugh that makes Callow bridle and snap her beak. "Y-Yes. I almost forgot."

I grapple for the first book I see, *History of Briar*. There couldn't possibly be anything incriminating in it. Or anything Laurel doesn't already know, for that matter. She accepts it with a slight frown, dusting off the cover with the sleeve of her jade dressing gown and clicking her tongue at the state of the pages.

"Are you also the curator?" She throws the question at Aurora, who shakes her head emphatically. "Well, whoever is charged with the care of these volumes should be ashamed. These books are in disgraceful condition."

The princess nods. And the three of us just look at one another. I'm sure Laurel can hear the battering of my heart. Feel the ache of my breath trapped in my lungs. But she only utters a hasty good night and glides out, her eyes never leaving her new prize.

The moment the door closes behind her, Aurora and I

collapse into each other, sides aching with a mixture of laughter and tears.

It's late when I'm finally alone, and I want nothing more than to drag myself upstairs for a few hours of much needed sleep. But every inch of me is on fire, kindled by the memory of my almost-kiss with Aurora. If it was an almost-kiss. She mentioned nothing about it before she left. I was imagining things, I tell myself. I leaned into *her.* She would have shoved me away, disgusted that I'd even thought she could want me.

But when our faces were inches apart, she hadn't seemed disgusted. I can still see myself reflected in the lavender pools of her gaze. Smell the hints of lilac and appleblossom clinging to her skin.

Dragon take me.

Since I have no hope of sleep, I turn my attention to the commission the king wants, questioning for the thousandth time my decision to work for him. I want nothing to do with Tarkin if he's plotting against Aurora. But I have no doubt he will seek his revenge if I refuse. Whether I stay in Briar or escape beyond the sea, I'd rather like to keep my head.

I'm just finishing, packing the bracelet back into its box and writing a note for delivery, when, for the second time tonight, my door opens unexpectedly.

"Come back later," I say automatically. It's near dawn, I think. The servants must be rising for their morning chores.

"I do not require an invitation."

That voice stops me cold. Thick and resonant, with an

accent that reminds me of the wind in the trees and rushing water.

"Lord Endlewild."

Callow shrieks from her perch, flapping her wings.

The Fae lord steps out of the gloom, hearth light striking against the laurel-leaf sigil pinned to his doublet. Illuminating the winter white and icy blue streaks in his neatly tied queue, the colors changed since I last saw him. His birchwood staff taps against the stones of the floor. "Will you not invite me to sit, half-breed? Offer refreshment?"

Half-breed. The insult sears the same as it did every time he uttered it during my treatments. But I force myself to breathe through the phantom pains, resisting the urge to clutch at my scar. Remind myself that he is not holding me down or cutting me open. Even so, Endlewild hasn't been to see me in years, and never in the dead of night. Terror claws its way up from my toes and thuds between my ribs.

Callow feeds off my energy, pacing back and forth on her perch. More tiger than bird.

"Your bird dislikes me." Endlewild studies her like he's deciding whether to roast her for dinner.

I angle myself to block the kestrel from his view. "She distrusts strangers."

The tips of his dagger teeth gleam. "But we are not strangers, you and I. Will you not welcome me into your . . ." His nose wrinkles. "Abode?"

Rage smolders in my guts. I want to take that false Fae politeness and strangle him with it. But I know better than to refuse him. I motion toward the worktable. He deigns to sit, running one of his unsettling, sticklike fingers over the surface of the wood and flicking the grime away. Then he slides an expectant look at the leftover bread and cheese.

Hands shaking, I toss what's left of Aurora's wine goblet into the fire and pour him another, then shove the entire platter of food toward him.

"My thanks." He inspects a square of cheese and the lines bracketing his lips, like the grooves in a tree trunk, deepen. "You do not eat well here."

"Apologies." I don't even try to keep the sarcasm from my tone.

"It is no matter." He starts in on the bread, picking out bits of seed and letting them fall. "I have come regarding some recent incidents I find alarming."

It takes every thread of my self-control not to react. "Incidents?"

"Do not waste my time with lies." The orb on his staff flares, tingeing the glass amber. My skin prickles, knowing that the orb can also burn crimson. That it can leave smoking, blackened marks on my skin. "Duke Weltross's death was most suspicious."

"He was sick."

"Yes. And others have fallen ill in the palace of late. One of the king's ministers suddenly went blind. Another could hardly recall his own name. The healing Graces could do nothing to aid them." Wood creaks as he crosses one leg over the other and I catch the faint scent of his power—dewy grass and sticky-sweet nectar. "It reeks of Vila magic."

"I don't know what you're talking about."

He blinks slowly, like a reptile. "Did you know, that when

you were first discovered and brought to the Grace Council, I advised the Briar King to kill you?"

I curse myself for the way my shoulders hunch and my head drops, submitting to this creature the way I have a hundred thousand times before.

"He obviously did not heed my advice." The Etherian selects another bit of cheese and chews it thoughtfully. "Humans are always so fascinated by magic. And yours was a new toy for him to play with."

Wind rattles down the chimney. Cinders sizzle as they fly free of the hearth and onto the freezing stone floor. Callow cries out and strains against her tether.

"Why are you telling me this?"

"Such a demanding half-breed," he croons, using that tone that has haunted my nightmares for over a decade. "Such anger. It will serve you poorly. Become your undoing, if you are not careful."

The magic in the Etherian staff whirls in time to the tempest in my ears. Aurora said the source of the Fae lord's magic was in that staff. How sturdy is the glass protecting it? My power aches to find out.

"I was but a child when the War of the Fae ravaged Etheria and threatened my own. But I know well enough that Vila magic is unpredictable. The power of a half-breed is even more wild and untamed. I told Tarkin that perhaps at first you would only be able to create elixirs—a Dark Grace, as they call you. But one day, your power might truly manifest. And when it did, there was no end to the havoc you could wreak."

"You're saying you're afraid of me?"

Endlewild's cruel, catlike eyes narrow, his easy grace chipped at the edges. "I am saying that if I find you are more Vila than I first perceived, I will not hesitate to put you down. And not even the Briar King can stop me."

I don't grant him a response. Callow rages from her perch.

"It would be a kindness to you," he goes on. "You do not understand your power. It will consume you, Alyce. And take everything around you down with it."

My own name shudders through me, colder than any winter wind.

Lord Endlewild rises. "I will be keeping watch. I hope I do not have cause to return. Or"—he pauses at the door, his profile lit up by the magic of his staff—"perhaps I do hope so."

The door snicks closed behind him, a lingering scent of meadows and rain the only sign that he was ever here.

An all-too-familiar shame scalds my chest, coupled with a wave of fury so strong that I have to dig my fingernails into my flesh to keep from razing this Lair—this house, the entire realm—to rubble. But it's not just the Fae lord. I hate myself. Hate the fact that I still cower before the Etherian. That I still fear him.

In all my training with Kal, in my time with Aurora, I thought I had shed that weakness. But I'm no better than the child I once was. Huddled in the darkness, just waiting for the next kick to land.

Unable to reenter Lavender House lest the servants see the red limning my eyes, I untether Callow and curl up in a corner by the hearth. Whether through need or by command, I Shift as I did when I was a child, making myself as small and compact as possible. Callow scoots close to me, wedging her body in the warm crook of my neck.

And then I let myself drift in the inky waters of my despair, until my bell rings and announces my first patron of the day.

CHAPTER TWENTY-SIX

There's a party held that evening to honor one of Tarkin's newly minted generals, yet another excuse for the entire Grace District to drink their weight in wine until sunrise, and so my patron schedule empties shortly after midday. I know I won't be seeing Aurora, either, and so I snatch a few hours' rest, gather Callow, and escape to the black tower.

If Endlewild knew what I was doing with Kal, he would have made good on his threats. And probably burned the tower down for good measure. But I know his promise to watch me was not an idle one. And so after I'm clear of the Common District checkpoint, I push my Shifter magic to its limits. For the first time, I'm able to hold a Shift for longer than a few minutes. I become a beggar woman with a weathered face that not even the guards at the main gates bother to question. Still, I think I feel eyes on my back with every step.

Between lack of sleep, restless anxiety, and spent magic,

I'm a jumble of buzzing nerves by the time I reach the tower and let my Shift fall away. Callow sails ungracefully to the ground, complaining when she lands at an awkward angle.

"Haughty Fae beast," Kal spits out when I've told him of Endlewild's visit. "He has no right to threaten you. His kin murdered your own."

"It's not the first time he's threatened me, and I doubt it's the last." I pull my cloak closer against the shards of icy sea spray. "When I told you of my childhood—all the tests and treatments were done under Endlewild's direction. He wanted the Briar King to kill me when they found me. Now he's just waiting for an excuse to do it himself."

Kal tenses with each word, his shadows like spears in the dimness. "He will not kill you. Not as long as I live."

I don't see that there's much Kal can do from this prison, but I hold my tongue. The sentiment means more than I can say. "He can't prove anything about my power, otherwise he would have already executed me. And the Briar King doesn't want me dead—not yet." When I escape Briar, he might change his tune.

"That will not stop the Fae beast." Kal paces along the perimeter of the chamber, which is submerged in the deepening indigo of twilight. "Does he know you are part Shifter?"

"No." Of that much, I'm certain. Being half Vila is bad enough for the Fae lord. If he knew I shared the blood of another creature of Malterre, he would have slit my throat on the spot. "And I would never betray you."

Dragon knows I've wanted to tell Aurora about Kal often enough. But I can't trust that she wouldn't reveal Kal's existence, even by accident. And if Endlewild wants to kill me simply because of my ancestors' perceived crimes, I don't want to think about what he would do to Kal.

"I believe you." His shadows roll like a tide behind him. "But we must be more careful."

"I'll Shift every time I come. I managed it the whole way just now."

He beams, a brilliant slash of white in the gloam, and for a moment I let his pride fill me up, replacing the queasy dread that's plagued me for days. "Wonderful news. But it is not enough. Not quite."

That shot of happiness fades. "What else can I do?"

"I will teach you a new Shift. It is difficult, but I believe you have the potential to master it. And you must."

My magic wriggles, already eager for the challenge. To prove that I'm worthy of Kal's confidence. That I'll do anything to keep him—us—safe from Endlewild's claws. "What is it?"

His jet eyes glow. "I will teach you to be invisible."

Difficult is an understatement.

I'm already bone-tired from my sleepless nights, and my power was stretched as thin as spider's silk after I held the Shift on the way to the tower. The key to invisibility is focus. The Shifter must be in constant flux, altering herself with each step to reflect the changing environment. The best Shifters, Kal tells me, are able to remain invisible even at a run. Even on horseback. But it takes decades of practice and patience.

The Shift itself is excruciating, requiring precise concentration on a hundred details at once. An ache starts at my temples and hammers down my tender vertebrae, into the exhausted muscles of my shoulders. My joints don't want to re-form into the molds I bid them take, and they balk and buck at every command.

But I reach deeper, ignoring the way sinew and tendon threaten to snap. Thinking instead of Endlewild's easiness when he promised my death. Kal is right. There's nothing the Briar King can do to stop him. Endlewild is beholden to the Fae courts, not the mortal realm. And the Etherians wouldn't punish one of their own for ending a Vila.

Spurred by the rage the Fae lord always kindles in me, when the moon is only a handsbreadth above the silvered waves, I'm at last able to make one of my arms disappear. Only one.

My stomach growls.

"That is the third time your belly has complained in the last hour," Kal observes. "You need food. And it will be easier for you to slip into Briar before the sun rises."

I settle myself on the stump of a column instead, where Callow has made her perch for the night. She opens one eye, bleary and irritated, before ruffling her feathers and turning her back on me. The sea is calmer than usual. Far in the distance, I can see the ghostly outline of one of Briar's trading ships as it skates across the moon-kissed currents. Months ago, I'd been desperate to be aboard, starving for a life away from Briar.

It feels like years have passed since that day.

In the black silk of sea and starlight, I picture Aurora's face. The freckle nearly hidden on the shell of her ear. The tiny dimple creasing the right side of her mouth. Her lower lip, always slightly swollen because she bites it when she's thinking. As the details take shape, the break of the waves against the tower becomes her laugh. The breeze on my neck her touch.

She wants to make me her advisor. Me, sitting at council. Deciding what's best for the realm. Taking back all the power the former queens lost and funneling it into Aurora's reign. Finding ways to use my power that help instead of harm.

A shadow rustles my skirts, sending a shiver up my leg. Kal. I don't want to leave Aurora, but I don't want to lose him, either. Maybe I don't have to.

"Kal?" I hesitate, choosing my words carefully. After his speech about his distrust of the royals, I know he wouldn't approve of my time with the crown princess. "If I free you from this tower, would you consider staying in Briar?"

He turns slowly, shoulders tight. "You want to stay in Briar?"

"No." The salty air scrapes my lungs. "Maybe. I don't know."

Kal's brow rumples. He joins me at the column. "I thought leaving this realm was your deepest wish. Do you want the Fae lord watching you forever? The Briar King demanding curses from you whenever the whim strikes him?"

"Of course not." Before I can pull them back, my wild, intoxicating hopes spill free. "But what if Tarkin wasn't the

Briar King? What if Endlewild could be leashed? Banished, even?"

Questions flash in the depths of his obsidian eyes, like lightning building in the heavy underbelly of a storm cloud. "What do you have in mind, Alyce?"

"Nothing." I squirm against the half-truth. "But if Briar was different. If it was a better place for people like us—would you stay?"

I can hardly breathe, anticipating his answer.

"It was not a random choice, to put me in this particular tower," he says at last. One hand moves absently to his chest, tracing the outline of his medallion through his doublet. "There was a time, before these walls began to crumble, that I could climb to the upper floors and see all of the realm. Even glimpse part of Malterre—or what remained of it. Years after the war, black smoke still rose from the wreckage. I could smell the scorched flesh. Hear the screams of the dying."

A shudder races up from my toes. I huddle deeper into my cloak.

"They selected this place as my prison so that I *would* see and hear and smell those things. So that I would watch as my homeland disintegrated, powerless to stop it."

I close my eyes against the pain his words bring. Malterre was my homeland, too, even though I never set foot on the soil. I can't imagine what it must feel like to know that everyone you loved had died. That you had to live forever with their ghosts. I reach for Kal, but he avoids me, going to stand at the gap in the wall and look out at the sea.

"The war was a long time ago," he continues. "And I understand that things have changed. That they could change even more in the coming years." He gives me a meaningful look, as if he knows the crown princess is hidden in my words. Heat clambers up my neck and bursts across my cheeks. "But, no, Alyce. This land holds too many ill memories. And I could never ally with a realm that utterly destroyed my own."

Shame sinks its talons deep. He'll never be able to separate Aurora from the humans who poisoned Malterre. And how could I ask that of him? After everything he's seen? Perhaps I should feel the same. I still don't know who killed my mother. Endlewild will execute me as soon as he has the chance. With Briar as Etheria's ally, could anything really change?

"I cannot tell you what to do or how to feel." Kal takes my face in his hands, and ice crackles along my jawline at his touch. I taste the sharp bite of frost. "But sometimes, Alyce, you must choose a side."

CHAPTER TWENTY-SEVEN

"Y-your Grace?"

I slam the Nightseeker book closed with a yelp. I'd been poring over another ritual Aurora wants to try and hadn't even heard the door open. One of the housemaids hovers at the entrance, her hand still braced on the door handle, as if she's debating whether she ought to turn and bolt. I've half a mind to give her a reason to do it.

"Your Grace?" the trembling thing repeats.

Dragon's teeth, I hate it when the servants address me that way. They always make it sound like they're spitting out something sour. Or begging me not to kill them.

"Well, what is it?" I give her my best glower.

"Mistress Lavender says you're to come at once."

I glance at the clock on the mantel. I'm expecting a patron before long. She wouldn't dare take me away from the business of earning coin for the house. Not when the midyear Grace standings have our rank dipping below the middle—lower than it's been in years, apparently.

"What for?"

But the maid doesn't need to answer. A muffled ringing chips its way through the stone walls of my Lair. High and grating, one toll clanging after the other in a discordant loop.

The alarm bells. They're used only when there's a sudden squall or storm.

Or an attack.

I'm on my feet and pushing past the terrified girl in an instant. The house is in chaos, servants tripping over one another as they try to keep up with Mistress Lavender's frenzied demands. Rose and Marigold are huddled together whispering, their mink-lined Grace cloaks already fastened and hoods drawn. Another maid shoves my own black cloak into my hands before flitting to her next task.

"Alyce, there you are." Mistress Lavender is breathless. A fine sheen of sweat glistens on her neck like quicksilver. "There's no time to waste. Come now, the carriage is waiting. The sooner we leave, the better."

"But where are we going?"

Sunlight streams through the main parlor windows—no sign of a storm. And I can detect no sounds of battle or invasion, not that I would recognize them.

"It's a Grace." Laurel is beside me, her voice low. "She's on trial."

My stomach sinks, more for Laurel's sake than for mine.

"Another?" Grace trials are rare. The last incident was a year ago, in which a Grace was convicted of supplying vials of her blood to a smuggler to be sold in other realms. I'd heard about it through the other Graces. She'd been sentenced to spend the remainder of her gift in one of the stricter houses, all her profits ceded to the Crown. Though to Rose, the true punishment was the fact that the Grace was banned from parties and royal events.

But there hadn't been any alarm bells announcing her trial. And we certainly weren't summoned to watch.

Laurel nods, and I can see the same thoughts etched onto the sharp lines creasing her forehead. "I don't have a good feeling about this."

We're forced to abandon the carriage. The streets are too crowded for it to be of any use. Marigold is quite put out. But even her rambling complaints are drowned in the swell of rumor and gossip that eddies like a reeking tide pool around us.

I hear that this Grace accepted bribes. That she took a lover and provided him with elixirs for free. That she drugged the other Graces of her house and bled them in their sleep to steal their gifts.

With each snippet of speculation, Laurel's jaw clamps tighter. And though I have no love for the Graces, I can't help but feel sorry for her. What if it was a Vila on trial? My own mother, for the emerald in her blood? Kal?

It takes nearly an hour to pass through the palace gates and into the throne room. The entire Grace District must be here, nobles and Graces pressed against one another like pickled fish in a jar. For once, no one seems to notice me.

Not even the guards, who can barely keep to their posts for all the jostling of the citizens passing through.

The Graces are steered into the first-floor viewing area, the rest of the court looking down from the mezzanine. Mistress Lavender prods us forward until we're as close as possible to the low gilded railing separating the rest of the room from the royal dais and thrones. If Endlewild is here, I don't see him. King Tarkin and Queen Mariel are already seated. Tarkin looks exactly as Calliope had when the ratty dog succeeded in dragging Rose's breakfast plate from the table and gobbling up every crumb. But Mariel looks thin and drawn despite her Grace gifts. And she's restless, constantly rearranging the pendant at her throat or smoothing her skirts.

Beside them—a jolt flashes through me.

Aurora.

Her eyes are more blue than violet today, like forget-me-nots in a morning sun. But there's a gray cast to her skin. She scans the crowd and does a double take when her gaze passes over me. Her lips twitch like she wants to say something, but she only gives a barely perceptible dip of her chin, and then looks away.

"Whatever this is, I wish they would get on with it," Rose mutters in annoyance. But her hands quaver as she fluffs the lace at her neckline.

We don't have to wait long.

Tarkin rises and the suffocating room falls silent. I think I can hear the patter of a hundred Grace hearts.

"My court." Candied sunlight glints on the jewels in his rings. The Briar rose on his signet flashes scarlet. "Graces."

There's a tremulous ripple in the sea of gilded eyes and powdered necks. Mariel's knuckles on the arms of her throne go white.

"Would you not agree, Graces, that the Crown shelters you?" Tarkin pins a cerulean-haired Grace with his attention until she squeaks out an answer.

"Yes, Your Majesty."

"Do we not honor you with our patronage? Value you above all else in this realm?"

Other murmurs of assent, laced with a slinking undercurrent of unease. I can smell it in the air. Like rotting seaweed.

"Then I am utterly befuddled," the king goes on, false concern dripping from each word, a tone I recall from our meeting in the war room, "as to why one of you would want to openly flout the laws that keep you safe. Why you would bite the hand that so lovingly feeds you. Surely such flagrant disrespect cannot go unpunished." He lifts the chin of a pleasure Grace with two meaty fingers. "What say you?"

The Grace's deep brown skin is waxy beneath her armor of golden paint. She hesitates, but only for a heartbeat. "The realm is generous to us, Your Majesty. It deserves our service."

Tarkin weighs the words. The tips of his crown shine like spears.

"My thoughts exactly." He releases the Grace, and I can just glimpse her shoulders drooping. "We *deserve* your service. The Grace Laws are in effect for your protection. To keep those away who would want to monopolize your gift. To keep you here, in Briar, where we can make certain of your well-being. Where we can keep you in the comfortable lives every Grace should enjoy."

"Not my life," I mutter. Laurel elbows me.

Tarkin motions to Mariel. The Briar Queen sits taller at his recognition, but her expression remains stony. "My queen and I are much distressed, then, to learn of a Grace who has defied those laws—not once, but twice."

Graces pivot right and left like snared rabbits, desperate to discern which one of them might be missing.

A side door bursts open and a Grace is hauled inside between two guards. Her simple woolen dress—a far cry from the usual Grace wardrobe—is torn at the sleeves, dirt smeared at the knees and bodice. I know I've seen that shade of hair before. A deep russet, with bright threads of crimson and gold.

A name begins to rustle at the outskirts of the crowd as soon as it lands in my mind.

Narcisse.

The music Grace I met at Aurora's dinner.

Laurel's fingernails dig into my flesh.

"Narcisse." Even Tarkin's booming bass is hardly audible over the rush of mutterings and shifting bodies. "Of Willow House. You stand before your peers charged with violating the Grace Laws. What say you?"

The guards shove her to her knees. Narcisse cries out, the heels of her palms skidding against the jeweled marble floor. Mistress Lavender inhales sharply.

"I did not mean to offend Your Majesty." Her voice is barely more than a kitten's mewl. It has nothing of the melodious ring I heard when we met before.

Tarkin looks to the mezzanine of nobles and shrugs. "She did not mean to offend."

Laughter follows, and I wince. It's the same fanged sort of laughter that's hounded me for years.

"I find that hard to believe, Your Grace." Tarkin rubs his chin. "Seeing as this was not your first offense against the Crown." More mumblings from the nobles. Narcisse looks confused. "Indeed, two years ago, you were accused of refusing to use your gift. Isn't that right?"

"I— I—" Narcisse looks to her sisters, chin wobbling. But no one can help her now. "I was never charged. I made a mistake. I was afraid."

"Afraid?" Tarkin presses a hand to his heart. "What have you to fear in this realm?"

Laurel and I exchange a look. Everything. She has everything to fear.

Narcisse is weeping openly now, tears leaving tracks in the dirt on her face. "Willow House was slipping in the standings. I didn't want to be sent to a lesser house if my elixirs were weakening. And so I asked our housemistress if I could limit my patron appointments. But I never—" She chokes on a sob. "I was taking two dozen appointments a day. I would have Faded if my patron list didn't lessen."

Two dozen appointments. That's more than even Rose might see in a day. Do all the greater houses require such a schedule from their Graces? Narcisse was cruel to me at Aurora's dinner, carelessly so. But I'd never thought of what she might be enduring beneath her mask of haughty vanity.

"Do we not provide for our Faded Graces?" A trap wrapped in velvet.

"It isn't the same," Narcisse insists. "The best a Faded Grace can hope for is a marriage or to become a housemistress. But I couldn't count on either."

"And so you acted out of greed?"

"No." She shakes her head. Bits of copper dance in her hair. "No, I—"

But Tarkin doesn't let her go on. He circles her like a winged Fae-beast from a story, gluttonous and ready to dive. "And then, after we granted you *clemency* for your infraction—allowed you to keep working and earning in your house—you attempted to leave the realm. No doubt to sell your blood across the sea and grow rich."

Narcisse swallows. Musters the last of her strength. "It was the only thing I could do."

A splash of heat lands on my wrist. I look to Laurel. A single tear quivers at her jawline, glittering in the sunlight.

"It was not, in fact, the only thing." Tarkin's grin is wolfish. He knows he's won. "It was betrayal. Treason to the Crown. And you admit it." His attention swivels to his audience. "I've summoned you today"—he rubs his thumb over the Briar rose on his signet ring—"because these Grace trials grow tiresome."

Tiresome? It's rare to hear of a Grace facing punishment, much less being brought to trial. A few Graces around me look puzzled, too.

"I have consulted with the Grace Council, and we are in agreement. No matter how severe the punishment, Graces continue to break the law. I mean to stop it. Once and for all."

A few cheers sound from the mezzanine. Probably from the members of the Grace Council. Laurel stands straighter.

"Narcisse." Tarkin wears the same look he wore when commissioning my service, and a chill needles between my shoulder blades. "You attempted to steal from the Crown when you tried to remove yourself from the realm." More grunts of agreement from the nobles. "And so the Crown is just in taking what it rightfully owns. You, obviously, cannot be trusted."

Dozens of vibrant Grace heads bend toward one another, trying to sort out what the king means. I find Aurora. Her lips are pressed together into a firm line.

"You, Narcisse, have forfeited your gift. You will be bled until you Fade, your blood used immediately in elixirs for the Crown."

A heartbeat of stunned silence. And then the room explodes. The nobles are shouting and jeering. A few Graces faint, falling into one another like wilting flowers. Narcisse begins to wail, crumpling in a boneless puddle as the guards work to heave her upright.

"She will die!" a Grace pleads. "You will kill her!"

And it seems even a few of the nobles agree. Cries against the king's decision ring sharp and clear across the hall. Tarkin ignores them.

My arm wraps around Laurel's waist, expecting her to sway and falter. But she is rigid, steel-spined and eyes blazing. Mariel rubs her temples, her true age eating through the veil of countless Grace elixirs and revealing a bone-weary woman Leythana would not recognize as her kin. And

Aurora—Aurora looks like it is everything she can do to remain seated. She closes her eyes and breathes in short, staccato bursts as several healing Graces enter the hall.

"Remember." The king's voice soars above the muddle. "She brought this on herself." He jabs a finger at the Graces. "Let it be a warning."

As if struck by lightning, Narcisse flares to life and tries to bolt, bare feet slapping the marble as her earsplitting shrieks threaten to cleave me in half. The guards are faster, catching her around the middle and swinging her back as her legs kick in the air.

And then one of the healing Graces pulls on a pair of thick leather gloves. She produces a wooden box, opens the lid, and extracts the very same golden bracelet I cursed for the king.

The room tilts and I waver with it.

No, no, no, no.

Dragon's teeth, it was never a bracelet.

It was a shackle.

"No, no!" Narcisse's screams are knives of panic.

The healing Grace fixes the shackle to Narcisse's wrist. The paralysis curse hits instantly. Narcisse stills all at once, the echo of her wails ringing against my eardrums. The guards strap her to a table, and one of the healing Graces begins arranging a series of elaborate tubes. The other produces a long needle and punctures the fragile skin on the underside of Narcisse's elbow. And then her golden Grace blood begins to flow, gushing through the tubes and dribbling into waiting vials.

Marigold collapses at the sight of so much Grace blood lost. Years and years of gift. Rose doesn't move to help her. Like Laurel, Rose is all defiance and fury, her hands clenched into fists at her sides. But I see beneath the gilt powder on her cheeks and neck, the sallow ravages of the bloodrot. Know that what she's doing, trying to alter her power, is a violation of the Grace Laws. She could be in Narcisse's place in an instant.

Some of the Graces press toward the doors, but the guards keep them back. Not even the swooning Graces are carried out. Soon, the hall reeks of rancid bile and salty tears and thick, musty fear. Even the nobles are affected. Some clamor for Tarkin to ease the punishment once a half-dozen vials are filled with Narcisse's blood. He does not. Not until that sparkling river of gold dulls. Until the roots of Narcisse's fire-touched hair bleed silver. Only then are the doors opened and the rest of us allowed to file out, dazed and sick.

But I cannot move, transfixed by the sight of the shackle I cursed. I helped do this. Narcisse is unbound, her wooden limbs falling in unnatural angles as she slides from the table. No one even bothers to keep her head from smacking the tile. Tarkin is the one who ordered the bleeding, I tell myself. He would have done it with or without my curse. And yet he used it. He used me. And I let him.

As if called by my thoughts, the Briar King's gaze finds mine in the thinning crowd.

He dips his chin to me, and smiles.

• • •

I cannot think. My skin feels too tight for my body. Narcisse's screams chase me through the rest of the day and night. The sticky-sweet scent of her blood scalds my nostrils. The next morning, the Graces and I drift through the corridors of Lavender House in a fog. Even the patrons are skittish and avoid eye contact. Many of mine don't show.

With nothing to do, I ricochet around my Lair, biting my nails to bits as I count the hours until nightfall, when Mistress Lavender takes the Graces with her to a party given at another house. After what happened yesterday, I can't imagine that it will be much more than dull-eyed Graces drinking away the blood-soaked memories.

But the trial will soon be behind me. When I first began cursing items for the king, it was easy to convince myself that it was his hand committing the violence. The same way that it's my patrons who decide how to use the elixirs I craft for them. But watching my curse used against Narcisse, her stiff, splayed limbs and silver blood pooling beneath her . . . I can no longer deny my own responsibility.

There is only one thing to be done.

Once I'm sure the house is empty, I gather the largest, strongest sack I can find, race up to my room, and throw in what meager belongings I care about. A few spare, worn dresses. An extra cloak. Then I'm back in my Lair, shoveling all my earnings from my safe into the sack—years' worth of gold, plus the king's commissions. When I toss the last coin in, the damn sack is so heavy I cannot lift it. I Shift, sending strength into my back and shoulders and arms. The muscles grow hot, stretching and expanding and bulging against the fabric of my dress. When I'm done, the sack is as light as a pillow. I sling it onto one shoulder, then take Callow from her perch and settle her on the other. Her anxious talons dig into my flesh.

I creep around the back of the kitchen and through the side gate, my hood close around my face as I tear through the Grace District, dodging late-night deliveries and irritable carriage drivers. The oil lamps are lit, casting slick pools of light on the cobbled streets. My skin itches, instinct begging me to Shift to invisibility. But I don't think I could manage such a difficult Shift the whole way to the tower. And it would make me even more conspicuous—my sack and Callow floating in midair. So I settle on my beggar woman disguise, spine protesting as it hunches under the heavy sack.

I look back only once, when I pass through Briar's main gates for the last time. The moon tonight is high and full, bathing the Grace District in its ethereal light. The shadow of the palace falls hard on its rooftops. Torchlight flickers over the openmouthed dragon gargoyles perched on the palace's eaves and ripples over stained-glass windows. One of them is Aurora's.

My heart stutters, urging me for the first time away from this plan. I'd written her a dozen notes, tossing each one into the fire when my nerve failed. I can't explain to her why I'm leaving—that I'm little better than the Briar King's minion. That he will require worse from me, and I'll have little choice but to comply. Aurora would hate me. Coward that I am, I can't stomach the thought.

Callow ruffles her wings against my cheek.

It isn't safe for us here anymore.

But I whisper a vow that I will return when Aurora is queen. When things are different.

The tower is easy to spot, jutting up against the obsidian of the calm sea. My heart beats faster with every step. Knowing that what I'm about to do will change my life forever.

Moonlight streams through the gap in the wall, glinting off bits of broken stone in the staircase. The tattered banners billow and sigh in the night breeze like wraiths.

The darkness undulates and Kal materializes, his worried gaze divided between Callow and the sack I dump unceremoniously on the ground. "What is this?"

"We have to leave Briar." I let my Shift fade away and relax back to my true form, muscles cooling and skin shrinking. "Tell me how to break your bonds."

Kal can only stare. His shadow chains move at haphazard angles. "What happened?"

Quickly, I fill him in on Narcisse's trial and the shackle I cursed, one eye on the entrance to the tower as I do. Part of me believes Endlewild or the king's guard will storm in at any moment and drag me back to the castle to execute me or lock me in a cell. But there is only the lapping of waves on stone. The brine-stained, wintry kiss of the night.

"I thought I understood what I was doing. But I didn't expect . . . I didn't know—"

"There is no need to explain." Kal's shadows coil into him. He pauses, looking out at the clear, star-crusted night sky. "And I agree. The king's requests will only worsen. I do not want him thinking you are a pawn he can control. But are you certain this is what you want? The last time we spoke it seemed—"

"No." I cut him off so suddenly that Callow clacks her annoyance. "It's time. I have enough gold for us to board the next ship out. The only thing left is to break your bindings—if I can."

He closes the distance between us. "You already know what to do."

"Can't you tell me anything more than that?"

But that infuriating stillness engulfs him again. His lips mash together until they're bloodless.

"Of course you can't," I mutter, raking my hands through my hair in frustration. "What kind of prison would it be if you could tell someone how to free you?"

I begin to pace back and forth, wracking my mind for what I know about Kal's past and his bindings. As if they know they're the subject of scrutiny, the dark tendrils curve and wend in a macabre dance around his body. My magic strains in its cage, aching to tear them to pieces. Grind them to dust.

I wheel to a halt, upsetting Callow.

Perhaps I can do just that.

The enchantment is bred from magic. And I can find magic. Control it. My power is Vila. Strong enough to build Malterre. To create an entire race even the Etherians could not crush.

Cobbling together what little confidence I have, I focus

on the writhing shadows, reaching my magic out to find theirs. It connects almost instantly. But instead of another cord or a beating heart, I feel a wall of black stone like those of this tower. Slimy and ancient and impenetrable. Protections, I realize, put in place to guard the enchantment.

But they will not stand against me.

With everything I have, I push against the walls of power. The shadows groan and creak, as if they are made of rusted iron. Kal winces, his body tightening. The enchantment gives way another inch beneath the pressure of my magic. Then another. My limbs begin to shake, sweat pouring down my neck and soaking the back of my dress. But I will not give in. I *will* sever these chains. The groaning intensifies, like nails against glass. The scent of ice and frosted stone that I know is the enchantment's magic burns in my lungs. I'm getting closer. The protections are so thin now. Beneath them, I can feel the brittle heart of the enchantment thrumming. All I need do is—

The sound hits before the pain. It's a whip-crack in the thick, misty air. I am thrown backward, my concentration broken. My back finds the opposite wall of the tower and my spine and skull connect with stone. My vision blares white. All I can think or see or feel is white. And then red. And then pain. Then nothing.

The moon is sinking when I finally come to. Callow nips at my elbows. Walks her taloned feet across my stomach, clucking like a worried hen. I'm crumpled in a shaft of chalky winter moonlight. My head is filled with molten lead. Embers smolder behind my eyelids. Every fiber of my body screams, like it's been cut to pieces and hastily sewn back together. And not well. There's a taste of ash and blood in my mouth. The lingering scent of charred wood. My tongue is sore. My teeth feel loose.

As soon as I am able, I drag myself out of the light and into Kal's embrace. His mercifully cool fingers stroke my hair and knead the angry muscles of my neck and shoulders.

"I should not have let you do that," he says over and over. "I am a selfish fool. You could have died." His voice breaks. "It would have been my fault."

I open my mouth to croak out a reply. But he pulls me closer.

"I want you to go, Alyce." He lifts me up so that I'm eye level. "You have the gold. The means. The cleverness. The harbor is not far from here. Hire a boat and leave while you can."

His reason is so tempting, especially now, when I'm spent and broken. But then a shadow slinks around Kal's wrist, like a shackle. Like Narcisse's shackle. A wind gusts in through the hole in the wall and billows my skirts. Somewhere, a rotting piece of this crumbling tower falls.

"You'll die if I leave you here."

He doesn't argue. Just runs his knuckles down the side of my face, pain and regret warring behind his eyes. "You will die if you stay."

"I'm not dead yet." Ignoring the hundred hammers in my head, I drag myself to stand. "And I won't let you die, either. Just a little longer. More training. That's all I need."

Until then I just have to hope the Briar King doesn't issue

another commission. And that I can keep the Fae lord's ruthless, gilded gaze off my back.

Dragon's teeth, this is a mess. I prod at a tender spot just above my ankle, discovering a developing bruise already the color and shape of an eggplant.

"Alyce," Kal says, so quietly it's almost lost beneath the cresting waves. "Just promise me one thing."

"Anything."

His shadows spread like wings behind his back. "Do not leave without saying goodbye."

CHAPTER TWENTY-EIGHT

It takes a long time to trudge back through Briar after that. My power is almost completely wasted, resulting in a weak Shift that is quickly slipping out of my control. Streaks of charcoal smudge the horizon as I reach Lavender House.

But when I arrive at my Lair I find I am not alone.

"Alyce?"

Callow screeches and flaps her wings, her feathers rough against the side of my face. I wheel around, dropping my sack as panic slices through the last, threadbare strings of my Shift. A hooded figure emerges from the wall of garden hedges, eyes bright even in the dimness of the morning. Eyes I'd know anywhere.

"Aurora? What in Briar—"

She hurries closer, glancing about to check for others. "I came to see you, but your servant was out and your door was locked."

"And so you waited all night?" How long had I been gone? Four hours? Six?

She shrugs, as if freezing to death in the bushes was the most natural thing in the world to do. "I wanted to make sure you were all right."

"I'm not," I grumble, unlocking the door and kicking the sack inside.

"Let me help you." She's dragging the damn thing in before I can stop her, grunting with the effort. "What do you have in here?"

But she gets her answer when part of the fabric snags on a nail in the doorway and splits. Several coins spill out. Aurora's brows draw together. She wriggles open the strings and gapes. Even in this gloomy dawn, the contents gild her cheeks.

"Alyce," she breathes. "Where did you get all this? And where were you going with it? This is enough to . . . to—" Her lips fall open. "Were you going to leave Briar? Leave me?"

Dragon's fucking teeth. She may as well have skewered me and roasted my traitorous body over my own hearth. And I'm too much of a coward to answer, instead busying myself with transferring Callow to her perch. Anything to keep from looking at Aurora.

"Is it because of the trial?"

Narcisse flits between us, my Lair suddenly far colder. I fuss with the hearth, striking a match and goading a weak flame. I can't tell her the real reason I wanted—needed—to flee. Or of the agony that consumes me now that I can't.

"Alyce, you can't leave. It's too dangerous. If my father finds out—and he will—he'll . . ." A thousand horrible possibilities swirl together in the heavy pause that follows. "I can't watch him do to you what he did to that Grace. I understand that—"

"What do you understand?" She looks at me as if I've struck her. "Do you know what it's like to live at the mercy of someone who can take everything away from you whenever it suits him?"

Her jaw sets as her shock heats to anger. "Perhaps not as well as you do, but yes. A little. You think I don't want to run away? From suitors and a cloistered life and the constant judgment and criticism of court?"

"I thought you wanted to be queen."

"Yes, but it's not the life I would seek for myself if I could choose. And after yesterday, when—"

"A Grace was nearly bled to death in your throne room?" I'm being cruel, but I don't care. Tarkin certainly didn't.

She flinches. "It's not my throne room. Not yet. And believe me, Briar is the last place I want to be right now. But when it is my turn . . ." She squares her shoulders. And not for the first time, I see the queen she will be one day. "Nothing like that is ever going to happen again."

My anger ebbs a little, souring to guilt. The trial wasn't Aurora's doing and I shouldn't punish her for it. "That was a callous thing to say. I'm sorry. It's just that it was . . ." An image of Narcisse, the bracelet I cursed clamped around her wrist, rears in my mind. Of Tarkin's delight as he watched vial after vial fill with her gift.

Callow's tether jangles.

"Awful." Aurora slumps onto a chair. "It was awful. I didn't know until just before. I argued with my father. Tried to stop him. His mind was made up."

That doesn't surprise me. The last of the fight goes out of me and I sit beside her. "It wasn't your fault."

She watches Callow. "Then why does it feel like it is?"

"Because you're a good person. And you'll make a great queen."

"Not if I'm dead." She traces circles over the place where her curse mark rests. "I kissed fifty men yesterday, and all that broke in me was my spirit."

Fifty. Would that I could let Callow return the favor to each of them.

"Don't." I put my hand over hers, stilling it. "You said you weren't going to give up. Your idea about the Etherium mines was better than anything this realm has done in my lifetime."

"It wasn't my idea, really," she says. "It was Elias's. He thinks that—"

My skin crawls. "Elias?"

Aurora gives me a look that Laurel sometimes reserves for Marigold. "The prince from Ryna. We've been writing. You know that."

The fire spits at us and Callow grumbles. "Yes. But you've never called him Elias before. Only the Ryna prince."

"Well, his name is Elias." The tiny beat of pulse at Aurora's throat quickens. "I don't see that there's anything wrong with using it."

There isn't. But something lurks beneath her words, and I do not like it. I think of the last time she was here, when we'd almost—

What a wretched fool I am. Too blind to see that I'm only a means to an end for the crown princess. A distraction until the right man arrives and breaks her curse.

"I suppose there won't be anything wrong with kissing him, either."

The sentence hangs between us, swiftly growing fangs.

"I don't know that I have much choice in kissing him," she replies slowly. "I can't exactly refuse my suitors."

"You swore you wanted to rule alone."

"I do." She flings a gesture at the trunk where we hide the Nightseeker books. "Why would I go to the trouble of all our work if I didn't?"

"I don't know." Anger builds inside me, picking up speed. I haul my sack of gold over to my safe and begin chucking the coins inside. Gold smacks against stone. "But this is different. You've never written to any of your other suitors before. Never learned their names or cared what they thought."

She doesn't argue. Tension masses around us, between us, like a storm lumbering in from the sea.

"Can you blame me if I do hope, just a little?"

I shove away from the safe and wheel to face her, my blood roiling in a way it never has with Aurora before. "So you're not interested in breaking the curse yourself anymore?"

"That isn't fair." Two spots of pink burst on her cheeks.

"Maybe not." I sense the recklessness driving me on and

I tell myself to back away. But I don't listen. I never do. "But it's the truth. A princess needs her prince."

Aurora blinks back tears, but her tone is hard as flint. "Why are you doing this?"

"Because I thought you were different. I thought you wanted Briar to be different."

I thought you cared for me.

"I am. And I do." She stands and paces in front of the hearth. "I also want to break this curse. And we're nowhere closer than we were when we started. I have months left. If Elias can break the curse, so be it."

I snort. "I'm sure his silk trade helps. More money for balls and gowns. You should tell him to hurry. Pay for a faster ship to go and fetch him."

The splotches on her cheeks blaze crimson. For a moment I think she will lash back at me. But then a single tear tracks down her cheek. It might as well be an ocean. I will drown in it.

"Enough," she whispers. "I won't do this anymore. Not with you."

And it's only now that I see just how tired she looks. The Grace elixirs keep her skin supple and healthy. But there are fine, dark lines under her eyes. A midnight tinge of exhaustion behind the violet. The hearth light illuminates the subtle hollows of her cheeks.

"If he breaks the curse," she continues after a while. "And that's in no way certain. I still want you by my side." Aurora kneels on the grime-slick stone next to me and catches my wrists in her warm hands. "I always will."

A smile falters on my lips. Aurora is sheltered and privileged. She means well, but she has no idea of the ugliness of the real world. Of my world. If this prince—*Elias*—breaks her curse, I do not know what she will do. But the vision of myself as her advisor, of a life in a realm that does not despise me, is already disintegrating. And as the pieces crumble to ash, I find that I cannot depend on what the future Queen Aurora might decide.

There is no one but myself.

CHAPTER TWENTY-NINE

Over the next few weeks, I funnel every free second into practicing my Vila powers. Teasing my fire into specific shapes and colors. Giving brief life to a tiny set of armor I find on a shelf in a parlor and even turning stolen quills into miniature swords. Anything that requires me to find deeply hidden magic and strengthen my control. I refuse to be in Briar when Elias arrives, which can't be long now. I won't watch him break Aurora's curse and burrow like an eel into her heart.

The princess visits only once. She is distant and taciturn, barely glancing at the armload of books she brings as she hands them to me, the fissures that formed during our last visit still raw. And she doesn't even stay long, making some feeble excuse to get back to the palace when she used to stay practically the whole night, no matter what time her maids were scheduled to wake her the next day. If she doesn't want to see me anymore, I wish she would just stop coming. It would be easier on both of us. But I don't say that, coward that I am. Just watch her disappear into the night as if she's one of the ships leaving the harbor.

A blizzard shoves in from the sea on the day of the Grace competition, its punishing winds battering the walls of Lavender House and smothering Briar beneath a snowfall so thick we can barely see the gates of our garden. My Lair is frozen solid, the fire utterly useless, no matter how many logs I pile up. Luckily, I have no patrons brave enough to face the weather. And so I move my miserable animals up to my attic room and hole up in the main parlor, hibernating under a mountain of furs.

Rose is implacable. She launches from room to room, squawking about how her enhancements aren't fresh enough. Her kit is misplaced. Something is missing from her stores. I don't envy the mousy servant who is herded out the front door with strict instructions not to return without Rose's exact requirements. I pray for his sake that Hilde is open.

It's a relief to everyone when Mistress Lavender at last announces that she's secured a snow carriage and that it's time to depart.

I can't help but notice Rose's face just before she hurries out the door. She's chosen a thick brocade gown the same color as her name, with golden ribbons latticed across the bodice. Her skin sparkles with Grace powder, as if dusted with fallen stars. Her eyes are limned in the stuff, even her eyelashes gilded. Every inch a Grace. But her movements are jerky and rapid, like an animal deciding whether to fight or flee. Desperate. As if she can feel me watching, her gaze cuts to mine. She scowls, daring me to call her out.

"Good luck," I say. Meaning it, for some unfathomable reason.

She only snorts, fastens the clasp of her mink-lined cloak, embroidered Briar rose sigil winking in the lantern light, and sails away.

Alone, I am restless. The Lair is too cold to work in, and I am desperate for something to do. I move up to my attic, thinking to look through some of Aurora's books, or read Kal's again, to remind myself of my true heritage. But the words slide under my eyes without sticking. Even Callow prefers to sleep rather than keep me company, the peevish thing. All I can think about is Kal and Aurora and Endlewild and the damned Ryna prince who is probably on his way across the sea right now. Maybe his ship will sink.

From my bed, I watch the snow still falling outside my window. It's too thick to glimpse the lights of the palace in the distance. The air too heavy to hear the music that sometimes floats from those royal parties. Aurora is there, I have no doubt. Once the prince arrives, there will be a wedding. And soon the time we spent together here will only be a memory. Her husband will not tolerate someone like me as an advisor. And Aurora will marry him, regardless of what she says.

Another bout of infernal tears scalds my eyelids, and I hate myself for it. The princess is impulsive, used to having countless toys at her disposal. I was one of them. Entertaining until the stuffing leaked from my seams.

I devour another cranberry tart, giving in to my own self-pity, even though I know I need to focus on Kal. On life after Briar, when I can shed the mantle of Dark Grace forever.

A crash downstairs startles me. I sit up straight, swiping crumbs from my lips with the back of my hand. I'm sure it was a servant. A dropped tray or a toppled chair.

Another crash.

The clatter of porcelain breaking. And then the dull thump of something heavy hitting the floor. I scramble out from beneath my blankets. Is it Endlewild? Has he come to kill me, as he swore he would if he found out about my Vila power?

I will kill him first, a feral part of my soul vows.

I hardly feel the steps beneath my feet as I slink down the stairs. The house is dark, with only a single taper lit at the front entrance for the Graces' return, which won't be for hours yet.

Where are the servants? Why haven't they come running?

The parlor at the end of the hall is bright, light from the cracked door spilling into the gloom. It's Rose's. Why would Endlewild be skulking in there?

Adrenaline rises to a high pitch as I approach the door. My magic is ready. I grip it as one would a sword hilt, ready to lash out at the slightest hint of danger.

Peering through the slit in the door, I hold my breath, worried Endlewild can hear even that. But there is nothing. The room is vacant. A vase is shattered on the floor. Grace-grown peonies, colors still changing from fuchsia to violet, lie in the wreckage. The armchair by the fire is overturned. And that's when I see it. The heel of a shoe. A rose-petal pink shoe.

I burst into the room. It's not Endlewild. No intruder at all. Sprawled on the floor, her beribboned gown sodden and ruined with muddy snow stains, is Rose.

And spreading beneath her, faster than I thought possible, is a puddle of glittering, golden blood.

"Rose!" I roll her over and slap her cheeks. She moans and tosses her head. One of her hands is bleeding, more than any hand wound ought to bleed, the source of the blood I'm kneeling in.

I keep calling her name, tearing off a strip of her petticoat and winding it around the slash in her palm. With the Grace powder caked on her skin, it's hard to tell how large the wound is. I count to three and the blood has already eaten through the wrapping.

The damn bloodrot, I realize instantly.

"You stupid fool," I curse at her, tearing off more petticoat and trying to rebind her hand. It's useless. "Where are the damn servants?"

"Sent them away." Rose's words slur together.

I roll my eyes, unsurprised. "Well, I'm fetching them."

"No." A crinkle forms between her brows. Her skin is like ice, lips tinged dark amber. Had she walked here? "No one can see."

Leave it to Rose to be concerned about appearances even in a moment as dire as this. But it's more than that. I haven't seen this much Grace blood spilled at once since Narcisse's trial. I wince at the memory of the molten gold dripping into the vials. The sound of Narcisse's skull hitting the marble. If I don't help, it will be Rose's blood tingeing silver.

"Damn it, Rose." I wiggle my arms under Rose's shoulders and haul her upright. She can stand, but barely, leaning most of her weight on me as I lead her out of the parlor, through the kitchen, and out the back door to my Lair. Her bandage is leaking, so I press her hand into her chest to catch the blood.

"It's c-cold," she stammers as I settle her in a chair by the hearth. It's only embers now and I stoke it, adding three logs.

"There's nowhere else to go. If you don't want anyone to see."

She quiets.

Quickly, I gather what I need from my stores. I'm no healing Grace, but I've burned and cut and bruised myself often enough doing my own work to have picked up some tricks to treat wounds. I just hope it's enough.

Her hand is a wet, garish mess when I return. She winces as I unwrap the makeshift bandage, resting her head on the back of the chair as her eyes flutter closed.

"Wake up," I say, thrusting a bottle of potent beetle dung under her nose. She curses, slapping my hand away and groaning.

"You'll thank me when you don't die."

Rose looks from me to her hand, face shading impossibly whiter under her thick layer of powder. "All that blood," she whimpers. "Just gone."

"Don't think about that," I say, digging out a handful of balmwood moss and pressing it hard into the cut. But I know she won't be able to think about anything else. The rug in the parlor was soaked. And who knows how much she lost before I found her. It could be years of her power drained away. Rose has been among the highest-ranking beauty Graces since she Bloomed. She had every chance of beating Pearl for the role of Royal Grace. But not after tonight. "What are you even doing here? You should be at the competition."

"I left."

"Because you won so handily?" I can't seem to resist the urge to bait her. "Why aren't you at the reception?"

Rose curses again as I pack down a fresh layer of moss. It seems to be working. The blood is slowing.

"If you must know, I didn't make it past the first round." Her whole body stiffens under my hands, the hollows of her collarbone deepening. "I couldn't even turn Lady Elipsa's hair a decent shade of ruby. And the other Graces . . ."

The walls of the Lair creak against the blizzard.

"It's because you've weakened yourself," I tell her, almost gently. The blood has finally clotted. I remove the moss and make to rinse the wound with a mix of mint water and chamomile leaves. "By taking those thinners and running yourself ragged."

"I stopped taking them," she snaps, trying to wrench her hand away.

"Be still or you'll open the wound!"

She relaxes, but glares. "I stopped. I knew my power needed to be at its most potent."

"It doesn't work that way." The water in my bowl is yellowing with her blood. "You can't just stop taking something like bloodrot without consequence. You'd been dosing yourself too long. You needed to taper off."

A jewel in one of her Briar rose earrings glimmers. "No one told me that."

"I'm sure they didn't." I dab at the slash on her skin. "Let me guess, you kept adding more blood to the elixir at the contest, hoping to make it stronger. And then—"

"It wouldn't stop," she confirms, trying and failing to keep a tremor out of her voice. "It just kept coming. I barely made it out of the hall without anyone noticing."

A strange sort of sympathy takes shape inside of me. But it is pointy-edged and uncomfortable. "Lucky for you, they probably all thought you were sullen and pouting."

She kicks me, but doesn't argue.

"How did you get home?"

"A carriage. Not one from the palace. I walked part of the way. I couldn't let anyone know."

"You're lucky you didn't die in the storm. Bleed out on the street."

"I understand, *Malyce*." Her usual venom returns. "I don't need a lecture from someone with green blood."

Much as I try to deflect it, the jab lands on a sore spot. But I hold my tongue. For a while, there is only tense silence. The fire pops and spits, doing little to combat the cold. The wind howls outside, moans down the chimney and into the room.

"Are you almost done?" Rose rubs her uninjured hand over her other arm, trying to warm herself. "I need to clean up the parlor before the servants find it."

"Why do you hate me?"

The question takes us both by surprise. She blinks a few

times. But she doesn't deny it. "You have no idea what it's like to be a Grace."

I nearly drop the bottle of rosewood ointment. "*That's* why you hate me? Because I'm not you?"

Rose flushes, the first color I've seen on her face since I picked her up off the floor. "I might have bled out five years of my gift on my own parlor rug. Five years, maybe more, when I could have beaten Pearl tonight. Will your gift ever Fade?"

The truth needles between my shoulder blades. "I don't know. Probably."

But I am Vila and Shifter, and will wield magic until my dying breath. Which, because I do share the blood of my ancestors, is a very long time from now.

"It won't," Rose snarls, as if reading my thoughts. And for a moment I'm sure she knows about me. But it's suspicion, not conviction, that paces behind her gaze. "Vilas don't Fade, even if you are only a half-breed. You will always be strong and powerful, even if everything you do is ugly."

"You—" The wheels of my mind click and spin. "You're *jealous* of me?"

Rose's color deepens. "Of course not."

But she is. I can see it in the shape of her shoulders, bowed and defensive. In the way she is suddenly fascinated with the books on my shelves. Rose, who has tormented me all of my life, always rubbing my nose in her precious golden blood, is jealous. A feeling I do not recognize simmers behind my sternum.

"I always wanted to be one of you," I say softly, unsure why I'm offering her this bit of myself. Her attention lashes back to me, sharp as a whip. "To craft beauty and charm and to make people love me instead of—" I bite the inside of my cheek. "We're not as different as you think. I'm a prisoner, too."

"I'm not a prisoner," Rose says quickly. Automatically—as if she's said it often to others. Or to herself.

"Aren't you?" I finish applying the ointment to her hand and begin to wrap it with a clean cloth. "Forced by law to spend your gift on nobles who have little interest in you once you've Faded? I was at the trial, too. What they did to Narcisse was . . ." I can't bring myself to go on. Narcisse's ghostly presence flickers between us. "You're worth more than your blood."

Rose scoffs. "You sound like Laurel. Soft and weak. We're nothing without our gifts. What do you think would have happened to you if that grotesque shade of green didn't mean you had power? You would have been killed. A mongrel not worth her own breath." The rage in my veins burns hotter. My wrapping is brutal, too tight. But I don't ease up. Rose doesn't, either. "And I've read my birth records. I would have been a sailor's daughter had I not been gifted. I would have had no fine things. No admirers or importance. I'd be barely better than the fish sold in the Common District. I want more than that. And so would you, if you had any sense."

"I have sense enough to know when I'm being used." I tie up the bandage roughly enough to make her yelp. "What the royals give, they can take away. And they will—as soon as it suits them. Just as they did to Narcisse."

For half a breath, I think I see anguish flash behind her

Fae-blessed eyes. Her fingers twitch, like she wants to reach out to me. But I must have imagined it. "If you're finished," she says, familiar acid back in her tone, "I need to go."

"You're not going anywhere but to bed." I toss the bloodied water into the fire. Ochre steam rises. Rose looks sick.

"The rug—"

"I'll clean it." Dragon knows why. I'm feeling generous, I suppose. Or I know what it's like to want out of your life so badly you'll do something desperate. Whatever the reason, it's not to ingratiate me in Rose's eyes. She doesn't even thank me.

Rose stands, still unsteady on her feet. She runs a shaky hand through the remains of her chignon and my insides clench.

"Rose."

"What is it?" she snaps.

I approach her slowly, as one would a cornered animal, and reach my fingers into her snow-matted ringlets.

"What is it?" But the question wobbles in a way that tells me she already knows.

Carefully, I tug a lock free, stretching it out under Rose's nose. She doesn't scream, but her mouth hangs open. And then a horrible, inhuman keening escapes her.

The once vibrant-pink curl is silver.

CHAPTER THIRTY

If any of the servants saw the evidence of Rose's accident before I cleaned her parlor, they have the good sense not to let on. It had taken me until the small hours of the morning to finish scrubbing the blood from the rug, marveling at my own stupidity all the while. A parting gift, I kept telling myself—not that Rose deserves one.

Before I herded her upstairs, Rose had taken a pair of my scissors and cut her silver streak, close to her scalp so her dressing maid wouldn't see any traces of the telltale color. It could have been the shock of losing so much of her blood so quickly that made her hair turn. She kept telling me so as I helped her to bed, shaking and whimpering and entirely unlike the Rose I've known for the past several years. For her sake, I hope it does grow back as rosy as ever. If not—a chill goes through me when I think of what she might do. Of her face at breakfast the next morning, when she found out Pearl was chosen as the ascending Royal Grace. The slump of her shoulders when Mistress Lavender offered threadbare condolences laced with disappointment about the loss for our house standings.

It makes no sense for me to feel pity for someone who has made my life a living hell since she stepped through the gates of Lavender House. But I do. Rose's gift is the only thing that makes her feel in control of her destiny. And it's slipping away.

A few days after the incident, I'm in my Lair, adding to my patron log—a fat book that I'll turn in to Mistress Lavender at the end of the month. Inside the wide columns, I note the kinds of elixirs I was asked to create, as well as the amount of blood I'd spilled, in drops, for each. Every Grace is required to report these details to her housemistress and the Grace Council, who then use the information to determine the strength of a Grace. Concerns arise when a Grace who once needed only three drops of blood to craft an elixir begins to need four or more. Or when her elixirs begin to Fade faster than in the past.

Given the pressure of house standings and the ever-present fear of Fading, it's tempting for Graces to lie about the amount of blood they expend per elixir. Rose has accused Pearl of such deceit when she thinks only Marigold can hear her. But if Pearl is lying, the Grace Council would know soon enough. Patrons aren't shy of lodging complaints with housemistresses if their elixirs wear off quickly or don't manifest as intended. And after Narcisse, I'm not sure if any Grace will be brave enough to anger the Crown by being caught in such a scheme.

There's a knock at my door and I admit a waifish servant carrying my earnings in a black velvet pouch. I take it and wave him off, spilling the contents onto the open pages of my book and counting. One hundred gold, more than a usual week's work. My patrons, it seems, are noticing my growing power. My schedule lengthens by the day. Let them take advantage of it while they can. The Dark Grace will not be in residence for much longer.

Sighing, I sweep the gold back into the pouch and go to add it to the rest. But when I unlock my safe, I freeze. The space inside, which houses all my years of earnings—the profit from every drop I spilled in service to a patron—is empty.

A small black box leers at me instead, a matching envelope resting on top.

Cold flashes across every nerve.

I lift the lid. It's satin-lined, the color like slick mortal blood. Nestled within the folds are a half-dozen brooches. Thin gold whorls and twists into the shape of a dragon, scales set with a myriad of opals and sapphires that flash in the hearth light.

I tear open the envelope:

The wearer dies an untraceable death.

A mad rushing—like a storm over the sea—roars in my ears. I cannot breathe. Cannot think. I'm back in the throne room after Narcisse's trial, Tarkin smiling at me in that calculating way that stripped me bare.

He knew.

He found out that I was trying to leave Briar and he took my gold so that I couldn't book passage on a ship. The message is so clear he might as well be screaming it from the palace. My throat clogs, an iron weight clamping around my neck and tightening with each breath. Tarkin's collared beast. That's what I am.

But how did he know? I've combed through the possibilities often enough, trying to figure out how his servants found a way into my Lair when they left his commissions. They also knew where I kept my safe. Discovered my plan to escape. But I've noticed no one lurking. No repeat patrons or new servants.

Unless.

The cord of my magic undulates.

It was someone inside Lavender House.

The kitchen staff scatters in my wake. Even surly Cook veers out of my way without bluster. A flighty maid drops an egg with a strangled cry and I don't even bother to dodge the splattered yolk. The other Graces are in the main parlor. I can hear their easy conversation. The high pitch of Mistress Lavender's vapid laughter. I plow through the glass-paned doors.

"Which one of you was it?" Rage crackles in the pounding of my pulse at my wrists. At the underside of my jaw. In my chest. It is everything I can do to keep my power contained.

The chatter dies, four pairs of eyes pivoting to my entrance. Mistress Lavender pales to a watery gray, her teacup frozen in mid-sip. I see myself in the silver of her gaze. Wild-eyed and hair flying. Teeth bared. A monster.

Laurel sets down her biscuit.

"What's happened?" she asks, unnervingly calm as her gift of wisdom guides her.

My magic is ready to explode. Ready to unleash my worst on these women who have caged me in this house my entire life and have now ruined my only means of escape.

"Someone has been spying on me. They've taken my earnings." I launch the words like daggers, watching carefully to see who bleeds. "Everything is gone."

Mistress Lavender lowers her cup, the soft clink of china like a thunderclap in the charged silence. "Are you certain?"

"Yes, I'm *certain*. It was all there a few days ago, more than twenty thousand gold, and now it isn't."

"Perhaps you miscounted." Rose remains stoic, unruffled. My first and only suspect.

She's jealous of my power, which will always be stronger than hers. It's not hard to guess that she'd be prowling about the house, watching me and reporting back to the king. And she'd been in my Lair the night of her accident. Had she seen where I kept my gold? But how? The questions trip over one another until I can't tell one from the next.

"Or she spent it." Marigold nibbles a scone. "Honestly, between you and Laurel, you spend your coin on the strangest things. I wouldn't be surprised at all if you lost track." She titters, but no one joins her.

"Twenty thousand is quite the sum." Mistress Lavender's brows draw together, and I can almost see the numbers running through her mind. "We are, of course, happy to search the house. The servants' quarters. And why don't you let me count what you have and compare it to our ledger? Just to make sure you're not mistaken. That's such a large amount, Alyce."

"Did you not hear me? I have nothing. *All* of it is—" My mistake registers like a shot firing. The twenty thousand included the king's payments. If she tallies up my earnings for the past years, even if I never spent a copper, she'll know I claimed more than I'm supposed to have. Panic douses my wrath. I'm such a fool.

"What a good idea. It should be easy to prove it that way. Unless you did spend it." Rose adjusts her necklace—a string of rare pink pearls only found on the shores of Cardon. "Or unless you're taking on unreported patrons."

Even Marigold gasps at the implication. Under the Grace Laws, patrons and earnings must be reported. In theory, this is to ensure that the Graces receive their rightful coin and to prevent anyone from abusing the system, as when Graces were bought by the nobles. But really it's to make sure that the Crown always gets its share of Grace profits.

Worry purses Mistress Lavender's coral-painted lips together. "Alyce knows such a practice is illegal."

So that's what Rose thinks I'm doing. Taking extra patrons to earn more money because my gift doesn't Fade. And so she betrayed me to Tarkin to punish me.

"She knows." Laurel pins me with a knowing look. "This is all a misunderstanding. A mistake. Alyce, why don't you look again?"

She's rescuing me. I can see it in the subtle lift of her eyebrows. I should be grateful. But resentment burns through me, turning my blood to liquid wildfire. I am trapped, my one escape route blocked forever. And I can say nothing. Because this is not simply a case of taking on illegal patrons. This is the Briar King keeping me in his clutches. I might as well be Narcisse, my magic available to be tapped at his pleasure.

A memory swishes at the edges of my mind, like a bright flag in darkness.

"You can't leave . . . If my father finds out—and he will . . ."

Dragon's fucking teeth. There's one other person who knew I wanted to leave Briar. Who saw where I kept my gold, how much I had, and knew what I was planning to do with it.

Aurora.

Understanding hits, swift and brutal. I have to grip the doorframe to keep from falling over. What a stupid, stupid wretch I am. I remember the creases of sadness on her face the last time we met. Were they traces of guilt because she had already betrayed me? Did she know what her father was about to do, but didn't stop him—the same way she didn't stop him from bleeding Narcisse dry?

"Alyce?" Mistress Lavender's voice cuts through my spinning thoughts.

"I will look again," I hear myself say. "As Laurel suggests."

"Ah, what a good plan," our housemistress says, relief

expelling a huge breath from her ample chest, the sticky situation already smoothing itself out. "Always so reasonable, Laurel. Perhaps you'll be the one to earn the house a royal crest one day? Think of what it could do for our standings."

She winks and Rose blanches, stirring her tea with vigor. But I can take no satisfaction in her discomfort. I make to leave, but Mistress Lavender isn't finished with me.

"Alyce. Do take care next time. These accusations are thoughtless and hurtful. Think of your sisters' feelings."

I don't even turn around.

CHAPTER THIRTY-ONE

For the next week, I am either in my Lair, my room, or at the black tower with Kal. I do not wish to endure the smug, sidelong glances from Rose and Marigold. They may not have taken my gold, but they're more than happy to reap pleasure from my misery.

Aurora doesn't come. I'm not surprised. With each new day I'm more convinced than ever that she betrayed me. Was anything between us ever real? The library, where she shared her deepest secrets and applauded me as I added tiny horns to mice. Her visits, when she told me her plans for Briar's future in a rush of excitement. Does she even want to rule alone, like Leythana? Or was it all just a ruse? A way to glean information about the Dark Grace on behalf of her father? And now that her duty is done, she has no reason to return.

It doesn't matter, I remind myself, though the questions chip at my heart until it's nothing but a hollowed-out stone.

Even so, I can still hear the melody of her laughter. Feel the velvet softness of her skin against mine when our hands met. If I inhale deeply enough, I swear I catch hints of lilac and appleblossom amid the sooty smoke and mold of my Lair.

Stop being an idiot, that ruthless voice inside me commands. *She never wanted you.*

The memories disintegrate like foam on the sea.

A few nights later, my Lair is too cold to inhabit and I find myself once again in the main parlor. Laurel joins me. She arranges herself on a chair in front of the fire with one of the books I'd given her. *Ancient Briarian Rulers,* I think.

"I wish you'd be more discreet with those books," I say to the snow, my breath fogging the glass.

A page turns. "You don't want anyone to know you're stealing from the old royal library?"

I whip around so fast I tip halfway out of the window seat. "How did you—"

She taps the inside cover of her book. "They're stamped. Do you think I'm a fool?"

"Clearly, I'm one." I resist the urge to beat my head against the window.

"I haven't told anyone, if that's what you're worried about." She sifts through a few timeworn pages. "If I did you'd stop bringing them."

"Well, enjoy it," I grumble, drawing my knees up to my chin. "There won't be more."

For a while, there's only the gentle cadence of the fire.

The soft ticking of the clock on the mantel and the glass creaking in the windowpane.

"I'm sorry about your gold," she says at last. And I think she means it. "For what it's worth, I don't think Rose took it."

"Why not? Doesn't she hate me enough?"

"She's too self-absorbed," Laurel reasons simply. I can't help but laugh. "The only gold she's concerned about is her own. If she wanted to steal yours, she'd have done it ages ago."

I agree with her, though I won't say who my true suspect is. "Maybe."

"It is interesting, though. Do you think your missing earnings have anything to do with the absence of the princess?"

She might as well have punched me. I jerk forward and my foot smashes into the window casing. Laurel just looks at me as if she'd asked what the weather might be tomorrow.

"You do realize I'm gifted in wisdom," she says. "And I saw her here myself."

The night she came asking after the books. "I—" I splutter, unable to latch on to a coherent excuse. "I thought . . ."

"You thought she'd properly disguised herself?" Laurel crosses one leg over the other, thoroughly amused. "Perhaps for someone less observant. But not when I saw the stamp on these books. And she took no trouble concealing her voice. I heard her before I entered your chamber."

I duck my head into my arms, muttering curses.

"No one else knows, if that's any comfort."

It is, a little. "Why haven't you told?"

"I already explained." Laurel adjusts her blanket. "You're entitled to your secrets. And the crown princess can do as she likes. Not everyone would feel that way, though." There's a warning in her tone.

"I'm aware." The cold leaking through the window has bitten through my clothes. I move to the chair across from Laurel, wincing as I imagine what Rose would do with such delicious knowledge.

"Is that why she stopped coming?"

I pick at the fringe on a throw pillow. "I have no idea," I lie, stubbornly refusing to admit my own naïve stupidity. "I thought . . . things were different between us."

"She's a royal."

"You're saying I shouldn't trust her?"

Firelight catches the bits of sea-green in the wisps of hair that escape her braid. "I'm saying she's as caged as we are. In a different way."

"You feel caged?"

"Don't you?" She tilts her head. "The Graces are commodities, the same as you. We both attended the trial."

Narcisse's frenzied pleas resonate in the whine of the wind outside. I pull the blanket tighter around my shoulders. "Aurora wants to change that. Abolish the Grace Laws and establish an entirely new system."

"Aurora?" Laurel smiles and a blush climbs up my neck. "She might. If she lives. And I hope she does. But there's a difference between being a princess, given free rein to traipse about the Grace District at night, and a queen."

Kal's words from a different mouth. I hadn't wanted to believe them then, but now—

"Don't mistake me," Laurel continues, tracing her fingertips over an illustration in the book. A Briar Queen, it looks like. I can make out the thorned bramble crown from here. "I expect great things from the princess. We need more rulers like the early queens. Leythana's daughter systemized the Etherium mining. Her great-great-granddaughter established the trade routes we still use today." She doesn't try to mask the disdain in her next words. "Of course, much was lost once the queens started doling out their responsibilities as wedding gifts."

"Aurora swears she wouldn't." But a bitter taste forms in my mouth. Can I believe anything the princess said?

"It would mean a new age." Laurel studies the fire. "The Lord Ambassador is also eager to see what would happen with the next queen."

Endlewild.

I swear I can hear his snide Fae laughter in the crackle of the fire. "I don't give a dragon's asshole what he thinks."

Laurel's eyebrows shoot up to her hairline. "You're not fond of the Fae lord."

I wrap my arms around my middle as tight as they will go, the phantom burn of that golden staff scorching my skin.

"You wouldn't be either if he tortured you a hundred thousand ways, deemed you a half-breed, and promised your death at his earliest convenience."

A flush smears across Laurel's cheeks. She looks away. "I know you have a history."

"That's putting it mildly." I cringe against the memory of

his coarse, bark-like touch. "And what are you doing talking to him anyway? He hates the Graces."

"I met him when I first Bloomed. He's partial to the wisdom Graces. I believe he views us as less . . . materialistic. And we've spoken several times at social engagements." She pauses, pressing her lips together as if considering whether or not to continue. "And he doesn't hate the Graces. That's a common misconception. He hates Briar's obsession with wealth and beauty. Ours is no longer the realm the Fae entrusted to Leythana. And he despises seeing light Fae magic bottled and sold."

"Sounds like something they should have thought about before they made the alliance agreement during the war." I burrow deeper into the blanket, that slimy feeling of Endlewild's gaze still oozing down my spine.

Laurel shrugs. "Perhaps. But I think you have more in common with the Lord Ambassador than you realize."

I huff out a laugh. "He wants me dead."

"He's separated from his kin and court. Made to witness his own breed of magic harvested for vanity and greed. Can you imagine what Narcisse's trial was like for him?"

Once again, the fallen Grace's ghost hovers in the shadows. It was hard enough to watch her gilded blood racing through the tubes, picturing my own kind in her place. And I'd noticed Endlewild's absence at the trial. I'd assumed he hadn't known about it, but perhaps he did know. And he stayed away because he couldn't bear the sight.

But anger quickly takes the place of any sympathy I might feel for the Etherian. "Can you imagine what it was like for me? To be half drowned in Etherium baths, fed every sort of vile remedy, tortured with that precious Fae magic—all because my blood was the wrong shade?"

A charged silence buzzes between us. The clock chimes the hour.

"I'm not defending what was done to you."

"Then why are you telling me this, Laurel?"

"Because." She leans forward, long arms folding over the open book. The scrolling laurel leaves stitched onto the sleeves of her dressing gown shimmer. "You would be stronger working with the Lord Ambassador than against him. The War of the Fae was ages ago. The past can be forgotten. Paved over with a new alliance."

Dragon's teeth, she's gone mad. "He'll never accept me."

"You don't know that," she presses. "And believe it or not, you want the same things. The Lord Ambassador abhors the Grace Laws as much as we do. I know they're the only thing keeping you in Briar. Do you want to spill your blood for the nobles forever?"

"We are *not* the same." Endlewild poisoned my childhood. My mind. We have nothing in common save a mutual hatred.

"The Graces are standing on a precipice, Alyce. Maybe we're not bought up by rich men, crammed into tiny rooms while our power is used for their benefit. But we are leashed all the same. And it would not take much for the scales to tip in their favor again."

I squirm under the weight of her logic. No, it had not taken much for the king's commissions to escalate into a curse for death. I've yet to complete the brooches, and I know I'm trying Tarkin's patience by stalling. But I just—can't. Even if some of the nobles do deserve a swift end. This commission is only the beginning. A slippery slope into becoming the monster the realm branded me.

"If there is anything you can do, you must do it." Laurel's gaze is fixed on the door, as if she's worried we'll be overheard. "Ally with the Fae lord. Prove that your Vila heritage is an asset to the realm. I know you're not what he believes you to be."

My fingernails dig into the upholstered arm of the chair. "You have no idea who I am." *What* I am.

"Yes, I do." The book thumps on the rug as Laurel slips from her chair and kneels at my feet, seizing my hands. I yank back, but she refuses to let go. "I know you hate being the Dark Grace. And the Grace system is bloated and corrupt. Think of Rose. I've seen the way she looks. The circles under her eyes. The thinness of her cheeks. She's using bloodrot." She keeps speaking over my surprised cry. "And she's not the only one. What happened to Narcisse could happen to any of us. The Graces are in danger. You are in danger."

I don't know what to say. How to react. I've never been welcome among the Graces. To ask me to be their champion is insane. But Laurel pins me like a specimen to a board, fear simmering stark amber in her gaze. It's the first time I've seen it there.

Against my better judgment, I want to help her. But what could I possibly—

The brooches.

An idea slams into me with a rush of adrenaline. Just because I received the king's commission doesn't mean I have to complete it the way Tarkin expects. The plan manifests abruptly, as if a veil is being lifted, and I'm almost ashamed I haven't thought of it before. The Briar King will be livid. Maybe even enough to let Endlewild lop off my head. But then he'd be without his Dark Grace. And I'd never be used as a weapon again.

It's a risk I just might be fool enough to take.

CHAPTER THIRTY-TWO

Another week passes with no sign of Aurora and I smother the smoking remnants of my heart with the promise I made to Laurel—sabotaging the king's request.

The very morning after our talk, I'd sent the dragon brooches back to the palace with a curse. But instead of death, the curse I set was for sleep. A sleep that mirrors death. A strange thrill ran through me when I watched the gems drink up the drops of my blood, imagining Tarkin's beet-red cheeks and twitchy mustache when he figures it out. But what can he do? Admit his plan to murder members of his own court?

A commotion stirs the Grace District when the Ryna prince sails into Briar. Everyone waving their caps and cheering as they follow the procession from the harbor to the palace. I watch the parade from my window, as sullen as Callow when I'm late to feed her. Not long after, a royal invitation is delivered to the Graces. There's to be a party during which Aurora's curse is sure to be broken. The entire Grace District erupts into raucous celebration, but I can hardly drag myself out of bed when the day arrives. Even the black wax seal on my schedule infuriates me. I snap it in half, wishing it was the face of the Ryna prince.

I shouldn't care about the party. Aurora befriended me only so she could spy for her father. Drew me in and let me believe there could be someone who accepted me. Wanted me. And then she stole my gold and cast me off.

And yet her absence in my life leaves a depthless hole, sucking everything else inside it like a whirlpool in the sea.

It's a dazed, unmoored feeling I can't shake as I slog through my heavy load of patrons, who are all in a frenzy over the coming festivities. I craft a dozen elixirs for various pseudo-illnesses and mottled complexions and bald heads and muted voices. The self-satisfied nobles scurry off with their prizes like the rats they are.

But as the evening quiets, the Graces long departed, my heart whispers fickle, traitorous wishes. To go to the party and see Aurora kiss her prince. To see *her* one last time before her curse is broken by someone else and I lose her forever. All of Briar will lose her, though the gluttonous vipers don't even understand what the realm could have been if only—

No.

Aurora played me for a fool. Toyed with me as if I were no better than Calliope begging for scraps of her attention. Abandoned me after she swore to be my friend. To make me a royal advisor. My blood heats, thudding against my temples as I remember every hollow promise. Every second I believed was real. But they were all calculated. Like Endlewild giving me that book on Vila and Shifters, sowing the seeds of my self-hatred.

That settles it. I will go to the palace. The crown princess of Briar deserves to see that I know what she is—no better than a common thief. A liar and a fraud. And if the truth helps her to see the poison coating her own actions—if it steers her at all to be the queen she vowed she wanted to be, all the better for Briar. I won't be around to witness her reign.

This celebration is not a masque, but I have other ways of obscuring my identity now. I concentrate on small Shifts, ones that won't require much effort to keep in place. I keep my skin pale, but conceal the blemishes and green webs of veins. My hair remains dark, but cascades in thick, lustrous waves down my back. I sneak into Rose's room and dab her golden, shimmery Grace powder onto my collarbone and neck and cheeks. I don't even bother Shifting a decent dress. Instead, I pilfer one of Laurel's, a gown colored like the depths of the Carthegean Sea with gold filigree racing along the hem and sleeves. I take one of her fur-lined cloaks as well before I leave, catching a glimpse of myself in the mirror and smirking.

No one will be able to pull a mask from my face this time.

If it's possible, the palace is even more riotous than on the princess's birthday six months ago. The ballroom teems with the press of bodies, the clink of crystal, the pop of corks. Servants barely have room to slip through the crowd, carting trays of goblets and delicacies and shallow dishes of Etherium. I spot a bulging pastry that appears dipped in real gold. A woman with a miniature ship nestled into her mountain of ringlets—arranged to resemble a storm-tossed sea—swipes it up and stuffs it into her mouth, squealing with delight as lemony cream bursts from the center and onto her chin. Fountains that must have been crafted by innovation Graces gush waterfalls of frothy peach liquid from spouts shaped like roaring dragons. Fizzy wine, I realize, when a man ducks his head below a jeweled snout and swallows down sloppy gulps, his group of friends laughing as it splashes over his doublet and onto his shoes.

Grace-grown Briar roses in honor of the occasion are wound around railings and climb up trellises and are suspended from the high ceiling in tight clusters. So many that the ballroom is redolent with their heavy scent. Live hummingbirds flit among the pearl and lavender petals like tiny gems flashing. Musicians keep up an endless barrage of waltzes and minuets, the dancers never tiring as they bend and twirl and swoop. Among them, I see Lord Arnley, his handsome face tipped back as he laughs and slings his arm around another man's waist. Part of me wants to ask him to dance again. To make him want me and then cast him off. To jeer when he feels exactly as I did that night—disgusting and worthless. My cord of magic hums and I tear my gaze away. This is not the night for that.

Just as the last time I visited the palace in disguise, hardly anyone pays me a passing glance. I've Shifted enough times now to be used to the feeling of anonymity, but it tastes no less sweet. I weave through the tipsy guests, drowning in the tide of perfumes and spilled wine. Searching for the shine of Aurora's dawn-colored curls, ears tuned for her laugh. She isn't here, though. She must still be in her rooms, or in one of the antechambers, waiting to be announced.

I pause at a column, studying the doors the royal family emerged from during the last event. Relieved that Endlewild doesn't seem to be in attendance. Snippets of conversation drift past me.

"Is Lord Selligan not with us tonight?" A male voice, sonorous and suggestive.

"No." A lilting, wine-tinged giggle. "I'm afraid my dear husband has caught the sleeping sickness everyone is talking about."

A stone lands in my stomach. Sleeping sickness. I edge closer, hiding myself in the gauzy swaths of purple and cream fabric wound around the column.

"What a pity." He doesn't sound upset in the least. "What does that make—five now?"

"Something like that," the woman drawls, bored. "At first I was alarmed. I returned from tea with the Countess LeSalle and thought the earl was dead! His lips were blue."

"My poor dear." The sound of a hand being kissed. "What an ordeal for you."

A sniffle. "It was horrid. And then, once the physicians arrived and determined that he was *not* dead, I was distraught over the thought it might be contagious. I've hardly been able to sleep for worry I'll not wake."

I roll my eyes at the lady's histrionics, quite certain there are a number of other reasons she's not sleeping while her husband is suffering under my curse.

"Lady Selligan, but your health is so dear to us. You must take care."

She blows loudly into what must be her companion's offered handkerchief. "I know, I know. And the doctor assured me all is well. The earl will wake in time, they promise. Not even the king appears concerned—even though Lord Selligan is a member of his council and a personal friend. His Majesty sent a gift just the day before. A lovely brooch. Quite expensive. I haven't had the heart to take it off of him."

I bite down on my tongue to keep silent.

"I'm sure the Briar King is beside himself, to lose such a prized courtier. One would like to know the cause," the man continues, thoughtful now. "If only to avoid such a fate."

The lady sighs. "Who knows, these days? Perhaps overindulgence is the culprit."

A loud, barking laugh. "If that were the case, my dear, the entire palace would be fast asleep, never to wake." She giggles again. "I'm happy to see your spirits restored. And I hope to help keep you occupied—while your husband is indisposed."

The woman murmurs something, breathless. And I move away, uninterested in the bed play of Briar's upper class. Foreboding thrums at the base of my neck. So the king has deployed his brooches. But he's sent no guards to arrest me for blatantly ignoring his orders.

I don't have time to puzzle out what that might mean. The herald at the royal entrance bangs his dragon-headed cane and announces the royal family.

Queen Mariel practically floats into the ballroom, the happiest I've ever seen her. And she certainly dressed for the occasion—as though the royal wedding might take place this very night. A collar of teardrop pearls and enormous diamonds glitters on her neck. Her bodice and skirts are studded with ruby Briar roses. From this angle, it appears as if her crown of bramble and thorns is drenched in fresh Etherian blood.

Tarkin is a step behind her as always, wearing enough jewel-encrusted chains and bright-ribboned medals to sink him to the bottom of the Carthegean Sea. Outrage shoots from the tips of my toes and tingles in the roots of my hair when I think of what he stole from me. It takes every ounce of self-control not to send my power into him and grind his magic to dust.

"Loyal subjects." The Briar King maneuvers around his wife. "This is a most anticipated night, when the stars have at last aligned for our beloved daughter and heir, Aurora."

There's a ripple in the crowd, a hundred necks craning, and then Aurora glides into view. I was not ready to see her. A gasp wrenches free from my lungs. Though most of the guests are dressed in their winter brocades and velvets, Aurora wears a close-cut silk that sets all the courtiers whispering. The gown is a deep plum color, riddled with hints of crimson that wink and glow like embers in the candlelight. Delicate lace sleeves hang from gilded straps on her shoulders. The neckline is square and low, exposing the elegant lines of her collarbone. A high garnet choker climbs the column of her neck.

I remind myself that I'm angry with her. Clench my fists, repeating the litany of wrongs in my mind. She used me. Discarded me. But all I really feel in the chambers of my treasonous heart is the desire for her to look at me. To speak to me again. To touch me. To—

I force myself to look away.

The king drones on, but his words are warped and run together. Something about the excitement of the curse breaking and the new royal family soon to be. And then there is another crack on the marble floor, loud enough to jar my attention back to the present.

"Prince Elias of Ryna."

Tall and broad-shouldered, dressed in the same colors I saw flapping on his standards—navy and bronze—is the star-chosen prince. The room is quiet enough that I can hear every thump of his boots like a hammer against my breastbone. He is handsome. Several nearby courtiers comment on his brushed copper skin and strong jaw. And he does not have the cruel look of the Briar King. The corners of Elias's lips turn up in a soft smile. His brown eyes are kind. He stops two steps below where Aurora waits and sweeps into a low, effortless bow. Waits until she offers her hand before he takes it.

When their fingers meet, recognition eddies between them. This is not some stranger Aurora's parents flung at her head. She knows this man. Anticipated his arrival.

And she is radiant.

Light glows from beneath her skin, more than any Grace could have gifted her. Her expression filled with something that makes the floor tip beneath my slippers—hope. She *wants* this, I realize miserably. Wants *his* kiss to break the curse. One by one, every moment we shared together wilts. Every promise she made crumbles to ash.

The room holds its breath as Prince Elias rises to Aurora's level and asks her permission to kiss her. She agrees—*blushes,* damn it all—and then he bends. Closer and closer, driving knives into my belly with each inch. Aurora's eyes close. Her chin lifts. And then the prince brushes a chaste kiss on her parted lips.

Nothing happens.

Tarkin's mustache jumps. He whispers something to the queen, who inserts herself between the couple and jerks Aurora's sleeve up her forearm.

Mariel's jaw sets. She shakes her head.

A chorus of disappointment begins to swell, the court launching into motion once again. Aurora's expression slackens. And though I should feel some measure of satisfaction in the way she blinks away tears, in the defeated slump of her shoulders, all I feel is pain. I want to go to her. Comfort her. And I hate myself for it.

What happens next is a blur. The king calls for order, trying to piece together a half-baked speech about hope and perseverance. The apparently not-so-star-chosen Prince Elias offers another bow and leaves, Aurora close behind him.

Is she chasing him? Consoling him?

I am quick on her heels, dodging clusters of courtiers and harried servants. Ducking under arms and narrowly missing dancers. I catch a glimpse of Rose, gossiping madly with some other Graces. Laurel, who takes a second look at me as I fly past.

The door behind the dais slams shut as Aurora's plum train swishes into darkness. And the two men guarding it, each of whom boast tree trunks for arms, don't look particularly inclined to let me through.

Summoning my courage, I veer around a pair of women who seem much more concerned about the taste of each other's necks than what happened with the princess, and huddle behind an opal-veined pedestal. A huge, heavy vase rests on top. Peonies and roses and dahlias overflow from the rim, petals brightening and dimming in every imaginable hue as the seconds tick by. What I need is a distraction.

I press my palms into the stone and send my power to search for the magic there. I think I find it, but the pedestal's drowsy heart is buried too deeply for me to command properly. And so I venture elsewhere, seeking instead the slippery current of magic in the water in the vase. That is simple to manipulate. It swells under my power, almost willing as I tighten my darkness around it and push through my command. The water churns. Steam rises from the lip of the vase, porcelain groaning as it heats. There's a rumbling gurgle. A scalding droplet leaps out and sizzles on the cold marble. A fissure races up from the rounded base of the vase. The colossal thing wobbles. Moans.

And then bursts in a deafening explosion of glass and

porcelain. An answering scream ricochets around the chamber as shards of vase and blistering water find gowns and exposed skin. The guards scatter toward the conflicting cries, swords drawn.

And in the commotion, for the first time and fueled by my overwhelming need, I Shift myself to complete invisibility and slip into the torch-lit corridor.

CHAPTER THIRTY-THREE

My feet are too slow.

Sweat tracks through the Grace powder on my face and neck with the effort of maintaining my Shift. My muscles are stretched tight enough to tear. One advantage the corridor affords me is its uniform walls, far easier to project onto my body than a more complicated landscape. Even so, a few times, a green-veined hand pops into view. The flutter of a gold-embroidered hem. I will not be able to hold the illusion long.

Hopefully, I will not have to. Soon enough, I detect the patter of heels. It must be Aurora, hurrying back to her rooms.

Hurrying after her star-chosen prince.

Her steps lead me up several flights of stairs and through a dozen winding turns, until they abruptly stop and I come upon a still-swinging tapestry. Mustering what little of my courage remains, I push through the narrow door and into the crown princess's private chambers.

Everything is quiet. Not even the candles are lit, and I have to pause for a few ragged breaths to let my eyes adjust. I clamp my hands over my mouth, smothering my relieved sob as I let my Shift slide away and my limbs reappear.

One hand on the wall to steady myself, I cling to the shadows of what I believe to be a sitting room. Lounges and chairs are arranged around small tables, books on every surface. The last vestiges of a fire wink from behind a grate. Sheer curtains do little to hide the tall windows, the star-scattered sky casting the room in silver. In the corner, there's a large rounded object covered by a thin cloth.

I inch my way across the rugs, toward a set of double doors. Rustling sounds leak through the opening, as well as the faint glimmer of a single taper. Aurora's bedchamber. A creaky plank of wood betrays me as I tiptoe inside.

"I said I wished to be alone!" Her voice is harsher than I've ever heard it. She wrestles off her necklace and tosses it away.

I don't move, frozen in place, and she whirls, mouth open to hurl another royal command. And then her jaw drops, one hand going to her throat, the other bracing against the dressing table.

"Alyce."

My name on her lips. Something runs through me, and I can't tell if it's longing or rage. Maybe both. "Are you surprised?"

"What are you doing here?" Her gaze jumps to the doors behind me and the darkness beyond. "How did you get inside?"

"I don't see how that matters." I push farther into the bedchamber, determined to keep control of the conversation. "You came to see me often enough—*un*invited. I thought it only fair to return the favor."

She looks away, flustered, and pulls pins out of her hair. "I've hardly been able to draw a breath of my own since Elias's ship was spotted." Silver clacks against the glass top of her dressing table. "Did you know my mother ordered a wedding dress made? Before the curse was even broken." She laughs, but it's stilted.

"It didn't look broken to me."

"No." Her arms droop to her sides and she sinks onto a stool. "It didn't break."

"What a pity. I know how much you were looking forward to the prince's arrival. And I'm sure it was a beautiful gown. How much did it cost? Twenty thousand gold?"

"Twenty thousand—" She blinks. "What?"

Even now, she lies to me.

"The gold you stole. My gold. My way out of Briar. How long were you and your father planning it? I want to know." Her brow rumples. What a clever, talented actress she is. Fury gallops through my veins. "Was it amusing? A romp—trick the Dark Grace into trusting you and then take everything she has?"

"I don't understand you, Alyce."

"You lie so well." My power thrums, spurring me to act. Her mortal magic would be so easy to destroy. It would feel like one of Rose's glass baubles shattering under my heel. "Did your father teach you? Your mother, perhaps. Was it after your birthday masque that they bade you visit me? Or after the duke—when they realized how much of a Vila I really am?"

She gapes at me like I'm speaking a different language. "You . . . you think I've been spying on you?"

"Why shouldn't I? My gold is gone. Conveniently after you saw where I stored it. After you knew I was planning to leave."

"You think I told on you?" She launches to her feet, setting the candle wobbling. Shadows dance over the walls, as they do in the black tower. "Even after the trial? When I knew what my father would do to you—that's what you think of me?"

Doubt cracks like a rotten egg and trickles down my spine. I shake it away.

"Don't look at me that way. What else was I supposed to think? Spoiled princess. You were done playing with your Dark Grace and so you threw me away."

I don't let myself feel guilty for the way she winces when the words hit her.

"Stop it, Alyce."

"Does it hurt you to hear the truth? It should. I hope you feel a fraction of what I felt when my whole world was ripped into pieces. My one escape blocked. Now I'm chained to the role of Dark Grace forever."

The argument is a living, wild thing between us. Aurora's chest rises and falls in an uneven, painful rhythm. "Do you really want to leave me?"

No, my heart answers. I roundly tell it to be silent. "There's nothing for me here. I'm tired of being a villain."

"You were never a villain to me."

It is enough to break me. I want to lean into her, feel her arms around me. Smell the appleblossom of her skin.

No.

I've let myself be reeled in by her charms too many times. All it takes is a kind word, a soft look, and I'm eating out of her hand again. Like the pet I am.

"You're part of this," I insist, stoking up the flames of my greedy wrath. "I don't know how, but you are."

"I'm not."

"But you stopped coming. Discarded me once you were bored."

"Is that what you think?" She reaches for me. But I will not let her near. "That isn't true, Alyce. I had no time. I was trapped here—as trapped as you."

"It's more than that." Every ill thought I harbor piles together until it is a wall of stone. "You wrote to Prince *Elias*. You never did with the others. Never even spoke of them." I barrel on when she opens her mouth to argue. "And tonight you looked . . . you looked—" It scores my heart to say it. "You wanted his kiss to work."

The accusation lands at her feet and quivers in the air. She pales in the quicksilver moonlight. "Is it so terrible? To want my curse to be broken?"

"We were trying to break it! The two of us, together. That's what you promised. And to see you looking at— at *him* like that." The air is too thin. There is not enough of it.

Aurora continues, so even and cool that it sends a shiver down my spine. "If I seemed happy to meet my newest suitor, it is because I knew he would be the last."

"Because you thought he would break the curse and you would—"

"Because I mean to refuse all others."

I have to repeat her words in my head before they make any sense. "You mean to . . . refuse?"

"I mean to refuse," she says, as smoothly as if discussing a choice of gown. "Queens of Briar are not technically obligated to marry their cursebreakers. And it turns out that Prince Elias wanted to marry me as much as I wanted to marry him—not at all."

My whirling mind cannot keep up with her. "Not at all . . . but—"

"It's something we discovered when we were writing to each other." Aurora crosses her arms and gives me a pointed look. "He agreed to come to Briar. If his kiss worked, we would *not* be married, but we would work closely together during my reign. As a younger son of Ryna, he likely wouldn't be king in his own right. But he could be an ambassador of sorts here. We could share ideas, strengthen relations with all realms, create a better world for both peoples. All without marriage."

The fight goes out of me in a single breath, leaving my limbs like rubber.

"You never told me."

"You never let me! Any time I mentioned Elias you did nothing but argue and bait me. You hated him as soon as I spoke his name."

I focus on the Briar roses stitched on the rug, ashamed. Dragon's teeth, I'd been so wrapped up in jealousy that I didn't believe in her.

"It doesn't matter now." She kneads her thumb over her thorned curse mark. "I decided before he arrived that I will have some control over my own life in these last months. Regardless of the outcome, Elias would be the last man I kiss."

"But . . ." My chin trembles, imagining Aurora's lifeless form laid out on a funeral pyre, her face waxy and body stiff. "Briar. You're the last heir."

"Yes, and I've been the last heir for some time now. My mother must have some arrangement with the Etherians. They have to start including me in those negotiations. I will do everything I can to help them establish the next ruler. I have a few months. We'll find a solution. Think of it this way"—she picks up a bottle on her dressing table and sets it down again—"I'll have no daughters. And there's no extended family remaining—my mother's sisters have all passed. And so I'm ending the curse forever."

My mouth goes dry. "No."

"For the last twenty years of my life, every waking moment has been centered on this curse." A stubborn curl spills out of a loose pin. The spun gold shines in the candlelight. "I may be a spoiled princess. But it hasn't been a life. Not at all. Did you know that even when I was a child, visiting dignitaries would kiss me? And their sons?"

A sour feeling churns in my stomach.

"Indeed." She smiles, but it's weak. "One never knows when a true love will appear. I had a great-aunt whose curse was lifted at the age of eight by a man thirty years her senior."

Eight. Hilde's long-ago words about Graces being cursed

instead of blessed float back to me, and I wonder if the same could be said about the cure for Aurora's curse.

"Since I could read, I've been drilled in the stories of the women before me. Who lived, who died, who found their true love and at what age and how." She sucks in a breath and exhales slowly. "I have had enough. Even with you, the one place I had a rest from court, all we did was talk about the curse."

No wonder she'd been only half interested in the books during her last visits. I'd accused her of giving in to the Crown. Of wanting Elias. The last stone of my doubt collapses into itself. I am a fool. A selfish, utter fool. "That's why you stopped coming."

"No." Aurora closes the distance between us and grasps my shoulders. "I told you the truth. My mother employed every snare she knew to keep me locked inside these walls. She even had a spinning wheel brought in so that I could better understand Ryna's silk trade." The veiled object in her sitting room. "But I should have sent word. I'm sorry for that."

She owes me no apology. Her hands fall away, leaving cold spots in their wake. "You can't just stop accepting suitors." I think of the king. Of how easily he outmaneuvered me. "They won't allow it."

Her expression hardens. She's thought about this a great deal, I realize. And the blood of her ancestors pumps from her heart. Warrior queens. "They can try what they like. But I will see no more. These last months are mine."

Aurora goes to the window, pulling open the gossamer

curtains and looking out into the garden below. It's the same one where we first met, though the fountain has been restored. The gurgling water has been dyed lavender for the celebrations—as though the incident with mud never happened.

"When I'm not helping with the succession, I plan to do exactly as I please. Until it's time." There's an undercurrent of anxiety in her words, but her body is rigid. She turns to me, moonlight lending a halo around her form. "And there's only one person I plan to kiss."

"I thought you said—"

And then her finger is on my lips. My heart kicks up, fire racing through her fingertip and into my bloodstream. I can only stare down, cross-eyed, at my nose.

"I want to kiss you, Alyce." I can hardly hear her over the stampede in my ears. I drag my gaze up. Her eyes are an indigo-amethyst and glimmering with something I can't name. The neckline of her bodice rises and falls in a rhythm that matches my own. "You're the first and last person I've ever wanted."

I cannot feel my feet. That is the only thought that loops through my mind as her face nears. I will fall. My legs are numb. This cannot be real.

But the scent of her washes over me, lilies and apples and cool, night things. Another lock of her hair wriggles loose of its fastening and drops to brush against my arm. Tentative, her hands cup the underside of my jaw, thumbs tracing my cheekbones. I close my eyes. No one has ever touched me like this before. I expect her to pull away at the clamminess of my skin. The flaky, scaly surface of me. But she only leans closer, the space between us as thin as any hope I've ever dared dream.

"Will you kiss me, Alyce?"

My heart is a wild thing. Fast as a hummingbird, steady as a hammer. It will break me in half. Burst out of my chest and flail on the rug like a caught fish. And I would be glad of it.

Logic and reason scream at me to pull away. This is the crown princess. We live in two different worlds and we could never—but my lips have other ideas.

Aurora yelps as my mouth crushes against hers, and then she tightens her hold on my neck. My own hands reach up, not sure where to go, but knowing that they must go somewhere. Must *do* something to pull Aurora closer to me. One snakes into her hair, uncaring as pins scratch and scrape me. The other finds her waist, wrapping tight and reeling her in. She tastes of warm sugar and the dry, fizzy wine from the celebration downstairs. Of hope and freedom and everything lacking in my life.

A rumble reverberates through my bones as I deepen the kiss, both petrified and electrified at my own boldness. An entirely new sound escapes Aurora's throat, traveling from her mouth into mine in a way that will be my undoing. She slumps a little. I hold her up, parting her lips with my tongue and exploring the velvet within. She pushes me backward, until I'm flat against the wall, her hands spreading wildfire down from my neck and over the sides of my breasts. Her teeth find my earlobe. The furious cadence at my throat.

It's then that I notice the shaking.

The rumbling I'd thought was my own tremulous body is real. The wall is vibrating behind my shoulder blades. The candle on Aurora's dressing table teeters, then whooshes out as it crashes to the floor.

Aurora is kissing the skin above my neckline, every nerve aflame, but I push her away, motioning at the fallen candle as I try to catch my breath. Her eyes fly wide, swollen lips parting in a silent gasp. The quaking intensifies. We grab for each other before we tumble to the carpets. Glass pops as fissures map their way across the dressing-table mirror. Windowpanes implode. I throw myself over Aurora, shielding her from soaring bits of glass. Books and vases clatter to the rugs. The walls groan, and for a moment I'm worried they will cave and bring the ceiling down to crush us both.

But then, just as suddenly as it started, everything stops. Aurora lifts her face from the crook of my shoulder.

"Was that—something from the sea?" It is the only thing I can guess. A massive wave, or a squall. A ship turned back into a dragon by some fantastical bit of magic.

But Aurora doesn't answer. She's staring at her arm, her sleeve yanked up to her elbow.

"Are you hurt?" I bend down, inspecting the spot, but there is only clear, unbroken skin. No glass. No cut or bruise.

And then it hits me.

Aurora's eyes shine as they meet mine. "It's gone." She lets out a sob. Tears glisten on her cheeks. "You broke the curse."

CHAPTER THIRTY-FOUR

"No." It seems the only word I'm capable of speaking. Because what *Aurora* is saying is impossible. "I didn't. I couldn't have. You must have done something."

She grins, pressing our foreheads together. "Yes. I kissed you. And you kissed me. And it broke the curse."

I pry her fingers loose and put as much distance between us as I can. "That's impossible."

Aurora laughs, giddy. "Why do you doubt it? The mark is gone. I feel—" She takes a long, deep breath in. "Incredible. Lighter than I've ever felt in my entire life. Because of you."

"Not because of me."

"Why not?"

"Because"—my chest tightens—"because my magic can only accomplish wickedness. I'm part Vila. I don't break curses." I cross my arms, choking on the bitterness of my next words. "I make them."

Aurora pads across the rugs. Glass crunches under her feet. A frigid wind snakes through the jagged holes in the windows, billowing the curtains.

"Maybe the curse breaking has nothing to do with your magic," she whispers along my jawline, "and everything to do with this."

Her lips meet mine and that same jolt of lightning forks through me. I want to wrap my arms around her and never let go. Lose myself in the honey taste of her mouth and the addictive scent of her skin. But this is madness. I push her back.

Aurora traces circles over the place where her mark used to be. "You know, I always wondered about the *true love* stipulation of the curse." She picks up a candlestick. A handful of pins. "Even before I lost my sisters, I would read about the queens who ruled before us. They had one thing in common: terrible marriages."

When I think of Tarkin and Mariel, I'm hardly surprised.

"It confused me. After all, it was the Etherians who softened the original death curse. Theirs is light magic. If true love could break the curse, why couldn't it last? Had the Vila's magic somehow soured that love even after the curse was broken?"

The back of my neck prickles.

"But then, as I grew older and watched my parents, I realized that it wasn't the light Fae or the Vila who were to blame for the love lost between the royal couples. It was the humans themselves. Briar is an isolated realm. Consumed with our own importance and wealth—that's what undermined the marriages of the other queens. Not some magical force outside their control." She relights the candle. "Once I figured that out, I stopped fearing my own death. Instead, I was afraid that I *would* find my true love. And that I would have to watch that love corrupt and re-form into something ugly. That's why I insisted on breaking the curse myself and ruling alone." She pauses. Holds my gaze. "But tonight that fear is gone."

I can hardly breathe around my desire to believe what she says. The distance between us hums, both too much and not enough.

"Do you trust me?" Aurora asks.

"Yes," my heart answers for me.

"Then you'll stay with me. Rule beside me?"

"Rule?" I hold on to her bedpost to steady myself. I'd barely begun to imagine myself as her actual true love, let alone ruler of Briar.

"Princesses always marry those who break their curse, don't they?"

"They marry dukes and earls and princes," I correct. "Who then become kings. And you said you didn't want to marry."

Aurora raises an eyebrow. "Well, I wish to marry you. Two queens of Briar. What could be better?"

A hundred thousand things. Even if I did accept her offer, the rest of Briar would revolt against me. I'd be dragged out and burned alive. Aurora has no idea what she's asking. There's never been a queen like me—never could be one.

But her lips land on mine before I can argue. "You said you trusted me."

And I do. Enough to drown myself in that depthless,

forget-me-not gaze, in the taste of summer berries on her lips, and never look back. Like a fool, I nod.

"Good." She threads her fingers through mine. "Come with me."

Does she mean to tell her parents tonight? This moment? My blood turns to ice water and I balk as she tries to drag me away. "We're not—we can't."

She waves away my worry, guessing my thoughts. "Not now, no. But they'll be coming to check on me soon. I'm surprised they haven't already, with all that racket. And I don't want them to find us yet."

Find *us*. My heart thumps.

"Tonight"—she pulls me close, whispers in my ear—"is only ours."

We take the servants' halls, keeping our heads down and our feet swift. But they all must be tending to other matters, for we pass no one on our way to the abandoned library. Anticipation skitters down my spine and burrows into my bones as we enter. I have never been alone with anyone like this. Never thought that I would be.

Aurora lights some of the fat, dripping candles, their paltry glow cutting through the gloom. It seems the blast that broke the curse reached even this ancient part of the palace, though it isn't as bad as in Aurora's rooms. Many of the books were shaken free from their shelves and lie in haphazard piles on the shabby rugs. A rusted chandelier groans as it swings back and forth, one of its moorings pried loose.

I need something for my hands to do, so I set a table right

and pick up the books that spilled. "Did you know it would be like this? The curse breaking."

"No." Aurora rubs her upper arms against the chill. "My mother spoke of a slight wind. And there are records of light. Music sometimes. It's different for everyone."

"But it was so violent this time."

"Yes." Aurora appears at my side, gently stilling me. I let the book fall, forcing my gaze to hers despite the flock of birds in my stomach. "Maybe it's ended for good."

Her long, graceful fingers comb through my hair, freeing it from its braid. I lean into her touch, craving more. Scared of the way my pulse races, chest aching like it might explode.

"You're beautiful, Alyce."

I stiffen. "No. Nothing like you."

She smiles softly. Sadly, almost. "Me? I have no idea what I look like."

"What do you mean?" The palace has no shortage of mirrors.

"The moment I was born, the Graces were summoned. Every inch of my body is planned. The length of my legs. The width of my hips. My hair color. I think I was born with black hair, actually. I know my mother was." She examines the tip of a curl. "So what you see isn't much better than a trick. Turning a regular child into a beautiful princess with a few drops of magic."

I turn this over carefully in my mind. In her own way, Aurora is a Shifter, too.

"Sometimes I think about letting the Grace elixirs wear

off," she muses. "But I've never gotten very far. Whenever anyone notices even a hint of a blemish, I find a fresh bottle of beauty elixir on my breakfast tray. And if I ignore that"—she grimaces—"they slip it into my tea."

A prisoner in a lovely cage.

"But you"—Aurora unbuttons my sleeve and traces the underside of my forearm in a way that makes my blood sing—"are entirely natural. I want you just like this. Always."

Before I can stop her, she lifts my hand to her lips and kisses each fingertip, slow and deliberate and sure. Heat bursts at that satin-softness, rolling up my arms and down my back. Her mouth moves to my palm. To the tender skin of my wrist, where every nerve is alive and thrumming. Her teeth bite down and I cannot wait any longer.

Letting all my jittery hesitation disintegrate, I grab Aurora by the waist and pull her close. My lips stumble into hers, bruising as the intoxicating taste of her fills my mouth. She deepens the kiss, her hands roving down my back and snarling in my laces. I let go of her only long enough to untie them, the front of my dress gaping open. She yanks at my sleeves until they're hanging at my sides, and then there's only my shift beneath.

Instinctively, my arms go over my body, hiding skin that looks like spoiled milk. Green veins like the poorly made seams of some grotesque doll.

"No. I'm—" *Disgusting. Hideous. Vila.*

The wounds from my early years split open and ooze. The horrified stares I receive from the courtiers at the palace—from my own patrons, paying me for the very blood that brands me a monster. I don't want Aurora to look at me that way.

But she does not. Her eyes are so bright, like violet stars. She steps away and fusses with the fastenings at her back. The gown drops from her shoulders and pools like ink at her feet.

I cannot breathe.

Her moon-stained skin, soft and unbroken and utterly perfect. Without thinking I reach out and run my fingers along her pearlescent bare arm, gasping at the sensation. At the image of my greenish, scaly skin against her unblemished marble. But Aurora is not repulsed. Gently, she tugs my other arm down, ignoring my noise of protest—or terror. Her hands explore my exposed chest, clever fingers slipping under the straps of my shift and easing them off my shoulders. My heart is beating so hard, I'm sure she can hear it. The entire palace probably can, and they'll storm in here at any minute and drag us apart.

But I can't think about that once Aurora leans in and kisses my neck. A sound I've never made before escapes me, and I grapple for purchase, finding the slippery fabric of her shift that is so close to her skin I might combust. Aurora finds the dip of my waist. The sides of my breasts, her thumb caressing those curves in agonizing circles. Her lips follow, on my sternum, over my stomach, until she is kneeling and looking up at me, her expression like she's worshipping a goddess.

"Are you frightened?" she asks.

Yes. Completely. But not of her. I'm frightened of this feeling that consumes me and promises to rip free of my body and set the entire palace ablaze. Of the way I want to taste every part of her. Devour her whole.

As if reading my thoughts, Aurora pulls her flimsy silk undergarment over her head and tosses it aside. Candlelight laps at her bareness. She is exquisite. I let my fingertips play in the hollows of her collarbone. Over her shoulders opalescent moonlight shimmers in diamond patterns, as if she is some scaled water nymph come to the surface. She leans into my touch, closing her eyes, her breaths shortening.

"Alyce. Please."

A tremor goes through my whole body, starting at my feet and rocketing upward. Heat pools between my legs, an aching feeling of fullness I've never experienced. I want more of it. Want to let it break me and remake me new. And so, before I can lose my nerve, I wriggle free of the rest of my clothing, leaving nothing between me and Aurora. Sparks canter over the backs of my legs, my calves, the insides of my thighs.

My hands bury themselves in her hair, desire and longing and a dash of breathless anguish mixing together in a dizzying whirlpool of color. My head drops back as her lips and tongue discover places I never dreamed could feel so tender. And then she moans as her mouth finds somewhere entirely new, filling my whole body with a vibration that will shatter me.

The feeling intensifies, and I arch backward, bracing myself against the edge of a table. Aurora's mouth moves quicker, tongue flicking against me, warm, wet heat traveling up the length of my body. My arms shake. Aurora grips the backs of my thighs. Sweat breaks over my chest and across my belly. And then, just when I want to beg her to stop, or to move faster, for the earth to yawn open and swallow me whole, my body goes rigid. An explosion begins where Aurora is inside of me, shooting through every fiber. Tingling in the roots of my hair. It is all I can do to sink to the floor, a limp puddle of soft bones and flaming skin.

We spend the rest of the long midnight hours wrapped in each other, ravenous. And with every shared heartbeat, I know that she is right—we are meant for each other. Two halves of the same whole, and I will not let my own uncertainty cleave us apart.

We don't sleep until the night tinges gray, and even then it is only an hour, perhaps. Dawn is just blushing the warped windows when I startle awake, woken by the unfamiliar sensation of another breathing body beside me. The air is saturated with the smell of her—of our joining—and for the first time I feel that I am exactly where I am supposed to be.

Aurora rouses slowly, blinking against the early morning and tossing her mussed hair out of her face. She scoots closer to me on the rug, beneath the moth-eaten blanket we found to ward off the cold, and drapes a long, slender arm over my belly.

"Go back to sleep," she mumbles.

"I don't understand how you can sleep, knowing what's coming."

She sighs, still half in her dreams. "I'll need my strength."

I laugh and snuggle in next to her, burying my nose in the crook of her neck and smiling as I catch my own scent mingled with hers. Closing my eyes, I try to lull myself back to slumber, pushing away the worries that rear up in the light of day. The knowledge that I will have to face the king and queen, perhaps in a matter of hours. I want a few more blissful moments with her, while it's just us, unsullied by the others.

A bell begins to ring in the distance. Then another, the tones clanging against one another and making the glass windows shudder. Aurora sits up, pulling the blanket around herself.

"What is it?" I don't remember the last time the bells rang in Briar. Not these, the huge bronze beasts suspended in the palace belfry. There are alarm bells spread throughout the streets, the ones that summoned us to Narcisse's trial. But those are sharp and brittle. These are deep and joyous, their calls rolling across the Grace District, all the way out to the sea.

"It's the curse." She stares up at the window as if watching the approach of an invading army. "They know it's broken."

Not two heartbeats later, a pounding rattles the library doors. Aurora is on her feet in an instant, pulling me with her, the blanket shielding us both. The massive, ancient doors heave open, and two guards clamor through, stone-faced and bleary-eyed.

"Your Highness." The first of them, a huge, barrel-chested man with eyebrows that look like caterpillars, bows. He rises, discovers me, and his expression falls.

The other guard skids to a stop, looking from Aurora to me with unconcealed horror. Aurora wraps her arm tighter around my waist. Stands up straighter, daring them to say a word. And they must be well trained, for they do not. Only divert their eyes to the floor.

"Your presence is requested, Highness. In the throne room."

"Leave us." Though a little rough, the words are clear and sure. The voice of a queen.

The guards bow again, stiffly, and retreat.

Aurora turns to me. The amber-kissed dawn catches in her eyes, lighting them up like dragon's fire. Apprehension simmers behind it, I think. The same kind that's turned my guts into boiled nettles. But her grip is steady as she takes my hand. Squeezes.

"Are you ready?"

Absolutely not. But I nod, squeezing back, and begin to dress.

CHAPTER THIRTY-FIVE

To my surprise, the guards do not lead us through the main halls of the palace. Instead, we keep to the servants' passages, taking enough twists and turns to leave me utterly disoriented. Aurora refuses to let go of me, even when the maids and footmen freeze in their duties, shock scrawled on their faces. Even when we're ushered through the discreet back entrance of the throne room and herded in front of the waiting royal couple.

The chamber is nothing like it was during Narcisse's trial, courtiers and Graces packed limb to limb. Even the servants are sparse, stationed with their backs turned at their posts. The air buzzes with an unnatural quiet.

"Aurora, my darling." Queen Mariel launches from her throne, her gaze fixed on our joined hands like it's a festering wound. She sweeps her daughter into a crushing embrace and I'm pushed to the side. Mariel seizes Aurora's wrist and slides up her sleeve, running her thumb over the spot where the thorn-riddled Briar rose once rested. "It's truly broken. Oh, what wonderful news. Tell us what happened. We've been looking for you all night."

"It is wonderful news." There's a slight hitch in Aurora's voice, but she clears it. Steels herself. "And it's true. I have found my true love."

"The prince?" The queen claps her hands, beaming. A taste like charred deathknot fills my mouth. "I knew that kiss Elias gave you at the celebration was too chaste. You found each other later. That's what did it."

"Obviously she did," Tarkin scoffs. "Showing up here in last night's rumpled gown."

Heat burns down my neck. Do they really not understand we were together? They must not want to believe it. They're hoping she'll feed them something—anything—that will contradict what's before them.

Aurora's cheeks color. She swallows, but does not look away.

"Don't be silly." Mariel's garnet earrings glitter. "Aurora wouldn't . . ."

But she trails off when Aurora finds my hand again, interlocking our fingers. "I did spend the night with Alyce. She broke the curse."

All air is sucked from the chamber in a single, violent whoosh. Aurora's pulse, pressed hard against my own, is rabbit-quick. Tarkin's eyes blaze, cinders in the morning sun. He reddens, his nose the color of a ripe strawberry.

"What are you saying?" Mariel speaks first, her hand falling from her mouth. "You don't mean . . ."

"I said exactly what I mean, Mother." Aurora doesn't

even look at her. She looks at me instead, funneling strength from her bones into mine. "Alyce broke the curse. She is my true love. And we mean to marry as soon as possible."

A mixture of horror and happiness twines tight around my soul. I feel the way I do when I stand at the top of the black tower, the sea stretching out before my feet, a strong wind away from falling. Or flying.

"Alyce?" The queen's shrill voice sends me hurtling back to reality.

"That's her name." Aurora bristles. "Though you so conveniently forget it when you're warning her to stay away from me and disinviting her to parties."

"You are mistaken, my darling."

"No, I understand very clearly." She rounds on them both. "You've been dictating my life since the moment I was born. I won't stand for it any longer. I am the future Briar Queen. You cannot stand in our way."

"And what about children?" Mariel blurts. "Your duty to Briar is to provide the next heir to rule. You can't possibly do that with—" She gestures wildly at me. "With *that*."

The word strikes me like an arrow in my chest. My shoulders hunch against the wound. But Aurora is stronger. Her arm goes around my waist.

"My duty to Briar is to improve the realm—and there's much to be done on that account, isn't there?" Her silent accusation prompts raspberry blotches to erupt on the skin above the queen's neckline. "We will establish the issue of succession later."

"This is a new curse." Mariel's wrath homes in on me. "You've tricked her into believing she loves you. You're trying to take the throne for yourself. You evil, malicious thing. Just like your ancestors. We should have put you down when we found you. I've always known what you are."

My head spins. This was a mistake. A terrible, awful mistake. Aurora steps in front of me, protecting me.

"That's *enough*. You will not speak to her that way."

Hot tears track down the sides of my neck.

"Tell me, daughter." Tarkin taps his signet ring against the arm of his throne, slow and deliberate. "You think you know the Dark Grace?"

A current of cold air snakes between us.

"What does that mean?" Aurora snipes back. "Of course I do. Better than either of you, blinded by your own ignorant hatred."

At that, the Briar King laughs. The tips of his teeth gleam. Numbness fizzes along the base of my scalp and between my toes. No, he cannot mean to—I hadn't had the chance to tell Aurora yet. I open my mouth to say something—anything that might prevent this from happening, but I'm rooted to the spot.

"Oh, Aurora. You think you're ready to be queen? You can't even see what's right in front of you." Tarkin rises, looming over us like the dragon doors of his war room. "Your precious Alyce has been working for me."

"That isn't true." Aurora turns to me, searching for an answer. When I don't respond, the first inky tinges of doubt bleed across her features. "Alyce?"

I cannot bring myself to reply.

"Filthy beast," Mariel spits at me. "This is how you repay our generosity?"

The question brings me out of my stupor. Anger balls inside my chest, fanged and livid. "Generosity? Is it generous to be placed in a Grace house, ordered to produce elixirs for every noble nursing a grudge? To be neglected, excluded from every social event, gawked at like I'm a creature from a nightmare? Treated as an abomination my entire life?"

"Save your dramatics. You were paid for your services." Tarkin waves me off. "Quite a sum, if I recall."

"That's not—"

"Quite a sum?" Aurora interrupts. Her forehead creases.

"Aurora, I . . ."

"The gold," she breathes. "The gold I saw you with. It was so much. I thought perhaps that's what every Grace earns, but . . . but it was from my father. Wasn't it?" She is too still. Her skin too pale. I reach for her, but she bats me away. "You lied to me."

Tarkin claps slowly and I recoil as though I've been struck. "I knew you were clever. Yes, Aurora. Now you see." Sunlight dances on the jewels in his crown. "Let me show you exactly what the Dark Grace has been doing. Boy!" One of the servants scuttles over. "Fetch our subjects from Master Gray."

Subjects? My insides curl.

An eternity passes after the gangly servant disappears through a side door. Tarkin strolls from one end of the room to the other, almost jovial. Aurora will not look at me.

Finally, there's a distant shuffle and clanking. The door opens again and three Graces are led before us. Dragon's teeth. They look exactly as Narcisse had. Ripped and dirtied clothing hang off their half-starved frames. Rough iron chains leave raw marks and scabbed blisters on their wrists and ankles. Their eyes are sunken and dull. Some of them are even sporting silver streaks in their matted hair.

Nausea rolls through me and I have to clench my teeth to keep from retching. What has the king done?

"Alyce has been helping me with an experiment," the king continues, circling his prisoners with a kind of sick approval.

He's lying. I never—but then the pieces of this awful game begin to click into place.

"That isn't possible," Aurora whispers. "She wouldn't do this."

"Really?" The king moves to the first Grace and trails one finger back and forth in front of her gaze. But the emaciated creature only stares ahead, eyes vacant and cloudy.

"As it turns out, our Dark Grace is far more talented than we first believed. She's been cursing items for me using her Vila blood. Like this ring." Tarkin lifts the Grace's hand. A golden ring glints on her first finger. "It causes blindness."

The ring I cursed for the king. Endlewild said it had been used on a nobleman, but I never thought—

"Alyce?" The distance between Aurora and me feels like an ocean. "Is that what you did?"

My tongue peels itself from the roof of my mouth. I cannot deny it. "I—yes. But it wasn't— I didn't mean to—"

There's nothing I can say. I knew the king would use the items I cursed. I convinced myself that it wasn't my fault who got hurt. But I thought he was lashing out against courtiers. Against those who deserved it. But seeing these

Graces—broken and spent—it is my fault. Utterly and completely.

"You understand what she is now," Tarkin says. "Self-serving and vindictive. I suppose the substantial gold I supplied to commission these items wasn't enough for her. The Dark Grace wants the realm for herself. And so she used that Vila magic to trick you into falling in love so she could usurp your throne."

"No." Aurora backs away, merciful certainty returning to her voice. "She wanted me to rule. She was helping me break the curse. We . . . we tried everything."

"And yet nothing worked. Except this convenient kiss?" Tarkin tilts his head at me. "I wonder, was she trying to help you, or merely pretending? Tell me, Aurora. Did the Dark Grace truly do everything in her power to free you from your burden?"

I feel the threads of this situation slipping out of my control, but I can't grasp them.

Aurora doesn't answer, but I can see her stitching together bits of memory. Each time I refused to use my blood for a healing potion or a ritual. Refused because I didn't want to hurt her. Because I was afraid of the ancient Vila summoned by my blood. But it must look like I was biding my time. Waiting for just the right moment.

"Aurora, please." But her lips are slack. Her arms wrapped around her middle, as if she's holding herself together.

"Were you using me, Alyce? While you were—" She looks to the battered Graces then back to me, utterly repulsed.

"No, Aurora, I—"

Her next words slice me to pieces. "Who are you?"

"Don't worry, my dear." Tarkin snatches up the reins. "You won't have to be troubled with her any longer. You will marry Prince Elias. As of yet, the court knows nothing. We will tell them the prince broke the curse with another kiss later in the evening. They will believe it."

"It's for the best," the queen chimes in. She pulls Aurora farther away from me, a ship on the horizon, leaving me behind. "You remember the story I told you. About Eva. We do not want another . . ."

"You can't." Aurora's cheeks regain a splash of fire. "I will not!"

But the king raises his hand, Briar rose signet an ominous eye.

"You will do as you are bid," he says, low enough to be a growl. "Or you will have a tragic accident."

The chamber thrums with his words. Even the queen looks confused. She stops mid-step. "What did you say?"

"You heard me, both of you." The king does not waver. Does not even skip a breath. "Aurora will marry the Ryna prince. We need some reason to explain the curse breaking other than the truth. And if she does not, she will go the way of her sisters."

Aurora extracts herself from her mother's grasp. "You wouldn't dare."

Oh, but he would. We are standing in the room where Narcisse's gift was drained. I can see her ghost flitting between us, her lips like granite and her eyes storm clouds. She is screaming at me to run. Hide from this mad Briar King.

"It amuses me how little you know." Tarkin laughs. "See

if you can wrap your mind around this: There is an edict before the small council, giving the reigning Briar King sole right to rule in Briar."

The hall is utterly silent. I think I can hear the dust filtering through the sunbeams.

"The council will not stand for it." The queen's voice tears through the void. Wretched. Feral. "I am the ruler of Briar. These are my people."

"Darling wife." The smile on the king's face sickens me. It's the same one he wore at the trial. "I don't see how this is much different from our current arrangement. You signed over most of your duties on the day we wed. This edict just cuts the last remaining strings. You'll hardly miss it, my pet."

Panic blooms bright in Mariel's eyes as understanding sinks its teeth into her. She did this. Every Briar Queen who surrendered her rights to her husband did this. "They will not vote against me." But she does not sound certain. "They will not support something in direct violation of the Etherian treaty."

The king sighs through his nose. "Perhaps not all of them. But it's such an interesting turn of events." He taps his chin. "Every council member who would not support the edict is somehow—indisposed."

The sleeping sickness. What did that woman say last night? That her husband was a valued courtier. A council member. "That's what the brooches were for. You poisoned your own advisors."

"*You* poisoned them, Dark Grace. And not even properly. They should be dead, the mutinous snakes. Don't think I don't know your slip was intentional. A deathlike sleep." He snorts, his mustache twitching. "Creative, I'll grant you that. But defiant. I've yet to decide what to do with you for that little stunt."

Mariel clutches at the king. "What have you done?" When Tarkin doesn't answer, she wheels to me. "What is he talking about?"

"He bid me"—I struggle to find the words inside the riot in my head—"to cast a death curse on some brooches. But I cast one for sleep instead."

"A . . . sleeping curse," she repeats. And then an idea sparks in the queen's eye. "Boy!" she barks at the servant who escorted the Graces. He steps forward cautiously. "Find those ill with the sleeping sickness and remove every article of clothing they wear."

The servant glances furtively at Tarkin, as if for permission. Mariel claps her hands. "Now, I said! It is the command of your queen! See that it is done or I will—"

"It will not matter." Tarkin dismisses the poor boy and he returns to his post. "You believe I am naïve enough to stake my plans on a piece of jewelry?" He laughs. "That I was not informed immediately when those who should have been dead suddenly woke—after what was attributed to a 'fainting fit'? Exhaustion?" He glares at me. "I visited those early victims personally to inquire after their well-being. Which is when I discovered that the brooches were not needed at all. Not when those council members were *pricked* with the cursed item. Sleep set in instantly—and hasn't yet lifted."

Because my curse entered their bodies directly. And my intent was clear. The nobles will be asleep for a long time.

"But they aren't dead," the queen attempts. "And so the healing Graces . . ."

"Cannot undo her magic." Tarkin grins.

Dragon's teeth. I could almost laugh at my own stupidity, thinking that crafting curses for the Briar King would come without consequences. I've put us in this position. Jeopardized Aurora's throne.

"You are forgetting something, husband." The queen gathers her strength. "My crown is blessed by the Etherians. It will only rest on the head of Leythana's heir. It will kill anyone else." She rips the crown free of her arrangement of coiled braids and thrusts it at Tarkin. "Try it on yourself, if you want it so badly."

The king glowers at the circlet of golden brambles, its thorns like so many gilded teeth. "Then we will get a new crown. For a new Briar. It's time."

A new Briar.

A hundred minuscule details sharpen into horrible focus at once. The war room, with the maps of Etheria spread over the table. The strategy markers strewn across them, indicating routes through the mountain range. The books Aurora told me the king collects, where she'd read about how the light Fae hold their magical hearts in their staffs.

The wheels of my mind begin to whirr.

Tarkin hates Endlewild. I recall the dinner here, where he asked the Fae lord about purchasing Etherian-made sails. His obsession with his army and ships and frustration with the limited scope of Grace power. His promise to grant me rank and prestige in return for my curses.

One of the shackled Graces whimpers. Dragon's teeth. I thought he was using Graces to test my curses because they're bound to obey him. Wouldn't be missed. But it's because they carry the light Fae magic. He wants to see what I could do against the Etherians.

"You're going to invade Etheria." The thought tumbles out as soon as it forms.

The Briar King looks at me like he sees me for the first time. One thick eyebrow raises. "Perhaps I misjudged your intelligence, Dark Grace."

"Have you gone mad?" Queen Mariel lunges at him, swinging her crown like a weapon. "The alliance. The Graces. The Etherians will flatten us into the earth. The treaty with Leythana—"

"Is over." Tarkin shoves her back. She stumbles and the Briar crown sings as it hits the floor. "Or it would have been. Once our last heir fell victim to the curse. Then there would have been no choice but to invade the Fae courts."

The king sounds like a child denied his plaything. Mariel hears it, too. She shades impossibly whiter. "Are you saying—you *wanted* Aurora to die? Your own daughter? Your blood?"

He doesn't deny it. Every inch of Aurora's body stills.

"Something needed to be done," Tarkin continues. "I knew it as soon as I arrived in this realm. Heirs dying off one by one because of that curse. There's only one way to end it properly—start a new line."

"A new—" Mariel swallows. "Seraphina and Cordelia. You wanted them gone, too? I always told you they didn't have enough suitors. Begged you to invite more eligible men to the palace. I even agreed to let Seraphina kiss those from the Common District, when she came to me in her final days. But you refused. I thought your lack of concern was because you didn't understand. You thought some miracle would happen at the last moment. But you . . . you isolated them on purpose. Sent them to their graves because of some—some bid for war?"

"What I understand, wife." If Tarkin feels an ounce of remorse over what he's done, he doesn't show it. "What every son of Paladay understands, is how to strengthen a kingdom. You have no idea how to rule."

"This is not a kingdom." Pride swells in my chest at Aurora's voice. Small, but laced with iron. "It belongs to a queen. And the curse was broken. Leythana's alliance remains intact. I will be the next Briar Queen. Your plans will come to nothing. And I will see you answer for what you did to my sisters."

"*You* will mean nothing soon enough." Tarkin narrows his gaze at his daughter. "If my edict passes in council. And I've made sure that it will. Then Briar will be *mine*. Etheria next." He jerks his chin at the line of prisoners. "The Graces are trinkets compared to the magic that's beyond those mountains. Magic that should be Briar's. Think of what we can do with sails that need no wind and ships that never sink. Lakes that grant immortality."

The story Aurora showed me in her book. Tarkin knows it, too. "That's what you want. To live forever?"

"To *rule* forever," Tarkin corrects.

The queen half laughs, half shrieks. "We'll be dead as soon as they suspect it. My people will never follow you. You'll have a civil war on your hands if—"

"We've beaten a Fae race once, wife. Or do you not remember the war?" He twists his signet ring. "Besides. We have something now that we've never had before. That no realm has ever possessed."

His attention spears through me.

"A Vila."

Some*thing*. The word slithers across the floor and into my blood. Because I am not a person. Not here. Not to him. Queen Mariel gapes at me.

"Yes." Tarkin watches me like I'm a meal to be devoured. "The Vila would have won the war were it not for human interference. And now we are the ones in control. With your dark magic, we will quash the Etherians. They cannot stand against you."

The cord of my power ripples. "I will not be your weapon."

Tarkin laughs, a low, lethal rumble. "And how will you stop me?"

I know exactly how.

My magic springs from its cage. Slams into the king's chest and finds his human power. The fragile thing quivers at my touch. The Briar King falls to his knees, eyes bulging and mouth flopping like a caught fish. His huge fingers dig at his neck, jowls going purple as his strangled gasps fill the chamber. I will end him. As I should have done in the war room. As I should have done as soon as I knew I could do it.

"Alyce."

My name knifes through the air. Aurora's eyes are glassed over and shining. A tear streaks down her cheek and hovers at her jawline. It trembles in the sunlight before it drops to the floor.

"Don't."

My hold on the king's magic loosens.

"Please."

And then it unspools, slinking back into my body like an injured dog.

The way she's looking at me. A crack forms in my heart and fissures outward.

I am a monster.

Tarkin heaves his mountain of girth to stand. No one helps him.

"Try anything like that again," he snarls, gesturing at Aurora, "and she'll be the one who pays for it. It's time to learn your place." He wheels to his daughter, his own heavy crown askew on his balding head. "And yours."

Aurora's jaw sets. A maiden facing a dragon and refusing to back down. "I will never—"

He doesn't let her finish. "You will." The king brushes his knuckles against her cheek. She slaps him away. "It's true. Things would have been easier if you had perished as your sisters did. Without another heir, the realm would have gone to war gladly in order to preserve the Etherium trade and gain access to the Fae courts."

"I'm sorry to disappoint you," she grinds out.

Tarkin shrugs. "But what does it matter if Leythana's line

is intact? You have no children. Perhaps you will have none. And it's clear enough that the Etherians will be of no help to us regarding the matter of succession—Endlewild refuses to discuss the matter with me, and the High King of the Fae ignores my letters. I know the tactic well enough. They're stalling. Waiting to reassert their control over these lands as soon as the last heir is dead. But I mean to take what is ours."

"The magic in Etheria is not yours," Mariel fumes. She picks up the crown and brandishes it at him. "And it will be a death sentence if you—"

"Obviously, your mother does not support my plan. But you." Those beady eyes comb over her and I want to pluck them out of his head. "The realm adores you. Young, beautiful, headstrong. They will follow your lead. It's a good match with Prince Elias. With a silk trade to supplement our coffers. If you dislike him, he can be on the front line during the war."

The implication worms its roots into my guts. Even Aurora cringes.

"There are riches beyond your wildest dreams on the other side of the mountain. Magic far more potent than the petty party tricks that keep your hair soft and your skin supple. In return for your support, I will let you rule beside me—forever. The whole world will be at your disposal." He takes her chin in two fingers. "Or you can fight me and die for it."

CHAPTER THIRTY-SIX

In the end, I am carted off to the dungeons.

The Vila in me yearned to attack the magic of my guards. To Shift and bolt from the palace, never to be seen again. But Aurora. I have no doubt the king would make good on his threats. And I will not let her die because of me.

So I find myself locked in a tiny cell, far below the opulence of the palace. It reminds me a little of my Lair. The slimy stone walls, smelling of mold and damp, rotting earth. The cold that seeps through the delicate silk of Laurel's pilfered gown and into my marrow.

The dungeon is worse than the Lair, though. By far. Rats have taken up residence in the mess of straw piled in one corner, their tiny claws scratching at the stone. And there's the awful stench—like perhaps the royal sewers empty nearby. This far inside the mountain, they might.

I try to think of other things, like counting the time in the dripping of distant water and the intermittent echo of footsteps. The guard changing, I assume. But they do not come to bait me, as I guessed they would. The Briar King's Vila pet must be considered too dangerous. And there are no other prisoners close by.

There's nothing to do but think and sleep. But sleep is as far from me as one of the realms across the Carthegean Sea. Instead, every conceivable thought burrows into my brain like the rats into the straw. How long before Tarkin starts to use me? He's been planning this invasion for some time. I was just the missing piece. The secret weapon he didn't even realize that he had. Until the duke. I curse myself again for my idiocy. I should have known this day would come. How many Etherian lives will I take? How many of Tarkin's enemies will I put down? My skin itches, as if it is already covered in their blood.

Every time I close my eyes, there's Aurora. The sound of her voice when she asked if I was using her to take over Briar. The look on her face when I had her father in my thrall. It had been as if she was seeing me for the first time.

I rest my forehead against the gritty iron bars of my cell. I must get to her. Explain—

What? A savage voice tears through me. That I didn't take her father's gold in return for curses? That I wasn't lying to her every time we met, making it easy for the Briar King to steal her throne and raze her realm?

Unbidden, a new image of Aurora seems to emerge in the darkness. Her kneeling and looking up at me like I'm a fallen star come to earth. Her skin gloved in moonlight. The taste of her mouth on mine. Our limbs tangled together in sleep. Tears burn down my cheeks as I crumple to the filthy ground. That night was my one slice of happiness. I'll never have another.

The sound of metal screeching against metal jerks my eyelids open. For a moment, I'm lost in the suffocating blackness, the place between waking and sleeping, and I don't understand why my back aches and I'm freezing and my head feels filled with lead.

And then it all comes careening back.

I'm on my feet as fast as my sore body will let me move. Rough stone nicks my palms as I wedge myself into a corner.

"Alyce."

My brain must be addled. I'm hallucinating. Because I know that voice. And it can't possibly be her. My cell door opens with a squeal and a cloaked figure slips inside. Another behind it. My eyes begin to adjust in the gloom.

"Laurel?"

She tugs her hood down around her shoulders, polished black skin drinking the light of her lantern flame. My arms are around her before she can answer.

"What are you doing here? How did you—"

The second figure registers. My veins flash fire and ice.

"Hello, Alyce."

I let go of Laurel.

"Aurora." Her name on my lips is a tenuous, fragile thing. But once I've spoken, everything else pours out in a fury.

"I'm sorry. I'm so sorry. I never wanted to make the curses." I choke on a sob. "I didn't realize. I just needed a way out of Briar. Of my life here. The whole world was closing in and I— I . . ."

She stays me with a raised hand. "I've had time to think. And I remembered what you said. About being at the mercy of someone who has the power to take everything."

Shame scalds down my throat. I'd been harsh with her that day.

"I don't forgive what you did." The fractures on my heart expand. "But I know my father. And I know you likely had little choice in the matter." She pauses. And her next words are so soft I almost miss them. "You did have a choice, though."

I clench my teeth against the truth that crackles between us.

"I know."

Now she will turn and go—leave me to the mercy of the Briar King. But then, "I want a new beginning for us. For Briar. One in which choices like that don't exist at all."

Hope wriggles in my chest. "You mean you still . . ."

She steps impossibly nearer. One hand cups the back of my neck. Her thumb trails my jawline. "Of course I do." Her lips brush mine and I am reeling. "This is the only thing I'm sure of. You aren't the Dark Grace. Not anymore. You're Alyce."

Carefully, as if she might disappear at my touch, my fingers bury themselves into the silk of her hair. And then I am kissing her again, gulping her down like sweet, fizzy wine. Desperate to be drunk.

"As much as I hate to interrupt." Another voice startles us both.

Mortification smears up my neck as I realize how close Laurel is standing, the three of us pressed together inside this tiny cell.

Cell.

"Wait." Beyond the iron bars, the passage is empty. "How are you two here?"

Aurora grins. "After I decided you needed rescuing, I sent for Laurel myself. It was easy enough to summon a wisdom Grace while I was supposed to be considering my father's offer." Her gaze brightens with that mischievous glint that lets butterflies loose beneath my skin. "The rest was your own doing. You know the sleeping potion you gave me for my guards? You were right. A jab of my sewing needle did the trick."

The draught I crafted when she first came to my Lair. Dragon's teeth, that feels like years ago. I can't help but laugh at the absurdity of this situation.

"Keep your voice down," Laurel warns. "We don't have much time. Here." She fishes something wrapped in cloth out of a pocket of her cloak and presses it into my hands. "I thought you'd be hungry."

Bread and cheese. I could kiss her. But I stuff the heel of the loaf inside my mouth instead, groaning as flecks of butter melt on my tongue.

Laurel doesn't waste any time. "It's been just over twelve hours since your arrest." My stomach grumbles, arguing that it feels far longer. "The princess told me about the Briar King's plan. He's made no overt declarations, but the guards have increased in the palace. And I heard there was a secret council meeting. I imagine things will progress quickly." She watches me, expectant. "Do you have a plan?"

"No," I say through the crumbs. "Not yet."

She squeezes the slender bridge of her nose. "Why would you? Fall in love with the king's daughter, get thrown in the dungeons. But, by the dragon, *don't* have a plan."

"Yet," I repeat, bristling. "My plan is to make sure Aurora gets her throne."

Her fingers twine with mine.

"With you by her side?" Laurel asks wryly. "Because she could ally with her father and get exactly that—a crown and a throne. Forever, if he's successful."

"I will not," Aurora answers, stiffening. "He let my sisters die. Wanted me dead, too, so that the realm would support his war. I do not trust him. And there will be no Briar if my father attacks the light Fae. My mother was right about that much—they will destroy us."

Laurel considers her for a long while, her gift working. "Good. Then there is only one thing to be done. The queen must regain her full authority."

"That's impossible." Aurora lets go of me. "The contract granting the Briar Kings their rights is ironclad. I've read the agreement often enough. The Briar Queen's place at council is ceremonial. The only political power she retains is of delaying the council's vote or swaying a member's opinion—and my father has taken care of those who would be loyal to her."

"There are some who care nothing for such contracts."

Hints of bronze in Laurel's gaze leap and dive with the flickering lantern flame. "Those bound by word and word alone."

Word and word alone? There's only one creature I can think of who fits that description. "Do you mean the Etherians?"

"I do indeed. As they cannot lie, the *verbal* agreements of the Fae are as strong as any blood oath. And they did grant Briar a blood oath, in the form of the crown itself."

I think of the statue outside the palace gates. Leythana's crown dripping with golden paint. But it wasn't paint when the Fae blessed it. It was blood. And not even Tarkin has dared wear the wreath of bramble and thorn, knowing the power behind it.

"The Etherians have never interfered with Briar's affairs before," Aurora argues, wrinkling her nose at the bed of straw when a rat tail swishes into view. "Catalina started giving away her duties centuries ago, and the light Fae did nothing to stop her. And my father says they've been no help with the matter of succession. They don't seem the least bit concerned that I'm the last heir."

"Honestly, did you two *read* the books you stole from the library?" When we don't answer, she utters a low curse and exhales slowly. "As part of Leythana's alliance agreement, the Etherians pledged to protect the rightful ruler of Briar. But she has to *ask* for that protection. The whole point of Briar's existence is so the Etherians don't have to meddle with the borderlands. They only come if they are called."

"But my father did call. He asked several times—"

"Your father is not the rightful ruler of Briar in the eyes of the Etherians," Laurel interrupts. "Queen Mariel is."

Aurora falls silent as realization hits. The handle of her lantern creaks in her grip. "Because the light Fae are bound by word alone. They don't give a dragon's tooth about the wedding contracts. Oh, I've been such a fool. How did I not see that?"

"It doesn't matter now." Laurel waves her off. "Based on the fact that the Etherians haven't intervened, I assume it's been only King Tarkin communicating with the Fae?"

"I—" Aurora is still dazed. "I thought my mother was negotiating with them about the succession, but . . . now I'm not sure. Whatever she's done, it's not enough for them to help us. Because they would help, wouldn't they? They would cast my father down as a usurper."

Laurel nods. "If Leythana's heir named him such, yes."

"How would Mariel do that?" I ask. "Endlewild?"

It's suddenly clear why the Fae lord hardly gives the time of day to most of the court. Why he refused to discuss Briar's future with Tarkin. He's bound only to Mariel, and she doesn't even realize the power she holds.

"The Lord Ambassador hasn't been seen for some time," Laurel says darkly. "I've been making inquiries."

I was wondering why I didn't see him at the curse-breaking celebration. And he wasn't at Narcisse's trial, either. In fact, I can't remember the last time I saw the Fae lord aside from his visit to my Lair.

A rat rustles in the straw.

"That can't be a good sign."

"There could be many reasons for his absence." Laurel sounds calm, but worry deepens the lines around her mouth. "Perhaps your mother has spoken with him and he's gathering reinforcements."

"Or he's dead," I mutter.

Laurel scowls.

"I doubt it. Mother was as shocked as I was when we learned of Father's plans. She can't have gone to Endlewild now—even if he's at court, Father will be watching. The council vote is in three days. If we can't summon the Etherians—"

The bread and cheese curdle in my stomach.

"Tarkin will be expecting resistance," Laurel cautions. An errant wisp of her emerald hair shivers in the dank chill.

"We need to distract him," Aurora says. She chews her bottom lip, as she does when she's thinking. "My mother can only stay the vote for so long, if she manages to stay it at all."

This is a mess. Not even a year ago, I could not have cared less if Briar smoldered to ash. Now I want Aurora to rule. Want the future we could have, one in which I don't have to spill my blood and curse brooches and—

An idea strikes, hot and cold at the same time. "The sleeping curse."

Two pairs of eyes pin me to the stone. "What?"

"I can make another, like I did with the brooches. We can put your father to sleep. For as long as it takes to call the Etherians and set things right." I'm nearly tripping over the words, the plan taking swift flight in my mind. "He'll wake up dethroned and powerless."

Or not at all. The thought brings me more joy than it probably should.

Laurel glances beyond the bars and presses closer. "You're talking about poisoning the Briar King."

The tips of my fingers tingle, but I can't tell whether it's from anticipation or fear. "I'm talking about saving the queens. Mariel and Aurora both."

"How?" Aurora demands. "He'll be expecting it. He already has tasters for every meal. And he obviously knows about the brooches. He probably has them in his keeping."

"Something else, then. It can be anything."

Laurel frowns. "You don't have your kit."

I swallow down a lump of guilt and rush on before I think better of it. "I don't need it. My magic works differently than yours."

"I see." She sweeps a weighted look from my head to my feet. "And if anyone guesses? I can't imagine that they would. The Dark Grace imprisoned and the king mysteriously struck down by the sleeping sickness."

"I'll leave, then. Hide."

"No." Aurora's hand lands on my arm, firm. "We can't possibly smuggle you out. I'm sorry, Alyce, but it was hard enough sneaking down here. If they know you're gone—"

"You don't need to worry about that." And then, ignoring the instinct tapping against my sternum, I hold out my hand and Shift it to invisibility, wincing as exhausted bones and muscle obey my command.

"You're a Shifter!"

"I knew it!"

They speak at the same time, Aurora batting cautiously at my missing hand. Gasping as her skin touches what her eyes tell her isn't there.

"You did not know." I glare at Laurel.

She shrugs. "I knew you were up to something."

I roll my eyes. My Shift fades, skin prickling as it reappears.

Aurora swats at my wrist, as if expecting it to vanish again.

"You're not—" The words are sticky. "Disgusted?"

She tucks a lock of my hair behind my ear. Smiles in that way that turns my heart into hot, melted wax. "Never."

She presses a kiss into my palm and memories of our night together flow unchecked into my mind. Of how those kisses felt elsewhere.

"Well." Laurel clears her throat, making us both blush. "Now that we have that settled. Shall we get back to the insane plan to poison the king?"

"Curse the king," I correct. "But she's right. It's risky."

"Everything is risky." Aurora lets me go. "No matter what path we choose, it ends in ruin. Briar's or mine."

"But this could end in both." Laurel begins ticking items off on her fingers. "If the king dies from the curse and you're implicated, the people will never trust you. His supporters in the council will overthrow you. If it doesn't work and he realizes what you've done, he'll kill you, ending your line. Or Briar will descend into civil war. Or the Etherians could decide to take back the land and kill us all. Consider this carefully."

"I am," Aurora snaps. Laurel raises her eyebrows in silent challenge. But Aurora doesn't waver. "I trust Alyce."

A thousand emotions whirl through me at once—love and frayed nerves and terror and everything else. It's difficult to tell them apart.

"How soon can you have the curse ready?" Aurora asks.

"As you said, Tarkin already knows about the brooches, so I'll need something else of his. Something he won't suspect. Can you get that?"

The light from her lantern stutters. "I think so."

"Good. Then have Laurel bring it to me. It's too dangerous to come yourself. I'll go to the black tower. The ruins at the edge of the sea cliffs. I—" My long-held deception stings. "I've been practicing there." But I still won't utter Kal's name. His secrets are his own.

"I'm afraid you two are forgetting a very important detail." Laurel snaps her fingers between our faces. "I have not agreed to this plan."

"But you're here!" I protest. "You brought her to—"

"To discuss our strategy. Not to go along blindly with whatever you two love-struck imbeciles cook up. I've already voiced my thoughts on this plan."

Aurora and I exchange panicked glances. We need Laurel for this to work.

"Do you have another, then? I'd love to hear it."

Laurel rolls her shoulders back. Adjusts her cloak. "No," she admits. "One is nearly as bad as the next. But I want assurances. A return on my investment."

"Anything," Aurora blurts out. I knock her with my elbow.

"Alyce is right." Laurel tilts her head. "A queen needs to be far better at negotiations. Never promise something you might not be able to deliver."

Aurora slumps a little, chastened. "What do you want, then?"

Laurel doesn't hesitate. "You will abolish the Grace Laws once you take the throne. Dismiss the men serving on the Grace Council and replace them with Graces. *We* will be solely responsible for the management of the system and the selection of the members of the new Grace Council. There will be no interference from the royals or nobles or anyone else."

"Done."

Laurel smirks. "You are not Fae, Princess. I require more than your word." From the inside of her cloak, she pulls out a tiny gilded knife. One the Graces use when preparing their enhancements. A ruby Briar rose glitters at the base of the hilt.

"What are you going to do with that?"

"A blood oath." She slices her palm. Molten gold blood trickles down her wrist. "There's just enough Etherian magic in a Grace's blood to make it effective." She wipes the knife on her skirts and offers it to Aurora. "Unless you refuse."

"You don't have to do it," I say, nudging her.

"No. I want to. I have no intention of going back on my word." She sets her lantern on the ground, takes the knife, and uses it to slit the skin of her palm.

"You will honor your promise regarding the Graces," Laurel says, holding out her hand.

Aurora takes it, not an ounce of nerve showing. And then

light erupts from their joined grip. A golden cord winds around their wrists, followed by a funnel of cold that gusts into the cell with a low groan. The lanterns gutter. Their cloaks snap in the current of wind. And then everything is still.

"Now," Laurel says to me once the gilded aura fades. "Let's get you out of here."

CHAPTER THIRTY-SEVEN

The guards are still drooling in their sleep when we tiptoe past them. We'd locked my cell door again and replaced the heavy key ring on the belt of its owner. Laurel even thought to bring me a fresh dress—stolen from the palace servants—and we arrange the one I'd been wearing so that it looked like I was curled up in the rancid straw. But we have no illusions. I have hours, if that, before they discover I'm gone. I can only hope Tarkin won't punish Aurora for my escape.

My power is waning, depleted from the harrowing events of the last night, but I manage to Shift into one of the guards to emerge from the dungeons. And then find a shadowy alcove to transform into a Grace to exit the palace with Laurel. But my magic is stretched farther than I've ever pushed it, and with each step I'm afraid that I'll lose the Shift and expose myself.

But it holds.

Laurel hails us a closed snow carriage and directs it to the Grace house nearest to the Common District checkpoint, as close as she can get to the black tower without raising suspicion. I let my Shift fall away as soon as the brocade curtains are drawn, sighing as my bones drift back into place.

"The princess will send for me again once she has something for you to curse," Laurel says as the carriage sets off. "As you said, it will be too risky for her to come to you herself. I will bring it. To the black tower. Where you've been training in secret."

Even in the charcoal dim of the carriage I can see the accusation etched in the angles of Laurel's face.

I pick at the stitching on my sleeves. "Yes."

"Alone?"

"Nearly."

The carriage skids over a patch of ice and I catch myself on the hand strap before I'm thrown forward. Laurel crosses one leg over the other and drums her fingertips against her knees, waiting for me to say more. I don't.

"I hope you know what you're doing," she says at last. Through a slit in the curtain, I watch the Grace District blur past. I wonder if it's the last time I'll see the pale brick façades and snow-frosted poplars. "We're in enough danger as it is."

I want to tell her that I do. That Kal is our ally. He taught me what I needed to flee Tarkin's dungeon. To control my power. But would she trust him? A prisoner locked in a tower since the War of the Fae. I keep the words back.

"You have nothing to worry about."

"We have everything to worry about." She snaps the curtain closed. "And if you don't understand that, we're in more trouble than I thought."

I use the dregs of my power to Shift into a dirt-smudged errand boy in order to talk my way through the checkpoint at the Common District and then the main gates of Briar. I wanted to stop by Lavender House to rescue Callow. Even set Prince Markham free. But Laurel refused. My Lair is in ruins, she told me. The palace guard arrived shortly after I was sent to the dungeons. And my animals are gone.

A fresh lash of guilt scores my conscience. Callow. Is she in an alleyway, pecking at scraps of food? Is she dead? Laurel promises to look for her, but I'm not optimistic. Another life on my hands.

Kal is waiting for me in the black tower, his shadows gathering like storm clouds. After the dungeons, the king, Callow—I come undone.

My threadbare Shift dissolves. Sobs wrack my body. Kal doesn't ask questions. He holds me, his icy body a comfort against the liquid fire of my own.

I don't speak for a long time, only clutch at Kal's chest. When I do, he listens. I keep nothing back, ashamed of myself for lying for so long. But he doesn't chide me, as he should. Doesn't rage. He pulls me closer, resting his chin on top of my head.

"I worried this would happen. And I suspected there was something with the princess." He strokes my hair, the frost from his touch tingling on my scalp and stinging the inside of my nose. "But I am sorry you felt the need to lie to me."

"I'm sorry," I mumble against his heart. It beats slowly, faintly, as always. "I'm a fool."

"For falling in love?" A shadow tickles my cheek. "I cannot agree."

I curl my fingers tighter into his clothes. A wave breaks against the cliff, the echo reverberating through the tower.

"I want her to rule. I want a different Briar, one where I'm respected and treated like an equal. I want—" I break off, shaking.

"You want her." Kal smiles, but it's sad. Shadows swirl around his shoulders like tentacles. "I understand. But is it worth everything, Alyce? Because that is what it will cost."

Anger swallows my grief in a single violent gulp. I shove Kal away harder than necessary and stalk to the other side of the chamber.

"Do not mistake me," Kal says after a while, a cautious hand on my shoulder. "I do not mean to discredit your feelings. Your kiss broke the curse."

I taste salt on my lips. "But why us? Why that kiss, when I'm Vila?"

Kal taps his index finger gently on my forehead. "I think you know. The union of a Vila and a human. Two races sworn to despise each other, who irreparably harmed the other during the war, coming together. That alone is powerful magic."

My head throbs. What he says makes sense, but I still do not fully believe it.

Kal runs the pad of his thumb over the crust of tears on my cheekbone. "Please. Think." He pauses, waits until my eyes lock with his. "Think of everything she has to lose by choosing you. How much simpler it will be for her to abide her father's wishes. Are you certain she will not take that path?"

"Yes." There are so many variables in our plan, but of that I am sure. "Invading the Etherian lands is madness. She will not let her father do it. She will not lose her crown that way."

"But will she keep you by her side? Or will she use you and discard you? As everyone else has done."

A taste like bile slides over my tongue and down my throat. Thunder rumbles in the distance, raising the hair on my arms.

"You are making a mistake," Kal continues. "I do not wish to lose you."

"Stay with me, then." I reach for him as white flashes through the gaping hole in the stones. "I will plead your case to Aurora. You've more than paid for your crimes, especially if you agree to help us. She's reasonable. She won't do what her ancestors did."

"You are determined, then." His jet eyes harden, shadows curling away from me like they've been burned. "I will not dissuade you."

It isn't a question. And I don't answer. My chest aches, but I don't try to explain myself anymore, beg his forgiveness, or win his favor back. I have made my choice.

"I will free you first," I vow. "I won't let you rot here if things go badly. But I hope you'll change your mind. I don't want to choose between you."

His next words, laced with misery, hurt worse than any torture the king could have devised. "Oh, Alyce. You already have."

In the upper floors of the tower, there is a small chamber where the ceiling is mostly intact. Its narrow window looks out over the black, restless sea, the moon like a silver coin hidden behind the clouds. I do what I can to make it habitable. The bed is in decent shape, although the bedclothes are moldy and reek of brine and dampness. But it's better than the disease-riddled straw of the prison cells. Rubble and broken furniture litter the floor, including the remains of an ancient spinning wheel.

Though I know I need rest for my magic to regenerate, sleep refuses to come. Each new fear crashes against my skull like the breaking waves below. My ears stay tuned for the tinny clang of the alarm bells. For the rumble of hooves on the ground, searching for the king's escaped prisoner. But Briar is quiet.

Once dawn begins to gild the whitecaps, the promised storm of the last night having done little more than grumble as it passed over Briar, I give up the bed and focus my energy on fixing the spinning wheel. It's a lost cause. A large chunk of the flywheel is missing. There's no belt. The footman is warped. And the maidens are crooked. But the impossible task gives my hands an outlet. By midmorning, I have the pieces mostly in the right places. I give the wheel a good spin, finding a strange sort of comfort in the way the spokes blur together. In the creaky, clacking sound it makes. Almost hypnotizing.

"Have you given any more thought to what I said?"

Kal's voice from the shadows pulls me back into the present.

I still the wheel. "Have you?"

His silence is answer enough. There will be no convincing him to stay—no more than I can be convinced to leave.

Letting out a sigh, I knead the shooting tension at the crook of my shoulder. I have no idea when Laurel will arrive with the king's item. When she does, things will move very quickly. Kal needs to get away while he can.

"It's time to free you, then."

One of his shadows slithers away from me, as if it knows what I'm going to do. "You do not have to try now. You are tired."

I push past him and down the stairs, inhaling deep breaths of the salty air and trying to center my focus. There's another storm coming. I can see the charcoal line on the horizon, heavy-bellied clouds trudging their way inland. A twinge starts behind my eyes, the pressure building.

"I'm well enough for this." Even I hear the fatigue in my voice. But I made Kal a promise. And my Vila magic has only grown in the past months. "We don't have time to wait."

Kal watches me with his arms crossed, the shadows wending and billowing around him like the beating wings of one of Leythana's dragons. As if they remember what happened last time and are daring me to try again. I cling to what little confidence I can gather and send my magic out, feeling for the protections of Kal's prison. The cord of my power connects in half a heartbeat, bumping against the stone buttress that encases the enchantment.

This time, I do not start swinging blindly as I did before. Brute force only alerts the binding magic to an attack. Instead, I skim the edges of the protections, feeling for weaknesses.

There.

A chink. A thin spot. It's all I need. I pull my power back before the shadows realize what I'm doing. Build my magic until it is a thick rope of darkness. And then, with every fiber of my soul, I let it loose.

Like a whip, my power cracks against the protections of the enchantment. The floor of the tower rattles. Kal groans and doubles over. The shadows hiss and scatter, leaving his body for the first time since I've known him. But his prison is not broken. It's angry.

The walls of magic build themselves back up, healing the wounds caused by my attack. But I am faster. My own power zips around the protections, puncturing their surface. The shadows howl, shriveling up like scorched parchment. The magic of the enchantment pushes against mine, iron meeting iron. I grit my teeth, sweat beading along my collarbone and drenching my back.

"Keep going," Kal gasps. He's on all fours, sides heaving.

My muscles stretch and tremble. My very bones shudder with the growl of my power. The smell of woodsmoke and charred earth and flint floods my lungs. The pain is nearly too much. Spots bleed and dance across my vision. But I ignore the agony. Dig deeper than I ever have into the core of my power and funnel the remaining vestiges of my strength.

And then I find it.

The heart of Kal's enchantment. It screams of otherness. My own metallic scent mingles with that of spring roses and dewed grass. The taste of loamy earth lands on my tongue. It's familiar somehow, but I can't place it. I push harder, my Vila power eclipsing the tiny pulse of Kal's cage, wrapping and winding and clamping until the shadows around Kal go perfectly, unnaturally still. Like ink frozen in the air.

And then, with a last shove of my magic, there is an explosion of light. The black tower goes white, the same way it did the first time I tried to break these bindings. Only a thousand times brighter. Like the sun itself is captured within these walls. I'm thrown to my knees in the blinding glare, hands skidding on the stones. My power recedes, limping and bruised. But victorious.

The room comes back into focus.

Kal is standing near the gap. For the first time since I've known him, sunlight spills over his shoulders. Lends an aura around his form.

"You did it." He turns his hands over, gazing in wonder.

I wobble to my feet. He rushes to me, scoops me up, and spins me around. "You did it!" Kisses rain across my forehead and down my cheeks. His body is unbelievably warm, the shadows taking the icy cold with them when they fled. And his skin is brighter. Pale pink touches his eyelids and lips. His once raven hair is an unfamiliar shade of rust.

He sets me down and all I can do is gape. "You're—different."

"Yes." He adjusts his waistcoat, now garnet with ebony filigree, still grinning. "I rather am." He tips his head back and inhales. Then grabs my hand and pulls me toward the entrance. "Come, I wish to feel the daylight after so much darkness."

But I pry myself loose. "I have to wait for Laurel. It won't be long now."

Kal's smile wilts. "Of course." An awkward silence settles between us. "Alyce," he attempts, and I know what he's going to say. "Will you not reconsider? Come away with me. Leave the humans to their messes. You owe them nothing."

I know he's trying to protect me, but I won't be swayed. "I love Aurora. I will help her."

"Her life is so short. Will you rescue her so that she can grow old while you remain young? Are you content to watch the years whittle her away?"

The thought makes me itch. I know he's right. But I cannot abandon Aurora simply because she is mortal. "I want all the time I can have with her—even if it's not much."

A current of wind slices through the gap in the wall, carrying the salt-stained promise of the storm. His onyx gaze gleams. "This is a fool's game."

"Kal." I go to him, wishing that I could make him understand. "I am utterly grateful for what you've done. I would never have discovered the depth of my power without you. But—"

"Then come with me." He grasps my elbows, and I swear I can feel the steady rhythm of his heartbeat through his palms. After the frost I've grown accustomed to, it's unsettling. "Together we can go anywhere. Be anything."

He wants this so much. I can almost smell his desire, like crushed nightshade berries—bittersweet and smoky. Part of me wants to give in. Kal deserves my loyalty. But so does Aurora. "No, Kal. I am staying."

"In a realm that despises you? What do you think they will do, even if your precious princess survives?" His grip turns harsh. "Do you think they will welcome you with open arms? Put a crown on your head?" He bends close. "They will burn you. Tear you limb from limb. You will always be a monster. A *mongrel.*"

Instinct taking over, I grind my heel into his toe and shove him back. He stumbles. Anger builds in my chest, its hot coals stoked with each breath.

"It is no business of yours." I rub the sore spots on my arms. "I trust Aurora. And I choose her. If you will not stand with us, then leave. But you will not speak to me that way. You will not hurt me."

A slow, languid smile stretches over Kal's face. A wave smashes into the base of the cliff, its spray like chips of ice. Warning bells clang through my mind.

"I had hoped you would come to me willingly. But I see you will not listen to reason."

The roots of my hair stand on end. I know this feeling well.

Run.

Obeying that primal impulse, I bolt for the entrance of the tower. But I don't manage two bounding leaps before a wall of shadow slams into me. I back away, dizzy and stunned. Are those the same shadows I'd just cleaved from Kal's body? But they can't be. Panic beats out a frenzied rhythm at my breastbone, sending me tripping over my feet.

"I just want you to listen." Kal's voice is too calm. "To hear me."

Darkness undulates in every corner, writhing like snakes. Kal snaps his fingers and strips of shadow peel themselves free and cut through the air. My mind spins. Kal *is* controlling the shadows. But how?

I don't stay to guess. Adrenaline thundering through me, I sprint up the stairs, scrambling for a plan. Kal's even, measured footsteps thud behind me. There's nowhere to go where he can't follow. Dragon's teeth, I don't understand. Kal is my ally. My friend.

You don't have friends, that awful voice seethes.

"I will not hurt you," Kal calls.

The blood searing through my veins says otherwise. I throw myself into my room and bolt the door, but the wood is rotten and I know it won't hold up beyond a few good kicks. Kal's steps are nearing. I scan the chamber, terror sinking its claws deep into me.

A gull cries, jerking my attention to the window, where the spinning wheel waits. The spindle. *Weapon,* my mind registers.

But I don't want to hurt Kal. He's confused, as I had been. He needs time.

The sleeping curse.

The thought lands in my brain like a drop of water on parched earth.

Yes. I could curse him. Just for a little while. Long enough for me to settle things in Briar. When he wakes, he'll see that Aurora isn't like other humans. He'll understand.

Wood pummels against wood and the hinges rattle. "Let me in, Alyce. I want to talk."

As the next blow lands, I pry the spindle free of its moorings.

Sleep, I push through my mind, harnessing my intent. *Not death. Only sleep.*

Guilt churns through me. I don't want to do this. But there's a crunch and the door buckles. Another kick splits the paneling in two. I hardly feel the stab of pain as the tip of the spindle pierces my skin.

Kal stoops through the wreckage, shadows at his heels like loyal dogs. I hide the spindle in the folds of my skirts.

"That isn't Shifter magic." I nod to the darkness, struggling to keep my voice level.

"A funny thing about magic." He knocks aside a section of the door with his boot. "Sometimes, when you live with an enchantment long enough, you absorb its power." A tendril of soot curls around his ankle. "And we have been so long acquainted."

The hand holding the spindle begins to shake. This is not the Kal I know. "Please. I don't want to hurt you."

"Nor I you." He steps closer. "Which is why I cannot let you return to Briar. We leave now. Let the mortals tear their realm to bits. Then the land will be ours for the taking. A new Malterre."

I blink in confusion. "You want to . . . to turn Briar into Malterre?"

"Should I not?" He sneers, betraying an ugliness I don't recognize. My instinct thrums, urging me to act before it's too late. "The humans razed my lands while I watched. Seizing theirs is only fair. And after that"—greed flashes bright in his eyes—"Etheria itself."

Dragon's teeth, he's lost his senses. I grip the spindle harder, searching for the best place to strike. "That's exactly the kind of logic that will get the Briar King killed."

"Ah, but we are not the Briar King." He laughs and it mingles with a roll of thunder. "We are Shifter and Vila. And we will seek revenge for those who have fallen." He extends a hand to me. "You must know this is right, Alyce. Avenge your mother's death. Take justice for all the wrong this realm has dealt you. I know you want to bathe in their blood."

I release an unsteady breath. When I first came to this tower, that's precisely what I wanted. Vengeance as a balm for the hundred thousand tiny wounds Briar had inflicted. But the sweetness of that future is bland in comparison to what I have with Aurora.

Kal doesn't understand. He's too lost in bitterness.

"You will see," he says. "Together we will—"

Before I lose my nerve, I lunge forward and slam the spindle into his side. Kal curses, jumping backward and flailing. His lips form the shape of my name.

And then he crumples.

CHAPTER THIRTY-EIGHT

For a long time, I sit and watch Kal sleep. The rhythmic rise and fall of his chest and the flutter of his eyelids. Relief soothes my guilt with each small movement, proof that my curse didn't kill him as I worried it might. This abysmal morning replays through my mind on an endless loop. I should have known better. Kal lost everyone in the war. And then my mother centuries later. I can't blame him for desiring vengeance. But I won't let him take Aurora's throne to get it.

The sleeping curse I enacted on the spindle should last about as long as one of my elixirs, since it was crafted out of need and not desire. I'll decide what to do with Kal when he wakes.

Throwing a tattered blanket over him, I go downstairs and wait for Laurel. It's evening now. Thunder rumbles, rattling loose stones in the upper floors. The storm has made slow progress. I hope Laurel arrives before it hits. If it's another blizzard, she could be locked inside for days—we can't spare that kind of time.

The skies are tinged navy, but quickly darkening to lead as I watch the clumps of trees hiding Briar's main gates. With the shriek of each passing gull, I wish that I could spot Callow coming to find me. It's a futile hope. My kestrel can't fly. But pain throbs in my chest when I imagine her lying sprawled in some alley, her neck twisted and wings splayed out. I fear I will never outlive the guilt that plagues me for her fate.

Lightning forks in the distance, Briar lit up in a blaze of white. If everything goes well, this time tomorrow, the king will be asleep. Mariel will call in the Etherians and—

A frigid wind sweeps underneath me and I'm knocked to my stomach, chin slamming against stone. Blood bursts in my mouth. I choke on the taste of wet, bitter earth. That same invisible grip flips me over onto my back. My arms and legs strain, but they are caught, bound in shadows.

"What in Briar?" I struggle and squirm, but the darkness only clamps tighter.

A ripple of movement catches my attention.

"No." It's all I can say. All I can think, as I watch *Kal* descend the stairs. "I cursed you."

The shadows bite into my wrists, the cold like a blade.

"You did." He grins. "But you forgot the key element to your power, as you have done since the day you set foot in this tower: intent."

Thunder rolls again, a sickening, haunting laugh.

"No, I—"

"You said it yourself—you did not *want* to hurt me. And

so your little sleeping curse caused nothing more than a nap."

Dragon's teeth. I wriggle harder against the bonds, but it's useless.

"Really, Alyce. By now, I expect more from you. It seems I still have much to teach you." With a grunt he picks me up and throws me over his shoulder. Pain spikes through my jaw and teeth with each of his jarring steps. "And I do not wish to be interrupted by a pesky Grace. Laurel, was it? Well. We shall deal with her later."

Terror drums beneath my skin. Now I do hope there's a blizzard on the way. Anything to keep Laurel from danger. We've reached my room. Kal drops me unceremoniously onto the floor in a corner.

"Kal, this is madness. We cannot take Briar by ourselves," I reason, trying in vain to keep my voice steady. "Whatever was done to you, it's not worth dying in some reckless act of vengeance."

"What do you know of it?" He snarls. "Your life was a garden party compared to the last several centuries locked in this rotting cesspool. Do you know who put me here? Have you managed to puzzle it out? The same creatures who tormented you for years—Etherian filth."

The admission snatches the breath from my lungs. Now that the enchantment is broken, Kal can speak of his captors. The smell when I reached the heart of Kal's enchantment. Dewed grass and spring flowers. I knew I recognized it. It's the same that lingered in my Lair after Endlewild threatened me. The same power that pulses in the Fae lord's staff. Dragon's teeth, I should have known. The scar on my torso aches. "But how? Etherians can only wield light magic. They couldn't have bound you in shadow."

Kal laughs, low in his throat. "Oh yes, the Vila have a terrible reputation for lies and trickery, but the Etherians are just as wicked. They only mask it better beneath the perfume of blessings and charms." He moves to the window and sets the spinning wheel turning, wood clacking on wood. "They managed to imprison me in this tower because they were caging a dangerous beast. A *beast*. You know something about that, I think."

Thunder growls and I shudder. I do know.

"But I was not alone here," Kal continues.

That doesn't make any sense. I've never seen anyone else in the tower.

His hand goes to his neck, fishing out the medallion I discovered what feels like a lifetime ago. The raw skin of his chest has healed now that the bindings are severed. But why is the medallion intact? It should have shattered along with the enchantment.

"I was in love with a Vila once," Kal says. "In the court of Targen, to which I served as a spy both before and during the war. But the Vila council forbade the match, insisting on keeping bloodlines pure. I wanted to leave them—start our own court, perhaps. But she wanted revenge. And she took it as ruthlessly as she could." He fingers the thick chain and watches the sea. "Her magic bled into the Etherian lands. It was the first time in decades that the Vila had encroached on Etherian territory, and so the light Fae saw it as an act of war and struck back."

War? But there was only one war in Briar's history. "You

mean the War of the Fae? Your lover *started* the War of the Fae? That's impossible. I would have read about her." Dragon knows I'd scoured every book I could find on the subject.

He wheels to me. A quick streak of lightning illuminates the crimson threads in his hair, like fine streaks of blood. "After the war, her name was scrubbed from all records."

"No. There was only one Vila who—" The next clap of thunder shakes me to my core. "The Vila who cast the curse on Aurora's family. She was . . ."

"Very good, Alyce." Kal leers at me. "Yes. I helped her. Disguised myself as a servant to enter the palace and plant the Vila's curse on the heirs. The royals deserved it. The humans poisoned our lands. Killed our kin. And so we did the same to Briar. Leythana's daughters would live to the age of twenty-one, one year for each year of the War of the Fae. Just long enough to make the pathetic humans think they could *do* something to save their children. And then the poor princesses would succumb to the Vila magic. Eventually, the curse would end the royal line. Briar would be thrown into civil war, allowing the borderlands to be sieged and the mountains to be breached."

A few pieces of the ceiling clatter to the floor as the wind howls into the chamber. Shame claws up my throat. All this time I've been trusting the very creature who branded Aurora's family with the curse. Someone who just wanted to use me to tear Briar apart. My jaw clenches and I embrace the pain. I deserve far worse.

"But the princesses lived," I grit out. "The Vila's curse didn't work."

"Not as intended, no. After the Etherians managed to

soften it so that it could be broken by *true love's kiss*." Kal waggles his fingers. "But it did damage enough. Quite amusing, actually, the way events unfolded. By forbidding younger daughters to produce children, the royals picked off potential heirs all on their own."

He's right. Aurora's aunts have all died—childless, in order to prevent the spreading of the curse. There's only one heir keeping the Vila's work from being completed.

"And now it is our turn."

"No!" I wrestle with the bonds. The shadows only wrap tighter. "You'll have to kill me before I—"

"Oh, not you and I." Kal laughs. "Someone far more powerful. Someone who deserves to witness the fruits of her labor."

Storm-charged air punches through the narrow window.

"Do you mean . . . the Vila? You told me she was dead."

"I lied."

Kal unlatches the medallion's chain and dangles it before me. Even against the pitch-dark of the storm, the gem shimmers, deep emerald and sapphire darting and whirling within.

And suddenly I understand. "That medallion had nothing to do with the binding enchantment."

"Clever, as always, Alyce. And correct. The Etherians thought it entertaining to imprison us here together." He taps the medallion. "This contains her spirit." He takes a breath. Releases it and closes his eyes. "Mortania."

Each syllable spears down my spine like a lightning rod, setting every nerve aflame. My Vila magic shivers, that strange connection between us thrumming.

"I nearly forgot the taste of her name. Like dark wine and rich blood." Kal licks his lips. "I waited centuries for just the right vessel." Gently, he places the necklace on the floor. "I was close once. But I am glad she did not suffice. You—so perfect. A Shifter as well as Vila." He looks at me like a starving man regards a feast. "Perhaps I might even see her face again."

"I was close once." There's only one other Vila I know of who had ever entered this tower—my mother. Kal claimed that Lynnore had been almost strong enough to free him, but not quite. That she was thrown into the sea on the day they were meant to escape Briar together—with me. He let me believe that her killers were the same people who trapped him here. That he couldn't tell me who they were because of the enchantment. But the horrible truth spreads through me like winter frost crackling over a windowpane.

"You murdered her." The words scrape against my throat. "You tossed her out of this tower and let her drown."

"Lynnore was weak." Kal looms over me. The walls groan against the anger of the storm. "She did not appreciate the power I laid at her disposal. Once it became clear that she would not be able to break my bonds, she decided to leave without me. It was not safe in Briar for her child." His jaw sets. "I did what needed to be done. You were Vila and Shifter. A powerful mix. And that mix needed to stay here, where I could mold and shape you. True, it was a gamble as to whether the people of Briar would execute you. Whether you would ever find me. But I won in the end. And Lynnore would never have trained you the way I could."

The sea hurls itself against the rock.

"We'll never know," I fire back. My magic is too weakened by the shadow chains to be of use, but it *wants* to go. It practically broils beneath my skin, aching to wrap itself around Kal's neck. "I could have had a mother. My entire life could have been different. You took that from me."

"You are just as shortsighted as she was. I give you the greatest power in centuries—"

"It's *my* power!" I shout, thrashing harder.

Kal throws his head back and laughs. "No, pet. Not the feeble abilities I coaxed out of you these past months. Like pulling pig's teeth, I might add. Those are nothing compared to what is to come."

A fresh lash of shame scores my heart. Kal was never proud of me, then. Never believed my gift was something of value. He'd only used me. Found those sore spots on my soul and exploited them. And I let him.

"So long I waited. Hoped. Dreamed. And today it happens." His hungry look returns.

My mouth goes dry, heart skidding to a stop as everything Kal has told me clicks into place. The Etherians imprisoned him here with the Vila, her spirit locked inside the medallion. He's been waiting for another of her kind. Someone strong enough to—

"Kal, don't—"

But it's too late. With a manic grin, Kal picks up his boot and brings it down hard on the gem. There is the sound of glass crunching. An unholy wail. And then everything goes dark.

CHAPTER THIRTY-NINE

I don't know how long I'm unconscious. Everything hurts, my muscles throbbing in time to the pounding in my head. There's a high, tinny ringing in my ears, and a low, rumbling noise like a growl. A hazy shape floats over me. I manage to blink once, twice. But even that small movement is rusty and stiff.

"Mortania." A voice croons. A soft touch brushes my forehead. My cheeks. "My love. Is that you?"

Mortania. The name is familiar. Is it mine? Heat surges behind my sternum and webs outward. I squeeze my eyes shut. Open them again. The hazy shape sharpens into focus.

Kal.

I am not Mortania. I am Alyce. The growl I heard when I woke is the storm breaking land. Sleet and hail ping against the stones of the chamber. Shards of the medallion's strange glass remain on the floor, tendrils of hemlock smoke curling between them.

Kal frowns. "Mortania?"

Once again, a charge shoots through me. And I think I hear the echo of a voice, the same one that I'd heard in my Lair when Aurora and I had attempted to summon the Vila. It is screaming, but I can't make out the words.

Kal rises abruptly, angrily from his place beside me.

"This is impossible." He grinds his teeth, pacing. "I saw the magic enter your body. She should be here. She should be *you*."

So I'd been right. He wanted to release the Vila's soul into my body in order to resurrect her. I smile, the corners of my dry lips cracking. "I'm sorry to disappoint you. She's not here."

It's a lie. Something is changed inside me. I can feel it in the humming of my bones. In the thickness of my blood and the molten, foreign current rushing like a second heartbeat through my limbs. But I take great satisfaction in the way Kal tenses, nostrils flaring. Centuries of plotting and waiting come to nothing.

His anger pours out of him. He picks up a cobweb-covered stool and hurls it across the room. It connects with the wall and bursts into pieces. A scrap of jagged wood lands dangerously close to my face. He does the same to a chair. Smashes a table as well.

"Alyce?"

Every fiber stills at the sound of that voice, half-smothered beneath the throes of the storm, but clear as day to my ears. What is she doing here? Laurel was supposed to come. Terror wraps its fingers around my belly and wrenches. Kal freezes, his head listing toward the door. He smiles at me, putting a finger to his lips.

"Aurora, ru—" But the shadows are in my mouth before I can finish, tasting of ash. Sliding down my throat, heavy and tarlike. I want to retch, but I can't. My lips move, but no sound comes out.

"This is better than I hoped," Kal says.

I reach for my magic, desperate to save Aurora from whatever he's planning, but it's buried too deeply beneath the darkness—as Kal's had been when he was bound here.

"All I need is a little of her magic." He roots around the chamber, tossing bits of debris right and left before settling on something. Not just something. It's the spindle I cursed—the one that forced him to sleep.

Kal comes to me and I try to kick him away, but my legs are still shadow-bound. I can only knock my knees together. Huddle my body as far into the corner as it will go. But he grabs me by the elbow and hauls me forward. Pries my hands out of my skirts, spindle ready.

I sink my teeth into his shoulder.

He howls, scrambling backward and dropping the spindle. Kal examines the wound with two fingers. I'd bitten through the fabric of his shirt. The taste of his Shifter blood is in my mouth, iron and silt. I spit it into his face.

Kal wipes away the inky flecks with his sleeve. And then, so fast I don't even see the movement, the back of his hand pummels into my cheek. Something snaps, a pain like I've never felt exploding through the fragile bones of my face. I cannot breathe. Cannot think. Stars trip and dance across my vision, and then there's another pain—a sharp, swift puncture on the pad of my first finger.

"There." Kal huffs.

My own green blood beads on my fingertip, and I realize that Kal stabbed me with the spindle. The wound feels deep. The ancient spindle's tip is wet and glittering.

What is he doing? The spindle can't curse me—not when it's coated in my own magic.

There are footsteps on the stairs—Aurora draws closer. Kal winks at me and waves his hands. A thick shroud of shadows engulfs me, and I whisper a silent hope that Aurora can outrun the Shifter. That she'll sense the trap.

But she won't get the chance.

A muffled cry manages to wriggle past the shadows in my mouth, too faint to be heard over the wind buffeting the tower, as Kal begins to shrink. His body whittles down, becoming thinner and narrower. His doublet and breeches morph into a black, worn dress. His hair lengthens and thins, and green veins expose themselves beneath paper-thin, scaly skin. And then it is myself staring back at me, a malevolent smirk fixed on my own lips.

"Aurora." The voice is so much like mine that I cringe. "I'm in here."

No. No no no no no no no.

Aurora enters the room, letting her hood fall down around her shoulders. I buck against the shadows. Against the darkness in my nose and mouth, the weight pressing down on me like iron. It's enough to crush me. I cannot feel my magic. Cannot do anything but stare in horror as she rushes to Kal and throws her arms around my body.

But she pulls back, a crease between her brows. She looks at the broken tables and chairs. "Are you all right?"

Hope flutters. She is suspicious. *Yes, Aurora. Flee. Go now.*

Kal nods, kisses her cheek, and then rubs at my temples. "Just tired. What are you doing here? I told Laurel to come."

Bastard. I strain harder, but the shadows don't budge.

"It was too risky to send word." She extracts a pouch from the pocket of her cloak. "I saw an opportunity and had to take it. If Father knows you're gone, he's keeping quiet about it."

"But he won't for long." Kal passes the spinning wheel and bumps it. The flywheel turns. "What did you bring me?"

"A ring." Aurora tugs it free, a gold band with a fat lapis stone set in the center, but her gaze doubles back to the wheel. "I'll have to return it before morning. I've made certain he intends to wear it."

The spindle gleams in the next flare of lightning. Kal smiles. Spins the flywheel again. A faint green aura limns the wood.

"Do you like it?" Kal asks, goading the wheel faster. Aurora inches closer, entranced.

"It's beautiful." Her lips hardly move. Her grip on the ring goes slack and it pings against the stone floor, far louder than any boom of thunder.

"Yes. Quite an old thing. But still useful, I think. Would you like to try it?"

Aurora nods. Reaches one hand toward the wheel. I scream, but it is only the crash of a violent wave.

There must be a way out of these bonds. Desperate, I dive beneath the shadows, searching once again for my magic.

Kal is saying something to Aurora. Telling her how to use the wheel. She is so close now. Just another inch.

You found me, pet. At last.

I nearly faint at the sound of someone else's voice in my head. A voice I know from the flames of the summoning ritual.

Mortania?

A laugh flutters against my eardrums.

Well met, my dear. Well met.

I am losing my mind. Can she read my thoughts? I wonder, verging on hysteria. Can she kill me? But the presence I feel is not ominous. It is strong as it pumps from the place where my magic lives. Comforting. Almost motherly. I swallow back the ache in my throat.

You and I will do wonderful things together. Wait and see.

And it's then that I notice something else tangled with my power. Something that is not entirely my own.

Yes, Alyce. Yes.

It's Mortania's magic. That's what had happened when Kal released her from the medallion. Why he needed a Vila—someone with a breed of magic hers would recognize. The ancient Vila's presence undulates within me, her power twining with the cord of my own and strengthening it until it is like that beastly vine I summoned in the royal gardens. At first, all I can feel is fear. Mortania's magic is foreign. I do not trust it. But then a warm sense of certainty spreads through every limb. Like the way I feel with Aurora. Like coming home.

Go. I tell it.

The magic—Mortania's and mine—responds in half a heartbeat. Surges out through my body and shreds the shadows like cobwebs. I retch as the darkness expels from my body.

"Aurora!"

She turns, startled, but Kal is faster. He lunges, slams her hand onto the waiting spindle. Aurora yelps, jerking back and staring at the trail of ruby blood welling on her palm.

A wound that has a thin green plume of smoke curling from its center.

I rush to her, catching her as she falls, both of us crashing to the floor in a heap.

"Aurora!" I scramble out from underneath her, pushing her hair from her face, batting at her cheeks. They're already going cold. Her eyes are closed. A deathly tinge creeps over her face. "What have you done?"

Kal Shifts back to himself with a cold current of air. "Finished what we started. She is dying, Alyce. The last Briar heir. All that is left is to watch the realm collapse."

"Not like this." I shake Aurora's shoulders. "What did you do?"

"Better to ask what you did." There's amusement in Kal's voice and I want to strangle it out of him. "Surely you remember cursing the spindle."

"That curse was for slumber. Not death."

"For someone so terribly clever, you never did listen." He laughs and it cuts me to ribbons. "The sleeping curse you put on this spindle was little stronger than a wish. But it was just the spark Mortania's magic needed. Her intent is far stronger. It negates whatever pitiful attempt you made."

Numbness trickles down my back. Dragon's teeth . . .

that's what he was doing with the spindle. It's the same as with the king's brooches.

"I knew she was inside you." Kal runs a finger down my cheek. I elbow him in the stomach, but he dodges the blow. "How else could you have freed yourself from the shadows? Her power could never be hindered by so simple a binding."

My own scalding tears splash against Aurora's marble-cast features. "You're lying. You've done nothing but lie from the start."

"It is not my fault if you were not adept enough to discern the truth." Kal clicks his tongue. "But you misunderstand. The princess's death is what we need. A new Briar. A beginning for creatures like us. Sacrifices must be made, Alyce."

A new Briar. Aurora's words, but twisted and ugly when Kal speaks them. I did this. Mortania's magic bolstered the curse, but it's *my* magic that will kill Aurora. My reckless plan that brought her here.

"She isn't a sacrifice." A massive gale roars against the tower. "And you're a lunatic if you think I would trust you again after this."

"Well." Kal shrugs. "I already know Mortania is alive inside you. It is merely a matter of bringing her out. And I will find a way. Until then." He snaps his fingers, attempting to summon the shadows. Frowning as they refuse to budge. Because I hadn't just freed myself. I'd obliterated their magic.

Cold understanding bleeds across Kal's features.

An exquisite rage builds behind my breastbone. Beats in time with my Vila heart. Dark laughter that is not quite my own bounces against the curves of my skull. Kal watches me, sensing the danger.

"Alyce." He holds up a hand, gaze flitting to the door behind me. And some feral part of me hopes that he runs. That I can chase him down. "You are upset. But what is one life when they took thousands of ours?"

We do not need him, Mortania's voice crows.

Confusion ripples through me. Kal said the Vila was his lover, and yet I sense nothing of affection in the jagged edges of her spirit. Did she love him? Or did that love fester and decay in the centuries she was locked inside the medallion, consumed with her own hatred and rage? Had the Shifter become a means to an end—the same as I was to him?

"I must thank you, Kal." He stumbles over a splintered chair leg as I advance. "You really have given me more than my mother ever could. More than anyone."

His back hits the opposite wall, chest working quickly. "You will consider what I offer? A new realm for us?"

I have considered. Listened and trusted and hoped. Let myself be leashed and controlled and manipulated. And look where it got me.

"I will let you die quickly."

My Vila power responds like a warhorse, the scent of woodsmoke and damp earth mixing with rich, heady wine and molten steel. The tang of charred iron fills my mouth as my magic careens into Kal. His eyes bulge, hands going to his neck. I could laugh at how simple it is. Mortania laughs with me, the peals warping as they collide with the sounds of the storm.

I take one last look at the Shifter who killed Aurora. Who used me and lied and pretended to love me. But all he ever cared about was himself. And so I find the treasonous heart of his power and smash it beneath the heel of my own.

Kal sinks to the floor in a boneless heap, not even uttering a cry.

CHAPTER FORTY

Aurora's lips are chalky against the dull wax of her skin. Her veins are showing through her cheeks, blue-black and brittle. Her limbs are stiff. Her heartbeat faint. I crush my mouth to hers, again and again, begging the magic that broke the first curse to work again. She doesn't stir.

Not even when I reach my own power inside her, searching for Mortania's curse, trying to call it back. I command the Vila's magic now. But it doesn't budge. It's as Kal said, Mortania's intent was death. An intent stronger than iron. Stronger even than my own desire to wake Aurora.

"Please." A sob works free of my lungs. "Aurora, please."

"What have you done?"

A new voice rumbles through the chamber.

Endlewild lurks in the doorway. The light from his staff swirls with streaks of russet and the scar on my middle aches. His knife-sharp gaze assesses the room. The smashed furniture. Kal's lifeless body.

"You broke the enchantment." It isn't a question. "I sensed it in Briar. The heart of our bonds breached and the Vila loosed." His attention cuts back to me. "You killed the Shifter."

So Endlewild had known about him all along. Kal hadn't lied about that at least. The Etherians really did chain him to this tower. And I wonder that the Fae lord didn't suspect my alliance with the Shifter long ago—especially after I attempted to free Kal the first time. But then, I hadn't destroyed the enchantment that night. The magic had fought me off. I cannot think of that now. I hiccup through my sobs. "Aurora. Please, she's dying."

"The crown princess?" It is the first time I hear something like surprise in the Fae lord's rushing-water voice. He steps closer, eyes widening when he realizes the woman on the ground is Aurora. "What is she—"

But the next gale hammers into the chamber, setting the spinning wheel in motion. It clacks away. A faint halo of green still clings to the spindle. Endlewild stares, open-mouthed. And then he descends like the storm itself, ripping the flywheel away and breaking it over his knee. The spindle glistens with my blood. And Aurora's. He snarls at it, picking it up and hurling it through the window.

"What did you do?"

"It wasn't me." I'm rocking back and forth, Aurora's limp hand cradled in mine. "I didn't know. He tricked me and lured her here."

"Worthless half-breed." He kneels to press his knobby-boned fingers against Aurora's temples. The hollow of her throat. "Did you not think there was a good reason that he remained in our bindings?"

"I didn't know they were yours! And even if I had known, why should your magic have kept me away? All you've ever done is torment me. And he—he—" But the rest crumbles. Kal loved me? Protected me? It was all lies. "I didn't know what he was."

"You know well enough now." Lightning flashes, glinting off the laurel leaves of the High Court's sigil on his doublet. "When it is too late."

"No." I bring Aurora's frozen hand to my lips. My tears roll down her wrist. "You must save her. She is the heir to the throne. You are bound—"

"I need no schooling in my duties from you, *beast*."

The insult makes me cry harder. Because it's true. I'm the one who brought Aurora here. Released her killer. My magic coated the spindle that cursed her.

"I should kill you where you stand." His pointed Fae teeth gnash together. And I brace for the impact of his burning staff on my heart, the scar on my middle blazing. But it doesn't come. He shoves me away from Aurora and folds her into his arms. "I lack the time. You will come with me. Later, I will decide this matter. It is clear enough you are more than you seem."

The unspoken threat sends a shiver racing across my shoulder blades, and every instinct begs me to run. But I will not leave Aurora. And so I follow close at the Etherian's heels, down the stairs and out into the storm.

Endlewild's Fae steed is waiting. Aside from his staff, the

horse is the only bit of Etheria that the ambassador is permitted to keep in this realm. Its massive silver hooves paw at the ground, sparking where they meet the rain-slick rocks of the cliff. Its mane is waves of liquid moonlight. Its hide glowing, so much so that it hurts to look. Though the storm rages, the Fae magic in the creature's blood protects it from the torrents of sleet and snow, which roll off its flank like rivers of oil. Endlewild positions Aurora over its back, climbs up afterward, and tosses me behind him.

I barely have time to wrap my arms around his torso before we're bolting toward Briar.

The Fae lord must know of Tarkin's planned coup, for he doesn't steer us toward the palace. We soar over the landscape and into Briar at a brutal pace only a Fae steed could achieve, faster than the wind itself. The guards at the checkpoints don't even look up. To them, we're only a steel-sharp gale blowing through the gates. It's everything I can do to hold on to Endlewild until we lurch to a stop in front of Lavender House and I'm practically thrown off the mount.

Endlewild bursts through the front door with a blast of his gilded power and heads toward the main parlor. A bleary-eyed servant pokes her head around a corner, then scuttles away with a squeak, and soon the sound of confused voices floats down the staircase. Hurried footsteps patter overhead.

The Fae lord settles Aurora on a chaise longue, and the Graces tumble in a heartbeat later, hastily wrapped in dressing gowns with their hair mussed and chittering like startled birds.

"What in Briar—" But Mistress Lavender stops when she realizes who is standing in her parlor. She sinks immediately into a curtsy. The others quickly follow, elbowing one another as if to remind themselves of the proper etiquette when you find a Fae lord in your home in the dead of night.

"Lord Ambassador." Mistress Lavender's nose is practically touching the floor. "How might we be of assistance?"

Endlewild flicks back the edge of his cloak to reveal Aurora lying on the jade upholstery. Her curls are spilling over the cushions, brushing the rug. One arm juts out at a painful angle. A collective gasp issues from the Graces.

"The crown princess." Rose hazards a step forward, clenching the neck of her dressing gown. "Is she—"

"No." The light from Endlewild's staff gilds the chamber. He runs a spindly fingered hand through his snow-white hair. "But soon. And we will need all our magic to save her."

Laurel looks to me then, eyebrows shooting up. This wasn't the plan. Understanding puckers her lips. She thinks it was my fault. That I cursed Aurora by mistake. Lost control of my power. I slide my gaze away, guilt heavy on my shoulders. It's close enough to the truth.

"Marigold." Mistress Lavender flies into action. "Go to Willow House and fetch her healing Graces. Rose, gather the kits. And, Laurel"—she ushers the wisdom Grace through—"I expect His Grace will need your gift most of all."

Endlewild begins speaking to Laurel in low tones, explaining the situation as he knows it. Laurel nods along, blanching. Calculating her own part in the mess, I expect.

"Keep the half-breed close," the Etherian commands over his shoulder.

Mistress Lavender sucks her teeth. Her Faded Grace eyes are flinty, a muscle in her jaw ticking. The last thing she wants is the Dark Grace to be found in Lavender House. Not with the princess practically dead on her parlor couch. But she keeps her objections to herself.

"Go to the cellar and wait," she instructs me, straightening the tie at her waist.

"I will not." I cannot. Not after what's happened. Not when this might be the last time I see Aurora—ever. Craning my neck, I can just glimpse the heel of her slipper peeking from behind Endlewild. A slice of her too-pale skin.

"Alyce." Mistress Lavender grips my elbow. "You will not speak to me that way. Not after this. Not after everything else you've brought down upon my head. I tried to do my best with you. I really did. And it was such a burden. No other housemistress would take it on. But I thought—what a poor, luckless thing. I would help her. And this is how you've repaid me?"

Heat tingles along my scalp. "I'm aware of how inconvenient my life has been for you." I am reckless. But I can't stop. "And I'm sorry you found me to be so much trouble, regardless of the amount of coin I brought you over the years. What was it you said, that Lavender House rose three ranks once I started working here? And I imagine that housing the dreaded Dark Grace came with its own healthy stipend."

Mistress Lavender takes a step back, as if my words physically struck her. My pulse thrums beneath my jaw, spurred by my smoldering rage. Her magic would be so weak, a normal human's now that she's Faded. I could—

"Get downstairs," she grinds out. "If you do not, I will call the guard myself."

Do it a thought that I somehow recognize as Mortania's urges. Her magic hums against mine like a plucked string, begging to leave my body and be the end of Mistress Lavender. It would be so easy to release it. And then the housemistress could never order me about again. Never look at me like I'm something she found on the bottom of her shoe.

But then Laurel straightens from where she has been examining Aurora. She holds my gaze and gives the barest shake of her head, golden eyes softer now. Pleading. This is not the way. If I ever want to see Aurora again, if she survives this, it will do me no good to have committed such a crime.

And so I push my breaths in and out, ragged and shallow. Close my eyes against the burning wrath simmering in my blood. Take one last glance at Aurora, and then turn my steps to the back door, through the kitchen, and down the stairs.

The cellar seems an appropriate prison for the Dark Grace.

I'm half tempted to try to sneak out to my Lair. See what can be salvaged. But I have no desire to know how the guards treated it. Callow's perch hacked to bits. Her feathers—or perhaps even her body—littered among the broken glass and ripped pages. Pain balloons in my chest and sinks to my toes. I did not imagine it would hurt so much—how quickly I could be destroyed. An unsightly mark immediately papered over and forgotten.

Without a hearth, the cellar is frigid. My breath clouds in front of my face as I stalk between bags of flour and crates of wine and cheese, arms tight around my body. Even down here, I can hear the storm bellow. As if the wind itself wants to punch through the stone.

I go to the top of the stairs and press my ear to the door, trying to catch snippets of what's going on with Aurora, but it is useless. I can only seethe and wait and hope that she is getting better. That she hasn't died by my hand.

Hours pass. I think. With no way to tell the time, I'm going mad. At one point, I might hear movement from the kitchen, the staff waking and starting the day. But I can't be sure.

At long last, the doorknob whines as it turns and light floods down the cellar stairs. Mistress Lavender descends, looking ten years older than she did when I arrived with Endlewild. Her eyes are leaden and bruised in the flame of her lamp. She still hasn't changed from her dressing gown. I bolt up from the crate I'd been huddled against.

"Is she dead?"

Mistress Lavender releases a long breath. "She survived."

A giddy relief washes over me. Tears sting in my eyes. "I must go to her."

"You absolutely will n—"

I'm flying up the stairs before she can stop me. Mistress

Lavender claws at my skirts, trying to pull me back, but I yank myself free, not caring if she winds up flat on her back. I must see Aurora. Smell the appleblossom in her hair and kiss the curve of her neck and tell her how wrong I was and how sorry I am. The words are practically bursting from my lips.

She isn't there.

I reel to a stop in the parlor. Pale morning light streams in through the windows, the storm having exhausted itself at last. The Graces' kits and instruments are strewn on every surface. The air reeks of potent herbs and the floral, honeyed nectar of Grace blood. But I see only Rose and Marigold, collapsed on divans with their arms thrown over their eyes.

"What have you done with her?"

Rose stirs, squinting at me. "With who?"

"Aurora." I study the chaise where I last saw her. One of the pillows still bears a head-shaped imprint. "Where is she?"

Marigold sits up. "You mean the *princess*. The one you cursed with your filthy blood?"

Rose smooths her dressing gown. "She's gone."

"Gone?" The question hitches. "Where? What's happened?"

"As if it's any of your concern," Marigold huffs. "We broke your horrible curse. She'll wake up and—"

"That's enough." Mistress Lavender appears behind me, setting her lamp on a table. The rose-shaped glass is chipped. "The princess has returned to the palace. Where she belongs."

"Back to the palace?" I repeat. "Without speaking to me? Did she ask for me?"

"She can't, you idiot." Marigold grumbles something else about Vila filth, and I bare my teeth at her. She recoils.

"Not yet," Rose adds quietly. There's something like guilt in her golden eyes, but it vanishes an instant later.

"What are they talking about?" I whip back to Mistress Lavender, who purses her lips, clearly giving away more than she intended.

"We were able to soften your curse."

"It wasn't my curse." But it was. "It was an accident."

Mistress Lavender waves away the explanation. "It's done now. The princess will wake soon, and nothing more need ever be known of this incident. You will not see her again."

Incident. That's all I'll ever be to Briar.

"Even if she did see her, it wouldn't matter." Rose again. Mistress Lavender makes a noise of protest, but Rose ignores her. "The curse, whatever it was, was altered. The princess is sleeping. She will wake again, with a kiss."

Hope canters through my limbs. "I can wake her. Our kiss broke the curse the first time."

"*Your* kiss?" Marigold's face is a mask of disbelief and disgust.

This time, I cannot stop myself. My magic lunges, finding Marigold's small heart of power in an instant. It feels like putty against mine, so easy to meld and mash. Marigold croaks, her mouth falling open as her lips darken. Agony explodes in her eyes, like falling stars.

"Alyce, enough!" Mistress Lavender's hands are on my shoulders, shaking me violently. My concentration falters and I let Marigold go. She slumps in her chair, head back and staring at the ceiling as her chest heaves. "What's gotten into you?"

"It was always there," Rose says. Her expression has not changed at all, her golden eyes cool and calculating. "We didn't call her Malyce for nothing."

Still primed, my power begs me to reach in and squeeze her golden Grace magic until her eyes are as empty as Kal's were. But what's the point? She's not worth the effort.

"Your kiss cannot break the curse." Rose picks a bit of fluff from her sleeve. "There are protections in place."

Protections. The word sizzles in my mind like acid. "That isn't possible."

"It was decided"—Mistress Lavender wrings her hands—"that the princess will wake with a kiss from a suitor of the royal family's choosing."

Of Tarkin's choosing. "They can't—"

"It's done, Alyce." Sunlight glints off the amethyst ring on her finger, as if the Briar rose itself is winking. Mocking me. "Your kiss will not wake her. In matters like these, the Etherians can use their power to put up shields. To protect the innocent."

The way they had bound Kal. Had trapped Mortania inside the medallion.

"No." I retreat until my shoulder blades meet the doorframe. "He couldn't have."

Rose shrugs. "I suppose we'll find out. I bet they wake

her this morning." She inspects the beds of her fingernails. "It's a shame you'll miss the wedding. The princess and Prince Elias will make a beautiful couple."

The wedding. As if summoned by Rose's words, the bells of Briar begin to ring. Full and majestic, the same bells that announced the breaking of the curse. How different they sound to my ears only a day later.

"There will be no wedding," I vow, as much to myself as to the others.

"Really?" Rose twirls a pink curl around one finger. "What are you going to do about it?"

That same feeling from the black tower washes over me. I am Vila. And I have Mortania's magic inside me now. Nothing will stop me. Certainly not these vain, vapid creatures.

"Rose, do you remember when your elixirs soured?"

The smirk on her lips disappears.

"You were right." I grant her my most saccharine smile, already beginning to Shift. A tingling starts in the tips of my toes and gallops up my legs. "It had nothing to do with your gift waning."

"You." She leaps from the lounge and reaches for the first sharp object she can find. A gilded knife, the blade still slick with the remnants of an enhancement. "I knew it. Beast. Mongrel. I will—"

But her rage melts to shock as my spine lengthens and my hair fills out, falling in lush waves around my face. The burn behind my eyes tells me they've changed from black to gold. Rose's knife thumps as it hits the rug.

"What I did with your elixirs was the very least of my abilities. For twenty years I've let this realm trample over my back. Keep me caged and controlled. But I am not a beast. Not a mongrel. I am Vila. My power will never Fade. And you're about to feel every bit of it come down upon your heads."

CHAPTER FORTY-ONE

Their astonished and outraged cries swell as the door to Lavender house slams behind me for the last time. I have no doubt that they will call the guards. Let them. With my Shift complete, I look like a cerulean-haired Grace. Limbs still buzzing, I slip into a carriage and direct it to the palace.

I spend the drive slapping together a plan. What if Aurora has already awakened? A chill shudders through me at the thought of her standing at the altar next to Elias. The white ribbon binding her to the prince, as much a brand as the mark of the curse.

No. I will not let that happen. I'll make this right. Destroy anyone who stands in our way—the Briar King himself if need be.

With the palace in a frenzy, no one thinks anything of another Grace sailing through the gates. The guards nod at me. One of them even winks at me. During the carriage ride, I'd altered my Shift slightly so that my illusioned gown is cut low and close, lending me the appearance of a pleasure Grace. And so it is easier than I imagined to stroll through the corridors and find my way to the royal wing.

At this hour, it's mostly servants scurrying back and forth. But there are some early risers. Nobles already dressed in their formal satins and velvets, dealing out gossip like hands of cards. What snippets I catch have to do with the dress Aurora will be wearing and the length of time it will take her to become pregnant. My ears burn and I quicken my pace.

Preparations are already underway for the wedding. Carts overflowing with Grace-grown Briar roses, their petals bursting violet, then gold, then white, are trundled down the halls. Intertwined *A*'s and *E*'s, probably embroidered overnight by bone-tired maids, glare down at me from columns and balconies. I can just make out the first sleepy strains of cellos and violins warming up in the distance.

I ask directions from a passing servant, a broad-faced girl who trips over her own tongue in my presence. She hesitates at first, bobbing curtsies at me right and left, unsure whether she should divulge such information. But when I explain my purpose—preparing the princess for the nuptial bed—the poor girl blushes beet-red and stammers out a series of turns.

The main entrance to Aurora's rooms is a set of doors carved from a pale, shimmering wood that looks like it's been harvested from Etheria itself. An engraved dragon soars across the opalescent surface, its eyes picked out with glittering rubies. I approach cautiously, doing my best to keep my chin up and my shoulders back. To look like I belong.

"The princess is indisposed," one of her guards explains patiently. The small kindness makes me flinch.

So they haven't broken the curse yet.

For a heartbeat, all I can do is stare at him. What would a Grace do in this situation? Turn around and leave?

Rose wouldn't.

I lick my lips. "I am here for that very reason." I let my fingers drift to the lace at my neckline, noting the way the guards' gazes follow the movement. "I'm told she suffers from an onset of nerves. And I am here to . . . assuage her."

It's enough for one of them to let out a snicker. The other guard clears his throat, shooting his partner a warning look despite the hint of flush beneath his stubble.

"We were given orders that no one comes inside without the queen," he says. "And you're not the Royal . . ." he fumbles. Clears his throat again. "Pleasure Grace."

Damn. But I try not to let my confidence waver. Only widen my smile and make my voice huskier. "No. I was sent as a replacement. The Royal Grace is . . . otherwise engaged. I could tell you what room she's in—if you need to check for yourselves."

The guard's color deepens. His colleague chokes and pounds his chest.

"Very well," the first says, utterly flustered. And with a mumbled warning about being quick, he opens the door.

Little has changed since the night I snuck in through the servants' entrance. Aurora's sitting room is tomblike, the veiled spinning wheel still crammed into its far corner. I want nothing more than to smash it to pieces—and every last spinning wheel in Briar, for that matter. But I'm not here for that.

Outside the bells continue tolling in their insufferable cadence. I turn the lock in the door, buying myself a few extra moments. And then I go to Aurora's bedchamber.

My skin tingles at the sight of her. She is laid out on her bed, still wearing the clothes she had on last night, a periwinkle gown with gold embroidery on the bodice and sleeves. A light blanket is thrown over her body, her hands folded on her stomach.

I hurry forward and let go of my Shift. Aurora's chest rises and falls in a smooth, deep rhythm. Her lips are dry, but pink. And she is warm, so wonderfully warm. I don't realize I'm crying until tears begin to stain the silk stitching of her blanket. I pick up one of her hands, the one that met the spindle, and kiss each fingertip. The way she had on our night together.

"I'm so sorry," I whisper, close to her ear. And then I kiss the skin below her earlobe, where her strong pulse beats. Find her lips with mine, channeling every memory of us. Calling on the love that sprouted in my barren wasteland of a heart. On the faith I have in her—in us.

But she does not rouse. What have I done?

"Alyce?"

I freeze. Out of the corner of my eye, I catch the glimmer of an emerald braid.

Laurel.

"What are you doing here?" My panic ebbs, swallowed by surprise.

She stands in the doorway to Aurora's bathing chamber, a bottle of some peach-colored liquid in hand. Her gaze travels to Aurora, then back to me. "I came with the Fae lord to deliver the princess. They don't want the servants to know what's happened, and so they left me to watch over her until . . ."

"You helped him with this?"

"You mean did I help save Briar's only heir from a Vila curse? Yes, I did."

I bristle. "I wouldn't hurt her—you know that."

"I know that you promised you had this situation under control." She sets the bottle down on a side table. "Clearly, you didn't."

"You don't know what you're talking about. It wasn't my fault."

"It never is, is it?" The tone of her voice feels like a slap. I crumple a fistful of blanket. "You craft curses, but the effects aren't your responsibility. You come up with some half-baked plan to depose the Briar King, and it's our future queen who winds up nearly dead."

"That was an accident! I would never—"

"I know you wouldn't," Laurel interrupts. Her expression softens. "But I also know this situation was entirely out of our depth."

"What does that mean? You regret allying with us?"

"We had no chance of winning. I knew that from the start. I should have gone to Endlewild right away and—"

"Endlewild?" Something slithers between my ribs. She's never used his name like that before, without the honorific. And she wouldn't. As full-blooded Fae, he ranks far above the Graces.

"Yes. I told you we've been speaking of late."

But I can tell from the way she picks at the end of her braid that it's been longer than that. "When was the first time?"

"After I Bloomed." She straightens her sleeves. "And then at parties."

"Liar." The black silk of my magic ripples. "Tell me the truth."

Fear simmers stark ocher in her gaze. Good.

"I did meet him after I Bloomed." Her fingers knot and unknot. I've never seen her so restless. "Alyce, you have to understand that—"

"Just *tell* me."

She paces. Halts. "On the night of my Blooming Ceremony, Endlewild asked me to report on your actions. I was placed in Lavender House specifically to watch you."

For a moment, there is only the sound of the bells pealing outside. The soft ticking of the clock on the dressing table.

"And you agreed? You . . . spied on me?"

"I was afraid of you," she rushes on. "Everyone was. In the nursery, you were the subject of nightmares and horror stories. And then I was placed in your house? I was terrified, Alyce."

Unwelcome tears graze the back of my throat. "All those years—you were telling him everything about me."

Bits of memory, like shards of glass, begin to fly together. My missing gold. The king's servants sneaking into my Lair without leaving a trace. Laurel appearing in my Lair in the dead of night—she never did tell me what she was doing "visiting" me. Now I know. She didn't think I was alone. She thought the Lair was empty. She'd been breaking in. Poking her nose in my affairs. She's the one who stole my gold. Who told the Briar King what I was planning to do. This is why Endlewild stopped coming to check on me after I started working for Lavender House. He didn't need to. Laurel did it for him.

"It wasn't easy," she says. "Not after I got to know you. You're not a monster. And I meant what I said before. You and Lord Endlewild would be so much stronger together."

"Get out." I can hardly breathe around my rage. Around the magic that swells and hums inside me, desperate for an outlet. "Leave us."

"Alyce." She edges toward the bed. "You can't think this is going to end in your favor. The curse is different this time."

On instinct, I move closer to Aurora, blocking the path to her body. "Why?"

She presses her lips together, as if debating whether to answer, but then goes on. "Because when the princess wakes, she will not remember you. Not as you are."

I glance at Aurora. The smoothness of her forehead. The untroubled lines of her mouth. "What does that mean?"

"When we softened the curse"—Laurel speaks to me as though I'm a frightened animal, each word deliberate—"we made sure that when the princess thinks of you, she will know you only as a Vila. As a threat."

"You can't do that. It's dark magic—to tear us apart."

But Kal's words in the tower come back to me. "*The Vila have a terrible reputation for lies and trickery, but the Etherians are just as wicked. They only mask it better . . .*"

"You know that my gift is wisdom. With my elixirs, I can shape the knowledge in another's mind. Help them make decisions." She swallows. "And with Endlewild's help, I reached into Aurora's memory and changed it."

"That is not your gift," I insist. "That is evil. You cannot have done this to us."

She lowers her gaze. "It is not evil, Alyce, if it was done for a greater good."

"What greater good?" I shout at her. "Keeping the princess away from someone like me? A mongrel?"

"No. I don't see you that way." She reaches for me but I slap her away.

"Then why did you do it?" I laugh, but it is a haunting, caustic sound. "Because you're Endlewild's special little pet? Because you hate me? Please, explain the price of your betrayal. I want to know what you're worth."

She recoils.

"You know how I feel about the Grace Laws. How determined I am to reform them."

"What of them? Aurora already made your precious blood oath. She will do whatever is necessary—"

"The princess is a human. And human promises are fickle, brittle things, easily broken, easily forgotten."

Endlewild's words if I ever heard them.

"You don't trust her? After everything we've done. After everything she did—"

"She is one person, Alyce!" At last, that veneer of stoic calm cracks. "And her hold over Briar is not secure. She was irresponsible, going to the black tower alone. Relying on only a few people when she should have united a realm. She has no idea how to lead."

"And you do?" I fling back. "Endlewild does?"

"Yes," she hisses. "He's witnessed queen after queen sit on the throne. And he's tired of the greed and the corruption—as tired as I am." She pauses. Takes several breaths. "It turns out that Lord Endlewild's sporadic absences from court have been trips to Etheria. He's been negotiating with the High King of the Fae to intervene on behalf of the Graces. To stop the humans from enslaving us. The Fae will unseat Tarkin and uphold the queen's reign. And we will have everything I asked for—a council composed of Graces, a new system, all of it."

"And what did you promise in return?"

But my heart already knows.

"He refused the arrangement," she says quietly, "should a Vila be on the throne. Or in a position to influence the queen."

I nod, numb. "And so you get everything you desire—in exchange for my happiness. What a simple bargain to make."

"It is for the good of all Graces. For Briar. We can't afford another ruler like Tarkin. Even you can see that."

"Even me? The beast?"

"That's not what I mean." Laurel tries to reach for me again, but the look on my face must have her thinking better of it. "I didn't do it to hurt you. After our first plan fell apart, this was the only deal the Fae lord would make. You must understand."

"I understand that I trusted you. That you took the one person in my life whom I love and traded her for your own gain." She opens her mouth to argue, but I press on. "Tell me, Laurel, who will head this new Grace Council? Will it be you? Will Endlewild perhaps grant you the long life of a Fae so that you may serve as the liaison between the Fae courts and the human world forever?"

A golden flush climbs like Briar roses up her neck, and I know I've hit my mark.

"Of course he did. You know, I thought you were above such vanity. But you're no better than Rose. Terrified of Fading. And now you've ensured that you never will."

A muscle in her temple twitches. "It isn't about that."

"Is it not? How silly of me." A harsh laugh, steel grating against steel, punches between us.

"You need to leave, Alyce." She glances toward the door and I know she is using her gift. Trying to wheedle me into reason. "They will be coming soon. Tarkin has days—hours perhaps—before the Etherians arrive and bring him down. And they will kill you."

"You don't care." I wave her off. "Now that your deal is struck. It makes no difference to you whether I'm alive or dead."

"That's not true." She risks a step closer. "I care about you. You know that."

"Why? Because you bought me a dress once? Because you kept my secrets? Plotted to stage a coup on Aurora's behalf? Oh, wait." I tap a fingertip to my chin. "All of that was lies."

She rounds on me. "I knew the princess was coming to visit you in secret. That you were reading forbidden books. I could have told Endlewild that, but I didn't. I could have left you to rot in the prison, but I broke you free instead. Went along with your foolish plan—"

"For as long as it was convenient for you." I shove her shoulder hard enough that she stumbles. Her golden Grace eyes smolder. "But the moment it wasn't, you disappeared. Just like everyone else. And now you've taken Aurora, too."

The tolling of the bells echoes in the room.

"The Graces are prisoners. Just like you. Remember Narcisse. Rose. You would have done the same if it was the Vila hanging in the balance."

Maybe. But I dismiss that logic with a shrug. "We'll never know."

The sound of the key meeting the lock tears through the room. The handles jiggle. Laurel looks toward the sitting room, then back at me. "They're coming. You must go."

I nod, smiling. That familiar, comforting anger building inside my chest. Making me feel powerful. In control. "Oh, I will. And so will you."

Her brow furrows, trying to sort out the meaning behind my words. Too slowly, for all the strength of her gift.

Mortania's magic shivers awake. I can feel it uncoiling. Yawning and stretching. As it unfurls, I can sense the humming energy of nearly every object in the chamber. The leafy, woodsy magic of the paper in Aurora's books, the souls of the trees still trapped inside each page, still smelling of pine and damp earth. The honey-drenched buzzing of the waxy candles. The molten ore inside the iron fixtures.

Laurel backs away one step at a time, her palms up. A sheen of copper-tinged sweat beads across her forehead and cheeks. "Don't—"

A hawk striking, my magic soars out of my body and into Laurel's. Her power is stronger than Marigold's had been, but it yields all the same.

"Alyce," she gasps. "Please."

"Don't worry, Laurel." I tilt my head at her garbled sobs, riding the intoxicating tide of Mortania's power. "You're getting what you want. You'll never be a prisoner again."

She opens her mouth to beg. To bargain. And then the last fibers of her magic give out, guttering once, and then going dark. With a muffled cry, Laurel collapses, her arms stretched out on either side of her like broken wings.

Hers is the second life I've ended in less than a day. But I feel nothing, save for the crackle of my own power. And the overwhelming desire for *more*.

Something hard butts against the wood. Voices, first one, then many—one of which might be the queen's—begin to crest. The door bows inward.

We cannot stay here.

Aurora is too heavy for me to lift alone, but I command my power as I did when I carried the sack of coins to the black tower, filtering strength into my back and arms. After I Shift, it feels like she weighs no more than a child. I scoop her up, careful to tuck her head under my chin.

And then, just as the door begins to splinter, I shove aside the tapestry on the far wall and duck inside the servants' halls.

CHAPTER FORTY-TWO

I break into a run. There's no help for it now. A Shift would do nothing to aid me. Even if I became invisible, the servants would see Aurora's body suspended in midair.

And so as we pass each wide-eyed and spluttering maid and footman, I reach into their bodies and snap their magic neatly in two. With Mortania's power inside me, it's as easy as popping the head off of a daisy. And I feel only a faint itch of guilt each time another purple-liveried body wilts. They would have done the same to me.

I count twenty before we make it to the old library, the only place in this wretched palace that is ours. The blanket is still where we left it. I lay Aurora down on top of it, fetching a stained pillow for her head. If I breathe deeply, I can still catch our scents twined together. Appleblossom and woodsmoke. My stomach flutters.

But we aren't alone. Footsteps stampede down the corridor, shouts ringing back and forth as the palace guards follow my trail of dead servants. Swords sing their way out of sheaths. But they will not reach us. No one will separate us again.

With unbelievable ease, my magic finds the hearts of forest in the books and sends them flying off the shelves and piling in front of the open door. Torchlight bobs along the walls outside, the guards closing in. I am ready. I coax that leafy, loamy magic out, melding the flimsy hearts together until they are strong and sure. And then I set it free.

Fully grown trees erupt from between the pages of the books. Not the green-leafed saplings like those beyond Briar's gates. But black, spear-limbed things that roar toward the ceiling. I push harder, thickening the trunks. Bidding spiky, poison-tipped thorns to pierce through the bark.

I remember a lifetime ago, when I was a different person altogether, and had wept because I could not heal Duke Weltross. Because I could only craft darkness and death.

What a fool I was.

These trees, their slick skins, twisted to form a deadly barrier at the library's entrance, are the most beautiful things I've ever seen.

A guard rounds the corner. There's the sound of flesh separating from bone as he's greeted by my thorns. I laugh, Mortania's power surging through my blood and filling my lungs with the scent of molten steel and dark wine.

Swords hack against the other side of my trees, little better than needles against stone. They'll never break through. I let the guards tire themselves and turn back to Aurora.

She sleeps so peacefully, unaware of the chaos surrounding her. I run my fingers through her silky hair. Trace the shape of her lips. The dip of her collarbone. The curve of her neck. Was it only days ago that we shared the night together here? I can still see her, luminous and soft and so perfect it makes my chest ache. She told me I was beautiful. Held my hand while her parents berated us. Risked everything to be by my side.

And what had I done?

Colluded with the Shifter who had helped murder her family. Believed his lies. Cursed the spindle that nearly killed her.

The tears come again, swift and brutal. I press my forehead against her knuckles. Plead for her forgiveness. For her to open her eyes and let this nightmare fade away.

I should let the prince wake her. Watch her velvet eyes cloud and darken when she thinks of me, the Vila who held her captive. Let her live a life with children and a throne and every other happiness while I waste away in some faraway place. As good as dead without her—the one person who was ever mine. It would be a fitting punishment.

"DARK GRACE!" I recognize the king's bellow as it reverberates through the barrier. "You will release my daughter at once and answer for your crimes!"

My crimes. Yes. I have plenty of those. There is a trail of bodies outside, soaked in my magic. Every patron cursed from my elixirs. And then Laurel. She would tell me to give up. That I cannot win against an army of the king's best men, plus the Etherians. I rub my thumb absently over the back of Aurora's hand.

"I warn you, Dark Grace. When we tear down this wall, my soldiers will rip you limb from limb. Your head will sit on the palace gates. The birds will peck out your eyes!"

"What of your plans to invade Etheria?" I volley back, wondering how far away the High King's army is. "Have you no more need for your weapon?"

A barrage of steel on wood answers me.

My magic shudders as an echo of Mortania's voice whispers through me. Is this the man I will allow to care for Aurora? I recall her hard-edged fury when she spoke of her suitors. How she did not falter when her father threatened her very life if she crossed him. And then there are the lives of her sisters, yielded for Tarkin's greed.

Aurora would not want her throne. Not like this.

"Bring down this wall!" The weapon strikes become more frantic. "You are nothing! NOTHING! A beast who needs to be put down. I will—"

But I am no longer listening. A glimmer on Aurora's bodice has caught my eye. A piece of embroidery on her neckline, so delicate and small I thought it was a floral pattern. A trail of forget-me-nots or a lily chain. But it's something else entirely.

Dragons. I trail my fingertip along the golden stitching. A horde of dragons in flight. One tumbling after the other, twisting and soaring, breathing fire. Magnificent, terrible beasts.

Just like me.

Yes. Mortania's rasping voice again. Both mine and not mine. A shadow dwelling in my soul. And an idea unspools from that darkness. Mortania's magic heightened my Vila power, making me stronger than I could have dreamed. Had it done the same to my Shifter abilities?

Using the magic I find in the books, in the shelves, in the tables, I create a bed for Aurora. It wraps underneath her, gently lifting her up, then winds over her head, melding into an intricate cage, the slats so close together that I can barely detect the slow rise and fall of her chest. Thorns spike out in every direction, ready to defend her against anyone who draws too near. The star-chosen prince, Elias. The king. Any fool who thinks to wake her and claim her for their own. She will wait until I can figure out what to do. A hundred years, if need be. When the rest of Briar is dead and we can start again. But for now . . .

The king is still shouting at me. Calling me all manner of names, so familiar to me now that they might as well be mine: *Mongrel. Beast. Abomination.* They burrow under my skin and spread their roots, sprouting painful memories. The looks on the courtier's faces when Rose revealed me at the masque. The disgust in Marigold's voice when she learned I broke the curse. The revulsion in the queen's eyes when she saw me huddled against her daughter.

Aurora could have created a new world. A realm worth fighting for.

They do not deserve it.

Endlewild and I agree on one thing: Briar is no longer the land Leythana claimed from the helm of her dragon fleet. It has become a tree bearing rotting fruit. And there is only one thing to do with such trees.

Burn them to the ground.

My Vila magic hurtles out of my body and pummels into the outer wall of the library. The ancient brick explodes. Part of the roof caves in, stone and wood raining down in an avalanche on the Grace District. The bells are still tolling in anticipation of the royal wedding. I grit my teeth against the sound. Remember what Kal taught me. I was cautious with my Shifts before. Hesitant. But I draw on my unfathomable rage now, letting it snap and spark and roar.

If they want a monster, they shall have one.

Without a second thought, before I can let myself doubt, I take a running leap out of the gaping hole in the wall.

For one heart-stopping moment, I'm falling. The wind tears at my limbs. My stomach lurches into my throat. But I concentrate on my Shift. Command my power to obey.

Now, I order.

There's a blinding pain in my back. A pair of taloned wings shreds the fabric of my bodice and unfurls from my spine, like the sails rumored to have graced Leythana's ships. Veined and scaled and beautiful. Nothing like the flimsy illusions I summoned in the black tower. They buoy me up on the current of wind. My breath halts at the sheer joy of it. At the feeling of winter morning against my skin. The sight of the Grace District spreading below me. Exhilarating. I sharpen my eyesight, reveling in the way the citizens are scattering. Pointing at the sky, their shrill screams like music.

I'll deal with them later.

Stones are still falling from the wounded library. I position myself in the air, calculating where the king and his men are trying to force through my barrier. Mortania laughs, low and knowing, as her magic unspools with mine. A single command is all it takes. The roof above the guards collapses, as if it were made of nothing stronger than sticks and mud. Death cries float their way up to my ears. Shouts to protect the king. But it's far too late for that. If I breathe deeply, I can scent the charred copper of blood and fear. It is only the beginning.

I'll give Tarkin credit. For a realm that hasn't seen war in centuries, his army is well trained. Within moments, archers line the battlements, shooting volley after volley of flaming arrows in my direction. I land on top of the library and let my Vila magic wrap around me like a shield. The blows strike the shimmery green barrier, then slide away. At the first break in their assault, I launch from my perch and streak across the sky. Find the fiery hearts of the soldiers' torches and build it up. Stronger and hotter. Until each one blazes green with the force of my power and leaps into the archers' faces. Men howl and topple off the towers like the markers in Tarkin's war room.

In the distance, a fresh wave of soldiers is readying a cannon. They pour the powder and stuff down the ball in a perfectly synchronized dance.

But they have never faced a Vila.

The shot booms, a blur of black coming straight for me. I tread the air. Let them think they have landed their hit. And then at the last moment I release my magic. It catches the cannonball midflight and sends it careening back toward the battlements. There's a deafening crack as steel thunks into the side of the tower. The whole thing groans and leans to one side. Half of the men plummet to their deaths. The others are scrambling. Shouting. I concentrate on my Shift. My fingernails lengthen into claws. A barbed, poison-tipped tail punches through the base of my spine. The soldiers are trying to ready the cannon again. Cramming down the ball and the powder. Fools.

I tuck my wings in and dive. Spears sail past me, but I am faster. The wind whistles against my eardrums. Fear setting in at last, the men abandon the cannon and flee. Not quickly enough. I bank. Swoop low. My tail lashes out like a whip and connects with soft throats and tender bellies. Just before I make for the skies, a brave, stupid soul jumps into my path, brandishing a sword. I tear him in two with my claws. His insides spatter on the stone.

More. Mortania's laugh trills with the clanging of Briar's alarm bells. *More.*

Yes. At my command, the powder in the cannon explodes. Green fire snakes its way into every crack and crevice of the tower. I leave it to do its work and circle back to the rest of the realm. The Grace District is soaked in the acrid scent of terror. Men with axes and blades and even pitchforks crowd the streets, swinging their weapons at me like they could possibly make a difference. Women watch from the windows, mouths hanging open. I want to taste the salt of their tears. Rend the plump satin of their Grace-gifted skin.

I find Lavender House first. Every moment I spent inside, chained to spill my blood in the name of jealousy, swirls in my mind. Every snide comment. Every cruel prank. In seconds, I've called the fire in the lanterns. Casings burst. Flame canters through the garden and climbs the walls of the house. The Grace pennants are cinders. Windowpanes shatter onto the snow-blanketed hedges. There's a chorus of screams as my fire plugs doorways and broken windows, ensuring that there is no way out—not for any of them. The same way they'd trapped me for twenty years.

A new cry splits the air, and I look up to find a speck on the horizon. No. Not a speck. A shape I know very well. But one I never thought to see above the rooftops of the Grace District.

My heart swells. "Callow!"

She soars toward me in the steely sky, her black eyes fierce and vicious. A warrior's.

"How did you get here? Where have you been?"

The kestrel lands on my shoulder. Nudges her head against my cheek in greeting. Callow. Come to fight beside me. Our wings were clipped, but we're flying anyway, two birds freed from our cages. Untethered.

"Come," I tell her. "Let's show them what we can do."

Callow needs no encouragement. She swoops and dives, talons slicing the faces of our enemies. Pecks at fingers and hair and arms. Before long, the Grace District is nothing but smoldering green fire and the sweet, addictive scent of blood. Already, ships are beginning to leave the harbor, frightened passengers falling over themselves to get below decks. I find the wooden magic of the masts and break them in half. Set the rest aflame, dragon figureheads charring black.

We wing back to the palace. The fires I set are growing steadily. Tendrils of black and green smoke curl in the air.

But the windows of the king's war room are yet untouched. Another familiar figure looms behind them, staff pulsing gold. Endlewild.

Fresh rage boils in my belly. The Fae ambassador regards me with cool detachment, as if he doesn't care that I've wrecked half the realm. As if I'm still something he can crush under the heel of his boot.

Show him who we are, Mortania urges.

With a feral yell, I send my magic into the famed windows of the war room. For glass that is said to be able to withstand dragon's fire, it carries a flimsy heart indeed. It cracks almost instantly, a long fissure spiking up the center and webbing outward. And then, with a last push of my power, the glass implodes.

Endlewild doesn't flinch. Not even as the storm of glittery shards whooshes into the room and cyclones around him.

Callow settles on my shoulder as I tread the air current.

"I see you have ignored my warnings once again," Endlewild says, indifferent as ever. "Your anger will be your undoing."

Callow shrieks at him, her talons digging into my flesh.

"It will also be yours, Lord Ambassador."

"Wicked creature. This is not over. You will have all of Etheria upon you. Kingdoms from beyond the Carthegean Sea. It will mean a war." He raises his staff. A gilded aura shimmers around the orb, where his own heart of magic dwells. "We will bring you down."

But for once, that staff doesn't make me wince. He can't hurt me anymore.

The Etherian snarls. The magic in his staff crackles. He draws it back, lips moving in words I can't hear.

I close the distance between us in a single wingbeat and give in to the beastly instinct coursing through my blood.

Endlewild's eyes widen at my charge, as round as the golden plates at the king's dinner. Within their reflection, I glimpse my own. Wild-haired and ravenous. Claws stained with blood. Tail poised to strike. The Fae lord throws his arm forward. An arc of his Fae power erupts from the orb like a shower of stars. It slams into my shields and sizzles away.

And then there is only the sound of flesh tearing and the splatter of gold among the glass on the war-room floor. The staff falls from Endlewild's grasp and cartwheels end-over-end toward Briar. The Fae lord's blood is smeared over my face. It tastes like the fizzy wine from Aurora's parties. I want more of it.

Deep within my soul, Mortania laughs.

Callow beside me, I return to the decimated roof of the library. The smell of woodsmoke engulfs me as I bid my trees stretch their limbs, steeling this place against the fire chewing its way through the palace. Command more thorns to grow. Strengthen. Keep Aurora safe. I can almost feel her heart beating with mine, as it was always meant to be.

Briar burns below me, nothing but emerald ash and plumes of smoke. A wisp of guilt coils around my heart when I think of Hilde. Of the innocents in the Common District, their lives upended through no fault of their own. But I wouldn't change anything.

It turns out Kal was right. Sacrifices must be made.

Screams roll in from the harbor, miniature boats pulling out to sea. One of them is Elias's, I think, his navy and bronze flags retreating toward the horizon. But I don't bother to chase him down. Let him go. There's nothing for the star-chosen prince here.

I know what they will say of me, those who escape to the realms beyond the sea. The Vila who cursed the lovely princess. Trapped her in a tower, never to wake. Razed Briar to the ground for spite.

Malyce. I laugh. Rose knew me all along.

But that is not your name any longer.

Mortania. Her presence brushes against the inside of my skin, a missing piece clicking into place. Her face in the cursed mirror surfaces in my mind like a wave breaking, green eyes ablaze and pointed teeth gleaming. And suddenly I understand. That connection I felt from the start. I was afraid of it. But I should have embraced it. Our fates have always been entwined.

And with her power inside me, the Dark Grace is dead. Alyce burned to dust.

And what shall we call you, pet?

All the names I've ever heard spin through my mind. Those meant to degrade and chain me. Callow ruffles her wings. No one will ever utter them again.

Yes. A new name. For a new age in Briar. Exactly as Aurora wanted. We will be like Leythana claiming Briar for her own when no one believed she could. Like the first Vila and her mate, establishing Malterre after the Etherians cast them out.

Who was that Vila, I wonder? She was never named in the books I read.

Mortania's voice slinks through my mind in answer, raising the hairs on the back of my neck. It's like a veil being lifted. A path illuminated after years of wandering. My lips sound out the syllables, sweeter than Etherian blood.

I lift into the air. Pump my wings higher. Shift in my lungs so that the entire realm can hear. A name for a dark creature like me. Dangerous and cruel. Hard-hearted and unyielding. A nightmare come to life. It roars around us, rattling the stones of the crippled palace. Gusting across the waves, so that even the realms beyond the sea will know:

NIMARA.

“My rule is just beginning.
It’s my realm now.
Watch me rise.”

Alyce’s story continues in Book Two
of the Malice Duology.

ACKNOWLEDGMENTS

Not so long ago, this book—and others like it—would not have found its place on a shelf. LGBTQ representation has been sorely lacking in our history, as have stories in which female main characters are allowed to be anything but beautiful and good and in need of saving (usually by men). Alyce is neither beautiful nor entirely good. And I think, at some point in our lives, we can all relate to her feelings of helplessness and rage. Feelings that, when unmitigated, can lead to dire actions.

Our world, like Alyce's, is a lonely place when we feel there is no one like us. And so I wrote this book with the goal that readers would see something of themselves in its pages. That I could create complexity in the black-and-white trope of "good versus evil." And imagine a well-known villainous character as someone, well—like us.

But I could not have succeeded in my endeavor without the help of many people along the way. First and foremost, thank you to every LGBTQ author who has come before me. *Malice* would still be a computer file lost in a folder if not for the trailblazers who made their voices heard first. I am indebted to every one of you, and hope I can contribute to continuing the practice of inclusivity in publishing.

Incredibly loud thanks and raucous praise are due to my agent, Laura Crockett, and the entire team at Triada US. Laura found me in her slush pile, pitching a completely different book, and saw something worth picking up. She has been a patient ear, whip-smart editor, and unfailing champion throughout this process. Laura, I am honored to have you on this journey with me.

Thank you to my brilliant editor, Tricia Narwani. I knew from our first phone call that she was the perfect match for Alyce and her story, and I have since been utterly amazed at the care and passion that she and her entire team have poured into this book. Thank you to every person at Del Rey and Penguin Random House who has touched this book and made it better. Every thought and second given to my imaginary world and the characters within it. As I said, only years ago, *Malice* would have struggled to find a home. Tricia and Del Rey not only gave it that home, but celebrated the diversity of the book. That means more than I'll ever be able to express.

Of course, I would never have reached this point in my life without the support of my friends and family. Thank you to every person who listened to me blather on about publishing and who asked how things were going. Every teacher—and you know who you are—who read my early work and helped shape me as a writer. Mrs. Ro, you always knew I'd get here. And Coach, I really wish you were around to see it. My agent siblings, especially Tasha and Chloe, who listened and celebrated and otherwise helped me navigate these uncharted waters. My nonwriter friends who cheered me on. Thank you to my brothers, who were as excited about this process as I was. And my parents, who weren't surprised at all (well, you were) when I told them I was being published.

Thank you to my best friend, Ashley. We've been wreaking havoc since high school, and she never once doubted where I'd end up. Most of all, thank you, from the bottom of my heart, to Lindsey. She's been there through every tear and triumph. Every giddy dance when good news came. Every grumble of frustration when things weren't going well. I can't imagine anyone else by my side, and I am beyond lucky that our paths crossed ten years ago.

If you're an aspiring author reading this, know that I was once you. I flipped to the end of every book, searching for some magical crumb of a secret about how to get my work published. Despite the fact that you're reading this, I never found that crumb. Magic, unfortunately, rarely exists outside the boundaries of a page in quite the way we'd like it to. But persistence, patience, and an unwavering work ethic do exist. If I have any secret to my bit of success, those are undoubtedly mixed in. Keep writing. Keep rewriting. Keep reading. Keep trying. I can't promise you an end date. But I know that every piece—and every draft of every piece—makes me a better writer.

Lastly, thank you to every librarian, blogger, fellow writer, and absolutely anyone who has helped this book to find readers. Readers, this book is only ink and pages without you. I hope you found something of yourself in Alyce's story, or that it was at least enjoyable. If not—good thing there are more books!

ABOUT THE AUTHOR

Heather Walter is a native Southerner who hates the heat. A graduate of the University of Texas at Austin, she is both a former English teacher and a current librarian. Perhaps it is because she's surrounded by stories that she began writing them. At any given moment, you can find her plotting. This is her first novel.

heatherrwalter.com
Twitter: @heatherrwalter5

ABOUT THE TYPE

This book was set in Sabon, a typeface designed by the well-known German typographer Jan Tschichold (1902–74). Sabon's design is based upon the original letter forms of sixteenth-century French type designer Claude Garamond and was created specifically to be used for three sources: foundry type for hand composition, Linotype, and Monotype. Tschichold named his typeface for the famous Frankfurt typefounder Jacques Sabon (c. 1520–80).